EVERYBODY
DIES
TOMORROW

Other Books by Matt Howarth:

*Red Sky Radio**
*The Eden Retrieval**
*My Name is Lesion**
*The Eiger Contagion**
*Western Promise**
*Tuners**

Progression
Enriched Visions
Itself
Toofer
Separation Anxiety
Beyond Meat Time
Hungry Thunder
Stalk Exchange
Dreamtime Awry
The Blue Light
Imaginary Numbers
Haunted

For more information on books and comics by
Matt Howarth, visit www.matthowarth.com

*published by The Merry Blacksmith Press

EVERYBODY
DIES
TOMORROW

a novel by MATT HOWARTH

The Merry Blacksmith Press

2016

Everybody Dies Tomorrow

© 2016 Matt Howarth

For information, address:

The Merry Blacksmith Press
70 Lenox Ave.
West Warwick, RI 02893

merryblacksmith.com

Published in the USA by The Merry Blacksmith Press

ISBN— 978-0-69274-347-8
0-69274-347-2

1

CAN'T BREATHE!

Everything's blue.

I have no idea where I am—

The last thing Barry Winsor *could* recall was drifting off to sleep, snug in his bed on a chill wintery night. Now, he was choking in a blue void—a cold one, at that.

Cold—and wet.

It came to him in a flash: *I'm not choking—I'm drowning!*

But then, knowing what's going on didn't always explain *why* things were happening.

Screw figuring it out—

Clearly, Barry's imperative concern was the immediate lack of oxygen situation. *More like a crisis,* he bemoaned. Already his lungs ached for a fresh dose of air. All those years of smoking were finally kicking in. It took most of his concentration to force himself to not gasp for breath.

Common sense won out.

Up! Water always had a surface.

Easier deduced than accomplished...

Barry found himself surrounded by barriers, smooth planes that refused to budge.

A vague familiarity with the angles and positions of this enclosure ultimately identified his prison for him. A car. He was trapped in a car—a car filled with water—a car sunken underwater.

Again, that notion of a *surface* came creeping back into his thoughts, a rippling vista of waves, beyond which lay open air, undoubtedly miles of it. If only he could reach that surface before oxygen deprivation forced him to pass out—or gulp for air down here. Either would be fatal.

His remaining seconds of coherency were slipping away. So far, Barry had not followed any of the guidelines for dealing with a drowning victim—followed, hell, he was in such a panic, he hadn't even thought of them. So much for that CPU class. He had to stop being dazed and become proactive.

His fingers reached out and found a familiar shape lurking in the liquid blue. A seat, the front passenger seat. His hands traveled across the sleekly contoured cushions, searching for the door and the knob that would release him from this sunken prison. Haste made him clumsy. The lever kept slipping from his grip.

When he finally succeeded in gaining a secure hold, the damned thing wouldn't move. Jammed, broken, locked—it didn't matter. This door offered no escape.

Twisting in the chilly water, Barry lunged for the opposite side of the car. He clawed his way past the steering wheel to assault the driver's door with fingers made frantic by fear. This release lever proved to be as slippery as the other, elusive in the cramped confines of the sunken automobile.

The driver's door was equally jammed, broken or locked.

This only served to season his panic with frustration, resulting in a flood of chemical despair coursing through his body.

Damn! Damn! Damn!

Locked in to perish.

Maybe he could kick out one of the windows.

Screw that, he told himself. *It'll be easier to shoot them out.*

But—to his dismay—he discovered no Glock holstered in his armpit. He never went anywhere without heat; it was more than basic caution, he'd been the target of several old vendettas, so knew carrying could save his ass. It came with the job. Whatever had made him forget his sidearm?

Another piece of the puzzle that just wasn't there in his head.

Shaking off such distractions, he marshalled his situation. Kicking out a door of the submerged car wasn't going to be as easy as it sounded. Basically Barry spent no time in the gym, but even if he had, kicking out a locked car door was a lot different from crunching weights. He could only hope that panic would empower him with adequate strength to do the job.

Attempting to steady himself in order to establish leverage for a kick, he flung his arm above his head and his fingers encountered a soft surface, one that gave under the pressure of his touch.

It's a sports convertible! With a cloth top!

He dug his fingers into the fabric of the roof, tearing through it after several frenzied struggles. The cloth was tough, but only to a point, and his panic had already driven him past that point. Once he got both hands through, he was able to rip a larger opening in the roofing tarp. He slithered into it and was free.

Free—but still choking for air.

How far away was the surface?

He glanced about but could tell nothing from the indiscriminate murkiness. At one point, a pair of fish approached him and almost kissed his nose before abruptly darting away, quickly lost in the expansive depths.

He momentarily steadied himself, getting a reasonably good footing on the fuselage of the drowned auto. Then he kicked off. With his limbs clasped tight at his side, his initial kick sent him zooming up through the blue environment. The color grew more pale, hinting that the surface was imminent.

Hold on there—

But he couldn't. He had *held on* far longer than his physiology could handle. An automatic choke turned into an unwise gasp for air. Water ran down his throat, threatening to drown his lungs. He sputtered and thrashed. His posture became more agitated, having less to do with streamlined movement through water and more to do with physically expressing *Oh-God-Oh-God.*

He was still sputtering when he broke the surface. All this effort spent reaching air and he couldn't immediately satisfy that need. He had to cease coughing before he could suck fresh air down his throat.

For a moment—or an hour, although the elapsed time seemed anxiously brief to him—he flapped about in the water, gasping and hacking and spitting up fluid. His head took a few more moments to clear as he gulped welcome volumes of fresh air into his soaked lungs.

Now that Barry could breathe again, the question of how he'd gotten here returned to his mind.

Although dusk had fallen, he could make out the nearby shore of the lake. (He knew it was an inland body of water, for the water he'd tasted had lacked any briny tang.) Woodlands lined the shore except for one raised embankment; from the latter dangled the gray shards of a broken guard rail. Undoubtedly, that was where the car came from—off the road and into the lake.

Yet, as he casually paddled to keep his chin above the water, Barry reminded himself that he didn't own a convertible sports car. He'd crashed somebody else's car in the lake. (Again, what lake? He knew of no lakes this big in Manhattan.) Had there been another passenger? The car's owner? Driving the thing? But if so, where were they? He'd been alone in the clautrophobic confines of the submerged car, and if anyone had been there before he came awake, they hadn't left their escape route open. No, he'd been alone.

A grateful shudder swept along his shoulders. There was no one else to worry about it.

He was about to swim to shore when it occurred to him that maybe he'd been run off the road. If so, someone might be hiding nearby, watching to verify his demise. That thought stopped Barry dead, his hands poised just beneath the surface but stilled by sudden caution.

This was silly. He was an excellent driver, certainly capable of avoiding such an accident. But then, by the virtue of that same fact, he wouldn't veer off the road on some wanton lark, sending a borrowed vehicle to a watery grave. No—whatever had put him at the bottom of the lake had been a manufactured accident.

It wouldn't be the first time he'd been engaged in a car chase that went weird. All part of a cop's life, and nothing had changed when he'd made Detective four years ago. He regularly put himself in harm's way.

It wasn't all that strange for Detective Barry Winsor to find himself being stalked by some nefarious villain. Someone he'd been tracking. Somehow they'd turned the tables on him, chased him through the woods until they got their chance to force his car off the road and into the lake.

As far as the suspect's name and crime, everything, in fact, pertaining to the investigation that had led him out here—he could find no scrap of information on any of it in his head. As far as his recent exploits were concerned, all he found was a big empty gap.

Could he be trapped in a dream?

Or worse—was this some booze-induced hallucination? Had he gone on an another binge?

No, after all he'd just been through, Barry knew for sure this was all real. Wrong, but real. He was clearheaded enough to tell the difference.

So…he had a new enemy. Well, he was quite used to dealing with such situations. Except this time, he had no idea of the identity of his enemy, nor did he have any familiarity with the circumstances that had brought him this far. Was the suspect smalltime street trash? Or a career criminal?

The smartest thing would be to treat this as a capable and dangerous adversary. Barry had no desire to let his anmesiac confusion make him sloppy after all these years on the force. *Expect the worst. Cover your ass.*

He decided to swim to one of the farther shores, and do so as quietly as he could. He would absolutely avoid this end of the lake.

Until I figure out what's going on, he mulled. *I need to be extra cautious.*

Moving slowly and with great care not to disturb the surface in any noisy manner, Barry crossed the lake—it wasn't a big one—and finally dragged himself ashore. He took refuge within the woodlands, hiding from any possible enemies but also in a symbolic expression of how lost and befuddled he felt. Cut off from the world he knew, he needed some alone time.

Despite the cold evening, he stripped off his wet clothes and squeezed as much water from them as he could. In the process, he found his pockets devoid of anything of consequence: no coins, no keys, no wallet, no scraps of paper inscribed with a cryptic message or clue, no nothing. The clothing itself puzzled him, for he did not recall slacks like these or this pullover sweater as being part of his wardrobe; wherever they'd come from, it hadn't been his closet. The frayed army jacket was too big for him. And he'd never seen these sporty sneakers before.

Something drastic had happened in the life of Barry Winsor. A new development had put a bloodthirsty enemy on his trail, a chase that had ended in this lake…and then cursed him with amnesia concerning all of the details of what sounded like a perilous adventure. Perhaps the crash had done it, a blow to the head could explain his mental gaps.

Wasting time was dangerous. But he had no idea where to go. He was stranded in a strange wilderness.

Which means, he pointed out to himself, *it doesn't really matter which direction I go. At this point, they all lead to the unknown.* Well, not all. No matter what direction he chose to head off in, Barry resolutely intended to avoid the region on the opposite side of the lake.

With a weary sigh, Barry climbed to his feet and set off pointed away from the lake. He hoped the woods weren't too widespread. He might even stumble onto a roadway buried in this unknown forest that would guide him to civilization.

And what the hell am I gonna do when I reach a town?

I'll call Frankie. He'll know what the hell's going on…

But after several hours of struggling through the woods, Barry found no sign of civilization, only a limitless terrain of entangled shrubbery and trees clogging his way. He understood the stupidity of trekking through the woods at night, but saw no alternative. He needed to find out where he was.

Darkness was prevalent, although Barry suspected the foliage was so thick that even high noon would have difficulty penetrating this musky environment under the canopy of leaves. Thickets grew into each other, forming impenetrible obstacles. Once he even had to climb a tree to surpass a region of clustered thorn bushes. He maneuvered more by touch than by sight.

The night's chill crept into his still-damp clothing, and he couldn't stop shivering.

With every sludgy step, his agitation grew. This gap in his memory bothered him. It was not something he could ignore, either, for the mysteries contained in that psychic breach explained the nature of his present predicament. He was itchy for anything that might be pertinent to his plight, but his mental searches kept coming up with nothing.

Inevitably, he reviewed his basic memory in order to determine the scope of these gaps. His self-evaluation was particularly harsh, fueled by years of low tolerance for weaknesses (of which he carried more than a few). Barry Winsor had been a widower for almost five years now, but they seemed like an eternity to him. At forty-three years old, he was five three tall (okay, but only with shoes on), 260 pounds (at least some of that bulk was muscle, albeit not a high percentage), dirty blonde hair, no beard or 'tache (his facial hair wasn't thick enough to pull off either), he liked football and could tolerate baseball if there was enough action. Lacking any paper degrees, he was a self-taught, well-read individual. He spent his off-duty hours in the same house he'd shared for eight years with Emily. While unable to rid himself of her things, neither could he face them, nor the memories they spawned, so most of the two-story ranch house remained unused these days. Those chambers collected dust while he limited his habitation to his den, which now doubled as his bedroom (he'd found it impossible to sleep alone in the bedroom he had shared with her), and the kitchen (where, he ruefully confessed, he spent alltogether too much time)—and the downstairs bathroom. But then, he spent most of his time at work. Ever since Emily's passing, Barry had immersed himself in work, knocking down case after case, putting dangerous criminals behind bars where they belonged. At any given time, he and his partner, Frankie Dumont, juggled more than four cases.

His current adversary could be any one of the perps they'd been tracking. Danny Gough, but then that slimebucket was into beating women, he was too gutless to tangle with a man, much less a cop. Jennette Lamprey, while she had armed assault on her rap-sheet, her thing was more credit card fraud. Theodore Banksy, oh, it would be super to be able to pin something like this on that gangster, but he was too clever to leave evidence that could link him to any crime—he had a boatload of shyster lawyers to make sure that never happened. Titus Roth, no chance, that kid was smalltime street trash, no more than a bagman that might lead higher up the foodchain.

Damn this stupid amnesia...

The night hosted a variety of tiny noises, evidence that the woods were alive with hidden critters, scuttling and scurrying about. Their lives weren't interfered with by any amnesia. Their existence wasn't threatened by uncertainty—they were hardly aware of anything beyond their own hunger.

His own appetite was strangely dormant, and that was probably for the best. Even in daylight, he wouldn't have been able to tell edible berries from tart poisons. In the darkness, his hunger had less of a voice.

By now his hands were covered with a thousand scratches, wounds incurred during his struggles against obstinate bushes and raw branches often as sharp as needles. From what he could tell, the arms of his jacket were similarly torn; the tatters flapped like small birds clinging to his ribcage. Without a doubt his pants were shredded by his trek through the wild woodland. He wondered how long his fancy running shoes would last being dragged through this nocturnal muck.

Previously, his hair had been plastered to his scalp from his time underwater. Now, though, sweat and worry maintained the integrity of his golden skullcap. Perspiration drenched the rest of him.

I'd kill for a smoke. Even if a pack lurked in one of his pockets (which it didn't; he'd checked, repeatedly), the butts would be all soggy and impossible to light. But this understanding did little to appease his addiction.

A strange noise came from ahead. Granted, most every sound tonight was exotic to him, a city-bred lad, but this one was singular by being new, not a repetition of small scurrying or scuttling. There was more mass behind whatever was crunching shrubbery out there.

He resolved to avoid it. He edged to the right, hoping that way would afford easier passage. Alas, the forest's determination to obfuscate his progress won out. For minutes he searched for a way through and past the approaching stumbler in the night. In vain, every front presented an impasse of tangled foliage.

The stumbler was getting closer.

Resisting the inclination to call out to whoever approached through the underbrush, Barry bit his lip and got more aggressive with his surroundings. He made some headway, and in doing so suffered a fresh score of lacerations. Unfortunately his breakthrough was a noisy one. He made a racket; consequently the stumbler changed direction in the night. There no mistaking the change in the shambling, it was coming closer with each second, while he struggled with twigs that were impossibly entwined into what seemed like rattan-thick barriers. Whoever it was, they were heading directly for Barry now.

He had to wonder what sort of person was stumbling through the woods at night... Barry had his own reasons, but he doubted they were shared by whoever stumbled closer now.

Could it be his unknown enemy? Had they tracked him through the woods from the lake?

Logic asserted that this was unlikely. No one could track a person through this stygian realm.

This was just some chance encounter. There was nothing sinister about it.

The guy's probably as lost as I am. Barry relaxed a bit. He was about to call out a tentative greeting when the crunching lurched closer and something bumped into him. The dark made catching any details impossible, but the stumbler seemed much lighter than he'd expected. Was it a kid?

An arm swung out of the darkness and barely missed catching Barry in the shoulder.

The woodlands possessed its own assortment of malodorous smells, but suddenly another stench had joined the olfactory chorus. This new stink reminded Barry of rotten meat. It made him gag; he partially doubled over as his stomach churned. That lurch saved him from the clutches of the stumbler as it took a second grab at him. The assailant staggered past Barry, crashing into shrubbery somewhere in the darkness.

Bolting, Barry smashed his way through numerous barricades of tightly-knit shrubbery without hesitation. A tree slammed into his right shoulder. He bounced off it into another. Its coarse bole rasped against his cheek as he scrambled to circumnavigate the trunk.

Any sounds made by the stumbler were lost in the ruckus generated by Barry's madcap escape. He didn't care how much noise he made. All he cared about was getting out of here. This person might not be a foe, but nobody that odious could possibly be friendly.

He tried not to dwell on how soft the stumbler had been when they'd bumped into him. Almost squishy

He ran.

He tore through shrubbery like it was wet cardboard. Branches shattered across his chest as he flung himself through the timberland.

His flight left the mystery stumbler far behind in this murky province.

Eventually, exhaustion took its toll, and Barry collapsed with his back against a tree, his feet and butt sinking into the marshy ground. His breathing remained feirce, all raspy and hoarse. He could literally feel his heart thumping in his chest, straining to match his racing metabolism. His entire body welcomed his collapse—it gave everything the opportunity to cope with his elevated level of hysteria. His hands clutched spasmodically, digging their fingers into the moist loam. His jaw felt like a band of harsh steel locking his teeth in a grimace, through which whistled his ragged gasps for breath.

As his heart rate stubbornly decreased and evened out, Barry became more aware of his surroundings.

A dim pallor crept through the woods, casting a ghostly light on the terrain. The branches glittered like icicle growths. Even the serrated tree bark adopted a tender demeanor, as if the effulgence had somehow softened the raspy wooden surfaces. A seeping mist hid the ground.

Contrary to common sense, Barry instinctively understood this light was born of no normal origin. It was just too ethereal, flickering as if comprised of millions of microscopic fireflies, lethargic ones whose dance was minimal and hesitant. Its color was off, too; a pale yellow, lighter than the glow of any electric bulb known to mankind.

A light in the woods. There were only a few things it could be: a nearby roadway, a country settlement, or maybe just a lone homestead.

It turned out to none of them.

He spent a long time scrutizing the bunker. Creeping from shrub to tree, Barry circled the strange structure. He was careful not to let himself be seen. He had no way of knowing if the bunker was occupied, much less by friend or foe.

It was a gray thing, drab and blunt. Its sole unique quality was the glow it gave off, for the light came not from windows in the concrete shelter, but from the building itself. What windows it had were shadowy holes, in striking contrast to the bunker's ambient radiance.

But even more peculiar was the RAM Charger sitting in the parking lot adjacent to the bunker itself. The presence of a conventional car parked next to the arcane structure seemed too unreal to him. That was the part he fixated on.

Someone else might have shown a modicum of curiosity about stumbling upon a radiant bunker out here in the wilderness, but Barry only had eyes for the Charger.

Please let the keys be in it, he begged the patron saint of people lost in the woods. (If there wasn't one, he was wholeheartedly willing to lobby for such a celestial appointment.)

He stumbled across the parking lot. Hidden beneath the flowing mist, a gravel surface crunched underfoot, a welcome change from the unpleasant squish of sinking his feet into mud. A symphony of these disgusting wet sounds had chased him through the forest. But—that part of the nightmare was over.

The car door was open. A key was inserted in the ignition. A lunchbox sat on the passenger side of the front seat. A small plush pig dangled from the rearview mirror like a totem for teenage Japanese girls.

He slid inside the car and closed the door; after a moment, he locked them all. Only then did he relax, slumping on the green vinyl cushions. His eyes drooped closed and a long sigh escaped his chapped lips. He wasted only an instant, though, on immediate recuperation.

As he twisted the key in the ignition, Barry felt a minor pang of guilt for stealing the Charger. The theft would strand its owner out here at this isolated bunker. On the other hand, Barry felt a visceral aversion for the bunker. He had no interest in its purpose, contents or history. Escape was his primary concern.

Under his guidance, the car lumbered from the parking area and disappeared down the narrow path that led into the woodland depths. The Charger's headlights documented a progression of tightly-clustered trees. It was like driving down a tunnel, deep underground. The path was rustic, unpaved and often overgrown. On more than one occasion, hungry ruts tried to swallow the car's tires, stranding the vehicle in this timber burrow. Barry refused to let the car remain stuck, almost as if he were afraid to abandon the security of the automobile. Each time the tires got fouled, he rocked the car violently, dredging his way back onto stable ground through a manifest stubborn refusal to accept defeat.

Eventually, he knew the path had to end, it had to lead somewhere. But the monotony of the trees lining the tunnel seemed to be eternal. On and on…how far from the maddening crowd was that glowing bunker? He had to suppose it was a long way from anything. You couldn't have a building like that near public areas where someone might question the place's eerie radiance. Or, for that matter, be affected by it.

Until now, it hadn't occurred to him that the luminescence might have been radioactive. Wouldn't that go hand-in-hand with an isolated bunker? Would he suffer from his brief exposure to the site? Would his hair fall out and his teeth turn putrid? Well, it was too late to worry about that. At least he'd hastily evacuated the area, hopefully before any permanent genetic damage had been inflicted on him.

This has been one weird night…

What he encountered along the wooded tunnel almost made him wet himself.

Emerging from the trees like a plywood cut-out, a figure suddenly appeared and stumbled directly in front of the traveling Charger. Moving along at a cautious 20 MPH, its velocity was still enough to do some damage. The front grill connected with the figure, and Barry swore he saw bits come loose from the fellow. Chunks of meat now clung to the Charger's fender. As he drove past the person, he gawked at their advanced state of decomposition. Very little flesh remained to hold everything in place. Certain organs, bloated with putrifaction, created unnatural bulges on the creature's abdomen. Flaps of muscle dangled from chipped bones. Its skull was partially visible in its almost hairless, skinless condition. Yet, despite the absence of flesh or sinews, the animated corpse grimaced and marked Barry's swift passing with a hostile gesture.

Then the night swallowed the monstrosity. Considering what he'd just seen—or *thought* he'd seen—Barry was utterly unwilling to stop and check on the status of the person he'd hit.

It had happened so fast, but the details of the encounter were scorched into his brain. The person he'd hit had been dead. From the looks of the guy, he'd been dead quite a while. His collision with the Charger hadn't daunted him in the least; being dead, losing a few chunks of rotten flesh probably didn't bother him in the least.

First, glowing bunkers in the woods—now, the walking dead. Would this preposterous nonsense never stop?

Perhaps the most frightening part was the fact that he knew all of this was real. He wasn't dreaming, nor hallucinating these fantastic exploits. Despite the inherent absurdity of these developments, he understood that they were all real, tangible, deadly. Oh, so very deadly.

Corpses shambling about the woods. He was fairly certain that he'd narrowly escaped another zombie attack back in the depths of the wilderness.

Encountering one dead guy might be attributable to some weird science experiment gone awry—but two dead guys walking, that meant plague. If there were two, there would be more out there…possibly thousands. In the movies, there were always hordes of them.

Driving off the road and plummeting into the depths of a lake—he'd been lucky the crash hadn't knocked him unconscious. Then he would've died instead of managing to tear his way through the cloth rooftop and swim to freedom.

If I had died, would I be a zombie now? Like those others…?

When the wooded tunnel finally reached a more conventional roadway, the transition only meant more worries for Barry. At least in the woodland pathway, the trees had offered protection; out in open countryside he had to broaden his alert scrutiny. Any shadow could suddenly turn into an undead monster.

Before, he'd sought safety in the arms of society. Now, though, society might not offer any degree of safety. Did he really want to seek out the nearest urban cluster?

Actually, if the world had suddenly been plunged into a zombie holocaust, his place should be at the sides of his comrades in blue, fighting to restore order in these chaotic times.

Which meant yes, he needed to find the nearest city and join forces with its constabulary. He drove on, hopeful but still wary. The roads were surprisingly barren of other travelers; he saw only a few cars abandoned by the pavement. The figures he did see moved with the stiff lethurgy of the dead. He did not stop to investigate them. When one took an interest in him, he simply accerelated the car and outran the creature.

The ease with which he had accepted this zombie apocalypse unnerved him. But then, as a Detective he'd learned to hone his observations and trust the deductions he made from those findings. As outlandish as it sounded, the dead were walking. Something major had happened, occluding his personal crisis. You had to go with the flow, reprioritize things as necessary. And as far as survival was concerned, adjusting to this new macabre world was pretty damned important.

He wasn't really all that surprised to find he had no wallet in any pocket. If somebody had taken his gun, they'd probably boosted his wallet and badge too.

When he reached a police station, they'd have to take his word that he was a fellow officer. They wouldn't refuse extra help in the face of an ongoing crisis.

But when he finally located a police station, it was abandoned. From the looks of things, it had been empty for some time. That was his first new surprise.

His second came when he plucked a newspaper someone had discarded on a desk. The paper was from several months in the future, and its browned condition implied it had been sitting around for some time. His amnesia gap spanned *months*!?

The headline was disturbing enough: Asteroid Will Hit Us!

What asteroid?

If an asteroid had hit the Earth, things would be a lot more screwed up than they were. An asteroid collision would've caused tidal waves, earthquakes—there'd be some physical evidence of such a catastrophe. Yet, the buildings he saw were intact, the asphalt uncracked along the highways. Although the night was overcast, the clouds lacked the density you'd expect from an apocalyptic sky.

What role could an asteroid have played in causing this zombie crisis? It boded ill that there was no visible police presence here, it implied how drastically civilization had decayed. If the people had fled, where had they gone?

According to the newspaper, he was in Milford, a town in Illinois. Where would a smalltown populace run to? Chicago? Far from his Manhattan stomping grounds, Barry was unquestionably lost here.

A quick search showed him the station had been cleaned out. No guns, no food, just a lot of dust. More bad news. Not only did that leave him unarmed, but it heightened the chances that anyone he might encounter out there would be packing serious heat. He'd have to rely on his wits.

A more thorough search produced some SWAT uniforms and armored vests in an isolated closet. He availed himself of whatever he found. The pants were tight around his belly and too long, so he rolled up the cuffs. The Teflon vest was heavier than he remembered.

Which only served to remind him that he—quite literally—couldn't remember his last meal. It was about time he got something to eat. Any moment could turn into a brutal struggle for life and limb—he needed to replenish his dwindled reserves if he had any hope of staying alive.

And find yourself some kind of weapon, Barry advised himself as he took his leave of the police station. The Charger's gas tanks were nearly expended, so he left it sitting where it was and ventured out on-foot.

Moving along, he investigated the stores and building fronts that shared the street with the police station. A clothing store and a pharmacy (both securely closed behind metal shutters), a corner deli (totally ransacked, and then somebody had gone on a rampage and smashed the empty shelves and the cash register), a sporting goods store—*this* was open, although it had been a long time since any clerks or customers had walked these aisles. The looters had struck here too, but apparently with a more discriminating want-list, for almost half the sporting goods were still in stock.

At least he was able to trade in his tattered jacket and slacks for fresh clothes. A camouflage jumpsuit fit him. He had to settle for a pair of hiking boots a few sizes too big, but padding his feet with extra wollen socks helped.

The display cases that had offered hunting rifles and archery sets were empty; even the knives in the kitchenware section had been cleaned out. As far as weaponry went, the best he could find were golf clubs. At least they would serve as bludgeons…until he found something better.

Like what? A machete would be nice. An automatic rifle even better. But for now, he'd have to settle for a metal rod with a hefty knob at its end.

He felt somewhat embarrassed, carrying a pair of golf clubs as he walked down the deserted street. He'd never played golf in his life, nor had he watched tournaments on television.

If he had to justify his sporty armament to anyone, well—would he really give a damn what they thought? If he found another person—a living, breathing, non-hostile person—he wouldn't argue with them. He'd gratefully accept their existence, commend them on their survival skills, and propose an alliance with them. Let then sneer at his pathetic arsenal. Survivors couldn't afford to be picky.

I'd kill for a smoke, he lamented. *Or better yet—a drink!*

All things considered, Barry felt he deserved a drink—a stiff shot of whiskey would steady his nerves. His meandering path now sought a tavern.

It took him three blocks before he spotted one. He entered the establishment with extreme caution. With a chunk of masonry from the sidewalk rubble, he wedged the front door open so that some light spilled into the bar's interior. The place looked reasonably untrashed. But as he approached the smooth counter, he saw that the shelves and racks behind the bar were all empty. Investigating the cabinets behind the bar, his hopes remained consistantly frustrated. Scavengers had long ago appropriated every bottle for their own consumption. Even the beer taps were dry.

Maybe now wasn't the best time for a drink. He'd start with one, then drain the bottle shot by shot until he opened another. A nerve-steadier would turn into a binge. And when the next zombie came after him, Barry would be too inebriated to defend himself. That made sense. Even so, he wished he'd found *something* to take the edge off this strange night.

Hunger only added to his discomfort.

The tavern had held no food, either. Same story with the next two places he hit: a meat market and another bar. Mobs of looters had swept through the places months ago, leaving not even a bag of nuts.

Where was everybody?

If he found somebody, then hopefully he could learn what had happened, at least get a general version of the events that had changed the normal world into a zombie exposition. Furthermore, he wanted to know how an imminent asteroid strike factored into the apocalyptic equation.

None of the radios at the police station had been able to pick up any broadcasts. And so far, every phone he checked offered only dead air.

Even the empty streets had a "dead"ness about them. The inert concrete, the uncaring facades of gray buildings, the muted shimmer of a few surviving florescent streetlights, the spooky silence and the uncomfortable wince that came when his lone footfalls destroyed that quietude. The air had a dusty taste. Only now did he notice how silent the night was. No insects chittering away in the woods. No traffic noise. Nobody'd left their TV on too loud. No domestic squabbles going on in some nearby house.

Distracted by this lifeless environment, he almost failed to notice the threat shambling up to him.

Almost.

The stench was unbelievable. And the thing moved so jerkily, how could Barry fail to dodge the creature's crude attempt to pounce on its prey?

So, this was zombie. He took this opportunity to examine the thing. Somehow he'd envisioned that they'd all be rotting and half-decayed away, like the one he'd hit with the Charger on the woodland path. But this one almost looked like a healthy person. Except for the weird way it walked. Oh, now Barry saw—the thing's left leg was broken, half of the time the knee wanted to bend in a direction contrary to its original design; that sort of impaired its stride, or shamble, as the case was. Its clothing was rumpled, but untorn and unbloodied. Naught but a deadpan rictus marred the man's stockbroker face; his unruffled hair was a testament to the long-term effects of whatever lacquer spray the dandy had used on it. With his mildly plump face and colorless eyes, he could have been somebody's middle-aged pop. But not today. Today, Pops was an undead threat. A slow-moving threat, but that hardly diminished its dangerous potential.

None of this made a lick of sense in the real world. Zombies only existed in horror movies.

While not especially a fan of the horror genre, Barry had seen a fair share of scary movies in his youth, like any average teenage boy. He couldn't remember many details from any zombie films, though. As far as he could recall, the outbreaks were never explained. The adventures concentrated on normal people struggling to survive. In the movies, loners never fared well in these types of situations. Granted, groups had their difficulties too, but at times of world-shattering peril, people wisely banded together against adversity. Reverting to the unity of the tribe.

Despite his general unfamiliarity with zombie movies, common sense outlined the basic rules.

Rule 1: Watch your ass.

Rule 2: Be ready to kill anybody you see—especially if they were already dead.

Rule 3: You better believe it was really happening. Don't waste time trying to figure out how or why the dead were up and walking. In the face of incontrovertible evidence, you had to accept such things with a dreadful certainty. Doing so could mean the difference between survival and becoming a snack for some departed soul. All that mattered now was basic survival—don't get eaten by a mob of hungry undead creatures.

That's what they always wanted in the movies—to eat the living. Why was that? Did they think if they consumed enough living tissue it would return them to life? Somehow, Barry doubted the things had any "thoughts" more complicated than autonomic responses: walk, attack, eat.

It was important to keep in mind that zombies were reanimated cadavers. The minds, personalities, the souls had departed their meat containers long ago. Whatever had reanimated this dead flesh was without intellect, without soul, without mercy.

Barry wouldn't be killing Pops, he'd be putting down a thing, a dangerous thing. You couldn't just kill zombies by shooting them in the heart, either; that was useless. You had to destroy the brain, or sever the head from the rest of the body. Why? How could a zombie's dead brain be animating its body?

Those type of movies rarely wasted screen-time with scientific analyses of things; they were gore fests, little more.

And now I'm living one, he grumbled.

He used his golf club to cave in the wretch's skull. It took several blows to take down Pops. Barry would have to learn to not hold back. He wasn't hitting a person, he was putting down a rabid thing…whose head turned out to be more solid that he had initially expected.

The one in the woods had been all squishy—maybe that one had been dead longer.

Pops was a much fresher corpse, robust and ambulatory despite his injured leg. So it took mightier blows to penetrate that calcified bone shell. Even then, a third strike was necessary to pulverize the cranial tissue, finally forcing immobility on the dead creature.

Others had followed Pops out of the shadows, creeping over to menace Barry. He stumbled back, swinging his staff wide in an effort to ward off the closest cadaver. But the thing kept on shambling, paying no heed to getting cracked across the nose with the golf club. Its hands clawed for him. It gnashed its snaggled teeth in eager anticipation of sinking those foul canines into Barry's neck.

Taking a more cautious step back, Barry adopted a better defensive stance. His next swing of the rod was two-handed and fueled by two invigorating breaths—it atomized toothy's head.

The other zombies continued to advance. They were not as slow as Pops. In fact, their agility was downright obscene. Zombies were supposed to be slow. You just couldn't trust movies—it wasn't fair. It wasn't as if the Academy had offered a class on Handling a Zombie Outbreak. You had to draw your facts where you could find them…and hope that some of them were accurate.

Learning on the job was helpful too.

He took out the other three zombies in similar manner, shattering their heads like rotten pinatas filled with jelly. One put up a fight, blocking his early strikes with its numb arms—but Barry blustered through that tactic and pummeled the audacious adversary.

"Nobody dines on me tonight, guys," he advised the scattered dead. The exertion had left him winded. His voice was weak, but it seemed important for him to make some clever quip at this point. After defeating these agents of darkness, sardonic remarks were almost mandatory.

The club's destructive capacity had outmeasured his meager settle-for-anything expectations. The knob on its end was just big enough to do real damage, and its ridged edges didn't hurt—actually, they probably did. Overall, he was rather pleased with his first face-to-face with a gang of zombies. They weren't all that hard to kill. He moved faster than even the spry ones. And he had his wits—all they had was a feral drive smoldering inside their dead brains. A smart man could out-maneuver and out-think these chumps.

When he finally strolled off, with his club perched over his shoulder, his step was jaunty and full-of-confidence.

That confidence completely fell apart when he tumbled out of bed.

2

THAT MUST'VE BEEN **SOME BINGE** *to turn my drunken stupor into such a twisted nightmare.* Alas, that explanation was quickly dispelled by the lack of a sour mouth and a heavy head. There were no traces of any hangover. So—it hadn't been a drunken nightmare. *Then it was just a normal dream—well, not that normal…*

Life would've been so much easier if Barry could have treated the entire experience as a dream—just a bad dream.

Alas, Detective Barry Winsor could not overlook the scratches that covered his hands, forearms, and (when he pulled his pajamas up) legs too. Evidence like that simply couldn't be ignored.

But then…that meant the "dream" had been real—and *that* was absurd.

By everything Barry knew, a zombie holocaust was ridiculous, utterly impossible. The dead couldn't walk.

Just to make sure, he switched on the television and checked for any emergency broadcasts—there were none to be found.

So how did he explain the scratches that covered him? He had received those injuries during his madcap flight through the woods, escaping that first stumbling creature…y'know, the type that couldn't be real.

Had he strayed from his bed during the night? There were no thornbushes hidden under the blankets. He must have scratched himself in his sleep.

Stumbling across his darkened den, he fumbled open a drawer at his desk. He withdrew a bottle of Captain Morgan's spiced rum. Wasting no time finding a cup, he took a strong swig right from the bottle. He sank down in the chair at his desk and let out a long exhalation.

Let's be rational about this, he counseled himself.

Zombies weren't real. There'd been no undead outbreak. The world hadn't turned into a horror film. So it had just been a dream. But he'd

19

scratched himself in the dream and he still had the scratches now that he was awake. They weren't self-inflicted. (He examined himself, just to be sure. No, there was no flesh caked under his fingernails. These marks were unmistakably attributable to running through brittle shrubbery.) Had someone broken in and whipped him in his sleep? Not only was that highly improbable, but how had the whip lacerated his flesh and not his pajamas? They were still intact, unshredded like the clothing he'd worn back in the dream. Was it some weird kind of religious experience? (He doubted that, having basically turned his back on God once Emily had succumbed to her cancer.) A dream that left physical residue of itself—was that any less ridiculous than a zombie outbreak?

If it weren't for the damned scratches, Barry could shrug off the bad dream and get on with his day.

After a few more slugs of rum, which fostered no greater clarity to his process of deduction, he decided to shelf the mystery for later. There really wasn't much he could do if it'd been real. After all, according to the newspaper he'd seen, the outbreak wasn't going to happen for a few more months. No one would believe him if he tried to forewarn anybody. He had no evidence. (He didn't even believe in it in the first place, why should anybody else?)

After taking a leak, Barry moved to the kitchen and started to fry two eggs.

I could tell Frankie, but then he'd think I'd gone whacko. Hell, it sounds whacko to me.

Dreams weren't the kind of thing cops shared with each other, so bringing it up that way was no better.

No, you're stuck with this one, he mused as he stirred the yellow lumps in the skillet. *Your own private little mystery nightmare.*

Eventually, he decided to put it out of his mind. They were, after all, only minor scratches; they would heal, go away, taking with them any reminders of the horrific episode.

He ate and took a shower, then shaved and threw on what passed as his informal detective's attirea grungy gray suit with a rumpled tan trenchcoat (his original urge to become a police officer had come from watching *Columbo* on TV). Then he fished his gun (guns, actually) out of their lockbox—*See? Here's my Glock. And my .28 automatic back-up piece.*

Loath to pass through the darkened, unused portion of the house, he let himself out the back door off the kitchen. It was a chilly morning, it took a few minutes for his car (an old Impala) to warm up. He tried to think of things other than zombie apocalypses.

Frankie wasn't in yet when Barry strolled into the police station; his partner was renowned for latenight exploits, so nobody expected Frankie the Wolf to show up before noon. For that matter, recuperating from his own nocturnal escapades usually prevented Barry from seeing the squad room by morning light. Being here this early made him feel somewhat uncomfortable. He wasn't sure what to do. He puttered with some neglected paperwork, but none of it held his attention. Or perhaps looking at his scarred hands as he typed made him uneasy. Traces of his dream kept sneaking past his denial barriers and contaminating his concentration.

He needed something more tangible than paperwork to divert his attention away from the somnambulist puzzle that had followed him back into his waking hours.

Maybe a visit to the firing range. Not that his shooting needed any improvement, he was a crack shot, but the idea was the first distraction to surface in his troubled mind. He was half out of his chair when he noticed the kid sidling across the squad room.

Although Barry vaguely felt he knew the kid, he couldn't put a name to the swarthy hooded face. What he *did* recall, though, was that the kid was somehow connected to the gambling ring that he and Frankie were after.

"Yowel," grunted Barry. The name came to him just in time as the kid approached to linger beside his desk. It was an old school, family name, uncommon among the turks who made the street their home. "Pretty early for you, isn't it?" Normally, turks like this were busy spinning deals all night; they crashed with sunrise and didn't rise until mid-afternoon.

The kid twitched. Swaddled as he was in his oversized jacket, it was impossible to tell the difference between a shrug and an epileptic spasm. "Couldn't wait, copper."

"What's up?" Barry eased himself back into his chair. He gestured for the C.I. to take a seat beside the desk. The snitch had come with information he thought was important—important enough to drag him in here at this ungodly hour.

As Yowel sank into the seat, his hands clasped in his lap and he muttered, "That Titus, man—he fulla shit."

Barry nodded without comment. Remaining silent was the best way to coax the kid to get to the point.

"He owe me two Cs," complained the Criminal Informant. "He claims he strapped, but I hear he's making a big run this afternoon…thinks he's so damned important, but he's just a glorified delivery boy…"

Having seen the kid dressed lighter before summer ended, Barry knew Yowel Fredrickson was a skinny seventeen-year-old. His face was equally emaciated, but the bushy mop of his hair disguised that gauntness. He had blunt features that reminded Barry of uncooked dough. He smelled of cigarettes and beer.

"Tell me about this run," Barry probed.

In a verbal flood punctuated with grumbled condemnations, Yowel revealed that Titus Roth was scheduled to make an extended pickup run today starting at 2PM, covering far more than his usual territory. Once he was done, the bastard was supposed to head over to Waldo's Gym on Wooster Street and make his drop there instead of the usual pool hall down on Canal. The word was: some hot shot gangster (Yowel was quite specific about that, painfully articulating "gangster" to make sure the copper didn't think he meant just some random "gangsta") would be there to take custody of the previous evening's take.

Outraged that Titus refused to skim from the collection bags to pay off his debt to him, Yowel had decided to snitch the bastard out to the cops.

The news brightened Detective Barry Winsor's day. He wasn't looking to bust Titus Roth; that would tip everybody off that the police were sniffing around the gambling ring. He and Frankie had been waiting for a chance to track the gambling ring to a higher echelon, and this sounded like the perfect opportunity. All they had to do was I.D. the "gangster" and then follow him. If the gang was sloppy, several upper levels could be uncovered by nightfall as the take passed from hands to hands. Even learning the location of a stash safe would satisfy Barry. A raid could hit the place and seize the money—that would rankle a few gangland feathers.

Once he was finished with his tale, Yowel tried to wheedle two hundred out of Barry as his pay-off.

Yeah, fat chance, punk, Barry stifled a guffaw.

Well aware that the slush fund was tapped out this week, Barry pulled out his wallet under the desk and checked its contents. He only had two twenties on him. Barry advised the kid he'd have to settle for twenty until the police could ascertain the value of his news.

For a moment, the kid subjected Barry to a bad approximation of a sad puppy expression, made all the more creepy by his doughy features, but when that ploy failed to up the ante, Yowel grumbled and snatched the bill from the cop's extended fingers. But he remained seated next to the desk.

Twitching again under his bulky jacket, Yowel was reluctant to leave. He intimated that he had more info to sell, news the cops would want to know about...a new gang in town...

Eager to get rolling, though, on taking down the gambling ring, Barry hurried the kid on his way. He had high hopes about this. He needed to contact Frankie and let him know about the great break they'd gotten on this case.

But Frankie didn't answer when Barry phoned him. Although he left an excited message to call in ASAP, Barry decided he was going to run out to Frankie's house and wake him with this good news.

Just in case Frankie came in before he could reach him, Barry left a note on his partner's desk.

Collecting his gun from its place in the desk's drawer, Detective Barry Winsor headed out.

No one answered the door at Frankie's place out in the Bronx, but not for the reason Barry guessed. Frankie Dumont wasn't still in bed, sleeping off a hot date. Barry found his partner bustling about the bedroom, fully dressed, stuffing other clothes into an overnight bag.

"I let myself in, Frankie. What's going on?"

Frankie Dumont was a burly fellow, an ex-boxer who'd been on the force for two decades. He had scars for every year, too, for Frankie'd been a real go-getter during his years on the beat. Now that he was a detective, his physical presence had settled into a nervous fidgetiness. He liked to pace while thinking. Right now, though, his movements were frantic for a new reason.

"Barry, hey, look—I won't be into work today—I'm in a big hurry too—" He didn't look up at Barry as he spoke. He continued to shove necessities into the canvas satchel perched on the unmade bed.

"What's the matter?"

"It's my mom—she's sick—really sick—"

"Your mother's in Dallas."

"Yeah—you won't believe this—she's contracted the ebola virus—I gotta go to her—"

"My car's outside," Barry exclaimed. "I can drive you to the airport."

During the drive, Barry filled Frankie in on the news about Titus Roth's special bagman run that afternoon. Both of them agreed it was an opportunity that couldn't be missed. With Detective Dumont out of town, Detective Winsor would have to handle it himself. They understood how important this lead was, it could crack the gambling ring case—but a sick mother trumped that, hand's down.

Much less—sick with the ebola virus!

So far, there had only been a few cases of it in the USA, each one with no apparent connection to the outbreak in Africa. Everybody was in a panic about the virus spreading on US soil. What were the odds that one of those American victims would be Frankie's mom?

"Take Pyle with you when you tail the Roth kid, okay, Barry? He's a good man in a pinch."

"Yeah yeah." Not that he any intention of bothering with that. He'd be conducting surveillance, there'd be no action today.

Driving like a maniac, Barry got back from dropping Frankie off at the airport—just in time to spot Titus Roth as he embarked on his run.

The punk's journey took him back and forth across town, hitting every dive and more than a few bars and delis. Another lanky teenager, Titus pedaled his bicycle through traffic that was (luckily for Barry) thin, enabling the detective to follow in his unwashed car. A few times, Barry had to pull over in order to remain behind the kid.

With each successive stop, the satchel strapped to the rear of the bicycle bulged more and more.

Barry remained cool and smooth for most of the crosstown run, but as Titus Roth approached Wooster Street, Barry found himself squirming in his seat behind the wheel of the Impala. It wasn't nervousness, it was anticipation. He itched to discover who this "gangster" was—another messenger boy?—or a major player in the gambling ring? In Frankie's absence, Barry was exhibiting his partner's fidgety habit.

He wasn't headed for a bust, just a bit of surveillance. He'd be using his camera, not his gun. No heroics this afternoon.

So, why was his blood pressure so elevated?

Digging out a fifth of whiskey from under the seat, Barry bolstered his resolve with a few stiff slugs. The brash liquid spread a warm calm through his body, easing the tension.

The kid's bicycle swerved off between two remote vehicles, vanishing into traffic.

No prob, mused Barry. They were just around the corner from the gym that was the delivery boy's ultimate destination. (Detective Winsor could have just parked across the street from the gym much earlier and waited for Titus to arrive, but Barry had preferred to follow the kid on his entire route, just in case he ended up somewhere else.) A minute more and traffic would move along and he'd have the kid in sight again.

But when he nosed his Impala through the intersection, there was no sign of Titus or his bike.

Damn! Where'd the punk sneak off to...?

He carefully scrutinized the block as he cruised past the gym.

Waldo's Gym was an ancient establishment; no glitz or chrome, no wall-spanning showrooms displaying the exertions of the gymnasium's patrons. A metal door painted dull green sufficed as the only feature breaking the archaic uniformity of the building's red-bricked facade. Aluminum sheets sealed all the second story windows. Only a few pedestrians moved along the neighboring sidewalk, none of them paying undue attention to the gym.

Had the kid gotten inside that fast?

Dammit—now, I'm going to have to go in there...

If he didn't take advantage of this opportunity, another one might not come along. He couldn't pass it up. Never once did he fret over the increased risk—all part of the job. If you wanted to catch the bad guys, you had to take chances.

Barry parked the car across the street. Before he got out, he unclipped the holster in his armpit; if he was going to need it, he didn't want a safety harness slowing down his draw. He fished his .28 from its ankle clip and stuffed it into one of his trenchcoat's side pockets. Maneuvering through the minimal traffic, he approached the gym's green door.

He slipped inside, and stood at the head of a short hallway. A gruff old man manning a cashier window asked him his business.

"Interested in joining the gym," Barry responded. "Wanna check it out first."

With a curt shake of his grizzled head, the clerk informed him the gym was taking no new members.

"Really?" Barry feigned confusion. "But my pal told me to check you out. He wanted me to meet him here—he should be right inside—let me ask him about this—" As he talked, he moved to the inner door and opened it.

"Hey!" yelled the old clerk. He leaned forward, sticking his head and shoulders from the window, and shook a warning finger at Barry. If the guy had anything more to say, Barry didn't catch it; he was through the doorway, closing it behind him.

What Barry found beyond the door stopped him cold. Of all the scenarios one might expect to find in a grungy gym, a festive party with strippers wasn't high on Barry's list. There were no grunts working out, nobody sparring in the dilapidated ring, just party people (mostly twenty-something guys in expensive suits) being fawned over by a flock of scantily-clad buxom ladies. In fact, in the five seconds he gawked (before somebody noticed him), several costume garments hit the floor. There, off to the right, dallying with the punch bowl, was Titus Roth, bicycle at his side; the stuffed satchel was no longer strapped in place.

"Hey!" Somebody challenged him.

Barry started to offer some bullshit line to justify his sudden appearance at what was clearly a private stag party. But all he got out was "I'm—" before somebody else bellowed "Copper!" and everybody went for their guns.

Somebody had recognized him. Tough luck.

Tearing his own weapon from under his coat, Barry curtly identified himself (a formality) and warned them that they were all under arrest (another formality). Now things were going to get ugly. Blood was going to be spilled, but—hopefully—very little of it would belong to him.

He thought he recognized a few of the men as they scuttled about like agitated chickens. Whoever's party this was had attracted an amount of minor bosses from uptown. Why, was that Theordore Banksy over there? Catching him here was a surprise—but certainly a pleasant one. Everyone on the force had ben trying to catch the gangster red-handed for a long time.

His gun blazing, he dove for cover behind a stack of exercise mats. Gunfire followed him, chewing gaps in the thick pads. One slug went by his nose so close that he felt its heat.

No point in waiting for a lapse, there are too many of them, and they're all firing together.

He quickly reloaded the Glock, and drew his backup .28 into play. Sucking in a deep breath through his nostrils, Barry leapt to his feet and immediately dodged left. Shots hit all around him. Both his weapons returned fire. His aim was trustworthy, but he hit nobody.

By the time he came to his feet, the gym was empty. Everybody gone, partiers and strippers. There were no gangsters shooting at him. In fact, no sign of the gala, either. The tables piled with food and cake and booze were gone. No banners dangled across the walls. Although the lights were out, enough illumination spilled through the open doorway for him to notice all this.

He stopped shooting at empty air.

What the hell—?

Down the hallway, no oldster lurked in the cashier's station. The green door hung open. It appeared to be night. The light ebbing into the building's interior came from a lone streetlamp.

Outside, the street was as empty as the gym.

3

HE FELT FOOLISH BRANDISHING his weapons at an empty street.

He lowered them, but didn't put them away.

What the hell is going on here?

One second I'm in the middle of a shootout—and now everybody's gone and it's night already.

Did I have some kind of blackout?

But wait...if I passed out during the shootout, those guys would've finished me off.

None of this made any sense.

He was reminded of the scratches on his arms that he'd carried beyond his dream—they made the same kind of no sense.

The empty street even fit with the abandoned world from that nightmare.

A movement caught his eye. Figures were stumbling out of an alley. Barry didn't need them to reach the streetlamp, he could tell they were dead from their rigid shuffle. A few seconds later, the stench verified his assumption.

Back into the land of zombies.

Despite the nocturnal ambience, everything was so vivid—too vivid to be a dream. Just as the first one had gone on too long to be a dream.

You're really here, Barry. Whether it made any sense or not, he couldn't question his senses. This was real, and he was stuck here.

He chose to save the ammo and just outrun these imminent zombies. He set off at a run; best to quickly put as much distance between them as possible. As he jogged along, he scanned the storefronts he passed. These darkened shops told a tale of looting and then abandonment. He saw no one else, live, dead or undead. He shuddered when he realized why there were no corpses littering the sidewalks. They all got up and walked off. Or got eaten by the ones who walked off.

It troubled him how unpopulated the avenues were. No sign of life at all. No lights in any windows. Had the zombies gotten everyone?

There have to be survivors. I can't be the only one left...

But he was reluctant to yell out something, lest he attract the wrong kind of attention—the shambling dead kind.

Just have to keep moving...until I find somebody...

There *had* to be survivors...

When Barry Winsor finally found somebody, they shot at him. They didn't care when he shouted to them that he was alive. They continued to shoot at him, driving him into a department store.

When he got around to thinking about it, maybe it wasn't all that outrageous. How could this person know Barry was a good guy—a cop, in fact—and trust him? It was probably a dog-eat-dog world in which many of the survivors had been driven to hostile behavior. While common sense dictated that strength lay in numbers, there were always going to be those antisocial ones who thought they could go it alone, themselves verses everything.

Not much point trying to convince this guy that I'm not a serial killer.

Move on—find someone friendlier...

His next encounter was with a dog, and it unsettled him much more than anything so far.

The mangy brown mutt came creeping from an alleyway, its head cocked at what initially seemed an uncomfortable angle, as if the animal were fascinated with something clinging to its back.

"Hey, boy," Barry called to the dog. Man's best friend was almost as good as another person.

But as the beast jerked to gawk at him, Barry was forced to reconsider that adage.

The creature's gaze was vacant, while its lips slavered with gruesome hostility. What had originally appeared to be clinging to its side turned out to be a metal rod impaling the beast. Going all the way through, the other end of the rod protruded from the lower chest. One of its legs was badly ravaged, but the creature put weight on it without wincing.

Because it was no longer alive.

With a snarl, the undead dog came at him. It shambled across the pavement, its jaws yawning with anticipation.

Barry put a bullet through its head.

Human zombies were unnatural enough. But—zombie canines? Never, in any horror movie he could think of had Barry ever seen undead animals. But—upon brief reflection, it sort of made sense. Some contagion had reanimated dead people—why would animals be immune to the same poison? What about birds? Or insects? He hadn't realized until now: this dog was the first wildlife he'd seen in this nightmarish landscape, here or in the Illinois woods. The rustlings he'd heard that night—had that been undead rodents on the prowl? Was this apocalyptic world populated entirely by undead species?

Somehow, the idea of zombie cats and dogs bothered him more than human zombies.

The next person he encountered was fighting off a swarm of hungry undead. This gave Barry the opportunity to prove his good intentions by going to her rescue.

Before leaving the department store (by its backdoor), Barry had sought out the store's sporting goods section and armed himself with a pair of hefty golf clubs. He remembered what efficient weapons they'd made last time…last time…

He had to shake off that annoyingly persistent sense of unreality (all this was real, dammit!) and focus on the crisis at hand.

In actuality, it was only a crisis for the girl. Barry had little difficulty bludgeoning back the swarm. As the zombies staggered about in turmoil, Barry grabbed the girl by her arm and hurried her away.

She came with him, dazed and possibly not completely aware of what was going on. A moment ago, she had faced certain death—and a gruesome one, at that. Her scrambled state of mind was no surprise.

As he led her along, he spoke to the girl, assuring her she was safe now. "My name is Barry, I'm a police officer. You're safe now. It's okay. I'm here to protect you." He continued his litany, intent on easing her out of her withdrawal. He'd released her arm from his grip and guided her now with a hand against her back. He tried everything he could think of to rouse the girl from her fugue.

She was in her twenties, somewhat mousy with uncombed brown hair and a pointy nose. Her eyes were cartoonishly large. She wore a camouflage jacket with a utility vest. An assortment of pouches hung from the two belts that circled her narrow waist. One leg of her blue-and-gray pants had come untucked from her Doc Martin boots. From her attire he would guess she was a student—but no, he suspected her clothing was a testament to her post-holocaust lifestyle.

If he could calm her down, return sanity to those huge eyes, maybe she could explain to him how the world had reached this state of decay.

At least this time Barry was on familiar turf. Last time, his transition had displaced him from his bed at home to a woodland lake in unknown territory. But here in his own city, he stood a better chance of survival. He could think of places that might be safe.

In fact, they were nearby one of those locales. Barry guided the mute girl in that direction. She offered no resistance. She wasn't even aware where she was.

Two blocks later, they were climbing the steps of the 9th Police Station. Here, the evidence of combat and destruction was more apparent. Apparently the precinct had fought off a siege. Numerous bullet holes pockmarked the charred concrete edifice. An assortment of rubble littered the entrance, among them an inexplicable baby carriage. Anyone who had died here was long gone, down an undead throat or shuffling off on posthumous feet.

The remains of a barricade piled in the entranceway presented Barry with a problem. The path through the broken barricade was labyrinthine; no way could he carry the girl through this maze, nor could he expect her to maneuver on her own in her present shell-shocked condition.

It was time to take some drastic action…drastic and unpleasant.

Facing off with the girl, Barry smacked her on the cheek hard enough to sting the palm of his hand. She recoiled, but her responses remained automatic. Her eyes were still glazed over.

He hit her again, this time giving an accompanying yell, "Hey in there!"

Her stare flickered. A cross expression came to her face. She made to push him away. He held her fast.

"Are you with us?"

After a moment, she pouted and nodded.

"You're safe now. My name is Barry. I'm a police officer."

"Those deaders…they came out of nowhere.."

"I took care of them. You've been rescued. Okay?"

Again, she gave a hesitant nod.

"Right now, we're relatively safe. I want to get us somewhere that's more reliably secure, okay?"

"Okay…"

"In there." He pointed to the barricaded entrance. "We have to climb our way through. Can you manage that?"

"I think so…"

"Let's give it a try, okay?" He urged her closer to the barricade.

He followed her, reassuring the girl by his immediate proximity.

At first, her movement was halting, her balance uncertain as she clambered through the gaps in the makeshift barrier. But eventually she grew nimble and moved ahead of him, out of his line of vision.

"Don't venture too far," he advised her.

He was relatively certain (more "unrealistically hopeful," actually) that the police station would serve as a safe haven, but who knew what lurked within the building? If any hostiles were inside, Barry needed to dispatch them to insure the safety of himself and the girl. He didn't want her blundering off and encountering anything nasty. He'd only just snapped her out of her daze, he wasn't eager to see her comatose again.

Several spots presented him with tight squeezes, but he got through. More broken furniture cluttered the foyer, another layer of the precinct's failed defense line. The girl was picking her way through this wreckage.

He found a closet and convinced her to remain hidden there until his return.

"I want to make sure the building is secure," he told her. *And empty.* But he didn't mention that part, fearing that the prospect of unwanted company might upset her.

"You'll come back…"

"Of course I'll be back." This wasn't just positive reinforcement; the smile he gave her was fueled by sincere confidence. The worst he could encounter would be a few starving zombies, easily put down by his pair of lethal golf clubs. There were only three floors and a basement; he could search the building quickly enough. Maybe first he'd lock the access points to the basement, leave that area for later.

His search produced no unsavory lurkers or surprises.

The building was empty. The arsenal stripped bare. The kitchen devoid of anything edible. Even the water bottles that went with the dispensing units were gone. The corridors and rooms looked as if a hurricane had hit them, leaving only debris of desks, chairs and filing cabinets. From a scrap of newspaper, he gleaned that the date was May 4th, which put him much closer to his own time than his last nightmarish visit. The lockup was equally empty and vandalized. One section of bars had been pulled from its chassis and tossed aside. Copious bloodstains decorated the cells, dried black and covered with a visible patina of dust—evidence of a massacre that had occurred here long ago.

There in the cells, he found the only weapons that hadn't been stolen by looters: three brutally bent truncheons, their metal cores kinked, their leather sheathes cracked by savage impacts. He could understand why no one had taken them. Their despoiled condition declared the severity of the slaughter that had ensued within these confines. They had apparently served someone well, but now were useless relics of that horrible bloodbath.

A more meticulous inspection would have to wait until later. Barry didn't like the idea of leaving the girl alone for too long.

Returning to the groundfloor, he released her from her closet hidey hole. She was visibly relieved to see him alive.

He took her into an office that was only minorly trashed and settled her on an undamaged couch. While she sat and fidgeted, he quickly checked the chamber for anything useful. He scored with the discovery of a stash of candy bars in the back of a bottom desk drawer.

"Here, but go slow," he cautioned her immediate haste once he gave her a candy bar. "Eat it too fast and it might come right back up. Sorry, but there doesn't appear to be anything to drink." Secretly, he hoped a few offices would yield up hidden bottles of whiskey and rum; that would quench his particular thirst, but not the girl's.

She grunted and fished a canteen from her belt.

"Thanks." Now that he held the sloshing container, he realized how dry his mouth was.

"Denise."

"Huh?"

"My name…it's Denise," she explained. "Denise Collard."

He grinned.

"Well, it's nice to meet you, Miss Denise Collard."

She tried to smile, but her mouth was too busy devouring the candy bar.

Settling himself cross-legged on the floor at the foot of the couch, Barry took a third welcome swig, then capped the canteen and handed it back to her.

"Say, Miss Collard, maybe you could answer a few questions for me...?"

He had hoped to learn more about the zombie apocalypse, but Miss Collard was not a news-hound. In fact, once things (whatever they'd been) had gone wrong, the girl's attention had been more concerned with daily survival. Things had started hard and, according to her, only gotten harder.

Right after the onset, there'd been days between encounters with zombies. But as time ground on, the encounters grew more frequent and more dangerous. Loners became pairs became teams became swarms, wandering the countryside. She presumed the "countryside" was infested, but being a native New Yorker, she'd never thought of leaving the city

The idea of heading out into the wilderness was not all that bad; at least, that was Barry's private opinion.

As far as any explanation for the outbreak, Miss Collard knew of none. It had happened so fast that society hadn't had much of a chance to publicly examine the crisis. News channels had all been blank by the time she'd thought to check them out.

"I was at a dance," she told him. "Me and a few BFFs hit this rave, hoping we'd meet some nice cool guys. Ha—the ones we encountered weren't nice and were even less cool. About half-past midnight, we decided to split. Despite the late hour, we decided to spare ourselves the cost of a cab; we would ride the subway home. We almost made it to the subway entrance, but this guy jumped on Debbie. He bit her—bit her right on the arm. We all freaked. I ran one way, the other girls scattered in other directions." She gave him a soulful sad look. "I never saw any of them again."

For days after that night, Miss Collard had hid in her apartment, nursing her traumatic shock. By the time she ventured out (for food), society had collapsed and everybody she saw on the street was undead. When the girl returned to her apartment, she found it overrun by nosy undead neighbors; her escape had been an ordeal. Since then, she'd lived on the run, pilfering what she needed and never sleeping in the same place twice. And choosing those places with vigilance bordering on paranoia.

So far, she had fared rather well. She was mildly vain about this point. Most people had fallen prey to the surprise situation, being set upon by strangers who wanted more than a handshake. But then, she confided, a previous boyfriend had been a big horror movie buff, so she'd seen a lot of zombie films and generally knew what to expect. She'd been quick to hit a police armory, taking as many weapons and as much ammo as she could carry. She abandoned her party dresses for camouflage outfits, although she admitted she didn't know if they helped hide her from the undead, but they helped keep her unnoticed by the nasties and the crazies. Oh, there were a lot of them. "Where," she wondered, "did all the polite people go?"

Barry could guess where they were, but held his tongue. The easy-going ones would've been among the first to go down, easy victims. Only the paranoid would avoid getting eaten, and paranoia bred other unpleasant mental states. It didn't surprise Barry to hear there were a lot of nasty crazies running around. It only made a bad situation worse. Worst case scenarios seemed to be the post-apocalyptic norm.

He had to respect the girl for surviving all that. Zombies and crazies, much less basic starvation. He'd expected her to be a skittish little thing, but it turned out she had grit

When he questioned her about a meteor threatening to hit the Earth, Miss Collard responded with a pixy laugh. Seeing his fixed expression, she coughed and apologized, "Oh, you're serious. I think I remember hearing something about that, but the news program dismissed it as a fraud."

At first Barry was glad to hear her cavalier dismissal of any meteor strike. But then it occurred to him, if one had hit since the fall of civilization, how would word spread of such an impact? There could be a gigantic crater somewhere in Europe and nobody Stateside would know about it. No volcanic clouds saturating the sky, so maybe it wasn't that big a meteor.

It bothered him how many gaps existed in his understanding of how things had gone bad.

Although his initial idea of holing up in an empty police station had been valid, Barry had to concede that this station had proven less than productive. Officers and/or looters had taken everything of value, food, water, weapons. The location might safeguard them from the zombies…but it might also serve to attract the attention of nasties looking to restock their arsenals or larders.

Miss Collard agreed with his line of thought. She'd witnessed gangs raid stores. "Not a pretty sight."

He could imagine so. Not all criminals were cunning, most were complete idiots—but there were always some who weren't utter fools. They'd be among the survivors. With society reverted to anarchy, these nasties would run wild, unchecked by any law enforcement. Anarchy came with an increase of vermin.

Barry proposed they leave the city. Beyond the concrete jungle, things were more spread out, not as heavily populated as the Big Apple. Less people would mean fewer zombies.

She grumbled, whining that she'd never been outside the city. "Never had any need to…everything anybody could want can be found here in Manhattan."

Ruefully, he had to agree with her sumnation. His job had taken him outside NYC's limits, but he'd always considered himself a city-boy at heart.

But the time had come to go.

He told her so.

They left the next afternoon.

"There's no way we're going on-foot."

The time had come to unlock the basement and explore that dark realm. There might still be some cars down there, but his gut told him the underground garage was as pilfered as the rest of the station. He had to check, though.

When he tried to get Miss Collard safely ensconced back inside the closet, she resisted and denounced his intentions. "I can take care of myself, dammit!"

He smiled, impressed by her defiance. He'd been raised to think of women as soft creatures who needed protection, and society had reinforced that antiquated attitude. But Miss Collard had a point—she had survived for months, fighting off living and undead assailants. It was unreasonable for him to doubt her ability to take care of herself.

"Okay." He led her to a doorway that led downstairs. It was chained shut. He unbound the door and slowly opened it.

Darkness ruled down there.

"Wish we had a flashlight," he muttered; there'd been none left at the pillaged precinct.

But Miss Collard produced one. The survivalist.

He took point and headed into the stairwell. Except for a few pieces of trash, it was empty.

He descended the steps. She followed, close at his back. They both held weapons ready for any sudden surprise—she, a gun; he, his trusty golf club.

All things considered, the club wasn't the smartest choice for a weapon in the stairwell's confined space. Luckily, he was given no reason to defend himself on the steps.

At the bottom, a broken chair propped open the door on the garage's stygian depths. When he tried the lightswitch on the wall beside the doorframe, none of the neon fixtures flickered to life. He moved through the threshold with the girl on his heels.

Swinging the flashlight beam in an expansive slow arc showed them a deserted parking area. Some scattered debris. No cars.

Behind him, Miss Collard expressed a disappointed sigh.

He pointed the light toward the far portion of the L-shaped chamber. "Let's see what's around that corner…"

Two vehicles were stashed around the bend. A dark van and a black-and-white cruiser. Three of the van's tires were flat. The black-and-white's windshield was riddled with fractures.

Despite the window's condition, the car was the obvious choice. While Barry clubbed the windshield to pieces and tossed aside the shards, Miss Collard stood by, fanning the flashlight back and forth, wary for any danger lurking in the darkness.

Naturally, the keys weren't in the ignition.

But they lucked out. The right one turned up in the batch Barry fetched from the key station.

The van was empty, but in the trunk of the cruiser he found a shotgun and a few boxes of shells. "Score!" These were welcome additions to their arsenal.

Once both of them were in the car and had it running, Barry gave a relieved sigh. "Ready?"

"As I'll ever be."

While he handled the steering wheel, Miss Collard cradled the loaded shotgun across her lap. She was ready to swing it into use at the slightest suspicious eventuality.

The gate to the street hung ajar. Barry nudged it open with the cruiser's bumper, then drove up the ramp.

The afternoon sun revealed the avenue in all its anarchistic glory. Several cars sprawled on the sidewalks, more than a few with their noses piercing storefront panes of glass. A stiff breeze sent trash scuttling across the asphalt. About a block away on the left, a few figures could be seen shambling along.

Barry turned right, heading down the empty street.

Their journey met with abundant obstacles.

Traffic jams of abandoned vehicles blocked numerous thoroughfares.

A wooden fence had been erected across one street. Eager to avoid contact with territorial fanatics, Barry took another route.

On one occasion, someone shot at them. A slug ricocheted off the cruiser's hood. Barry hit the accelerater. Miss Collard raised her weapon…but neither of them spotted the shooter. The black-and-white swiftly left the locale behind.

Their most common problem came from zombie encounters. Single ones were easily avoided; if they got in the way, they got run over. Groups were the real difficulty. Even smaller gangs could become troublesome, but swarms were outright deadly.

Twice they ran afoul of swarms.

The first time, the entire avenue was clogged with zombies. It was like some undead rally—*we're monsters and proud of it.* Barry prudently threw the cruiser into reverse before more than a few corpses on the fringe of the crowd noticed the car and started to shuffle in its approaching direction. That avenue was relatively unblocked, granting the black-and-white a hasty retreat.

The next time there were about forty of them. They all milled around a toppled school bus. This time Barry took bolder action. Instead of retreating, he guided the black-and-white along the opposite side of the street, up onto the sidewalk. Anything in his way got pushed aside or driven over, like a display stand of handbags and a stray shambler. An abandoned hatchback stood between the distressed bus and Barry's intended path. A number of zombies noticed the black-and-white's passage and lurched to throw themselves at it, but the sedan acted as a barrier. Barry zoomed away, leaving the swaying cadavers to batter their brittle fists in undead frustration against the sedan's flank.

Once they saw someone who didn't try to attack them, but the old woman fled, vanishing in a maze of deserted automobiles. When Miss Collard suggested they track down the old woman and add her to their party, Barry countered, "She clearly wants to be left alone."

Each obstacle was met with stoic resolve. Both Detective Barry

Winsor and the wayward Denise Collard were capable survivors. Armed, sharp-of-wits, and riding in the police cruiser, they were a force to be reckoned with.

Having left Manhattan far behind, they drove through marshes colored by chemical spills.

Initially, Barry had been daunted by the profusion of dead out for a country stroll. Somehow he'd assumed there'd be less contagion in rural territory, or that at least the infected individuals would be more loosely scattered. But no, the roadways on the Jersey side of the Hudson were as crowded as Broadway had been. At some point, the abandoned cars had presented such a problem that they'd been bulldozed aside to clear the routes leading away from the Holland Tunnel, but since then fresh wrecks had taken their place; at least this new tangle wasn't a complete impasse. Barry succeeded in winding the cruiser through a frustrating obstacle course, ultimately bringing them to the open highway. Except, these highways weren't all that open. More than just hundreds of deserted autos littered the asphalt, a loose horde of undead occupied the terrain with their aimless shuffling.

Here, Barry applied brute force, sending the black-and-white barreling through the crowd like a merciless juggernaut. Concentrating on veering around the abandoned cars, he wasn't worried about hitting any zombies—that was acceptable collatoral damage. But if he accidentally rammed into one of these metal monoliths of the road, a collision could damage the cruiser and strand them in the midst of this cadaverous mob. He had to balance speed (to keep the bastards from snagging onto the car as it passed) with acute navigation (to preserve their transportation).

The crowd seemed never-ending as he plowed through it. He guided the cruiser onto a ramp, hoping the elevated interstate might be less populated, but no, here too there were undead crowds aplenty. From this higher vantage, Barry could see for miles.

What he saw brought a deeper scowl to his already grimacing face.

The throngs did indeed stretch on forever. As far as he could see, the landscape swayed with reanimated corpses.

Not good…

How long could he expect the cruiser to hold up under this savage barrage? For that matter, how much gas was left after their circuitous escape route from the Big Apple? How far could he push the car before something killed it?

And then, we'll be next.

He'd intended to burn rubber on the open highway, putting as much distance as he could between themselves and the dead city. The farther into the countryside they could get, the better he'd feel. Alas, the highway wasn't open; it was a perilous maze of murderous impediments.

He wondered if the scenic backroads would be as crowded.

Desperately careening along the interstate, weaving frantically around immobile metal hulks and plowing through the undead mob, leaving behind a debris trail of decayed flesh and brittle bones, Barry drove like a madman. Beside him, Miss Collard remained alert for any clingers-on, which she summarily dislodged with a brusque-but-efficient poke of one of Barry's golf clubs.

A green sign emerged from the distance, announcing an imminent exit. That was enough for Barry; he didn't even notice the name of the exit. When the exit sign loomed, he cut over abruptly and took the ramp that descended from the elevated interstate.

For a block or so, the crowd remained constant, but eventually Barry's hopes paid off. Soon they were cruising down empty lanes. Greenery surrounded them. Further back from the roadway, large houses could be seen through the thick landscaped shrubbery. (Barry briefly entertained the notion of using one of these mansions as shelter for the night, but he decided it was wiser to put the highway horde far behind them before they stopped.) These roads were less cluttered with abandoned vehicles. Some rubble existed, but overturned benches offered no real hazards to the cruiser.

He pulled into the first gas station he spotted. Their pumps were dry, as were the pumps belonging to the next three gas'n'go's he hit. Finally, however, he found a station that hadn't been drained. He fed the cruiser's depleted tank, then filled three plastic jugs which he stored in the trunk.

Miss Collard wandered out from the convenience store attached to the depot, lugging bundles of plastic bags with each hand. Food," the girl informed him as she dumped the bags in the cruiser's backseat. Retaining one bag, she set it in her lap and pulled it wide open to reveal its contents. Mini bags of chips, shrink-wrapped sticks of beef jerky, candy bars in wrinkled wrappers, small cans of undoubtedly warm soda.

"Junk food," he mumbled.

"Munchies for the road." She flashed him a knowing smile and declared, "Trust me, this is a feast compared to what's left out there."

With a shrug he grabbed a bag of chips. He bit it open and poured the contents into his hungry mouth. Normally, he had no problem with a diet like this, as his flabby middle attested, but how long could anyone seriously survive on intermittent junk? Sooner or later, they would have to locate some real food.

Back on the road, he cruised along, pensively surveying the neighborhoods through which they passed. He moved quickly through the tenement districts, not trusting the squat structures that had homed so many unfortunates. His cruising speed lowered as he trolled along more opulant avenues. Like before, there were ranks of mansions, each discretely removed from the roadway and many guarded by stone walls and brass gates. Again, it struck him what a perfect hiding place one of these opulent domiciles would make, but again he shelved the idea until he had gotten them farther away from the crowded highway district.

Deeper and deeper into the wilds of rural America he drove.

So focused had Barry Winsor been on driving the black-and-white, he'd failed to notice the girl drift off. Snoring mildly, Miss Collard lay asleep next to him.

Maybe it's time, he told himself, *to find a safe haven for the night.*

The girl needed the rest, and so did he.

Unfortunately, his drive had taken them away from upper class real estate and into more plebian realms. He drove past arrays of rowhouses, block after block of them. They seemed to stretch on forever, and twilight was darkening into evening. He'd have to settle for a more rustic hiding place tonight.

They all looked alike. Red-bricked facades, uniformly squashed together to the point that each home's front door rubbed intimate elbows with their neighbor's. Some of the lawns had been decorated with potted shrubs or children's swimming pools, but now the plants were withered from neglect, the pools deflated and coated with scum. No windows betrayed any trace of interior lighting, but that hardly convinced Barry of the uninhabited condition of each residence.

No prudent criteria occurred to him that might determine which domicile was the safest choice. He was just going to have to pick randomly.

Miss Collard came instantly awake when he pulled over to the curb and shut off the cruiser's engine. Her eyes were alert. She clutched the golf club in one hand, ready for any immediate threat, while her other hand scooped the shotgun from where it had been propped between her legs.

"It's okay," he quickly assured the girl. "No swarms, no crazies. Time to pack it in for today, catch some sleep."

When she started to protest, he smiled and qualified his intentions, "Some comfortable sleep."

Reaching up to rub a crick from her neck, she gave in. "So...where are we?"

"I have no idea. Somewhere in New Jersey." He was honestly at a loss when it came to their location. He'd driven long and hard, all day and well into the night. His concentration had been focused on selecting safe routes. He'd noticed several signs—Welcome to Lincoln Park, Riverdale, Butler—but they meant nothing to him. "Maybe there's a map in the cruiser's glove compartment." But when they looked, they found no map. "I suppose we should've grabbed a map while refueling at that gas station." He shrugged. "We can get one tomorrow."

Standing beside the black-and-white, Barry and Miss Collard surveyed the street for a long moment.

"Okay...which one?"

"I haven't decided yet," he replied.

Scoping out locations which might possibly harbor hostiles was not new to him, but in those instances his judgment had been primed to watch out for signs of criminal activity. Here and now, he was actually searching for signs of *un*inhabitation. It was a completely different game, one that momentarily stymied him.

They all looked alike: run down, weathered, empty.

But that's exactly what someone hiding in there would want us to think, he mused.

"Can I make a few suggestions?"

He turned to stare at her. What he saw was a twenty-something innocent, but her tone marked her as a skilled survivor.

She proceeded to point out the signs of possible habitation. Every windowshade closed, that was a giveaway. Suspiciously clean doorsteps, evidence of human traffic. A trail of smoke rose from the chimney of one home, advertising the naivete of the poor wretch hiding therein. Another family had converted their puny front lawn into a garden that appeared somewhat healthier than the surrounding vegetation. There were a total of twenty-two homes lining this block; Miss Collard deftly identified five of them as sheltering someone.

"Potential hostiles," was the way she put it.

He arched a fluffy eyebrow at her. "They could be people—like us—just looking to survive."

"It's a new world," Miss Collard admonished him. "These days, you can't trust anyone."

"Sooner or later, we'll have to trust *somebody*."

"Maybe...but we'll have to be *really* careful. Even a BFF could turn out to be hostile."

Again, Barry's eyebrows converged, this time crowding the bridge of his nose with a reflective scowl. His cop sense detected some trauma underlying that last remark.

"You sound like you speak from personal experience," he remarked.

"Remember those girls I told you about? The ones I went to the rave with?" She turned to show him a sad face. "About a week after the outbreak, I ran into one of them. The one that crazy guy bit. He must've been among the first wave of deaders. He infected Donna. She came after me. She didn't recognize me. All she wanted to do was...hurt me."

After a moment, Barry ventured, "Did you...put her down?"

"Killing Donna's corpse was a turning point for me." Her sad eyes had hardened. Her lips were drawn tight. "After that, I armed myself and learned how to fight...how to survive."

The incident did not sound like a pleasant one. But—instead of scarring her, the encounter had only strengthened Miss Collard, helping her to survive this post-apocalyptic world. Barry admired her spunk.

Relying on the girl's judgment, they selected a domicile they could safely occupy for the evening. It was farther down the block, away from where he'd parked the cruiser. A crude wooden porch flanked the structure, offering a raised barricade to guard the threshold. The first-floor windows were high and locked behind iron grating, adequately securing them against forced entry.

Despite his new trust in the girl's survivalist expertise, Barry conducted a thorough recon of the interior once they were past the stout oak door. He made Miss Collard wait in the foyer (telling her she was guarding the entrance, when in fact staying there hopefully put her out of immediate harm's way), while he moved from room to room, up the stairs to examine a pair of empty bedrooms and a bleak-looking bathroom. As he went, he made sure that each window was locked. A backdoor led off the kitchen onto a balcony that hung onto a dilapidated alleyway; the former tenants had blocked this exit with piles of heavy furniture. Back in the foyer, he found wedges had been nailed on either side of the threshold; a stout plank of hardwood rested in a corner, it clearly fit into the wedges, securing the door against bellicose entry. Whoever had lived here had taken measures to protect their home from the nasty new world. So...where were they? Why had their fortifications failed them? He saw no trace of blood splattered about, so the family's exodus had not been a violent one. So...what had forced them to flee? Despite the apparent unthreatening nature of the domicile, Barry could not discard a vague sense of caution about the place.

"As safe as it's going to get," she told him.

He nodded gravely. He assumed she had made her own examination and had decided the home would serve as a shelter for them.

Did Miss Collard share his curiosity regarding the fate of the family? If so, she made no mention of it.

They transferred their bags of food into the house. After a brief debate, they decided to take all of their weapons indoors, but left the extra jugs of gasoline in the cruiser's trunk.

Barry took first watch. This afforded him time to brood. While he had only a few things to brood over, they were annoyingly momentous.

What the hell happened to the world?

What the hell happened to me? How did I get here?

No matter how many times he ran these frustrating puzzles in his head, he could find no logical answers.

Eventually, he grew weary of torturing himself with this fruitless pastime. He wandered through the house, rooting for possible supplies. He found no weapons, no food, no old newspapers offering explanations for the cataclysm, but he didn't expect to. He did, however, find the family's liquor cabinet, and was surprised to find it still reasonably stocked.

He took a pair of whiskey bottles back to his post in the living room. Sprawling on the sofa, he proceeded to drown his mysteries.

When the first bottle only served to soften his discomfort, Barry relied on the second one to finish the job.

He got smashed.

Instinctively, he sought unconsciousness to silence his nagging frustration. If he could only achieve this catatonia, he'd've languished there forever.

But alas, his worries bullied their way into his drunken fog, salting his blurred mind with their obnoxious stink. Zombies cavorted like devils, goaded on by criminals he'd once arrested. The apocalypse had freed them from prison; now all of their schemes were devoted to tormenting Barry Winsor. But when he shot them, they became zombies and continued to torment him. He longed to pass out and escape this misery, but that proved to be impossible. No matter how hard he tried, a trace of bleary consciousness lingered for the demons to abuse.

A few times, darkness embraced him, but it didn't last, oblivion dancing away, leaving him to further victimization.

At one point he thought he woke up in his home bed, but he was too drunk to be sure. The incident might have been just another inebriated whimsy. Anyway, before he could rally his focus, he was back on the sofa in the safe house.

Safe from zombies.

At least, that was the intended reason for hiding there…

But how safe was it really? The room seemed filled with undead figures lurching about, blindly pawing at the furniture and the walls, moaning like crumpled leaves. Their stink was repellent.

The stench dragged him from his stupor.

The room really *was* filled with zombies! Somehow, the undead bastards had gotten in! They milled around him, clumsily bumping into each other.

Why hadn't they attacked him?

Was it because he lay unmoving? Did they think he was already dead? After so long on-the-road without a bath, he smelled pretty ripe, but the odor of alcohol covered that smell.

Most of their arsenal was upstairs with Miss Collard. Barry's golf clubs had been propped against a lounge chair, undead jostling had knocked them to the floor. He knew grabbing for them was futile, the weapons were lost now underfoot as the zombies shambled to and fro. That same crowd made frantic flight impossible too. He might shove his way past two or three of them, but the others would swarm and drag him down and begin dining on him.

Well, he fumed, *I can't stay here…*

But his booze-addled brain couldn't squeeze out any viable courses of action. After all his prior failure to pass out, now he had to actively struggle to remain conscious.

This isn't fair…

You're a drunk, he accused himself. *You screwed up, and now you're paying for it.*

He was about to muse that his plight couldn't get any worse—when it did.

Flickers of light wandered into the living room from the foyer. Although the details remained hidden by the shambling silhouettes, flames were engulfing the doorway.

You've got to be kidding me.

The fire crept into the living room. The zombies recoiled from the blaze; panic overwhelmed their dead brains and their aimless milling about swiftly became a frenzied rabble.

Now or never, idiot.

It would've been nice if he'd leapt from the couch and dashed through the undead mob, but he was overweight and drunk. The best he could manage was struggling to his feet, his body suddenly seemed made of inert dough. Once erect, he had difficulty staying there. His legs were asleep, they wobbled beneath him. He inefficiently steadied himself by leaning against (more like collapsing into) the back of the nearby lounger. The zombies thrashed about him, engrossed in their frantic-but-futile efforts to flee the inferno; they blindly clawed at each other, seeking exits where there were only solid walls. Barry's head swam in a murky swamp. The room was spinning…looming flames contributed strangely stuttering illumination, rioting zombies surrounded him.

Okay, you're up—do something with that…

But—which direction should he go? The pyre blocked the front entrance. The windows and backdoor were all secured. Upstairs was all that was left.

And he had to alert Miss Collard. Their sanctuary had been violated, first by the undead and now by a fire.

He launched himself toward the stairs. His progress was tottery. Normal bloodflow returned to his legs, replacing numbness with an infuriating tingle. He needed to rely on external things to maintain his balance. In order to to cross the crowded room, most of the things he grasped to steady himself were undead. He tasted bile and forced it down. Contact with the zombies was unbearable. They were soft and squishy and rotten and they reeked. They blindly struggled with each other, and he joined that melee. Hopefully none of them would notice the living person in their midst. No, this pandemonium flooded what rudimentary awareness they had with earnest alarm, occluding all other stimuli. He staggered from corpse to corpse, squeezing past cadavers locked in pointless combat. Each step was a grotesque ordeal as Barry made his way through the throng.

Finally—Barry fell upon the stairs. He immediately crawled up the steps. Smoke was just beginning to creep along the upstairs hallway.

There was no point anymore in staying quiet.

"Fire!" he bellowed.

As he reached the door of the bedroom she'd chosen, it jerked open. She stood there, her bleary eyes wide, rudely awakened to face sudden disaster. She still wore her gray-and-blue camouflage outfit, having crashed fully dressed.

"And zombies," he added.

That got Miss Collard moving. Darting back into the bedroom, she hastily (but quite efficiently, he noticed) gathered their arsenal together. Their bags of food were downstairs, beyond any chance of rescue.

He remained poised in the doorway, uncertain what to do next.

"The window," she hissed.

Following her lead, he helped her out the window. They jumped into the back alley, landing atop a coup sedan. They took off along the alley, dodging between parked cars and rubble spilling from back porches.

To reach the police cruiser, they were going to have to travel to the end of the alley, then backtrack along the front block to where Barry had parked it. That was an awful lot of distance for them to be exposed. At this point, Barry was worried about more than just zombies.

Where'd that undead crowd come from?

And what about the fire?

Pyromania was unlikely behavior for the undead.

A living person *started that fire, presumably the same villain who herded those zombies into the house.*

A crazy.

A crazy who might still be hanging around to see what gets us—the zombies or the fire...

As he ran, Barry scanned for signs of trouble. He saw nothing amiss.

When they reached the end of the alley, he pulled her behind a brick wall and confided his deductions to her.

Miss Collard agreed with his suspicions about a living mastermind behind tonight's assault. She was quick to suspect that one of the others holed up on the block had pulled this stunt as some brazen attempt to drive off competition. "And of course we need to reach the car. We can't afford to lose all the stuff stashed in it."

Somehow, Barry was less concerned about "stuff" than he was about overall escape. The cruiser offered them the fastest means of getting the hell out of here. Finding alternative transportation was a risky prospect that would take too much time. Without the black-and-white, they were screwed.

Together, alert and suspicious of every shadow, Barry and Miss Survivalist edged around the corner and surveyed the length of street that separated them from the cruiser. Uneven rows of abandoned automobiles lined the avenue, inky hulks in the flickering light from the sole operational streetlamp. Barry paid extra attention to the five abodes which the girl had earlier identified as "potentially occupied."

They advanced slowly, their eyes sweeping back and forth in tandem with the nozzles of their weapons. The only noise to break the night's canopy was the crunch of their boots on the asphalt. Halfway along the avenue, the sound of a brittle leaf crumpling under an unseen foot brought Barry and the girl to an immediate halt. He stood with one foot inches off the ground, frozen in position, acutely alert to his surroundings. In the corner of his eye, he saw Miss Collard nod in the direction of the next rowhouse on the right. Her hunter's expertise had located the sound's origin.

Moving in an arc, he positioned himself before the house. The girl came in from the side, close to the wall.

What are we going to do? he pondered. *Force whoever it is to come out with their hands behind their head? Damn, I hope she doesn't intend going in after whoever it is. She's got that edgy spunk, I wouldn't put it past her...*

But before Miss Collard could show how recklessly couragous she was, the noisemaker leaped into view and scampered off down the street. The cat disappeared around the same corner that had brought Barry and the girl to the thoroughfare.

Barry expelled a gust of air. The muscles along his shoulder relaxed. He lowered his gun.

Miss Collard remained silent. Still cautious, the girl stayed where she was against the house's redbrick wall.

A few moments passed and nothing happened.

Finally, Miss Collard emerged from shadow and joined him in the street. Without exchanging words, they resumed their march up the block.

They reached the cruiser without further incident. Barry unlocked the car.

An automatic reflex had made him lock the cruiser in the first place. Thieves had no need to open the doors, they could crawl through the open windshield and easily take possession of the black-and-white.

Once their gear had been stashed in the backseat, Barry slid behind the steering wheel, while Miss Collard slipped in beside him on the passenger side.

This is it, he warned himself. *If there's anybody out there waiting to do us harm, this is their last chance to strike.*

Next to him, he could sense that the same pessimistic notion had gone through the girl's mind too. She twisted about in her seat, surveying the sidewalk and the street behind the car. She cradled the shotgun in both her hands. Barry saw a box of extra shells nestled in her lap. She was ready for anything.

But nobody came lurching or leaping from the darkness. No sudden assault targeted the cruiser. No one bid them "get outta here!"

The key in the ignition fired up the engine. Barry pulled away from the curb. He navigated the black-and-white along the roadway, cutting around the automotive and rubble obstacles. He continued on the same road for two more blocks before taking a hard right, then a left, two blocks later another left. His serpentine exit route persisted for a while, more than logically necessary, but it made Barry feel good to leave their enemy far behind.

Our enemy...

He'd never thought of anybody as an "enemy" before. As a cop, the criminals he went after were adversaries, but the basis for their mutual hostility lacked any personal vendetta—usually. Even so, the concept of an "enemy" was new to Barry. But, he realized, it was a valid term in this post-apocalyptic world. Few individuals could be considered allies. Most were just terrified victims waiting to be slaughtered. And the zombies— the slaughterers—their aggression was mindless, governed by undead urges. They were hazards, but not necessarily enemies.

But—whoever had let those zombies indoors and then set fire to the house—that person was a bonafide *enemy.*

It was possible that *enemy* had been only another scared person, striking out to drive off competitors. Had they just been defending their turf? Had Barry and Miss Collard been inimical invaders in their eyes? The detective in him had to consider these options.

But he quickly dismissed them. No, the attack had been an act of premeditated malice. An excessive one, at that. There was every chance the fire might spread and take out the rest of the neighborhood—including whatever turf the *enemy* was defending in the first place. This person was more dangerous than the usual crazy or an undead swarm.

If they were still in Manhattan, Barry might have suspected the *enemy* was someone with a personal grudge against him. But they were far from the detective's usual stomping ground; the chances of running into a familiar criminal out here was astronomical.

No, whoever the *enemy* was, they were a stranger. A mean stranger. A murderous stranger. Someone best avoided.

The odds were good, though, that Detective Winsor would never know who they were or why they'd over-reacted as they'd done. In the normal world, it was a single random assault among thousands in a crowded city. Now, however, the attack was a needle in a haystack—going in search of it would only get your fingers pricked.

Yes, best to avoid people like that.

Sadly, Barry ruminated, *most of the people I've encountered here have been nasties or crazies. I wouldn't go drinking with any of them.* Only Miss Collard had turned out to be friendly. But—how much of that was gratitude for him saving her from that zombie mob? Could she be biding her time, waiting for the most opportune time to strike?

Cut it out, he admonished himself. *She's the only decent human being you've found—don't defame her with paranoid suspicions.*

Bad enough he had a suspicious mind—it came with the job. But this damned world was eating away at his civilized nature, turning him into a dog.

A dog on the run.

4

A DAY'S DRIVE BROUGHT THEM OUT of New Jersey and into Pennsylvania, trading rural realms for farmland. It had been several hours since they'd seen any zombies, driving past the things' futile attempt to attack the cruiser. Fields already stripped by harvest spread out on both sides of the autumn roadway they traveled.

Barry was beginning to relax, to imagine they might have somehow outdistanced the contagion, reaching districts unpopulated by the undead. But then, he saw no signs of the living, either. The countryside was noticeably devoid of any apparent wildlife. He saw no deer grazing. No birds drifted across the sky.

At his side sat Miss Collard, alert, armed, anxious despite their recent peaceful drive—or maybe because of it.

The afternoon wind basked Barry's face through the vacant windshield. He was doused in the pastoral smells of the country. These scents were foreign to his city-boy nose, but he enjoyed them. They marked territory that seemed devoid of the undead plague. This reassured him, gave him hope.

The black-and-white rounded a bend in the road. Clusters of innocuous shrubbery masked the proximate countryside. Around the bend, though, the barricade was plainly visible. Even by night the thing would have stood out. A broad strip across the top of it was painted a vivid yellow. The barrier consisted of a large sheet of corrugated metal drawn across the roadway; several welded together supports secured the wall in place. Additional sheets of metal flanked the barrier, fencing in wayward travelers.

Barry hit the brakes, but did so in a casual manner. *Best not to show surprise. Don't let this intimidate you.* He sat and studied the barricade, waiting for something to happen.

A few moments later, a voice challenged them from the barrier.

"We're refugees," Barry answered. "But then, who isn't these days? We're not looking for any trouble."

"You're armed," accused the sentry.

Indeed, at Barry's side, Miss Collard was resting the barrel of her shotgun on the dashboard, pointed out the open windshield, in plain view.

"Everybody's armed these days," Barry replied. "It helps keep us alive."

The sentry made a grunt of agreement.

A stretch of silence ensued. Barry finally broke it with: "So, can we pass? Or should we turn around and detour around this area?"

After another pause, a second voice inquired, "Where you headed?"

"Away from trouble." It seemed a suitable ambition, unthreatening and amiable.

"Don't get trigger-happy, okay?" he cautioned the girl in a whisper. "They could've just shot at us, but they didn't. That's a good sign."

"I'm not trigger-happy," she softly defended her vigilance. "I'm justifiably wary."

"Just chill, okay?"

With a piercing rattle, the metal barrier trembled, then slid slowly aside to reveal the rest of the roadway. Three men stood there, all scruffily bearded under floppy hats, all dressed in denim overalls and lumberjack shirts, all armed. At the moment, their rifles were lowered, but clearly ready if needed.

Barry calmly drove the cruiser through the open gate. Once they were through, the metal wall rumbled back into place. He pulled to a halt about two meters from where the three sentries stood blocking the way.

Adopting his best friendly face (the one he used when questioning little old lady witnesses), Barry climbed from the cruiser and approached the men. Miss Collard remained seated inside the car, but at least she had moved the barrel of her weapon to a less aggressive position.

"You a cop?" asked the eldest, whose gray tresses were gathered into a plump ponytail. "Or did you boost that vehicle?"

"A bit of both, I'm afraid," was Barry's cordial response. "Detective Barry Winsor, with the Manhattan Police Department—or at least, I was before the apocalypse. And the car...? There was no one at the Precinct Garage to ask permission, so we just borrowed it."

The tall man extended his hand with a solemn smile. "Henry Templar," he identified himself. Barry could immediately tell from his authoritive voice: this was a leader among this enclave. His lanky stature made him seem taller than he was. Tufts of a robust mane hung in the shadows of the brim of his hat. His beard was trimmed short; its sandy bristled blended with his sun-browned face. "I'm the local mayor.," he added, confirming Barry's estimation. Templar indicated his companions. "This is Ben Fulton and his grandkid, Joey."

Once Barry had clasped hands with the two adults (the boy hung back), he inquired, "If you don't mind my asking, what kind of setup do you have going here?"

"We're peaceable country folk," Henry Templar announced. "Just defending our homestead against those dead things out there."

So, Barry reflected, *they're out here too. We just haven't seen any lately.*

"When civilization crapped out," the mayor continued, "we retreated to our farms and fortified them against invaders, living and dead. We've set up roadblocks to limit access to our land. There's three farms in all, spread out through the valley."

"We ain't about to discard the idea of civilization just 'cuz the rest of the country's gone to hell in a handbasket," asserted Ben Fulton. In contrast to his farmyard attire, he had the look of a college professor with his high forehead and articulated lips.

Templar remarked, "We've successfully maintained order in our territory."

"We got the firepower necessary to defend our land," declared the younger Fulton. He shook the rifle he held, as if it represented a hundred more like it.

A fleeting frown colored Barry's brow. "I assume most of your clashes are with the zombies?"

"More'n once, we had to fight off living bad guys," claimed Joey Fulton. A hint of pride lurked in the tone he used. After doubtless years of computer gaming, the fidgety lad clearly relished the opportunity for some real combat. He was a wiry kid, probably in his late teens. His beard consisted of little more than patches of peach-fuzz along his chin. He had the look of a homeboy itching to leave the farm and explore the world, but any wanderlust had been curtailed by the apocalypse.

Adopting a more sober disposition, Henry Templar informed Barry that, sadly, gangs of hoodlums wandered the countryside, looting and pillaging instead of doing anything to help rebuild society. "So far, we've been lucky enough to repel their attacks."

"The last bunch tried to burn our fields," chirped Joey Fulton, "but we ran them off and saved our crops."

"A little bit of determination tossed in with that luck," Ben Fulton commented.

Barry couldn't help but notice how open the kid was, gushing with bluster over his accomplishments, while the other men tried to downplay their successes.

The elder Fulton bent over to peer at Miss Collard where she still sat in the nearby car. When he squinted, the rest of his face was dwarfed by his prominent nose. "And who's your traveling companion?"

"Too young to be a wife," mumbled Henry Templar. "Maybe a daughter?"

"No relation," Barry explained. "Just a friend." He waved for Miss Collard to come forth from the cruiser, but she stubbornly remained in the black-and-white.

"Nice to have friends," grunted the elder Fulton. "These days."

Barry mused, *These folk see so few strangers—rational strangers— they're mesmerized by the novelty of new people.*

"You're welcome to pass on through if you like," announced Henry Templar. "Or," the man took the hat from his head and smiled, "you might want to stick around, rest up from your hard journey."

"Umm…" Despite these folks' sociable manner, Barry was leery to trust anybody. Rule #1: Watch your ass.

"At least join us for dinner," urged the elder Fulton. "After all, when was the last home-cooked meal you had?"

This drew Miss Collard from the cruiser. She edged forward and hesitantly asked if they had running water. "I'd kill for a bath."

"Bath, food, even beds for the night, if you're so inclined," chuckled the mayor.

Feeling a tug on his sleeve, Barry glanced down and found the girl wearing an expression of intense longing. Her eyes were huge, beseeching him to accept the offer put forth by these folks.

No matter how much his gut churned at the thought of trusting anyone in this post-apocalyptic land, Barry could not ignore the hungry fervor in her gaze. Food, shelter, safety—all of these things were clearly necessary to support life, but for a young woman, bathing transcended these valuations. It went beyond cleanliness. It was a feminine need, not something he could readily comprehend. Only by summoning forth memories of his time with his lost wife could he place the girl's earnest desire in a recognizable context.

Concealing his wariness behind a polite smile, Barry accepted the mayor's gracious offer.

"You can leave your car here," Mayor Templar advised. "It'll be safe."

The cruiser contained all of their worldly belongings, besides what Barry and the girl carried on their persons. He wasn't too comfortable leaving the car alone. It might be safe here behind the barricade, but it would be safest if it stayed within his sight. Alas, he couldn't think of any excuse to disagree with the mayor's assurance. All Barry could do was nod as he fell into step beside the man.

Trotting alongside him, Miss Collard seemed totally unworried by separation from their vehicle. Avid fascination for her impending hot bath had occluded everything else from her mind. He couldn't help noticing that she'd left her shotgun back in the car.

The Mayor escorted Barry from the blockade. Young Joey Fulton accompanied Miss Collard. The elder Fulton remained at the roadblock.

From his awkward behavior, it was obvious that Joey was smitten by Miss Collard. He chattered away, eager to impress her with accounts of how well the unified farms were flourishing. But she was still lost in her bathing fantasies, and his inept bravado was wasted.

Mayor Templar was engaged in his own brag-fest, regaling Barry with tales that revealed how well the colony (as he called the unified farms) had survived—not just survived, but they had managed to maintain certain aspects of civilized life in this land of hardship. "We have our own wells, so clean water is no problem. The same is true about foodstuffs. Each farm contributes different crops, fleshing out our dining pleasures." He gave Barry a creepy smile. "There are three farms, totalling six hundred acres, so we have more than enough pastures. The Dudleys have a herd of cows, and the Frey's have an abundance of pigs—the outbreak hit a week before old Hank Frey was going to deliver a shipment to a meat processing firm upstate."

Mention of the "outbreak" prompted Barry to inquire about that.

Henry Templar shrugged. "Don't expect an explanation from me— I'm just a simple farmer. People started acting weird, then they showed up dead but still moving around. At first, it was scary."

"It still is," muttered Barry.

"Ah, but when the three farms banded together, we had strength of unity. We helped each other barricade all the incoming roads. We police the fences surrounding our properties. We fight off any invaders. Our lives are no longer ruled by fear, just caution to guard our territory."

"An impressive achievement," Barry conceded. "How many people do you have in your little colony?"

"Over a hundred," Templar beamed.

Not really a lot, mused Barry. *Hardly enough to start a new society, especially with three families making up the bulk of their numbers...*

"Do you get many individuals wandering in and joining you?"

"We have to be careful." Templar's brown features darkened as a serious frown crept across his face. "As a unified colony, we're targeted by a lot of roving gangs of marauders. One gang, Dusty's Raiders, takes a run at us at least once a week. Other gangs think they're smarter—they keep sending spies to undermine our security. We don't give these intruders the chance to join...but neither do we let them leave."

Barry nodded. Suddenly he was glad he had identified himself as a cop, a person who the mayor had promptly seen as a welcome addition to the colony instead of a potential invader. These people jealously guarded their sanctuary and dealt harshly with anyone who threatened their safety. It was a laudable stand, but only if you stood with the colony.

Am I willing to join them? he reflected.

On the surface, things looked wonderful, a sane oasis in a lawless land of undead turmoil. But Detective Winsor knew better than to judge a book by its cover. *There's always hidden layers,* he reminded himself, *and people don't hide nicities, just the parts they're embarrassed about.*

The walk from the roadside barricade followed an agrarian fence beyond which grazed a few healthy looking horses. (Barry was glad to see that not every animal had succumbed to the undead contagion.) Beyond the idling equines Barry could see rolling hills covered by fertile pastures. Mounds of cottony clouds dominated the far sky, muting its afternoon blue with their white fluffiness. If his eye traced the path upon which he trod, it wound ahead to a cluster of manmade structures: a rustic farmhouse beside a squat red barn with a grain silo looming from it like a fat chimney. Figures bustled about this far scenario, too small to discern any details of their appearance or activities. As the mayor and his party rounded a copse of trees and approached the homestead, Barry half-expected a dog—probaby a collie or a golden labrador—to come bounding from the front porch and race out to greet its master, but no canine fulfilled that fanciful suspicion; nor, in fact, did any of the farmhands seem to take notice of Templar's advance. Things continued untainted by the arrival of outsiders to this exclusive settlement. As the group drew near, only a gaggle of chickens on the lawn paused their pecking to scurry away.

The group had almost reached the porch before someone stepped from the house to welcome the newcomers. It was a matronly woman in a long peasant dress with a white apron around her waist. Her hair was hidden beneath a scarf tied around her head, although a lone stray lock dangled from her forehead to tickle her pug nose. Streaks of flour decorated her smiling cheeks.

"My wife, Agatha," Templar informed Barry.

"Henry," she hailed her husband. "I see we have guests."

Ascending the entry steps, Henry Templar gave his wife a mildly affectionate squeeze and planted a kiss on her floured cheek before he confirmed her supposition. He introduced Barry and Miss Collard, identifying them as a police officer and his traveling companion.

While he conducted these introductions, a pair of children sidled out onto the porch to huddle by the farm's matron. They wore faded denim overalls without shirts, despite the chilly afternoon; both of the lads needed haircuts, or at least the application of a comb. Their faces were devoid of expression, not even showing the curiosity or trepidation youngsters showed toward strangers. Their slack features bothered Barry, but he couldn't attach any obvious danger to the children's emotionless state.

"And two of my grandchildren," announced Henry Templar. "Jake and Little Aaron."

Barry gave the children a smile and an amiable nod, but these actions failed to enliven the kids' vacant dispositions. They stared at him as if there was nothing interesting about meeting strangers.

Miss Collard's greeting was more physical; she slipped forward to clasp Agnes Templar's hand and tossle the kids' already-unruly mops. She and the matron exchanged pleasantries, while Young Joey Fulton, eager to advertise his prior claim on the female stranger, danced around them, repeating Miss Collard's remarks in a chattering squeak.

An elbow gently nudged Barry in the side. "The boy's smitten," the mayor confided in a whisper. "I wouldn't worry about it. She's a new face, and he's just acting his age."

"I'm not worried," replied Barry. He knew the girl could take care of herself.

"You're staying for dinner—of course," Agnes Templar exclaimed.

Her husband answered for the visitors, assuring his mate that their guests were road-weary and would welcome the amenities of a home-cooked meal.

"And a hot bath," Miss Collard chimed in. "I'd kill for a hot bath."

Mrs. Templar smiled. "No need for any bloodshed. Come, I'll show you to the facilities." Slipping an arm behind the girl's waist, she led her indoors.

"I imagine you'd like to refeshen up too," guessed Henry Templar. "After so long on the road."

Barry shrugged. After so long on the road, he knew he was rather ripe, and mayor was too polite to complain about this. Now that the opportunity presented itself, however, he would welcome the chance to wash away the sweat and grime and stress of his journey.

"The house only has one bath." Henry Templar guided his visitor around the side of the homestead, revealing another structure behind it: a bunkhouse for his farmhands. "But I'm sure the men won't mind you using their shower."

Only following him into the bunkhouse to point out the shower's location, Templar then retreated to allow Barry some privacy.

The bunkhouse bathroom was designed to accommodate a group of individuals. The bathing area was a long chamber divided by flimsy plastic barriers; each cubbyhole featured its own shower nozzle, fed from a long pipe that ran the length of the room. A plank walkway ran the length of the room; in the shower stalls, a floor of spaced wooden slats provided easy drainage. Off to the side, an auxiliary room contained a series of toilets opposite a long sink with a wall-spanning mirror. That mirror was old, its surface mottled by fading patches. Strips of fluorescent light fixtures ran along the raftered ceiling, but none of were turned on; adequate daylight flowed through a series of short windows that bordered the upper walls.

Everyone was still out working the farm. He had the bath all to himself.

Disrobing, Barry draped his clothes on a nearby rack. He padded barefoot along the rows of shower cubbies.

Bars of scented disinfectant scattered about failed to completely overcome the "fragrance" one associated with public bathrooms, a stink locked into the wood paneling from years of use. Barry found the odor reassuring. After so long in a world of undead hostility, the smell of people was a welcome thing.

He chose a cubbyhole and turned on the shower, standing back to avoid getting drenched by the cold water that always comes first. He reached out a few times, testing the stream with inquisitive fingers to gauge when the water reached the desired warmth.

While he basked in the refreshing stinging-hot spray, his mind toyed with the prospect of joining Templar's colony. On many levels, doing so seemed to be an obviously desirable choice. From what he had seen, this group of farmers had achieved miraculous stability in this post-apocalyptic world. Their pastures and herds provided them with ample food. The unity generated by the three families was a bastion against the horrors walking the landscape, horrors dead and alive. If the mayor was to be believed, they had successfully warded off repeated invasions by hostiles. He had no reason to doubt Henry Templar's claims, the man was cheerfully open about things. Even the countryside—what little he'd seen so far—was idyllic.

Yet for some intangible reason, Barry's gut didn't like the place.

It was nothing he could put his finger on, just a nagging hunch. As a detective, Barry had learned to heed his hunches.

What he needed was more information.

Over the course of the evening ahead, he would collect more cogent observations, enabling him to better ascertain if the colony had a hidden snake in the orchard. This was standard operating procedure: observe, collate data, review what you found…but most importantly—trust your gut.

Normally Barry was not one to heed the basic practice of apply soap, rinse, reapply soap and rinse again. He usually limited his bathing routine to a vigorous lathering up and a long languid rinse. Today, however, something told him the grime he had accumulated during his time on the road would require a second scrubbing. He lathered up again.

Later that evening, Barry would find a way to privately confer with Miss Collard. Considering what he'd seen so far, he trusted her survivalist instincts and was curious to learn if she shared his vague unease regarding this place. Barry assumed it would take more than a hot bath and the attentions of a gawky farmlad to sway Miss Collard's innate caution.

And what if she wants to stay? Barry asked himself. Well, she was an adult (albeit a young one), entitled to make her own decisions. *I guess the real question is: if she chooses to stay, do I stick around too?*

Water splashed across his face, clearing away the soapy foam from his features. He turned around so the shower spray could rinse the lather from his hair. Although his eyes were free now of soap, his vision remained momentarily blurred. He blinked away that haze—

Just in time to see a baseball bat careening toward him.

He didn't feel the impact, nor his collapse to the slatted wooden floor.

He remained oblivious to being hoisted up and removed from the bunkhouse. He did not feel the lacerations he received as he was dragged across the coarse ground. He was bound and a rope was secured around his neck. Then he was thrown into a pit. His landing only served to perpetuate his period of insensitivity.

Once he awoke, though, an inventory of his aches told him what he'd missed.

The "pit" turned out to be a sectioned-off part of the barn's cellar. His bindings didn't allow him much movement to investigate his prison, but there wasn't much to discover besides the rotten straw under him and the putrid stench of old urine. Although the pit was closed off by a trapdoor, some light filtered through between the wooden planks, granting him a sketchy idea of his barren surroundings.

I knew there was something wrong about this place, he remonstrated himself for not heeding his initial hunch. *But no—they suckered me in with their utopian commune.*

I shouldn't take it so hard. Little Miss Always-Cautious Collard was lured into the same trap by the prospect of a hot bath.

He presumed she had fallen prey to the same fate.

An angry shout confirmed this.

Muted by the walls, Miss Collard's voice answered him.

Once their stories were traded, the pair found they'd both been victimized in basically the same manner. Someone had crept up and knocked her unconscious while she'd languished in a warm bathtub, just as Barry had been coldcocked in the shower. (He wondered if their captors had bothered to dress the girl before dumping her into her pit, but he refrained from asking such indelicate questions.) Bound like him, she could not free herself of the rope that constricted her neck.

"What are we going to do?" she asked.

"We wait and see what happens."

Under their current circumstances, there was nothing else they could do.

"Why would they do this to us?"

That part stymied Barry. "If the colony wanted us dead, why didn't they just shoot us at the barricade? For that matter, if they don't tolerate visitors, why'd they let us in?"

"Well, obviously to capture us...but why?"

"If they're looking to convince us to join their colony, this is not the way to go about it..."

"They were so nice to us," she grumbled.

"Yeah." That part really rankled him. *Their sweet welcome was a sham designed to lure us in...so the farmers could take us prisoner. But—for what reason?* His inability to theorize their logic frustrated the detective. He was used to fathoming the thought processes of criminals, but these farmers weren't burglars or embezzlers or racketeers, although they *had* turned out to be guilty of mugging and con artistry.

"We're going to get out of here, aren't we, Mr Winsor?"

Although his personal confidence was currently a dormant sentiment, Barry assured the girl that they would survive. Despite her normal grit, she was still a scared young woman—he could hear it in her voice. No reason to throw gasoline on her smoldering anxiety. If they *were* going to get out of here alive, they'd both need to stay sharp, unclouded by defeatist dread.

Easier proposed than achieved, he reflected.

He understood that what he felt wasn't defeatism...more like pragmatic helplessness.

Barry needed to muster a forced sense of conviction that everything would turn out alright, that somehow he and Miss Collard would find a way to escape whatever fate these farmers had in store for them. He hoped for such an outcome, but he knew how little effect "hope" had on tangible matters.

No more discussion was necesary between Barry and the girl. They both understood that it was a waiting game now...waiting to learn the farmers' intentions.

Barry *really* wished he had a cigarette.

The impulse was still strong when Barry woke up back in his bed.

Here I am back home, he told himself, *not a prisoner curled up in darkness with a noose around my neck. As usual, it was all just a stupid dream.*

He sat up and rooted in the dark until he found the bedside cabinet. A crumpled pack of butts lay there. His rattled nerves made his fingers clumsy as he fumbled a cigarette from the pack. Popping it between his lips, he struck a match. He closed his eyes and inhaled deeply...but no smoke filled his throat. The cig wouldn't light. It was slimy in his grasp.

He suddenly realized that the fingers of his left hand shared that oily texture. He reached out with his right hand to switch on the nearby lamp.

To his surprise, Barry discovered the bedsheet was damp and sticky. He recognized it right away: blood.

I've been wounded. He remembered the shootout at the gym.

His dizziness escalated into a rich numbness. Buried within that tingle was pain, muted by desensitivity.

How did I get home and into bed if I was shot?

A more practical portion of his brain shoved aside these questions and ordered: *Call 911—*

That aching wave almost carried him into unconsciousness as he reached for the phone. His hand fell to the bedside table to steady himself. A vortex of darkness swelled inside his head; he fought through it, pushing himself back to a weak but cognitive state. His vision remained blurred. His efforts to grasp the bedside phone were clumsy, the unit eluded his bloody fingers. Eventually, his fumbling pushed the phone, lamp, everything from the table.

Dammit—

He stared at the phone on the floor, or at least the dark smudge he assumed was the toppled phone. A dial tone screeched from the dislodged receiver, its banshee wail battered his feeble focus. He winced. He doubted his ability to retrieve the phone from the floor. But he needed to get it before bloodloss made him pass out.

So he reached down from the bed. With his fingers inches from the loose receiver, a murky vortex surged through his concentration. The pain was too uniform, he couldn't tell where he was wounded. The darkness encroached on his concentration. He faltered…

And found himself face-down on the floor. The scream of the phone's dial tone had roused him, summoning him from the warm embrace of oblivion. Opening his eyes, he saw the receiver near his cheek. Barry didn't bother to waste energy rolling over or trying to sit up. He dragged his arm from its out-flung position, drawing it in, searching for the rest of the phone—it had to be close. His fingers found the coiled cord and followed it back to where it was plugged into the main unit. He pulled the phone close and turned his head so he could see its shaky approach. His fingers crawled over the surface of the phone, searching for the call buttons. Laboriously, forcing the muscles of his hand to follow the directions of his bleary vision, he punched 9 once and 1 twice.

The phone rang five times before a terse female voice spoke.

"Officer down," he choked at the receiver. "Send ambulance." He gave her his address.

She responded with a string of instructions that failed to penetrate Barry's barely-conscious condition. Ignoring the woman's advice (he knew it from experience anyway), he rolled over until he lay on his back. He stared at the ceiling, or at least the blur that was probably the ceiling.

Stupid fool...you're gonna bleed out before the ambulance gets here...

He became aware of a collection of small towers looming beside his supine head. Squinting didn't bring them into focus, but he guessed what they were: his bedside bottles of booze.

Now, there's some immediate medicine, he told himself.

It took a while, but he finally succeeded in grabbing one of the bottles and worrying its cap off. He was too weak to sit up, so he just tipped the bottle to his lips and gulped the liquor that spilled into his mouth. It was whiskey, it went down hard, but spread warmth from his gut to the rest of his body.

Nice...

This time he welcomed the darkness as it crept forth.

He didn't hear them break down the front door, nor their bustling search through the house, nor their thunderous ascent of the stairs. He never saw or heard the paramedics that swarmed to find his collapsed body next to the bed.

The next time Barry woke, he wondered where he was.

His surroundings were dark.

Am I back in the farmers' pit?

No. He was no longer bound, no noose encircled his neck.

So—where am I?

He could tell he lay on a bed, not a layer of putrid straw.

Am I back home?

No. The bedsheet drawn up to his neck was crisp, not his own worn linen. What he see of the gloomy room revealed it was not the den he had made his bedroom.

Then he remembered the pain...and realized it was gone.

Eventually Barry figured out where he was. He had to sort through two sets of memories, struggling to determine which were real and which belonged to those strange blackouts he was experiencing. Since he didn't believe in his time spent in that post-apocalyptic nightmare, it was fairly easy to push those recollections aside and concentrate on what was left.

Waking up dazed and bloody...fumbling for the telephone...falling to the floor...struggling to call 911...having what he'd thought was a final toast...

Apparently the ambulance had arrived in time. The paramedics had stopped his bleeding, gotten him to a hospital where surgeons had healed his bullet wounds.

Now that the crisis was past, Barry pondered on how the hell he'd managed to survive that shootout back at the gym. He'd been outnumbered and outgunned. But apparently not… Somehow, he'd gotten away, albeit wounded, and had made it all the way back to his home.

Why did I go home and not to a hospital? Didn't I realize I'd been shot?

Sudden illumination disrupted his speculations.

As the lights came on, the door opened, admitting a woman in white—a nurse. Wearing a comforting smile, she approached Barry and stood beside his bed. She checked the readings on the blipping machines stacked beside the bed, then checked the IV that ran into Barry's elbow.

"How are we feeling, Mr Winsor?"

"Fine," he rasped. A cough cleared his throat, so his next words rang with a more normal timbre. "How long have I been here?"

"Only since yesterday." She momentarily busied herself adjusting something out of view. "Frankly, a big man like you, I'm surprised they bothered to admit you in the first place."

Huh?

"The slugs the doctors took out of me," he instructed the nurse. "They're evidence. I'll want to see them."

The nurse gave him a strange look. "Slugs? Do you mean 'bullets'?"

"Of course."

"I'm afraid you're mistaken about the nature of your injury, Mr Winsor." She lay her hand on his forearm and whispered, "You weren't shot. You lost a finger."

"A finger?"

A tremor danced along his spine.

"Yes. I can't imagine why you did nothing to bandage it. You almost died from bloodloss."

He lifted his right hand, but all five fingers were still attached.

"Your other hand," advised the nurse.

Indeed, when he wormed his left hand from beneath the covers and examined it, only four fingers protruded from the knuckles. His pinky was missing. A medical bandage swathed where it should have been.

"My finger…" Barry croaked, his voice constricted this time by shock.

"Your neck and buttocks were badly abraded too."

The nurse and the rest of the hospital room receded into a shadow realm. His left hand filled his tunnel-vision.

I wasn't shot...?

I lost a finger...

How did I do that in a shootout?

Too stunned and overwhelmed by this development, he gawked at his wounded hand.

At some point, the nurse must've left. When Barry finally emerged from his mystified shock, he was alone in the hospital room. She'd probably had more to tell him, but lost in his daze, he'd missed it all.

Left alone, his thoughts remained fixated on the mystery of his missing finger. How had he suffered a wound of this nature during the shootout, yet escaped getting hit by a hail of angry bullets? It made no sense. Granted, he was startled to discover he'd lost one of his digits, but he was more upset by the amnesia that surrounded this injury.

Barry returned to a retrospective evaluation of his memories. They were spotty when it came to the shootout.

He'd trailed Titus Roth, the bag-boy, back and forth across Manhattan until the punk had finally made his drop at Waldo's Gym on Wooster Street. He'd followed Titus inside, where he'd found himself stumbling into some kind of gangster stag party. Someone had recognized him as a cop before he'd been able to offer any bluff. A shootout had immediately ensued. He'd ducked behind a tall stack of padded mats. He could vividly recall the barrage of bullets that had tracked him. The gangsters' gunfire had torn the mats to shreds. So, he had...

He'd done something, but he couldn't recall what. Here, things became cloudy, uncertain...almost as if nothing had happened. But *something* must have occurred, otherwise the gangsters' volleys would've killed him.

Had he found a way to sneak away?

Had some unexpected development stopped them from shooting at him?

He seriously doubted he'd outshot them.

Had additional police officers showed up, joining the face-off?

What troubled him was how this cerebral loose end fit with the onset of his latest post-apocalyptic nightmare. His memories of the gym shootout ceased...and the nightmare relaunched itself without a glitch. As if they were two ends of a thread that had been severed.

He wished he had a smoke.

Or a shot of whiskey to steady his nerves.

The prospect that the two ends of the thread belonged together was madness. Zombies were impossible. But then, so was surviving the shoot-out at the gym.

In violation of all logic, he dragged out the memories of this latest nightmare and rifled through them. Eventually, he discovered events after his incarceration in the pit…

Near darkness made time elastic. Barry had no idea how many hours passed before the wooden trapdoor lifted and blinding light spilled into his pit.

He squinted up, but could make out only hazy forms in the glare.

Daylight, he noted. So—he'd been a prisoner at least half-a-day.

Laughter accompanied the harsh light from above. Whatever they had planned for him had put them all in a jovial mood.

The rope around his neck suddenly tightened. It jerked Barry hard, forcing him to scramble to his feet—not an easy maneuver with his hands tied. The pull continued, dragging him erect. For a moment he stumbled, coughing, then his toes left the straw and he dangled at the end of a hang-man's line. He tried to gasp, but the noose refused to allow any air to pass in or out of his throat. With jerky movements, he was hoisted aloft and withdrawn from the hole.

The laughter became even more enthusiastic as the captors enjoyed Barry's blue-faced discomfort.

Finally, he was hauled over the edge of his prison. He sprawled on a floor of coarse wooden planks scattered with dirt and snatches of straw. No one was pulling on the rope now, but it remained tight, choking him still. Again, he tried to gasp, but could only manage a strained hiss.

Through the thunder of his own pulse, Barry heard: "Okay, enough fun, men. Better uncrimp that noose. We don't want him dying on us too early."

Someone leaned down and loosened the rope from its lethal hold on his neck. Left sprawled on the ground, he gulped air into his starved lungs.

Gradually, his vision cleared. The men stood around him, four of them. Their agrarian attire marked them as farmhands. Past their boots he could see another pair hauling Miss Collard from her pit. She was na-ked.

Before he could react, the rope yanked him to his feet, and he was led away. They exited the barn and crossed the graveled pathway, moving onto the lawn and around the house, where a gaggle of people clustered around a collection of redwood picnic tables. Poles were decorated with gaily colored tassles. The overall mood of the crowd reflected a similar tone of celebration.

As the newcomers approached the party, the throng parted to reveal Henry Templar. With an oversize chef's hat perched atop his head, he looked ridiculous. He waved barbecue tongs at them and welcomed them to the picnic.

Although Barry longed to make some snide retort, his hurt throat refused to utter more than raspy breaths. Besides, he felt it unwise to antagonize the man. Iritating him would only worsen whatever he had planned for the visitors.

Miss Collard, though, exhibited no such wisdom. She snarled and called Templar a most unladylike thing. She went on to ridicule his sexual prowess and then blaspheme his maternal heritage. She used language he'd never expected her to know; under other circumstances, it would have made Barry blush.

The mayor just laughed at her insults. In fact, he encouraged more from her.

She readily complied.

Mrs Templar stepped forth to object, reminding them all there were children present. Miss Collard ignored her protest.

After a few minutes, however, the girl ran out of steam.

"Exhausted yourself, have you, girl?" chided Henry Templar. "Good. It'll help things move along smoothly."

Emboldened by her outburst, Barry grumbled, "Nice way you treat guests around here."

"Oh, you were never really guests, Mr Winsor." Henry Templar broke into a gruesome grin. "From the moment you entered our territory, you've been *livestock*."

The implications of this remark made Barry blanche.

Beside him, Miss Collard cursed vehemently and launched herself against her captors. Her hands were bound, so all she could do was kick. Curtailing her outburst, the man holding the rope attached to her noose subdued her with a hard jerk on that tether. She struggled to clamber back to her feet, snarling obscenities, but another man struck her down. This time she lay immobile, powerfully dazed or possibly outright unconscious from the blow.

"Aw," bemoaned the mayor. "I was hoping to do her first, so Mr Winsor could watch."

One of the men poked Miss Collard with a booted toe. She remained slack.

"Yup," grunted the man. "She's out."

"Then we'll have to settle for starting with our esteemed city lawman." Templar turned away and led the way through the tables to a large brick barbecue. In its wide bed, a layer of coals glowed with fierce heat.

Barry was brusquely induced to follow the mayor. When he resisted, a tightened noose compelled him forward. Ultimately, he was forced to his knees before the open barbecue. At this point, two men appeared to hold Barry in place.

"So—this is where you kill me," Barry accused them.

"Oh no," protested Henry Templar. "It's important that the meat be alive as it's prepared." He raised his hand and a carving knife twinkled in the afternoon sun.

"It adds a delightful tang to the meat," added someone in the crowd. It was Old Man Fulton. His eyes twinkled like Templar's knife. "We've learned that from experience."

Going to cut me up and cook me while I'm still alive—and conscious! Horror and disgust dueled in Barry's mind for prominence. *And they've "learned from experience"—we aren't the first victims these sick bastards have butchered.* He gagged, but with no food in his stomach, only raw bile tickled his throat.

It really wasn't all that surprising that a post-apocalyptic colony might resort to cannibalism to feed its citizens. But Barry couldn't accept that, at least not so soon after the undead outbreak. He was certain enough grocery stores remained out there to be plundered for foodstuffs. Besides, this was a conclave made up of three farms—what about Farmer Dudley's herd of cows or Farmer Frey's pigs or the recently harvested crops? With all these natural food sources, why was this colony practicing cannibalism?

Because they want to. They're deviant by choice.

And Miss Collard and I had the misfortune of walking into their clutches.

As Templar leaned close, Barry strained back, but the men flanking him held him in place. Reaching around, the mayor severed Barry's bonds. While one captor twisted his right arm against his back, the other man forced Barry's left arm out, offering it to the chef. With a sadistic smirk, Templar pinched Barry's pinky finger between two fingers and then lopped it off.

Agony shot through Detective Winsor like wildfire. He thrashed and cursed, but his captors restrained him. They chuckled at his sides.

Stepping back, Chef Templar lifted Barry's severed finger aloft for all to see. The rest of those gathered at the picnic cheered.

Preparation for dinner had begun.

At some imminent point, Barry had lost consciousness, for that was where the nightmarish memory ended, delivering him from the barbecue tableau into suffocating darkness.

Letting go of the memory, he opened his eyes and stared at the acoustic tiles covering the ceiling of the hospital room without really seeing them. After a moment, he reclosed his eyes and rolled over on his side. Despite the fact that the evidence came direct from his own mind, Barry had difficulty accepting the tale told by his reverie.

All along he had scoffed at these nightmarish interludes, but maintaining that dismissive attitude was no longer practical. He had to accept the validity of the evidence. It was hard to ignore a missing finger. And hadn't that nurse mentioned something about bruises on his neck? These injuries matched his experiences in that post-apocalyptic realm too closely. Injuries he had incurred months from now.

Those crazy farmers…

At this point he was forced to take these temporal displacements at face value. He didn't understand them, but apparently he was stuck with them.

And these no-longer-deniable displacements had delivered him into the future suffering a zombie plague. Civilization had fallen as survivors fought off undead scavengers—and the survivors fought among themselves too, some even took their hostility to deviant extremes. Law no longer existed, nor common decency. It was a dog-eat-each-other world, unpleasant and deadly—a terrible future to look forward to.

Mixed in with his fundamental despair, he felt acute regret over Miss Collard's fate. By returning to his normal time, Barry had left the girl to the mercies of those cannibal farmers, who had no mercy, only a deviant appetite. Without him there to defend her, the mayor had undoubtedly sliced her into strips and cooked them—all the while forcing Miss Collard to watch as the crowd chowed down on her flesh. They were sick bastards, gratuitously sadistic in addition to their vile dietary habits.

I promised her we'd escape, he castigated himself. *But in the end, I abandoned her. And now she's dead…or at least, she will be dead months from now. I failed her.*

It didn't matter that his departure had been involuntary; the process—whatever it involved—was entirely beyond Barry's control. Regardless of this, he still blamed himself for the girl's grisly end.

I'd kill right now for a stiff shot of whiskey…

His mourning depression slowed his recovery.

Under normal circumstances, the loss of a finger was hardly a near-fatal injury. Yet, Barry had almost died from bloodloss, all because he hadn't realized he'd lost the finger. After all, he'd thought the dismemberment had happened in a dream. Now he knew better.

Once his stump had been sutured and bandaged, they should have discharged him from the hospital. But his vital signs were shaky; the doctors wanted to hold him for observation. Perhaps some vitamins added to his intake might help boost his blood pressure and heart rate.

The truth of the matter was that Barry's guilt over Miss Collard's fate had plunged him into a serious depression, resulting in his unhealthy condition. While his hand healed, the rest of him waned.

His first visitor besides hospital personnel was his precinct's Chief of Detectives, who was curious to learn how he'd lost a finger while raiding a gangster gathering. This was the explanation Barry had included in the sparse report he'd submitted on the incident. In his despondant state, he could offer his superior no further details concerning the matter. The man would never believe the truth. Captain Humphries was not satisfied with this lack of further disclosure, but he restrained himself from pressuring Detective Winsor on the matter, respecting his present unhealthy condition.

A day later, a police psychiatrist came, but she was more concerned with Barry's depression. In Dr Gellon's intrepretation of Winsor's report, the detective was suffering from post-traumatic distress caused by having shot so many criminals during his shootout (although no bodies had been found at the gym to support Winsor's account). She made no headway with Barry. He had no desire to engage with this disguided healer. Dr Gellon's best miracle cure could never assuage Barry's visceral grief over the loss of Miss Collard, nor was he foolish enough to confide to her the reasons for his emotional lassitude. (And if she took his tale at face value, she'd consign him to extended psychiatric evaluation.) Badly concealing her frustration, she departed, but promised to return to continue his therapy.

Visits from the doctor assigned to Mr Winsor's care were no more productive to anyone involved. Barry remained withdrawn, almost surly, which only served to alienate Dr Phillips. He remonstrated his patient for his seeming disinterest in his own recuperation, reminding Barry that a positive attitude was considered integral to the healing process. But Barry perceived no way that his recovery could possibly bring Miss Collard back to life, thus paid no attention to his physician's obstinate guidance.

Bt the third day, the nurses adopted an aloof demeanor with Mr Winsor. They alone seemed to realize the futility of their cheery dispositions and left Barry to stew in his self-generated isolation. Had he been aware of this, he might have respected them for their sagacious treatment, but as it was Barry languished in a realm apart from the real world.

His thoughts churned with confusion. Trying to fit his nightmares (now proven to be more than fanciful hallucinations) with orderly reality was still difficult for him. If he could discredit that apocalyptic future, Barry might find release from his self-appointed blame for Miss Collard's gruesome demise. But the evidence (fantastic and impossible as it seemed) fit his situation too snugly, leaving him no escape from his guilt.

Conversely, acceptance only heightened his despair. For if there was any veracity to his temporal displacements, then it meant this appalling cataclysm loomed in mankind's future, as unavoidable as exhaling a deep breath. What a terrible thing to occur, the death of human civilization… and Barry was the only person who knew it was coming, although he really didn't fathom how it had transpired.

He harbored no illusions of going out and spreading the word. Nobody would believe him; they'd laugh at his wild forecast. And if he persisted, he'd end up thrown into a psycho ward with daily electroshock treaments. For all the good that'd do—the apocalypse would happen regardless of Barry Winsor's mental health. And the survivors would be much too busy coping to remember his warning.

Emergences from his maudlin reverie were rare, usually prompted by the need for food or to go to the bathroom. He watched no television, ignored the magazines and newspapers which the nurses left as distractions for him. He barely took notice of the hospital staff's coming and going: the custodians emptying the trashcan in his room whether or not it contained any trash, the nurses checking his blood pressure or taking his blood to monitor his recovery. The passage of day to night and back hardly made an impression on him, so vivid was his introspection.

Early in his hospital stay, several calls had come in, all of them answered with reluctance and trepidation, for Barry really had no desire to talk with anyone. Most of those calls had been from fellow police officers wanting to convey their wishes for his speedy recovery. While not particularly close with any of these individuals, he understood their need to share support for a fallen comrade. More than half apologized for not stopping by the hospital to visit him, but, "y'know how it is, Barry, with so many cases piling up, leaving us no real free time." Indeed, he knew what it was like; in fact, their remarks served to remind him of his own case load, now languishing unattended while he was laid up. "You get better quick, okay, Barry? We need you back on duty." Barry found himself disturbed by how little these cases meant to him now that he knew how little time was left for human society.

Only two of the calls came from non-work-related people. Ever since he'd become a widower, Barry had neglected most personal relationships until they'd lapsed. The majority of these people had been primarily Emily's friends with whom he'd found nothing in common without his wife as the active interface. "I heard you were in the hospital, are you okay? What happened?" Barry had assured them he was okay. Rather than reveal the true nature of his injury, which would have led to explanations he could not offer, he had relied on the vague response: "I can't talk about it—it's still an ongoing case." One caller actually sounded disappointed, probably hoping to thrill to tales of the seedy underworld.

As far as family was concerned, Barry Winsor was almost the last man standing. These days, he had only one living relative: a cousin who lived in San Francisco and was an interior decorator or something like that. They'd never been close; he'd heard from Neil when Emily had passed, but before that more than a decade had crawled by since their last contact. While Emily's kin were many, they'd all withdrawn from contact with Barry once the cancer had taken her out. It wasn't that he was disliked, more so they didn't like the drunk that Barry had gradually become. Sometimes, when Barry wasn't drunk, he shared their opinion…but since losing Emily he had adopted a constant camaraderie with the bottle, so those sympathetic moments were as rare as swimwear designed for Eskimos.

Only one call managed to spark Barry's interest.

"Barry—it's me, Frankie."

"Hey, Frankie…"

"I called Captain Humphries to let him know my stay in Dallas was going to be longer than I'd thought—and he told me you were laid up."

Three days stranded in the hospital and Barry hadn't once thought of his partner. *What an asshole I am…*

"What the hell happened?"

What do I tell Frankie? The absolute truth is too absurd…but then the cover story I put in the report isn't much more believable…

"I—uh—there was a shootout." He proceeded to tell his partner how he'd followed Titus Roth to Waldo's Gym on Wooster Street, where he (Barry) had stumbled upon a gathering of gangsters. "I mean 'gangsters' like the New Jersey kind. There were strippers and party decorations and cake and one of the bastards spotted me. Everybody pulled on me. I returned fire. It was a fiasco."

"But Humphries told me you didn't get shot. You lost a *finger*?"

Barry feigned a chuckle, but it was unconvincing. "Yeah, well, mishaps happen." He promptly sought to change the topic: "How's your mom doing?"

Frankie Dumont's tone changed, exchanging concern for a sad sobriety. Frankie was unsure of his mother's status. The appearance of ebola victims on American soil had everyone freaked out. To squelch panic, the Center for Disease Control was being very cagey about what information they released. The possible victims had been immediately quarantined, Mama Dumont among them because she worked in a hospital where another victim had been discovered. Nobody was telling the press much of anything, and despite his direct relation to the woman, Frankie was equally being excluded from any news. Whether or not his mother had actually contracted the ebola virus was still uncertain; tests had confirmed nothing. The doctors were waiting for her to manifest more advanced symptoms before they publicized any diagnosis.

"It's driving me crazy," his partner confided to Barry.

"The bastards…"

While both detectives ordinarily had nothing but respect for physicians, neither Barry nor Frankie held any degree of affection for the bureaucracy that hovered like a dark cloud ready to descend and smother all compassion with their procedural murk. Obsessed with national security, the CDC remained oblivious to Frankie's concern for his mother's health. The least they could do was confide in him and swear him to secrecy; after all, he was a cop, not someone who might leak the data in an attempt to seek celebrity.

After a few more platitudes, they agreed to keep each other apprised of any developments, Barry with his convalescence, Frankie with his mother's health.

Replacing the receiver in its cradle on the bedside cabinet, Barry sank back into the embrace of the crisp hospital sheets and stared off out the window as dark clouds rallied to obscure the afternoon sky. While his eyes appeared vacant, emotionless, Barry's mind churned with fresh suspicions.

He remembered the reports of widespread ebola outbreaks in Africa from newscasts from before the onset of his time displacement adventures. Although he was no medical authority, Barry understood that the severely deadly virus was some form of flesh-eating malady. Several nations had dispatched medical relief teams to help in the African crisis, so modern medicine must be armed with a cure for the disease. Even so, every nation had overzealously tightened their security. Most countries had absolutely refused entry to anyone traveling from the infected areas. Proud of their screening process, America had not been so draconian concerning travelers from contaminated territories. That pride had proven to be more pompous than effective when cases of ebola were detected first in Texas, then later in New York City. Barry wasn't sure about the latest developments; his attention had been monopolized by his own activities, here and in the near-future.

The newspapers offered by the nurses (which he'd agressively ignored) might contain further information, but the girls-in-white had summarily removed them when his disinterest had become apparent. Now, though, he wished they were still strewn on the window-ledge of his hospital room.

A vague dread was surfacing in his mind, gathering synaptic fragments along the way to formulate a terrible tapestry of suspicious events.

He searched for the bedside buzzer. He located its cord, but after a laborious process of tracing it through the tangled bedclothes to its end, what he reached was where it plugged into the unit mounted on the wall above the bed's metallic headboard. With a sigh, he reversed his search and ran the other end of the cord through his questing unbandaged fingers. Somewhere along the semi-hidden way, he must have gotten fouled up, for his search only brought him back to the cord's wall-plug.

This time his sigh was less pragmatic.

For a few minutes he fumed and mulled over this obstructive development. Eventually, though, he just yelled for someone's attention. No one responded to that or his second and third bellows.

He sat forward, but still could not see the door around the fulcrum of the L-shaped room. Odds were the door was closed, explaining why no one at the nurses' station at the far end of the hallway could hear his summons.

He entertained the notion of climbing from bed and taking his call out into the corridor, but numerous tubes and wires tethered him in place, IV feeds and wires transmitting his vitals to the bedside array of machinery. He wasn't confident about the consequences should he sever any of these connections.

Frankly, Barry was mystified that he was still in the hospital. While the loss of a finger might be considered to be a serious injury, once tended and sutured closed, the wound shouldn't have warranted any extended stay in the hospital. So—why hadn't he doctors released him to recuperate and heal at home?

Was there some aspect of Barry's condition the physicians were withholding from him?

He'd asked the nurses about this, but they had professed no knowledge on the matter. Strangely, no doctors had come to see him in over a day, so he hadn't been able to accost them with the question.

So many questions…and not all of them concerned his health. Barry's worries were divided between the here-and-now and the nightmarish future he had unwillingly visited. Was it any wonder his overall state of mind was downcast?

Frustrated but stoic (*What choice do I have?*), Barry watched the minute hand crawl around the clockface twice, until a nurse finally came to check his blood pressure and temperature.

When he asked to see a newspaper, the woman smiled with open approval. Apparently she took this interest in current events as a sign that Mr Winsor was emerging from his withdrawal. (Maybe she would report this turn to his doctor and the idiot would show up again so Barry could challenge him on his patient's extended hospital stay.)

Promising to see what she could find for him, the nurse hurried through her duties and departed. It was fifteen minutes before she returned; an anxious Barry clocked her reappearance.

She gave him ragged copies of a *New York Times* and an issue of *The Globe*.

He thanked her. Before the beaming nurse could withdraw, Barry asked her help finding the buzzer. "Somehow, it's become tangled up in the sheet." She deftly fished the buzzer from the bedclothes, clearly this was not the first time a patient had needed similar help. She looped the cord around the bed's metal safety rail so the button hung within easy reach.

He examined the papers she left in his lap. They were all a few days old.

Setting aside *The Globe*, he barely glanced at its ribald headline: Banker Red-Handed in Sex Scandal!

The *Times* was missing its Sports section, but that didn't bother him; he doubted the information he sought would have been among any itinerary of football scores. He devoured each article that mentioned the "ebola crisis," as it was now being called. Unfortunately, these items offered little in the way of details. Their main gist involved criticizing the government for how badly it was handling the affair. The writers assumed every reader knew the specifics by now.

To his surprise, he derived more substantial information from the coverage in *The Globe*; albeit here each kernel of data had to be scraped free of sensationalized hoopla.

A television crew had visited a potential victim in a New York hospital; afterward, ignoring quarantine regulations, one of the newscasters had gone out for dinner at a posh restaurant. Public opinion exploded with outrage. This celebrity had risked spreading the disease to other dining patrons. The paper called for this woman's swift punishment—her arrogant actions had endangered the entire populace.

From this news story, Barry was able to deduce that the number of victims on US soil had increased. More specifically: the contagion had reached Manhattan.

While he found no reference to any ebola-related fatalities, the level of hysteria lurking in each article indicated that a swarm of ghastly deaths was expected any day

This news coverage seemed awfully irresponsible to Barry. Instead of attempting to calm the anxious public, all the media appeared interested in was goading everyone into overt panic.

An unrelated article reported that the Mount Palomar observatory had detected a celestial body passing the orbit of Mars. In typical *Globe* fashion, this scientific account was distorted by horrific implications when the story promised that the deadly asteroid was on a collision course with the Earth.

Another part of my nightmare confirmed.

He needed more current news concerning the ebola crisis.

Using the buzzer, Barry summoned a nurse.

"These are all old papers," he complained when the woman arrived. "Don't you have anything more recent on hand?"

"Well, yes, Mr Winsor," she replied. "I just assumed you were interested in what's been happening this last week."

He bit back the urge to condemn her stupidity; instead he requested a copy of today's newspaper.

It took her another twenty minutes to reappear with a fresh *Times* (again minus the Sports section).

The articles Barry scanned only escalated his boiling irritation. There was no mention of the ebola crisis, as if overnight the disease had vanished. Every story dealt with yesterday's mid-term election, in which the Republicans had reclaimed control of Congress.

Again, he buzzed for a nurse.

She came promptly this time, wearing an expression of thinly veiled annoyance. "What is it now, Mr Winsor?"

"The crisis—what happened to it?"

"Excuse me?" The muscles of her matronly face relaxed from consternation to bewilderment.

"The ebola crisis!" Barry rattled the newspaper at her. "The other papers were full of stories about the crisis, but today's has no mention of it."

"Oh, *that.*" Her puzzlement melted away and she gave him a congenial chuckle. "Well—clearly it wasn't the crisis everyone thought it was."

He stared blankly at the nurse.

"You shouldn't worry yourself over things like that," she told him. Stepping near, she reached around him to fluffy the pillow that supported his back. "You have your own recuperation to think about."

Before Barry could inquire how an international health crisis could vanish overnight, the woman had flashed him a reassuring smile and then withdrawn from the room. He stared at the corner that hid the room's doorway from his direct view.

What the...

He had wondered if there might be some connection between the ebola and zombie outbreaks. Over the months ahead, could the disease possibly mutate, transforming from a flesh-eating virus into something that could kill a person but keep them animated? Granted, it had seemed like a spurious stretch...but then, Barry was a police detective, not a medical expert. He harbored no clinical understanding of germs and mutation. A lot of modern science simply astounding him. He knew the real world wasn't populated by freakish mutations like in some Fifties monster movie, but that didn't rule out the existence of smaller, more subtle aberrations. Perhaps weeks from now some attempt to battle the ebola virus would go awry, some experimental chemical mixture might warp the virus into an entirely different type of contagion.

A stretch or not, the entire hypothesis was groundless if there'd never been any ebola crisis.

But—why would the media report a crisis if none existed?

Maybe the election had momentarily replaced the ebola crisis in the news. After all, swinging Congress from Democratic to Republican control signaled a major change in the country's political climate. That was significant news. Significant enough to completely eradicate all mention of the ebola crisis?

Unlikely, unless…

Unless the crisis hadn't existed in the first place, but had been a fabrication of political spinmasters. In several of the articles he'd read in the older papers, the media was blaming the ebola outbreak on the current administration. If the public came to believe that, it might sway their vote. Was Barry letting his mind get too fanciful with these theories, stretching deductive connections into conspiracies?

No, the ebola epidemic in Africa was real. There was no way anyone could reach from behind locked doors in Washington DC all the way to Africa and convince each foreign country to fake an ebola outbreak. More likely, the spinmasters had simply capitalized on the outbreak to alienate a fearful public to the hapless administration.

Back and forth, pursuing lines of possibility, however outlandish, until their irrationality was exposed, nullifying them from his mental inquisition. But then—the entire equation was irrational. He was looking for evidence to support a zombie outbreak—before it had happened.

The freshly fluffed pillow accepted Barry as he sank back in bed. He'd gotten too emotional about things, inadvertently draining his strength.

Staring at the clock on the opposite wall, he gradually lost his battle with exhaustion and fell asleep.

At first, Barry thought he had returned to the zombie-infested future, but within minutes he realized his perilous circumstances were only part of a dream—a real nightmare this time.

Scenes changed without logic, he started out crossing an empty train station, only to find himself standing in the middle of a football field. Swarms of zombies flowed from the stadium seats, rushing out across the astroturf, closing in on him and someone at his side. When he fled, it was down a narrow corridor lined with books; the tunnel brought him to a desert at high noon, where he couldn't spare the time to divest himself of his winter jacket. Sweat blinded him, but his efforts to wipe it away only revealed he was now underwater, surrounded by undead sharks.

One second Miss Collard was his companion, the next his deceased wife ran beside him, and soon she was replaced by Frankie and then the matronly nurse from the hospital—on and on, an endless series of variable partners in his struggle to ward off a zombie horde.

It was a harrowing dream, breathless and frightening—but being a dream, it induced only abstract anxiety. Here, the zombies were unreal, their bites wouldn't infect him or tear away actual chunks of his flesh. It didn't matter how hard he fought, victory over these undead creatures was illusionary.

The terrible outbreak still loomed in the future. Nothing Barry might do in his dream could have any effect on that imminent doom.

Despite the knowledge that it was just a nightmare this time, he woke covered in perspiration. Something drastic had happened in the dream, jolting him awake…but he couldn't remember what. As he lay there, the details of the dream evaporated from his head, leaving him with just a frustrating sense of dread that grew more vague with each passing moment.

Eventually, he even forgot he'd had a bad dream and slipped off to slumberland again.

This time, his sleep featured no internal distractions.

When he finally roused, he was rested, ready to put an end to his extended hospital stay.

That afternoon, his doctor visited him.

Barry immediately demanded to know why he was still here.

"Your injury has not entirely healed yet," Dr Azred rebuked his patient's rude salutation.

Barry swatted aside this excuse. "I only lost a finger. I should've been back on the street the next day."

"You need to trust our diagnosis of your condition, Mr Winsor."

"Not if it makes no sense," Barry threw back at the man. Normally, he respected members of the medical profession, but this guy wasn't being straight with him. "You're keeping something from me."

Dr Azred frowned, but not in a manner that conveyed doubt. His expression communicated a sense of annoyance.

"What is it? What's wrong with me?"

The doctor coughed, then pretended to soften up (but Detective Winsor easily saw through his pretense). "There is nothing wrong with you, Mr Winsor. Nothing besides your missing finger, that is."

"Then why are you keeping me here?"

"Your tests have included some…curious readings."

"What do you mean 'curious'?"

Oh my God, fretted Barry. *I was admitted to the hospital because of a missing finger—and they found something worse-- Cancer? Or—damn—am I now one of the ebola victims?*

"Nothing you should worry about," Dr Azred announced dismissively.

"What were these readings?"

"You wouldn't understand their—"

"Try me," he growled. He was already sitting erect with his legs dangling over the side of the bed. He scooted forward so that his ass was perched on the edge of the mattress. "I'm a cop, doctor. Do you know how much trouble you could get in by withholding important information about the health of a police officer?" He put on his best "dangerous" look.

Dr Azred faltered, flustered and uncertain how to respond.

"What's wrong with my test results? Put it in layman's terms, okay?"

"Your potassium count is high. As is the amount of red corpuscles in your bloodstream." Having finally unleashed his secret, the doctor proceeded to attempt to trivialize the matter "Now, while those readings aren't common with the traumatic loss of a body part, they do not indicate anything drastically wrong."

"So—they're not an indicator of, say, cancer?"

"Oh no!" His response was flavored with a touch of disdain.

"Or any other disease…like ebola?"

This time, his denial was vehement.

"So—why are you holding me here?"

The man waved his hands before his chest, as if the gestures would somehow reinforce the veracity of his words. "We want to conduct some more tests, Mr Winsor, to further investigate these biochemical imbalances in your system."

"Are these imbalances in any way dangerous to my health?"

"Well…no, not really. You might feel periods of an energized state, but nothing hazardous."

"Then you really have no reason to legally hold me here," asserted Barry.

"But I just told you—" again Dr Azred floundered. "We want to do additional tests—"

"Unnecessary tests. According to you, this imbalance isn't a danger to my health, so there's no reason I can't leave."

"Admittedly, this imbalance is non-threatening, even trivial, but the advancement of science is always important, Mr Winsor."

"I'm not your lab animal, doctor. I'm an officer of the law with a long list of criminals that need tracking down and apprehending. I think doing my job is more important than letting you poke me and take my blood."

For a protracted moment, the doctor glared at Barry. He pursed his dark lips, then chewed on them. His hands dug deep into the pockets of his lab coat.

It's my life, buddy, fumed Barry. *You've no right to lock me up and stick needles in me.*

It was clear that Dr Azred resented Barry's refusal to help science. Barry could see it in his eyes, that sneaky internal search for some piece of logic that would trump Mr Winsor's objections. Barry'd seen that look before, in suspects when they wracked their brains for a suitable alibi when the evidence against them was insurmountable. Consequently, Barry was ready to reject any response made by the man.

"As you wish."

So easily…? Barry was instantly suspicious. What distraction was the doctor going to pull out of his sleeve?

"I will see about authorizing your discharge papers, Mr Winsor."

Another long moment passed as a defiant Dr Azred met Barry's stern gaze, then the physician turned on the heel of his expensive shoe and marched from the room.

I won?

Somehow, Barry was unconvinced. The doctor did not strike him as the kind of fellow to give up so quickly; in fact, his reading of Dr Azred told him the man was used to always getting his way. He'd already bent the rules to keep Barry locked up in the hospital. Was he stubborn enough to resort to *breaking* the rules to serve his purpose?

Honestly, Barry didn't want to wait around to find out.

I'll check myself out.

He hopped from bed, but could move no further. An assortment of wires and tubes tethered him to machines located on the far side of the bed. *The hell with this—* He took some care extracting the IV needle, but otherwise detached the rest with savage yanks. Disconnecting himself from the monitors would undoubtedly summon a nurse to find out what had happened. *So I better move fast. I need my clothes.* He stepped around the corner of the L-shaped room. Three doors confronted him, each easily recognizable: the door of the left was ajar, revealing the bathroom it guarded; the center one's inset window portal indicated it as the room's exit to the corridor; while the accordion leather-covered-cardboard nature of the panel on the right identified it as a closet. Reaching out, Barry pushed aside the folded barrier. Hanging there and folded on a raised shelf were the clothes he'd been wearing when the ambulance rescued him from his bed…his bloodstained pajamas.

They'll have to do for now, he grumbled.

Suddenly, a thread of new conjectures surfaced in his mind. What if the doctor's concerns were valid? What if Barry really was sick? If there was actually something wrong with him, could it be the zombie contagion? Had he picked it up during his (still debatable) trips to the apocalyptic future—and brought it with him back to now? A knot caught at the base of Barry's throat. *Am I the cause of the undead outbreak?*

No, such speculations were absurd. How could a figment from his nightmare manifest in the real world?

Having shrugged out of his open-backed hospital gown, he drew forth the pajama pants and shook them out. He was lifting a leg to insert it in the trouser sleeve when he felt a sharp bite on his butt. His leg trapped halfway into the sleeve of the pants, Barry's hand flew to his ass. A wooziness crept upon him.

He whirled in time to see Dr Azred dance back from him, a hypodermic held aloft. The man wore a grim smile…a satisfied smile.

You bastard—

The dizziness started to overwhelm Barry. He wobbled as he reached out to grab the mad doctor and went down. From the floor, he thought he heard a voice remark something about how Mr Winsor's imbalance was clearly impairing his judgment and how he now needed others to make his decisions for him. As he wobbled on the edge of anesthetized oblivion, he watched a pair of glistening Italian shoes move past him, accompanied by a call for help getting this poor deluded man back into bed. The last thing Barry saw was the door swinging closed.

Summoned by the doctor, a pair of attendants came to return the patient to his bed thirty-seven seconds later. But the room was empty.

5

THE FIRST THING HE NOTICED upon waking was a cold hard surface pressed against his cheek.

The floor—right, I passed out...

No, I didn't pass out! That bastard tranqed me!

But when he raised himself on his elbows, Barry discovered he was
no longer in a hospital room. He lay on the floor of a jail cell.

He was about to wonder how he got here, but then the answer was
obvious. Technically impossible, but nevertheless obvious.

He didn't need the abattoir stench to tell him he was back in the
zombie-infested future. The bandage where his little finger should've been
was enough of a reminder how real this nightmare could be.

Scrambling to his feet, Barry found his clothing consisted entirely
of a pair of pajama bottoms—the ones he'd been trying to step into when
that bastard doctor had snuck up on him with a tranquilizer. *The bastard—* Exchanging embarrassment for anger toward the renegade physician, he stumbled about getting his other leg into the cotton trousers.
Now, at least, he felt a little better prepared to face whatever lay in store
for him this time.

The jail cell was empty and—luckily—the barred gate hung open.
Outside, he found the desiccated corpse that was the source of the mal-
odor. He moved along the row of cells, alert for any surprises, but the rest
of the holding cells were unoccupied by anyone, living, dead or undead.
A staircase delivered him to a door that opened upon a squad room. Its
meager size told him this was probably a small-town police station.

A sweater dangled on the back of some officer's swivel chair; Barry
appropriated it. Oversized, it hung on him like a poncho, reaching halfway to his knees. Alas, he found no one's discarded shoes, resigning him
to a barefoot existence for a while.

He conducted a swift search of every desk in the squad room. In one
drawer he found a revolver, a .45. Ammo for it lay in that desk's bottom

drawer. He stuffed his pockets with bullets. Now he felt even better prepared to face things.

By this point, Barry had learned: if it looked looted and abandoned, it probably was. But that didn't stop him from inspecting every drawer and closet and cubbyhole in the building. He unearthed another pistol, but no ammunition for it. He found a jacket that fit. He saw a few corpses that had served as meals for some undead creatures. He paused to congratulate one cadaver on its choice: faced with an imminent tide of hungry zombies, this officer had turned his gun on himself and blown his brains out.

From paperwork lying on abandoned desks, Barry identified the police station's whereabouts. From the floor of a Manhattan hospital room, he had been displaced to Upper Darby, which a map told him was located just south of Philadelphia.

Outside, it was day; mid-afternoon from the look of things. The air was crisp with a stern chill, too cold to comfortable go around barefooted in pajama bottoms. It must be around July, he estimated. He needed to upgrade his attire soon if he wanted to avoid frostbite. The streets were cluttered with discarded automobiles and trash flung from nearby building windows, but empty of anything that was or had been human.

Rather than waste his time with any of these vehicles, Barry set off on foot. Later, when the roads cleared up somewhat, he might grab himself transportation. For now, he would remain light-footed and wary.

But where am I going?

Of course, that was the prize question. What destination would he choose in the post-apocalyptic land? Remembering how rotten the Big Apple had become, he saw no point in returning to Manhattan. In fact, as a rule, cities in general were to be avioded. The zombies seemed to cluster in urban areas. *And on highways,* he reminded himself. He needed to get out of the city, into the country, primarily using back-roads

Which direction should he go? West? North? South?

Did he want to wander aimlessly across this devestated landscape?

And what was his long-term goal?

While wandering aimlessly had a certain appeal, Barry knew what his first order of business should be—had to be. His honor depended on it.

He had to find that farm commune and slaughter every overfed cannibal there.

There was more at state here than just avenging Miss Collard's death. This was a matter of decency—and *justice.* Those people were all culpable to serial murders. They must be punished for their ghastly crimes.

It looked as if Detective Barry Winsor was the only lawman left to care about this.

He headed north.

Before leaving town, Barry broke into a sporting goods store and added a pair of golf clubs to his arsenal. Every little bit helped, and with the terrors he would have to contend with out there, he needed every edge he could find. Anyway, these weapons had served him very well during his earlier visits to the future. He knew how to handle them. They felt good in his hands.

He discarded the flimsy pajamas for a pair of warmer sweatpants. Now, he wouldn't feel so foolish facing danger dressed for beddie-by. Again, none of the store's shoes fit him properly; he was forced to wear oversized boots stuffed with extra socks.

On the edge of town, Barry passed a tavern that didn't look all that trashed.

The prospect of a shot for the road lured him inside. He picked his way past toppled tables and chairs to reach the bar. Like everywhere else, the place had been hit by looters, but here they'd overlooked a pair of bottles of brandy liqueur.

A stiff drink to launch me on my journey...

Tearing the seal from the bottle, he brought it to his mouth and took a hefty draught. It was far too sweet for his palate, and the buzz it induced was too trivial to count. He was about to take another swig when he paused, then set the bottle on the bar counter.

Although he would never admit it to anyone, Barry knew he was an alcoholic. After Emily's passing, he'd sought relief from sorrow in intoxication. The problem was: that relief never lasted very long. Sooner or later, he would sober up and feel rotten again...and hung-over. But instead of doing the sensible thing, Barry would give booze another chance. Maybe this next time it would succeed in washing away his misery.

Was now really an appropriate time to get drunk?

Of course not—the question itself was ludicrous. Danger lay around every corner. Intoxication would guarantee that he wouldn't survive the first adversarial encounter he stumbled upon.

Even taking that one swig had been a risky move, considering Barry's predilection to keep on drinking until the bottle—and the next one—were empty.

But, he argued with himself, *one swig isn't enough. I need more...just to get me started...*

Oh, shut up—you'll get us killed? he chided his addictive self.

He knew what he had to do, but he couldn't bring himself to leave the bottles where they sat on the counter and get the hell out of here. He was frozen in place, his anxieties riveted on the open bottle of brandy. He could smell the liqueur from here, its cloying aroma made him sick—but it also inspired a thirsty spasm in his throat.

He strained to step back, but his legs ignored the command. He remained where he was, staring at the bottles. After a few minutes, he reached for the brandy, but sight of his bandaged stump made him stop. He snatched his hand back before his fingers could make contact with the contoured bottle.

No!

This was stupid. No addiction was worth getting killed for. Especially when the only booze available was such a vile concoction. Sobriety was advisable on every level—so why couldn't he heed his common sense and leave the bar?

Because you don't want to...

But I do want to—I need to!

He closed his eyes and forced himself to remember Miss Collard. Her oval face formed in his mind, although somewhat hazy in detail. He could remember her eyes—her large blue eyes with their piercing fire and stern wariness—but her nose, her mouth were homogonized features, blurred by his faulty memory. Usually Detective Winsor was good with faces...so why was her likeness so elusive?

He focused on the girl's strength of character, her resolute sense of survival, her plucky need to fight her own battles. If Barry could be half as strong...

But you weren't, sneered the Barry that lusted after the bottle's contents. *You left her behind, you left her in the hands of those cannibal farmers. You failed her. She's long dead by now—slaughtered to feed the farm folk.*

"I didn't leave her behind!" So vehement was his denial that Barry bellowed this aloud.

I didn't leave her behind...I was yanked out of the future and dumped back into the past—my present— Whatever happened was completely out of my control.

This time his addictive side had crossed the line. Taunting him about Miss Collard's grisly fate had been intended to goad Barry into despair—

but it had only served to tighten his resolve to remain sober. The truth of the matter was: he *did* feel guilty for abandoning the girl. He understood that whatever had happened had been no fault of his, but nevertheless he couldn't shake the visceral remorse of losing her. He owed her something, and justice was all he could offer. To achieve that justice, he needed to stay sober. There was no way a drunken Barry was going to overcome a whole community of armed farmers. He wasn't even sure a sober Barry could pull that off—but he had to try. For her. For him. For justice.

When they're all dead, he promised his addictive self, *we'll get back together and tie one on.*

Finally strong enough, Barry turned away from the brandy and strode from the wrecked tavern.

He resumed his northward course. At the edge of town, he found and followed train tracks going his way.

As he walked, he struggled to remember exactly where the cannibal colony was. He and Miss Collard had driven along miles of country paths before they'd encountered the colony's roadblock. He hadn't been navigating by any map. His course had been governed by avoiding undead swarms and seeking avenues unclogged by forsaken traffic. If he ever got the chance to plot that journey on a map, he expected the line would be impulsively crooked.

The best he could do was travel north into farm country and hunt for familiar territory.

Only now did it dawn on Barry that no one had ever identified the name of their exclusive colony. Nowhere among Mayor Templar's bragging had he mentioned what they called their commune. At first, this seemed odd to Barry, but then he deduced it was a way for the colony to remain hidden. Without a name, anyone looking for the commune of farms would have to rely on geographic guidance—like he was doing right now.

En route north, he encountered a few zombies, but each was alone and easily eluded. Although his pockets jangled full of ammunition, Barry was loath to waste any slugs on undead meat.

He was saving his bullets for live targets.

While he kept his personal compass locked on north, Barry knew this course was only a crude approximate direction. Templar's colony lay north, but it might be slightly to the northeast, or even northwest. He hoped to recognize some landmark that would guide him closer to his desired destination.

After a few miles, the train tracks veered east, so Barry abandoned them and set off across a country pasture. When he discovered a stretch of woodlands in his northward path, he turned west and followed the edge of the forest.

The boundary between pasture and woods seemed like a suitably safe course. Should zombie or any other rogues appear, he could easily duck into the woods and hide among the shrubbery. He never expected trouble to come from that direction.

Twenty yards ahead of him, a figure burst from the woods, stumbling into the open field. From their agility, it was apparent this was a living person, not a zombie. Without pausing to survey their surroundings, they dashed across the grass. An instant later, three others tore through the leafy wall and bounded in pursuit, waving an assortment of unconventional weapons—there was a construction hammer and a fire ax and what looked like an African tribal hunting spear.

As these hunters appeared, Barry slipped unseen into the shrubbery. From there he watched them run down their prey. They tormented the runaway before bashing in his head. Exchanging jokes and callous praise, the hunters returned to the woodlands. The body was left for the undead to pick over.

They must belong to one of those roving marauder gangs Templar mentioned, reflected Barry from his safe hiding place. *At least they don't eat their victims.*

On impulse, Barry decided to trail them and get a look at the entire gang. He moved cautiously through the bushes, but both (caution and foliage) slowed him down. Within moments he had lost the hunters' trail. Now he was lost in the woods.

Not the first time for me.

This time, however, he was able to backtrack and locate the green pasture. From there, he continued to follow its edge west. He pointedly wouldn't look at the red stain that marked the fresh corpse sprawled out in the field.

Maybe it's for the best, he mused. *They were a bloodthirsty crew. I don't think I'd've gotten a polite welcome if they spotted me. I might've ended up like that poor fellow out there.*

On he trudged, over hillock, through fields, across a small creek, past the burned-out husk of some kind of warehouse, always keeping his nose aligned to the north.

He topped a rise as night fell and found a modest settlement laid out before him. He stopped to look it over. A country hamlet, consisting of two streets that intersected as an X and were lined with quaint shops. Only a few cars were visible littering the roadways in a disorderly fashion. No lights showed in any of the windows. Barry guessed that the town was relatively deserted.

It would provide him with shelter for the night.

Granted, he hadn't seen a zombie for hours, and those had shambled along in the far distance. But if he camped outdoors, something bad was bound to happen. He just knew it.

Now that he thought about it, he'd seen very few wild animals or birds during his cross-country trek. The territories he'd traveled through should have been alive with squirrels and rabbits and other beasties scurrying through the underbrush. Yet, he could recall only a few sightings.

Had the human zombies wiped out the wildlife as they shambled across the countryside? Or had the rest of the animal kingdom fallen prey to the same zombie affliction? Were undead squirrels and bunnies lurking in the bushes?

Another reason to avoid camping outdoors. He didn't want to be pounced upon by a ravenous killer bunny.

So he trotted down the hill and approached the little hamlet. He saw no "Welcome to Our Town" sign, so he decided to call it simply Rest Haven. Strolling its streets, Barry passed a homey pastry shop, a frilly pink nail salon, an old style pharmacy flanked by peppermint spirals (turning no longer), a mom'n'pop restaurant whose sidewalk cafe had been plowed over by a runaway car that protruded from the window of a shoe store. Rest Haven was so sylvan and quaint it made Barry shiver. It was creepy to encounter such a pastoral hamlet in this apocalyptic land, this niceness was in direct opposition to the rest of the world's deadly ambiance. Yet, he couldn't shake the feeling that someone—or some*thing*—was watching him.

A bed-and-breakfast sat at the intersection. *As good as any place to crash,* he decided. Inside, the establishment had escaped damage by scavengers. All of the furniture stood neatly in place, albeit covered by several month's worth of dust. The kitchen proved to be fully stocked, and although a lot of the stuff had gone rotten, Barry managed to cobble together the best meal he had eaten in the future. Upstairs, he found comfortable beds. He saw nobody, smelled no corpses. The B&B was a satin island amid a landscape of thorns.

Barry immediately distrusted the entire affair—the seemingly plush shelter, the quaint hamlet, the aura of pastoral calm that permeated Rest Haven. None of it fit with the rest of the world. Barry found it difficult to believe this town had somehow escaped the brutal attention of any bands of marauders—especially with the hunters' gang presumably camped out just the other side of the woods.

He had to temper his suspicion with practicalities. He wasn't going to go camp outside beyond the town and risk being found by a roving zombie. But neither was he going to curl up in one of these perfectly inviting comfy beds and wait for the hidden sting. The town was a gigantic spider's web, waiting to snare passers-by.

Scorning the comfortable bedrooms, Barry took a blanket down into the basement and made it his hidey-hole for the night. He dozed, never falling completely asleep, his .45 revolver cupped in one hand.

No monsters disturbed his evening.

They waited until morning.

Something jarred him awake. Noise—a cacophonous bedlam!

His shock was so great his finger constricted on the trigger as his hand swung his .45 into defensive play. He fired two slugs into a wall of shelves, shattering a jar labeled "bath salts." Released from its container, the powder poured forth, spilling from the shelf onto the cement floor. A sensuous fragrance filled the basement.

Recoiling with embarrassment for his unprofessional reaction, Barry snatched up his golf clubs and crawled under the steps that led upstairs. He cowered there, fighting to regain a modicum of composure so he could deal with whatever was going on.

What *was* going on?

Another boom sounded. It was loud, but remote. A gunshot for sure, high caliber from the sound of it. He estimated it came from more than a block away. He was in no immediate danger, but danger could move on fleet feet, arriving fast and furious.

Time to leave Rest Haven, Barry told himself.

Pity. He'd've enjoyed another abundant meal before returning to his journey. But a prompt departure was called for. Barry had no interest in meeting whatever was shooting up town.

Up the stairs he went, along a homespun hallway, past pictures of ancestors in ornate oval frames, past dead floral displays atop antique tables, through the cozy kitchen (where he grabbed a box of crackers he'd left out on the counter), out the backdoor (wincing and hoping the distant gunfire covered the noise of the screen panel slapping closed behind him) and down the alleyway (wading through drifts of brittle fallen leaves). This delivered him past an array of shabby storage sheds to a modest asphalt spread behind the shops. Here, the town gave way to wilderness, spotty grass becoming scrub that was swallowed by the nearby woods. Loose leaves, orange and crisp, blew across the dewy field.

He didn't spare a backward glance until he was safely inside the forest. When he paused to peer through the foliage, he saw nobody was following him. In fact, he saw no sign of anybody; yet the ongoing blasts proved someone was there, raising hell in Rest Haven.

It could be anybody, but Barry suspected the hunters gang was responsible. From what he'd seen of their behavior, trashing the town would certainly be what they'd call "fun." After all, they were the closest group of marauders he knew about. But then…it could be anbody.

Ah, whoever it was, Barry understood the wisdom of avoiding contact with them. He wanted no perilous adventures before he tracked down Templar's colony. Afterwards…well, he'd have to wait and see if he survived the confrontation before he started making future plans.

So intent was Barry on studying the backs of the town's row of shops, he never sensed his attacker's approach. He was turning away, ready to move on, but when he pivoted he came face to face with someone. An involuntary yelp of surprise escaped his lips. The stranger's face still retained most of its flesh, but the man's deceased condition was evident in his cloudy gaze. And the shotgun hole in his chest that went all the way through—my god, Barry could've poked his arm through the hole without scraping the edges of the wound. With less than a foot separating him from the zombie, Barry gagged at the stench that rolled off the animated cadaver.

It reached for him. During some previous scuffle, the zombie had lost its fingernails. The raw stumps wavered in Barry's direction.

He recoiled, but his withdrawal was blocked by the shrubbery at his back. He floundered, fighting the thorny branches that threatened to engulf him, kicking out with his unstable feet as he fell. At least the bushes hampered the creature's efforts to pursue Barry. Those same entangled twigs kept him from using one of his golf clubs to brain his swaying adversary. He was loath to use the gun, worried not just about wasting a precious bullet, but fearful that the shot would be heard by the hoodlums trashing the nearby town.

Scrambling through the foliage, Barry tumbled from the edge of the woods. He scuttled on his ass across the damp grass. Within seconds, though, the zombie succeeded in forcing its way through the bushy tangles. It lurched clear of the shrubs and tottered toward Barry.

Now that he was clear, Barry could use a golf club against his assailant—except he'd lost one crawling through the scrub—and the remaining club was trapped underneath him. There was no time to roll and free the weapon; the undead creature already loomed over him. Fumbling his gun from where it was shoved into the front waist of his pants, Barry lifted it to bear on the menacing figure.

A loud crack rolled across the pasture, and a sloppy hole appeared in the zombie's forehead. The creature wobbled, then slumped forward in final death. Stunned by this sudden event, Barry remained frozen, and the dead zombie collapsed onto him.

Mouthing guttural curses, Barry fought free from the corpse's dead weight. He kicked the body aside. Sprawled there, he gasped and gawked, still in the thrall of utter surprise.

Barry had not fired the shot that had taken down the zombie. He'd never had the chance to squeeze the trigger of his .45.

Slowly rotating his head, Barry scanned the landscape until he spotted the shooter. Halfway from the hamlet, a figure was approaching. The man stopped a few yards away, but continued to hold his revolver pointed at Barry.

A subtle gesture, no more than a twitch of the wrist, ordered Barry to discard his own gun. Reluctantly, Barry heeded the instruction. This man had fired a single shot and hit the zombie square in the forehead from five-hundred feet away. The fellow was no novice to firearms; extreme caution was advised while dealing with him.

Now that he believed Barry was unarmed, the shooter advanced closer. His revolver remained aimed at Barry's chest as the detective carefully clambered to his feet. The two faced each other.

A proud rockstar mane spilled down to the stranger's shoulders, sequins glittered all across the black leather vest that confined his fluffy blouse. Rows of manly studs ran down the outsides of his designer jeans to be swallowed by a pair of brocaded boots.

The din of whoever had been trashing Rest Haven had ceased at some point during Barry's frantic encounter with the zombie at the edge of the woods. Silence reigned throughout the morning now.

"Thanks," Barry ventured, slightly inclining his head in the direction of the dead zombie.

Another figure had crossed the field and stood now at the shooter's elbow. The newcomer wore what appeared to be leather chaps over no underwear. A leather vest draped from his wiry shoulders, its fringe tassles dancing in the morning breeze. Two Western Colt revolvers, complete with ivory handles, hung from a pair of belts at his waist. Was he supposed to be an Indian?—or a cowboy?

"What's that he's got there?" he grunted.

Barry responded: "Huh?"

"There—at your belt."

"Oh—a golf club."

"Lose it," the arena rocker.commanded. Another wrist twitch jerked the gun in his grasp, stressing the severity of the consequences for failing to follow his orders.

"Okay, okay." Barry slowly pulled the golf club free of his belt and tossed it aside. "Chill, okay?"

Although he was loath to admit it, the costumes worn by these two guys connected them to the hunters Barry had witnessed brain that runner yesterday outside of the hamlet. They'd been outlandishly dressed too. Could he expect these guys to share the same bloothirsty attitude?

The newcomer came forward and snatched up the discarded club. He held it aloft for a moment. "Sporty," he remarked. Stepping back, he gave the club an experimental swing at the grass, then lifted it to swing at empty air.

"Nasty," commented the shooter. His revolver stayed centered on Barry.

"It's a dangerous world," Barry muttered. His fresh nod toward the dead zombie emphasized his statement.

"Ain't that the truth," proclaimed the newcomer.

Barry turned to face the man, but all he saw was the bulbous head of the golf club zooming at him.

Then darkness swallowed the dangerous world.

He expected to wake up back in his own time, but the air that accompanied his gasp was too malodorous to belong to a world uncluttered by dead things. For a dreadful second, Barry feared he was back in the prison pit beneath Templar's barn, awaiting the barbecue. Had whatever cruel demon that was moving him back and forth in time decided to drop him into a sequence he'd already lived through? But no, he felt clothing against his skin. His hands were bound, but no noose encircled his neck. And the stench was bad, but different.

My God, he bemoaned. *I've become a connoisseur of awful smells.*

.His left temple hurt like hell—that was where the stranger had caught Barry with his own golf club.

After a few minutes, his eyes adjusted somewhat to the dark. He was in some kind of concrete enclosure. A cellar?

"You're awake," someone spoke behind him.

What the—

And he wasn't alone!

"I can tell. Your breathing changed."

"Uhh..." Barry chose to keep his comments vague until he learned more about the owner of this voice. "...okay..."

"My name is Sheldon. Who are you?"

"Barry." The darkness was too murky. All he could see was a gray smudge in the omnipresent darker black. He tried analyzing the fellow's voice, but couldn't get a handle on him. His voice was high and reedy, his words articulate, but something in his tone conveyed a defeated soul.

"Where are we?" ventured Barry.

"In Dusty's panic room," came the mystifying reply. "Dusty keeps things he values in here. I'm important—that's why I'm here."

Something about the name Dusty seemed familiar...but Barry couldn't attach a significant memory to it.

"Why are you here?" asked Sheldon.

That was a good question—one Barry was unable to answer. Clearly, the rocker and the cowboy belonged to the same group as the costumed hunters. From what he'd seen of their behavior, he'd expected the rest of their gang to be equally bloodthirsty...but why would a band of bloodthirsty marauders take anyone prisoner?

"Oh no—" he blurted. "Don't tell me I've been taken prisoner by another bunch of cannibals!"

"What?" grunted Sheldon. "Dusty and his crew aren't cannibals. Who told you that?"

"I—it was just an assumption."

"Well, you've wrong. Okay, not all of Dusty's habits are socially proper, but he's not *that* sick."

"So," mumbled Barry. "You're a prisoner too."

"No!" The voice grew strident. "I told you—I'm important. Dusty locks me down here to keep me safe."

"Safe from what?"

Sheldon made a derisive sound in the dark. "From everything! You've been out there—you know what it's like…"

"The zombies, you mean."

"Everybody's killing each other out there! It's too dangerous. But Dusty protects me—because I'm important. I keep things working. Without me, Dusty's crew wouldn't have electricity or running water."

Over the years, Detective Winsor had interviewed thousands of witnesses. Their accounts were always fragmentary, vague. With Sheldon's stream-of-consciousness babble, it took Barry a while to get an idea of what was going on.

He listened as Sheldon rattled on, revealing how Dusty ran a twisted but efficient crew. His men had their eccentricities, "like their inclination to dress up in silly costumes, as if make-believe garb granted them new identities in this new world," but they were all able warriors. Glendale needed able warriors. Everyone envied the utopia Dusty had established here. "But then, without my help, none of it would have been possible." A comfortable sanctuary like Glendale needed amenities that required technology. Someone was needed to repair things around town and jump-start engines and restore the basic utilities. "Right now, I'm working on souping up a Ferrari for Dusty to use as his command vehicle instead of the truck he boosted from that Army base." Dusty valued Sheldon's expertise with machinery. Sheldon was Dusty's most valuable associate. "That's why he locks me away, to protect me from danger." The world out there was filled with so many dangers now. Not every band was as peaceful as Dusty's men. If any of those rapscallions ever learned of Sheldon's existence, they'd surely try to kidnap him and put him to use bettering their own gangs. "But," Sheldon insisted, "I'm loyal to Dusty." Dusty had rescued him from the madness at the university. He'd claimed to know about a peaceful oasis, removed from the flow of civilization, off the beaten track, isolated and perfect for their purposes. Dusty and his rowdy drinking buddies wanted to escape. The world had gone insane. That damned asteroid had set off a chemical change in the atmosphere and suddenly the dead were up and walking around and trying to bite the living. "Why don't they just bite each other?" It was a crazy new age, but Dusty had led his crew through precarious ordeals, ultimately bringing them to the promised land: the idyllic town of Glendale. "While the crew set to cleaning up the place (there were gnawed-on corpses to dump and a few living squatters to roust), I applied my genius to restoring the town's power and water and heat. That's why I'm was so important to Dusty." As a physics professor, Sheldon Bowman was invaluable, the new age's perfect fix-it man. Sometimes, though, Sheldon was locked away for long periods of time. "I don't like these occasions." He'd gradually realized that Dusty and the rest of the crew went away during those times. They conducted forays into neighboring territories, looking for supplies and other survivors. Sheldon was surprised how few of the latter were found and brought back. Clearly, the undead had slaughtered everyone out there. It was a terrible new age.

From Sheldon Bowman's rant, Barry constructed a mental image of the man: tall; thin, but not emaciated (Dusty would keep his valuable Fix-It man well-fed); like most intellectuals he undoubtedly paid little attention to fashion, so his attire was probably not a conscious concern (Barry pictured him in tan corduroy pants and an olive green sweater with elbow patches); his fingers were most likely long and nimble, enabling him to single-handedly handle his Fix-It chores; facially, he might have tiny eyes made creepily huge by thick-lensed glasses, an almost nonexistent nose, a tight unsympathetic mouth, and naturally a high forehead. Barry suspected that when Sheldon spoke, he tilted his head back to better project his dry voice from those indifferent lips. His acerbic attitude demonstrated his complete lack of any sense of humor—also an utter disdain for anyone stupid enough to doubt any of his opinions.

Later, when he finally got a glimpse of Sheldon, most of Barry's presumptions were validated. The man was tall and gaunt, indeed his clothing was rumpled, coarse and earth-toned, his hands were sleek with articulated fingers. It was the face that Barry got all wrong: he didn't wear glasses, but his squinty gaze made it seem as if he should, below his blunt nose sprouted a weak mustache that was not strengthened by his otherwise unshaven cheeks and chin. While his hair was of medium length, its tousled configuration made the tufts seem longer than they was. And that chin belonged on a hillbilly, not a pompous intellectual. Barry was spot-on, though, concerning the man's unsympathetic lips.

"You should be glad Dusty chose you," Sheldon assured Barry.

"If only I knew why Dusty chose me."

Glendale was the hamlet he had called Rest Haven, that much became obvious early on.

Sheldon was a college professor who Dusty had enlisted (kidnapped and brainwashed?) to be an all-purpose handyman. And when Good Ol' Mr Fix-It wasn't busy fixing stuff, Dusty locked him away in the dark—to "protect" him. But Dusty was an "okay guy," something Sheldon had repeatedly asserted.

To Barry, this Dusty clown sounded like a typical gang leader. Apparently, however, he was smart enough to surround himself with capable men in these torturous times. And he'd bagged a Fix-It man. All he needed then was a place to call home. Enter Glendale and set Sheldon loose on the dilapidated mess—and he'd lived up to his self-professed "genius" and rebooted civilization in this remote pastoral corner of the Pennsylvanian farmlands. Consequently, Dusty had appointed himself the feudal lord of the restored hamlet.

Barry had seen no evidence of the gang when he'd arrived in Glendale because they'd been away. *"Scouting for supplies" my ass*, Barry mulled. They were off marauding, raiding some nearby settlement, raising hell somewhere else.

Raiding!

That was where Barry had heard Dusty's name before. Mayor Templar had mentioned the man among his bragging about how successful his colony was at defending itself against invaders. Dusty's Raiders. They regularly attacked Templar's farms, but were always fought off.

That meant Barry had finally reached the region of Templar's colony of deviants.

All of this was immensely helpful in comprehending his current situation, but something Sheldon had mentioned sparked him to initiate a more detailed inquiry.

"You mentioned an asteroid…"

"Hmm?" mumbled Sheldon's voice in the darkness. During his entire ramble, the man had kept his distance. "You don't know about the asteroid?"

Besides the hints Barry had stumbled across in old newspapers, he knew nothing about the thing.

"Nobody listened," Sheldon told him in a hushed tone. "They warned that the asteroid was going to hit the Earth, but nobody paid any attention."

"Who's 'they'?"

"Scientists of course. Specifically the astronomers and astrophysicists."

"So—this asteroid—did it hit the Earth?"

"Nooo," Sheldon scoffed at his ignorance. "But it almost did. It came close enough to dip through a portion of Earth's atmosphere. That's when it happened."

"When what happened?"

"Don't you know anything? That's what caused the zombie outbreak."

"I…I've heard a number of theories that are supposed to explain the zombie oiutbreak," Barry lied to draw forth more details.

"All rubbish," Sheldon snidely dismissed. "You'd have to be a fool to believe in other people's wild theories. The asteroid was the real cause, don't let anyone tell you otherwise."

"But…how could an asteroid raise the dead?" This was the point that weakened his faith in the ex-college professor's knowledge. Barry couldn't fathom any possible connection between an asteroid and the dead suddenly walking. On the other hand, if such a near-collision had happened, Barry wanted to learn the details, even if they weren't germane to the zombie outbreak.

"It came swooping down," Sheldon continued, ignoring Barry's question. "Almost surfing across the ionosphere, until it finally gouged a chasm through the Earth's upper atmosphere. That's when it happened, when it released the contagion."

"A contagion?"

Sheldon issued an exasperated sigh, expressing his displeasure with Barry's relentless interruptions. When he resumed his explanation, his tone held a touch of command in it, as if now he was lecturing to a class of idiots. "The asteroid contained a pocket of some unknown chemical. Surfing through the upper atmosphere eroded away a layer of the meteor's surface, until that pocket was exposed. The contents emptied into our atmosphere. I know all this because a friend told me and he watched it happen through the telescopes at Mt Palomar. The chemical spread, catalyzing in weird ways with the elements that comprise our air. By the time it settled across the globe, the mixture was volatile enough to wake the dead."

Although the exposition was delivered in scientific terms, sounded like mysticism to Barry. His gut told him that no chemical concoction, however weird and alien, was capable of reanimating dead flesh. Sheldon had heard this tale and accepted it because it played into his need for physics to be the root of everything. But this time, the professor's philosophy had failed him. This asteroid's near-collision and the chemical payload it had dumped into Earth's atmosphere (if such a contamination had actually taken place) were interesting incidents, but it was dubious that they played any role in the undead outbreak.

At least now, though, Barry finally had an explanation for the headlines he'd seen in discarded yellowed post-apocalypse newspapers.

Now that he had a full load of data to reflect upon, Barry decided to try to address some more pressing physical inconveniences.

"Umm…" He adopted a friendly tone. "If we're not prisoners, do you think maybe you could untie me?"

"No, I couldn't do that," protested Sheldon. "If Dusty tied you up, he wants you tied up. I would never contravene Dusty's wishes."

Definitely kidnapped and *brainwashed.*

"But what if I have to go to the bathroom?"

"Do you?"

"Well…" Alas, he wished his bladder offered some heaviness that would validate his claim, but that was not the case right now. "Not yet," he confessed. He could do many things, but get pee out of an empty bladder was not among his skills. "But really…c'mon…give a guy a break…"

Sheldon's silence conveyed his persistent unwillingness to help Barry.

While discussing the world and things with the ex-college professor in the dark, Barry had been testing his bindings. They were tight, but the ropes were inexpertly knotted. A bit more squirming and he might just be free on his own.

Best to keep Sheldon talking, distracting him from possibly noticing Barry's escape act. The cellar was too dark for Barry to make out any details, but by his own admission, Sheldon had been locked up here for a while; *his* eyes were probably more accustomed to this murky gloom.

Barry probed for more details about Dusty's crew. What kind of setup did he have? What were his long-term goals? Did he even have any?—or was basic survival his major concern?

While Sheldon's answers were verbose, they contained little in the way of useful information. This Dusty had the professor so bedazzled that he couldn't stop praising him long enough to qualify why the gang leader deserved acclamation. Sheldon objected to Barry's use of the term "gang leader." Dusty was no hoodlum, the professor asserted, he was a visionary who had assembled a "crew" who were adept at survival. Having understood the changes that were in store for society, Dusty was acting to insure that some fragment of civilization persevered. And without Sheldon's help, that laudable ambition would never be attainable.

After a few minutes of tooting Dusty's horn, Sheldon invariably switched to crowing about his own importance. Barry had to verbally nudge him back on track.

But again, all of the professor's exclaimations boiled down to: look at Dusty, he's great, he's doing great things, especially with Sheldon's help.

Barry had hoped for something more informative…like how many men were in Dusty's crew?—what was their arsenal like?—when they'd grabbed that Army truck, had they picked up any other military gear? But none of Sheldon's adulation touched on any of these subjects.

Finally—Barry's managed to slip the ropes from his wrists.

He proceeded to conduct an examination of the chamber. When he found a wall, it was cool to his touch—the room was definitely some kind of a basement, probably beneath one of Glendale's buildings. Barry felt along the wall; moving to the right, he made a circumference of the room, detecting its sparse furnishing. Most of the walls were covered with shelving and most of those shelves were crowded with cartons and jars—presumably supplies stolen by Dusty's Raiders. A sofa sat against one wall, he found Sheldon sitting there. The man yelped when Barry fumbled across him, and continued to protest as the detective moved on to finish his blind surveillance.

"You were tied up!" wailed Sheldon. "How did you get free?"

"I'm a resourceful guy," Barry remarked offhandedly. He was searching out the doorway he had encountered during his circumnavigation of the chamber. It had no handle, no lever that might open the portal—which was as he'd expected. It was, after all, where Dusty stashed Sheldon while he and his crew were off marauding and raiding and raising hell. An interior doorknob would give the smart Fix-It man a way of escaping. For that matter, if even half of Sheldon's claims of genius were accurate, the man was intelligent enough to have already searched for a hidden exit. If he hadn't found a way out in all that time, the odds were that none existed.

"Dusty isn't going to like this…"

"I'll be honest with you, Sheldon—I really don't give a shit how Dusty feels about things." Relying on just his fingers in the dark, he gave the door frame a closer inspection. There was no trace that any inner latch had existed. The seal was tight; as he'd thought, the door only opened from outside.

Yet—suddenly—a white line appeared before him as the door unsealed itself. When the hatch swung wide, the glare of afternoon illumination momentarily blinded Barry. For a second he thought his examination had somehow triggered a secret release—but as his vision cleared, he saw the error of that assumption.

The silhouettes of several figures filled the now open threshold. At least two of them held guns aimed directly at Barry.

Out of the frying pan...and into the fire...

Recoiling, he took a step back, as if the figures gave off genuine heat.

"I believe I told you to leave him as he was, Sheldon," announced one of the figures.

"I didn't help him, Dusty!" came a tragic moan from the dark behind Barry. "He did it on his own!"

The burlier figure bid his comrades inside the dark chamber, then withdrew from the doorway. Entering, the pair immediately flanked Barry and forcibly steered him out into the daylight.

"Dusty, wait—I—" But someone shut the door in Sheldon's face, cutting off his beseeching whine.

After hurrying Barry up a short flight of concrete steps, the thugs presented him to their leader.

"So you freed yourself," Dusty challenged him.

For the moment, Barry remained silent. He carefully studied the gang boss, measuring him up.

This man exuded authority, a palpable charisma radiated from him. He had the physique to back up his pomposity too. His arms were thick and sturdy. The open front of his sleeveless black leather jacket exposed a bodybuilder's chest. In striking contrast, Dusty's face was almost cherubic. His sweet features somehow managed to twist into a haughty mask of arrogant command. His mouth was small, but housed an array of oversized teeth. Barry was reminded of Al Pacino in that movie about cruising gay bars. Whatever his proclivity, though, this was a dangerous man.

The others had stepped back from Barry, but kept their guns ready.

"You appear to be a resourceful guy," remarked Dusty. "Let's see how smart you are..."

"I don't need to be a genius to know who *you* are," Barry threw back at him.

His quick assessment of the gang boss told Barry his smartest move would be to stroke Dusty's ego.

"I was coming to see you," proclaimed Barry. "And well, this turned out to be a roundabout way, but here I am."

"Here you are..."

Knowing that any hesitation would undercut the tale he was swiftly concocting in his head, Barry launched into an account of how he'd managed to flee Manhattan. Fighting his way west, he'd heard about the exploits of Dusty's Raiders from a family he encountered in Philly. Barry intentionally cluttered his story with needless details, all derived from personal experience, just presented in a completely different manner. He knew that most people will accept anything as truth if you piled on enough graphic minutiae.

"I decided you sounded like the kind of fellows I'd like to run with." He gave them his haughtiest smile.

"So here you are," grunted Dusty.

"Yeah."

In the end, Barry was surprised by the success of his bluff.

His judgment to pander to the gang boss' pompous center had paid off better than expected. Apparently Dusty was easily duped by gratuitous flattery. "You've got this whole town revived—that's an awesome accomplishment." All his praise won Barry an invitation to join Dusty's "crew," as he called them.

Barry put on a convincing show of gratitude as he accepted this call to arms.

He was not allowed to carry any weapons, though. After a probation period, the crew would decide whether or not he could be trusted; only then he would be given back his gun.

"And my clubs," he requested.

"Those silly golf clubs?" scoffed Red Ryder.

"I like them." He gave the man a serious scowl and added, "I'm good with them too.

Having been the one who'd shot the zombie that had attacked Barry out by the edge of the woods, Red Ryder had seen what damage the clubs could inflict when his cowboy comrade had smacked Barry with one of them. "Yeah, guess they pack quite a wallop."

Barry gave a knowing nod.

He also thanked the fellow for saving him from the zombie.

Brushing aside Barry's appreciation, the big-haired rocker gave him the penny tour of Glendale.

The B&B and a YMCA around the corner served as barracks for the crew. A tavern and the small movie theater provided entertainment. A diner at the edge of Glendale fed everybody, a mid-town cafe offered coffee and doughnuts. One morning, Barry was asked to help restock the restaurant's larder. This consisted of hauling cartons from a nearby shoe store, now devoid of any footwear, but filled with stacks of different cartons. Barry presumed these had been accumulated during previous Raiders' outings.

The number of women Barry saw around town surprised him. When questioned, Red Ryder admitted that most of the broads weren't technically Raiders, just groupies who hung around for the luxuries and the protection. "In return for—" He nudged Barry's side with a friendly elbow and giggled, "—y'know."

The hamlet's remote location put it out of the way of most passers-by. Except for the line of woods behind the row of shops, the surrounding terrain was open and flat, bad news for anyone trying to assault the settlement. Later, Barry found that several of those storage sheds he'd seen behind the shops harbored machine gun emplacements, ample defense against rear attackers. He also learned that numerous cameras were scattered around the hamlet and its perimeter, monitoring goings-on. One such camera had alerted the crew to Barry's presence when he'd crossed to the stretch of woods. (He privately wondered why no other lenses had caught his original approach to the hamlet. Also, he marveled at the luck he'd had not running into anyone that night, for although most of Dusty's crew had been off on a raid, the concubines and a few men had remained behind in Glendale, but he had encountered none of them—and none of them had seen him. Not placing much faith in luck, the entire affair made Barry suspicious.) From everything he saw, it was clear that Dusty had a real tight operation going here.

So—how had Barry managed to get past its security web?

If they'd spotted him last night, then why had they waiting to capture him?

He was reluctant to probe Red Ryder for these answers; he felt such questions exhibited too much interest in the hamlet's security protocols. As the newest addition to the Raiders' ranks, Barry knew such curiosity might trigger suspicion among the crew.

A brief consideration, though, brought the answer to Barry: They *had* spotted him last night, but with the bulk of Dusty's warriors out-of-town, the on-site crew had decided to await their return before dealing with this invader.

All in all, Barry needed to be especially scrupulous. They had accepted him as a comrade, but that acceptance was tenuous and depended on him not overstepping his role as a new recruit. All the while, they were watching his behavior to determine whether his loyalties were long- or short-term. If for an instant they suspected his allegiance was a pretense, Barry had no doubt they would put him down—not unlike the man he'd watched be chased down and dispatched by those two hunters.

The truth of the matter: his fealty *was* entirely bogus. Besides fast-talking himself out of a quick death, Barry had ulterior motives for joining this crew. These men conducted regular raids on Templar's colony of cannibals. They knew its location, but questioning them about it would certainly raise a red flag of distrust in the marauders. Barry's best bet was to stick around until he could accompany the Raiders on their next assault on the united farms.

Until then, he had to blend in and gain the crew's approval.

He conformed with the others in their rowdy pastimes, raising hell, carousing, gambling, and drinking.

This last recreation posed potential trouble for Barry. While he still refused to brand himself as a full-fledged problem drinker, he wasn't foolish enough to overlook his weakness for the bottle. Ever since Emily's passing, he had grown too friendly with alcohol, even though he understood that the peace it fostered was fleeting and completely illusionary; a binge might force him to forget his sorrows, but they returned in the morning, often more boisterous than before. Barry couldn't risk getting drunk with the crew and slipping out of character. So he mastered the art of nursing a single drink for hours, making it appear as if he was matching his comrades' consumption rates.

He freely helped himself to the marauders' stockpile of cigarettes. Initially, he told himself smoking would help him better fit in, but in truth he enjoyed having a smoke when the urge came upon him. It made up for all the other times he'd wanted a cig in this wretched post-apocalyptic nightmare but there'd been none available.

Periodically he selected women to serve as his concubine, but rarely the same one twice.

At Dusty's request, Barry demonstrated his proficiency with the golf clubs. A mannequin was dragged from some store display and set up in the street. With a few casual blows, Barry smashed the painted figure to bits, but the baby-faced leader wanted to see the weapons in real action. Later, when a zombie was spotted wandering toward Glendale, they let it approach the town so that Barry could show his stuff on some "dead meat," as Dusty put it. He dispatched the creature with ease, raising awed exclamations from the onlooking crew.

"Nice," remarked Dusty. "Next time we hit one of the regional towns, let's visit some sporting goods stores and stock up on those things."

The other Raiders supported his proposal with a lusty cheer.

"Time we paid the farms a visit, boys," Dusty announced one evening at the tavern.

Most of them (including Red Ryder) applauded this.

At Barry's elbow, a black fellow (who called himself Petey Pete and wore a jet-fighter pilot's outfit) grumbled under his breath, "Just stupid, wasting our time hitting those farms again. Every time, the bastards fight us off."

"But don't these raids help keep Glendale stocked with foodstuffs?" Barry asked, remembering to add a touch of slurred sloppiness to his words.

"You've seen the town's back-up pantry, man. Restocking supplies ain't never the reason for these runs. Dusty wants payback—and the chance to loot their arsenal."

Not to mention, mused Barry, *letting these fellas vent their pent-up hostilities.* Dusty might have assembled an able crew of fighters, but in many of them Barry detected a streak of cruelty that could only be sated by mayhem. And he could tell that Dusty belonged to that group of latent sadists.

As far as Barry was concerned, though, "paying the farms a visit" was exactly what he had been waiting for.

Before leaving the bar, Dusty named the Raiders who would be going tomorrow. To his annoyance, Barry was not included in that roster.

"Hey," he complained. "What about me?" His minorly inebriated state (or maybe being pissed off by that same feeble degree of intoxication) emboldened him.

"You hear your name, Winsor?" retorted Dusty. "No—so you stay here with the women."

"Don't I get the chance to whack a few farmers' heads with my clubs?"

Someone lustily grunted that they'd like to see that. Someone else seconded that opinion.

Lowering his chin, Dusty stroked it with his limber fingers before he commented, "I suppose that would be fun..."

"Damn straight," crowed Red Ryder. "Good Ol' Bar'll splatter farmer brains all over the place!"

The others muttered in support of that prospect.

"Alas," Dusty decreed, "Winsor's still on probation…so he won't be joining us tomorrow." With a curt nod and a loud snap of his fingers in the air, the leader twirled on his heels and marched from the tavern. His toadie, a weasely guy called Runt, followed him.

"Aw, man" groaned Red Ryder. "Really wanted to see Good Ol' Bar' brain a few farmerboys."

While others shared his lament, clearly no one was willing to officially challenge Dusty's decision.

Dammit, Barry grumbled to himself.

But when tomorrow came, bad weather sabotaged the outing.

Dusty and his chosen Raiders departed well before dawn, hoping to surprise their drowsy victims before the sun came up. Most of them set off on-foot. A panel truck brought up the rear; while it carried a few men, the vehicle was otherwise empty—its cargo space was earmarked for whatever booty the raid would secure.

Just before they left, Sheldon appeared and argued with Dusty. From the window of his room, Barry covertly observed the confrontation. He couldn't hear their dispute, but Barry presumed the professor was probably protesting being locked up while the rest of the Raiders were away. Whatever reasoning Sheldon had presented did not sway Dusty's will; the professor was consigned to the custody of two men who dragged him away while Dusty set off, leading his Raiders from the hamlet.

Barry had considered sneaking away and following the Raiders on their trek to Templar's colony, but the consequences could be too dire if he got caught. If it'd been a matter of tracking them through an urban environment, Barry'd have had no worries, but the local terrain was a far cry from orderly concrete avenues. He was no wilderness expert. For that matter, one of the left-behinds might spot him slipping from town and, mistaking him for a zombie, shoot him in the predawn dark. If Barry were caught, they'd do more than eject him from the crew, they'd probably cut his throat too—and then he'd never get to mete out justice on the cannibals that had slaughtered Miss Collard.

So, chain-smoking his way through a pack of cigs, he remained where he was, stuck in-town with the women and crewmen too clumsy to be counted on in a fight.

As the sun rose over the wooded horizon, snow began to drift from the lightening heavens. Within an hour, the storm had intensified into a blizzard. Half-an-hour later, bedraggled and twitchy with frustration, the Raiders emerged from the white-out and stumbled into Glendale.

This time, Barry was nearby when Sheldon challenged Dusty upon his ignoble return.

"I warned you," yelled the professor. "I told you it was going to snow—but no, you didn't believe me. How could you doubt the veracity of my forecast?"

Annoyed by the raid's cancellation, Dusty was clearly in no mood to be berated. He punched Sheldon in the nose and then withdrew to the toy store that served as his private abode. A gaggle of the groupies argued among themselves before the ones who'd drawn the short straws followed the leader indoors to attempt to assuage his disappointment.

Everyone else herded the dissatisfied raiders into the tavern. Hot rum was promised to warm them up after their long and fruitless trek. Barry joined this gathering, but nursed a single mug until noon, when the celebration broke up and the drunken marauders dragged their asses to bed. Barry ended up sleeping alone, for the girl he favored had been among the cadre sent to lift the leader's spirits.

The storm reigned for several days, forcing everyone to stay inside. While the groupies provided some measure of distraction for the men, by the end of the third day, even the randiest Raider was suffering from cabin fever. Fights broke out. The men vied for sentry duty just to break the monotony. Many ended up in alcoholic stupors, seeking escape from boredom at the bottom of bottles. Although sorely tempted, Barry managed to avoid joining them on the floor.

When Dusty finally left his toy shop to wander the town, he stomped about and cursed anyone who got in his way. Apparently the groupies' wiles had failed to mollify the man, his frustration had boiled into a rage. Everyone avoided him. Everyone except Runt, whose habitual sniveling only earned him a brusque beat-down.

After kicking ragged paths back and forth through the snow-clogged streets, Dusty disappeared into the library, which was Sheldon's haunt (when he wasn't locked away—"for his own protection").

Withdrawing to a window booth at the diner, Barry toyed with a slice of lemon pie as he monitored the street. Half-an-hour later, Dusty emerged...alone. Barry watched him wade away down the avenue. Even from this distance, he could tell the leader was in better spirits; his step was bouncy as he trudged through the knee-deep snow. Dusty had gone to consult with his all-purpose Fix-It man, and Barry had to wonder if, irritated by Sheldon's huffy arrogance, he'd strangled the professor.

Curious, Barry finished his pie. Wrapping himself in a warm jacket (provided by the hamlet's clothing store), he left the diner. Outside, he lingered and lighted up a cigarette. Once he was confident there were no witnesses, he wandered across the street to climb the library steps. He doubted whether a knock would be heard. Before entering, Barry discarded the cigarette in a nearby snowdrift.

It was dark inside. Barry maneuvered the entrance hallway by the snow-glare that seeped in through the foyer's tall vertical windows. This led to a similarly murky chamber, one that he knew from experience housed most of the library's books. A small town had little use for an overstocked library. Here, Barry would find Sheldon, sulking in a corner, or dead on the floor.

He ventured softly, "Hey, Shelly…"

This informality was risky. Ever since the time they'd shared confinement in that dark basement, the professor had given Barry the cold shoulder. The detective deduced that he resented Barry for dismissing some of his beliefs. As far as Sheldon was concerned, every word he spoke communicated only irrefutable facts. To doubt Sheldon was to deny his superior intelligence—absurd and highly insulting.

A low grumble came from deep within the book-infested darkness.

So—he's alive, Barry noted. *Then what was Dusty all elated about?*

"It's me, Barry Winsor," he called forth softly. "You okay?"

Maybe Dusty just beat him, left him bloody on the floor.

What was his obsession with a dead or bloodied Sheldon sprawled on the floor of the library? The professor wasn't Barry's favorite person, probably not even in the top hundred, but the detective harbored no ill will for the man…at least, not consciously. What subconscious animosity fueled Barry's eagerness to find a bloody beaten Sheldon Bowman?

Maybe I've been hanging out with the other Raiders too long, trying to fit in with them has made me cold and heartless.

Now that Barry knew the professor was still alive, he could easily have turned and left…but something made him linger. It took him a moment to recognize the opportunity at hand.

Without a doubt, Sheldon considered himself to be an invaluable asset to Dusty's operation. But from what Barry had witnessed earlier, it was clear that the leader was pissed off at his Fix-It man. Maybe Barry could capitalize on this fall from grace. By playing on whatever rancor the professor now felt for his bossman, it might be possible to draw some practical data from him.

Moving carefully, Barry edged deeper into the library. A few more groans guided him down darkened aisles to Sheldon's location. Here, a feeble shaft of light fell from a snow-covered skylight to bask the professor in muted illumination. The man *was* on the floor, but not dead, not bloodied—just on his ass with his long legs splayed out and his back slumped against a book-laden wall of shelves. Sheldon seemed to take no notice of Barry standing there.

Here we are again, he mused, *in the dark.*

"You okay, Sheldon?"

The man gave no verbal response, but did tip his head to the side, turning his emotionless features on Barry. A large bruise marked his face.

"That was kind of…uh…harsh," Barry ventured. "Outside, y'know… earlier…"

Sheldon remained aloof.

"It sure smelled like snow was coming. Y'know, how the air gets that crisp odor right before it snows. What's that called? Ionization?"

The professor's stare remained deadpan.

"Only an idiot would ignore that, right?"

He refused to be drawn out of his surly shell by Barry's sympathic remarks. No amount of sucking up would crack the professor's distrust.

"Okay…" Barry mumbled. "Well, if you need anything…you let me know, okay?" He withdrew as he spoke.

Sheldon's vacant stare followed his departure.

A notion occurred to Barry as he trudged through the snow after leaving the library. By the time he found Dusty, Barry had sculpted the notion into a scheme, finessing it with a pitch that would appeal to the man's not-so-latent hate for Templar's farm community.

A hate we both share, reflected Barry.

His search for Dusty took him up and down the snowbound street, but his target was not in the tavern, nor the B&B, nor the theater or arcade. The bossman had retreated to his toy store domicile. Considering Dusty's foul mood, bothering him there was a risky move, but it was that very distemper that Barry hoped to fluff.

Entering without knocking, Barry found the leather-clad man drinking alone.

Although he'd passed it on the street several times, Barry had never given much attention to the place. From outside, the bay windows were opaque with posters advertising toys. Inside, though, Dusty had made meticulous changes to the store's original layout. The aisles had all been moved back to project from the side walls. A cavalcade of figurines and mini-vehicles decorated the shelves. Each toy had been removed from its wrapper and carefully posed, many of them interacting in lewd manners, elephants buggering cars, monkeys being inappropriate with winged pigs, rockets invading dolls' dresses. The shelves had been shortened, granting more room for the tableau that now occupied the shop's center. Tables arranged in descending tiers swept from the display aisles, all converging on a dais where Dusty's throne sat. It was an actual medieval throne, made of ornately sculpted wood and most likely stolen from some local Renaissance fair. Display stands loomed behind the chair like a theatrical backdrop—these offered toys of a more adult nature. Somewhere, Dusty had pillaged a sex shop of its most grotesque wares. Overhead hung an assortment of blow-up plastic women dressed in glistening S&M latex. Dildos and fake vaginas were glued all over these dangling dominatrix. Additional life-sized dolls flanked his throne, their postures expressing a parody of awe over the seated figure.

Amid this giant diorama devoted to deviant behavior, Dusty sprawled on his throne and nursed a bottle of vodka in his lap. In his sex club leather, he was the most conventional thing in the shop. At his feet lay a few headless dolls (of the variety cuddled by normal young girls); there was no sign of the missing heads.

Barry assumed the man's sleeping arrangements lay in a back room.

From the propensity of female dolls surrounding the man, Barry reassessed his judgment concerning Dusty's sexuality. But being straight hardly vindicated his weird sense of decor. His black leather outfit must have been just an affectation designed to confuse observers looking to draw conclusions from simple appearances.

He made a mental note: this rowdy was smarter than he acted.

Proceed with caution...

Dusty's volatile nature was in full bloom when he lifted his head and glared at Barry. "What do you want?"

"I want to smash some farmer heads."

"Piss off, Winsor. I'm in no mood to—"

"So do you."

"Huh?"

"You want to smash some farmer heads too."

Lips drawing back to reveal grinding molars, Dusty growled, "You here to rub it in, Winsor? I'll—"

"So why aren't you out smashing farmer heads?"

"The snow, you idiot. Or haven't you noticed the—"

"The snow isn't an impediment—it's an advantage you're not using."

"What?"

"You're passing up a prime opportunity to finally catch these farmers with their overalls down around their ankles." Barry leaned forward and spread his open hands before him. "I mean, they'd never expect a raid in the middle of a blizzard, would they? Their guard would be down. They'd be helpless farmers, huddled indoors, enjoying their warmth and peace of mind. You could sneak up and wham."

"Wham…"

"Wham!" Barry pounded a fist into the opposing palm.

The angry furrow of Dusty's eyebrows deepened, but the glow in his piggy eyes indicated that the focus of his rage had shifted from Barry to the farmers.

The helpless farmers.

Barry suppressed a smile. His scheme had titillated the gang leader's bloodthirst. The beauty of it was: the tactics were actually quite cunning. The attack strategy he'd suggested would definitely bring the Raiders victory over the colony of vile cannibals…if Dusty were crazy enough to venture out into the storm. Oh, the man was unquestionably that crazy—especially when goaded on by his manic hatred. Barry wasted but a fleeting second on self-congratulation, though. Now, he needed to strike while the iron was hot.

"Yeah—you know a good idea when you hear it, huh?"

Dusty's eyelids hooded his fierce gaze. He pursed his lips.

"Is it good enough to earn me a chance to smash some farmer heads?"

"You're a persistent one, Winsor."

"I want to smash some farmer heads." Barry despised the farmers' colony as much as the head Raider, just for different reasons. This hatred imbued his words with a fervid urgency.

"Okay." Dusty released a long breath, then rose from the throne. "Let's slaughter some farmers." On vodka-diluted legs he descended from the porn dais and staggered across the toy shop. Barry stepped out of his way. Dusty swaggered out of the shop and into the snow, waving his bottle at the sky between swigs.

Barry followed the man through the snow drifts to the tavern. There, Dusty barged in and loudly announced, "The raid's back on!"

Drunken crew members and their attendant concubines all faced him with puzzled looks.

"What— Now?" grunted someone.

"Now!" the leader snapped.

"But—the storm's still—"

"Exactly!" crowed Dusty.

"But—"

"This time, the storm will be our greatest weapon against those bastard farmers!"

This time, Barry let a smile sweep across his face.

He might have been a disturbed individual, but Dusty possessed a degree of cunning. He took Barry's scheme and added some rather ingenious refinements.

This time, the panel truck served as more than just transportation for the marauders. Dusty had the men drag a metal scoop from a civil storage garage and attach it to the front of the truck, transforming it into a snowplow. Now the Raiders could travel across the frozen terrain.

But this was only the beginning of Dusty's craftiness. Loaded with men (among them Dusty), the truck did not head directly for the farm colony. Instead, he took the Raiders to a neighboring town, where they looted a fleet of snowmobiles from a sporting goods store. Now, the marauders could maneuver through the storm as a swarm.

To insure that Dusty could distribute guidance to the Raiders during the assault, each man was given a walky-talkie appropriated from the store's electronics department.

The truck's tank was topped off from the garage's fuel pump; In case any of the snowmobiles needed refueling, several plastic containers were filled with gas and stashed aboard the panel truck.

Before the Raiders left for the farm colony, Dusty ordered all the men to familiarize themselves with the operating manual for the snowmobiles. "The last thing we need is to be slowed down having to dig one of you guys out of a ravine because you didn't know how to handle these things."

When Barry's turn came to review the user's manual, Runt protested, "Not you, probation boy." But when he yanked the pamphlet from the detective's hands and tossed it to another waiting marauder, Dusty retrieved the booklet and handed it back to Barry.

"Hey," grumbled one of the others. "What's to stop him from taking off and abandoning us?"

"The strategy we're using on this run was Winsor's idea," Dusty tersely declared. As he spoke, his hand dropped to cradle the handle of the revolver holstered at his side. "I say he's earned the right to be a mobile attacker."

The men shared a reluctant shrug. Nobody was willing to challenge the boss over such a trivial matter.

Across the courtyard, a shape lurched out of the storm. Nobody paid much attention to the zombie. Its progress was hampered as much by its cadaverous condition as by the high snowdrifts. Even if it doubled its speed, it would take the creature fifteen minutes to reach the garage's open bay where the men stood.

"Besides," Dusty continued, "I want everybody familiar with these vehicles, even the men who won't be riding one into battle. Last thing I want is for somebody to slow down our charge by taking a tumble, okay?"

This time their reply was less reluctant.

Barry had to admit, Dusty might have been a hotheaded psychopath, but he was a smart psychopath.

Once everyone had digested the user's manual, they all gathered by the idling truck for final instructions before heading out into the storm.

"Stick close and follow the truck. Runt knows this territory best, he'll be at the wheel. When we get close to the farmlands' perimeter, you'll be dumping the snowmobiles and proceeding on-foot. I don't want the mobiles' engines to warn them that we're coming."

The men nodded as a group.

Standing at Dusty's elbow, Runt puffed up his puny chest with pride over his role in the raid. Even in this expanded version and up on his toes, Runt was a runt. Barry doubted the fellow measured even four-feet-six. Hunched over as he always was only made him look smaller. At first glance, one would take him for a kid dressed like a gnome. Only when you saw his pinched face would you realize he was an adult—an ugly one, too. His chinless face swooped out to a pointy rat-nose. Coarse stubble covered the bottom of this visage, while permanant furrows occupied the upper portion, at least the part that wasn't covered by his knit cap. His flesh routinely glistened from oily perspiration.

Catching Barry looking at him, Runt scowled with malice. From the very beginning, Dusty's sycophant crony had disliked the detective.

Dusty reminded his crew to be careful. "We'll be catching the bastards unawares, but that doesn't mean they won't fight back."

This time, the group's communal acknowledgement was accompanied by a few snide sneers. They were all looking forward to finally geting the chance to kick some farmer-butt.

None of their bloodlust matched Dusty's, though. He had tried time and again to hit the farms, but the Raiders' assaults had never been able to get past the colony's defenses. This time, he expected full penetration and, at long last, the chance to punish the bastards for their arrogant opposition.

Meanwhile, that zombie had kept at it, dragging itself through the drifts the wind had piled along the street. It was still more than ten feet away, no immediate threat, but Red Ryder detached himself from the group and strolled over to brain the thing with a baseball bat he had recently added to his personal armory. Leaving the corpse where it fell in the snow, he rejoined the other marauders.

Finishing up his briefing, Dusty delivered a pep talk. His words reminded the men how many times these bastards had thwarted earlier raids, how many Raiders had fallen during those failed excursions, how the men owed these absent comrades vengeance. "Spare no one—but try to avoid property damage, especially to the barns and storage silos. Remember: blood isn't our only goal. Glendale needs their stockpiles of supplies."

As far as Barry was concerned, the more farmers the Raiders slaughtered, the fewer cannibals he had to deal with himself. They were all guilty in his eyes, they all deserved to die. Men, women, children—all had added human flesh to their diet, which made them all culpable for their victims' murders.

Finally, the Raiders set off.

The fleet of snowmobiles nimbly cruised across the terrain, kicking up clouds of ice crystals amid the still-falling snow. The truck, with plow lowered, gouged its own path through the snowbound hills.

While the Raiders had left Glendale well before sunrise, their detour had eaten up most of the morning. Not that it mattered. As long as the storm persisted, the heavy snowfall masked the landscape as well as darkness would have. Despite the snowmobiles' headlights and growling motors, the farmers would never see or hear the marauders coming.

Swaddled in new attire (a parka, winter pants and gloves, all picked out at the sporting goods store, along with an Arctic hat and googles), Barry grimaced as he raced through the storm. The snowmobile roared and throbbed beneath him. Large glacial flakes pelted him as the vehicle flung Barry across the iced landscape. It seemed as if the very air had crystallized; anything beyond the feeble reach of the headlights remained thoroughly hidden by the white-out haze. Veering around trees and clumps of shrubbery that suddenly loomed into view, he kept his vehicle within visible proximity of the next snowmobile in the advance line, lest he get lost. He needed to stay with the Raiders…until they hit Templar's farm. After that massacre, he and Dusty's crew would be parting ways.

Eventually, the walky-talkie in his pocket squawked. He drew it from his pocket in time to hear a crackly version of Dusty's voice instruct everybody to ditch their snowmobiles. "We're only twenty yards from the farm's perimeter. From here, we progress on-foot." As Barry powered down his vehicle, further squawks advised the marauders that the homestead lay due east roughly a few hundred feet past a field of cornhusks. "Converge there. And—if anybody spots you, try to kill them quietly. Let's hold onto our element of surprise as long as we can."

Climbing from the snowmobile, Barry set off into the white haze. He drew his golf clubs from his belt and advanced with them held ready for action. If he was going to encounter one of the farmers, it would happen fast, their figure emerging from the dense icy swirl, almost close enough to touch before they became visible.

The going was difficult. Wading through drifts that almost reached his waist, each step was a major exertion. Despite the cold environment, an uncomfortable sweat drenched Barry before he reached the edge of the cornfield.

Maneuvering through the cornfield was even more arduous. With their bases embedded in the thick snow-cover, the corn stalks became a maze of obstinate obstacles. At one point, the clustered stalks congealed into an impassable tangle, forcing Barry to veer off-course to go around this barrier. After a few feet, he found himself stumbling into a ragged ravine etched through the snow—the wake of another Raider's advance through the cornfield. He followed this course; doing so reduced the adversity of his own struggle. Although he could now move faster across the field, Barry slowed down. He had no interest in surprising a trigger-happy Raider from behind. Whoever it was, let them forge a path for him, let them be attacked should they stumble upon a farmer sentry.

When he reached the edge of the cornfield, he paused to survey the immediate territory. The storm still raged full-force, but a series of dull lights boosted local visiblity. These lights marked the location of the homestead roughly thirty yards ahead. The choppy path made by his predecessor led away toward those gray shapes in the ivory tapestry. Although he saw no sign of that individual, on both flanks he could detect man-shaped smudges moving through the white-out, all converging on the homestead.

From his previous visit here, Barry recognized the nearest structure as the farmhands' barracks. That put the family house around back of it from where Barry stood. The left side of the barracks converged with the barn, leaving him with the right as the easiest way around the building.

The device in his pocket squawked directions, but Barry ignored them.

He waited until the other Raiders had assembled beside the barracks, then slipped along the edge of the cornfield so he wouldn't be seen. Rounding the yard, he came to a virgin expanse of snow. He was reluctant to boldly cross it. Doing so would leave a trail betraying his departure from the rest of the marauders. A wiser path, which would leave less obvious evidence, was to travel along the lee of the barracks' southern wall. The drifts there were minor.

As he crept along the wall, a series of outcries sounded from within the building. Then gunshots rang out, followed by a cacophony of more terrified shouts. The slaughter had begun.

The farmhands were as guilty as anyone here, all had practiced cannibalism, all had cheered as they'd cut up, cooked and served poor Miss Collard, all deserved extreme punishment for their crimes against humanity. Barry felt no remorse as he listened to the farmhands scream and perish on the other side of the log wall.

This was one of the collatoral pay-offs of the scheme he had suggested to Dusty—a private pay-off. Every one of the farmland colony's residents deserved execution for their murderous habits. Barry had sworn to mete out this justice, but he understood how improbable it was for him personally to get every evildoer. After all, he was only one man. By using the Raiders as an auxiliary execution squad, however, more of the guilty cannibals could be taken down.

He hurried on. The family house was *his* target. Let the Raiders kill everyone else, but Barry wanted Henry Templar's blood on his own hands.

He knew personal emotion was distorting his sense of duty, but he didn't care. Templar was the one Barry blamed for everything—from torturing and maiming Barry to Miss Collard's awful fate. Wanting revenge against the degenerate fiend was purely human nature.

Well before Barry reached the family house, its doors were flung open and figures crowded the porch. Drawn forth by the ruckus at the barracks, they gawked and squinted, but saw very little in the swirling snowfall.

Barry put some speed into his skulking. The element of surprise was gone. He needed to reach the house before the family fled back indoors and fortified it against invasion. They would see him coming, there was nothing he could do about that, but by angling to the right, he approached the porch from an unoccupied side. The family members were clustered on another side of the building, looking away, not behind.

Arriving undetected, Barry clambered over the railing and crept along the porch. Instead of heading for the front of the house where everyone was gathered, he sought the rear of the building. There, a back door granted him access.

While there might have been a warped sort of cinematic drama in killing Templar with his golf clubs, Barry stuck them back in his belt and drew his revolver. Considering the frantic nature of this impending confrontation, Barry suspected speed and lead would produce the best results. Flinging back the hood of his parka, he pushed his goggles up on his forehead.

He stood in an empty kitchen. Past it, he saw a dining room, a repast set out on the long wooden table. For a moment he cringed, but relaxed when the twin drumsticks protruding from the bulbous browned mass identified the main course as a chicken, not a human body part. Not this afternoon. The chairs all stood back from the table, as if their occupants had risen to depart with haste. A few of the chairs lay on their sides on the floor.

Through the arch at the far end of the room, Barry saw a foyer. Agnes Templar was herding her children inside. As Barry watched, she hurried them upstairs and out of sight. The rest of the family followed her indoors. Stepping back behind a tall armoire, Barry heard the front door slam and a series of locks and latches engage. The family members all chattered with anxiety, creating an unintelligible babble. Then a loud voice shouted them down. Barry instantly recognized the voice: Henry Templar, mayor of this farm colony and villain extraordinaire. Barry listened as Templar ordered everyone not to panic. "It's just another marauder raid."

"But—they're at the barracks!" wailed a twenty-something man. "They've never gotten past the perimeter before!"

"We've fought them off before," growled Templar. "We can do it again."

"But—" somebody croaked.

But Templar ignored any disapproval and commenced ordering them to battle stations. Windows and doors needed to be secured. Weapons must be fetched from the armory closet.

As the family members scattered to attend to these tasks, Templar strode from the foyer into the dining room. He was muttering under his breath, but Barry didn't need to comprehend the words to tell he was cursing the invaders.

Today, Templar wore a gray suit. That was nice: the family dressed up for meals.

The man stood by the table, his head lowered, his brow furrowed. He reached out and plucked an already-carved slice of chicken from the carcass' breast. He bit off half the hunk and chewed it while his frown deepened. Apparently, High and Mighty Mayor Templar had evaluated the present situation and did not like what he saw.

With a smile, Barry asked aloud: "How's it feel to be *in* the frying pan instead of holding it?"

Templar jerked at the surprise accusation. Stumbling back a few steps, he spat the half-chewed meat from his mouth so he could sputter, "What— Who—"

"Every other time somebody's tried to attack your precious colony of deviants, you've managed to repel their assaults—but not today." Barry stepped forth from his hiding place.

Mystification washed from Templar's square face, to be replaced by horrified recognition. "You!" he gasped. "But—it can't be you—you disappeared—"

Barry had no desire to rehash his mysterious disappearance from the cannibals' cookout. "This time the barbarians are inside the gates." He raised his revolver and aimed it at Templar's head. "It's the end for you and your depraved colony."

From every logical angle, Henry Templar was a monster, fully deserving of a painful and capital punishment, but…Barry couldn't bring himself to do it. He couldn't shoot an unarmed man, that would reduce him to Templar's unholy level—a totally unacceptable moral devolution.

Before Barry could goad himself to violate his ethics in the pursuit of justice, the window behind Templar exploded with a burst of automatic gunfire. Barry had distracted the man before he could secure the window. And now bullets shattered the glass windowpane and ripped through the mayor's body. He crumpled to the rug and died with an expression of vivid disbelief, his hand still clutching a fragment of roast chicken.

The angle of the shots tore up the ceiling, missing Barry by yards. Even so, he edged back into the kitchen.

The bastard's execution had been wrestled from Barry's responsibility and delivered by one of the attacking Raiders.

As Barry watched, Red Ryder crawled through the violated window. Other Raiders followed him through the breach. Murderous glee twinkled in their manic eyes. They loitered for a moment to gloat over Templar's corpse. Unaware that they had cut down the leader of the colony, they just celebrated killing another anonymous farmer.

Barry stepped back into the room. "The rest of the family's off fetching weapons." He pointed toward the hall leading off the foyer. "Their armory is that way."

The Raiders stormed off in that direction, bellowing and shooting holes in the portraits adorning the walls. Barry was confident that their fervor would outgun any resistance offered by the rest of the cannibals.

Barry stared down at Templar's corpse. His body lay twisted. Blood seeped from innumerable gaping wounds. Death had frozen his face in a grimace of denial.

Well, Miss Collard, Barry reflected, *your murderer has been punished.* "What the—" he choked.

Templar had moved! His body was riddled with bloody holes—but he was still alive!

But no—as the mayor struggled to untangle his akimbo limbs, Barry spotted his glassy gaze. No, Templar wasn't still alive. He'd been killed... and now he was reanimated—a zombie.

Grinding his teeth, Barry remonstrated himself for forgetting about that. Kill somebody and they would only return as an undead creature. For all the slugs that had killed him, Templar needed one more to ultimately put him down.

This time Barry moved without hesitation. He faced no ethical dilemma regarding dispatching an undead thing. He put a bullet into Templar's head. The bastard finally collapsed for good.

Not that the afternoon was completely silent, what with the Raiders shooting up the farm, but that din became a muted background bedlam for a moment as Barry relished Templar's ultimate downfall. That brief moment was destroyed by a shrill outcry, followed by a shotgun blast.

Wheeling about—and just barely escaping the trajectory of the murderous salvo—Barry discovered Agnes Templar lurking in the foyer archway. She held a smoking shotgun, which, as he watched, she cocked for a second shot. Her face was contorted with rage and horror. In all the confusion, she had come downstairs too late to see the window barrage that had killed her husband, but in time to witness Barry shoot him in the head.

There was no moral quandary this time. The woman was about to fire off another shot. Her last one had only missed because he'd whirled around to face her. This close, her next shot wouldn't miss.

He fired his Glock at her.

She twitched and fell down. But from the direction of her spasm and her fall, it was apparent that it hadn't been Barry's shot that had caught her. He'd missed. And somebody else had shot her.

And there they are...

Several Raiders rushed into the foyer to grin scornfully over the woman's corpse. One of them shot her again, in the gut. Then they all rushed up the stairs in search of more victims.

For a few breathless minutes, Barry was a statue. He couldn't believe how close he'd come to death. Another half-second, and Mrs Templar would've pulled the trigger and blown him away. He owed his life to one of the rowdy marauders.

What finally roused him from his fugue was Mrs Templar's jerky post-mortem activity. She twitched, thrashed about a bit, then clumsily started to stand up.

He shot her in the head.

God, I need a drink.

The blizzard was still going when the Raiders finished their massacre. In the fervor of the bloodthirsty moment, every resident of the farm had been slaughtered without hesitation. Barry had accurately gauged the unleashed wrath of the marauders. The cannibal colony no longer existed.

The Raiders were all wired up from their killing spree. Dusty judiciously let them blow off some steam trashing the barracks, which contained nothing of value, and putting down the newly-dead-now-zombies produced by that spree. Once the men were less rambunctious, he directed one group to gather up the farmers' weapons, and another group to search for the best selection of plunder. Others were directed to fetch the truck to load with the booty.

"You," the leader summoned Barry from the throng of Raiders milling about on the snow-covered lawn. When Barry came to stand beside him, Dusty grunted, "Come with me."

"What's up?"

But Dusty offered no answer. Grimly, he led Barry around the main house to an added-on concrete structure.

An uncharacteristically pale-faced Runt guarded the doorway of this annex. No words were exchanged between crony and leader, but as Dusty brought Barry near, Runt opened the door and stepped back. The crony did not join them as Dusty ushered Barry inside; in fact he seemed unwilling to even cast a glance through the opened door.

Murky shadows prevailed indoors, but a peculiar smell was overwhelming and unnerving. A bad feeling crept up Barry's spine as he stood there in the musky darkness. That itch became a vivid twitch when a click heralded the wash of illumination from a series of fluorescent tubes set into the ceiling.

The light disclosed that the chamber was a smoke house, where meat was treated for long-term preservation. Rows of slabs of meat dangled from large iron hooks

A cursory examination of those hunks revealed their unholy nature. While some were conventional sides of beef, the majority had clearly come from human bodies. Arms, legs, and more than one torso hung on display.

Now Barry understood Runt's uneasiness concerning the chamber.

The gruesome selection elicited protests from Barry's own stomach.

"You knew about this, didn't you?" Dusty inquired from just behind the stunned detective.

Repressing the urge to study these body parts closely, seeking to identify if any of them belonged to Miss Collard, Barry turned to address the boss Raider's accusation. Barry found himself staring down the barrel of a pistol clutched unwaveringly in the man's grasp.

"Umm...yeah."

There didn't seem to be any point in denying that. Clearly, Dusty harbored some serious doubts about the Raiders' latest recruit. Barry's interest in "whacking a few farmer heads" had triggered some deeper suspicions. In Dusty's mind, Barry was linked somehow with Templar's colony. With the discovery of this human charnel house, those potential connections had taken on an unsavory character.

"I'm not one of them, if that's what you think," Barry assured the man.

Dusty's suspicious stare remained fixed. "I'm going to need more than your word on that, Winsor."

"Like what?"

The two faced each other, unflinching, untrusting, but unwilling to make a move.

"How can I prove a negative status in this situation?" offered Barry. "Yes, they were cannibals. Yes, I knew that—because I came close to being their picnic dinner a while back. I escaped. My companion didn't. I came back here looking for justice. You and your men helped me achieve that."

"And now," Dusty countered, "all the cannibals are dead, leaving no one to corroborate your story."

Barry nodded, but gave him an ironic twist of his jaw as he pointed out, "More likely, if any of these degenerate bastards were still alive, they'd lie, claiming I was their brethren."

"Anything to cause more bloodshed," grunted the leader.

"Something like that."

"Which leaves you no way to prove your innocence."

"I guess not."

The face-off continued. Barry was careful not to make any sudden movements that might unnerve the other. Standing just beyond arm's reach, Dusty kept his gun on the detective.

From outside came Runt's irritated complaint, "Oh, just shoot him and be done with it, Dusty. We all know he's guilty."

"You're not well-liked among the crew, Winsor."

Barry gave a slow shrug. "His opinion is hardly representative of any sentiment held by the rest of the crew. Besides, I wasn't here to win any popularity contests. And now that justice has been served on these deviant bastards, I plan to move on."

"Just like that."

"Unless you have some objection…"

After a terse moment, Dusty released a gusty laugh. He stepped out of the doorway and holstered his gun. "You've got balls, Winsor. I like that."

"Aw, c'mon, Dusty," moaned Runt. "You're not gonna believe any of that shit he just told ya—"

"Actually, Runt, what convinced me was your dislike of him." Dusty turned to smile at Barry. "Little Runt is a terrible judge of character. I keep him around as a sort of reverse barometer. The more he doesn't like somebody, the more I can trust them."

"Okay…" Barry could appreciate the man's twisted logic. *Especially since it appears he's using it to exonerate me.*

"Wait!" railed Runt. Pulling a pistol from beneath his bloodstained parka, he approached the door of the charnel smoke house,. "Ya can't let him go—"

"No!" Dusty's barritone command halted Runt like an electric shock. "If I say he's okay, he's *okay*."

"But—"

"Are you challenging my decision, Runt?"

The crony hastily backed down. He lowered his weapon, but didn't put it away.

Turning to Barry, Dusty snarled, "Get the hell outta here, Winsor."

"For real?"

"Don't push it," was Dusty's verification. "Take one of the snowmobiles and get gone."

Barry moved past Dusty and out the door. He scowled at Runt, who returned the negativity but backed it up with no action.

Squaring his shoulders against possible last-minute turnarounds, Barry walked away from the Templar massacre without a scratch.

There was no chance that Barry could locate the snowmobile he'd ridden to this place; he had to settle for another of the Raiders' stolen chariots… if he could find one in the icy maelstrom.

He crossed the cornfield, fighting through the snow mantle that covered everything. When he came to the outer edge of the field, he hunted for any of the trails gouged in the snow by the marauders as they'd crept upon the farm. Subsequent snowfall had all but buried these paths. Spotting a line of bushes, he immediately recognized a break in the foliage as being manmade, probably when one of the Raiders had barged through the shrubbery instead of detouring around it. From that point he managed to trace a mostly-obscured path up a hillock. There, he lost the trail. An afternoon's worth of snowfall and wind had obliterated the rest of the trail.

"Damn…"

He surveyed the landscape, but no amount of squinting bestowed useful definition to any of the white uniformity around him.

"Dammit..."

Stomping about in frustration, Barry lashed out and kicked at nearby drifts.

His boot struck something hidden beneath the snow. A spark of *what-the* blossomed into a wave of *yer-kidding*. Attacking the drift, he swatted away frozen layers until finally a portion of metal fuselage was exposed.

"Aha—gotcha!"

He proceeded to undo the storm's entombment of the vehicle. The top layers were easily brushed aside, but deeper down the snow had hardened, requiring more forceful removal. It seemed to take an eternity to free the snowmobile.

Its key still protruded from the machine's ignition slot, but when Barry twisted it, nothing happened.

"Aw, c'mon—"

Repeated twists failed to bring life to the cold machine.

The frigid temperature had fouled up the snowmobile's ignition. He was familiar with such things from Manhattan winters, but in those instances he'd merely grabbed a can of Unstickit, and after a squirt, stubborn locks would function properly. But here in this post-apocalyptic nightmare, he had no can of aerosol to use.

Hunkering back on his boot heels, Barry fought to quell his annoyance and force his brain into more practical pursuits. A cigarette would help him think. He searched through his pockets until he found the pack he carried. He had to take off his gloves to be able to open the box's top flap and withdraw a cig and the Bic lighter stashed alongside these last few butts. (Knowing he wouldn't be returning to Glendale after this raid, he should've stuffed his pockets with additional packs while he still had access to the hamlet's surplus.) So now each cigarette was a precious resource. With a certain reverence, he put the butt between his lips and lifted the lighter. He clicked it to life, but did not touch the flame to the end of the cylinder of tobacco. He stared at it long after the wind had extinguished the tongue of fire.

"Aha!"

Crawling forward, he clicked the lighter again and applied the flame to the key sticking out of the machine's dashboard. The persistent wind refused to grant the flame more than a fleeting flickering existence. He bent close, shielding the dashboard from the brunt of the storm. A few repositionings were necessary before his body provided adequate shelter for the tiny flame. He held it to the key. His naked hand shook in the cold, but he endured the discomfort.

A few minutes of this treatment succeeded in returning functionality to the obstinate ignition. The key turned and the machinery responded. The snowmobile's engine roared to life.

"Yeah!"

He climbed aboard and backed the vehicle away from the top of the hill. He took a moment to orient himself. The farm lay ahead of him, to the east. As far as he could gauge, that put Glendale to the south. The easiest direction away from both of them was to head west. Steering the snowmobile in a U-turn, Barry headed into unknown territory.

He rode through deserted farmlands and past sinister woodlands and around miniature mountains where chunks of granite thrust forth from the snow-covered loam to disappear into the storm's heights. He saw no signs of civilization, old or revived. Nor did he encounter any undead complications. He suspected both lurked out there, though, hidden by the thick blizzard.

The storm gave no indication of letting up. If anything, it got worse with each passing hour.

The snowmobile ran out of fuel at nightfall.

"Dammit."

Abandoning it, he set off into the white-out. As he trudged along, night brought a murkiness to his frozen surroundings that matched his dwindling optimism. He had no idea where he was, nor any real hope of finding shelter out here. But this defeatist mood didn't stop him from trying. He pushed on, bullying his way through mammoth drifts of snow to find only further icy obstacles to combat.

I guess this is it, he mused. He no longer had the stamina to vocalize his thoughts. *At least I got the chance to punish Miss Collard's murderers.*

His legs strained to keep him moving. His breath rasped painfully in his throat. Tears froze on his face. The chatter of his teeth became a never-ending soundtrack for his diminishing progress.

At some point, Barry's apathetic exertion faltered. Exhaustion and the cold brought him down. Closing his eyes, he let darkness envelope him. The howling wind propelled his consciousness into oblivion.

6

BARRY NEVER EXPECTED TO WAKE UP, but he did.

These reprieves from death were becoming tedious.

An emotional and physical weariness held dominion over Barry Winsor. He'd been through too many horrifying ordeals, seen too much death, witnessed too many examples of humanity's inhumanity. The world had gone to shit and getting through each day had become a worthless struggle. No matter how awful today was, tomorrow turned out to be worse. His interest in survival had diminished with each subsequent calamity.

If only he could go back to when there'd been no point in believing in a zombie outbreak. Not that those days had been stress-free, but chasing crooks was a thousand times easier than coping with post-apocalyptic horrors.

With a resigned sigh, he opened his eyes, but his whereabouts were not at all what he'd expected.

On prior occasions, he'd woken in his own bed, but this time he sprawled on a grassy surface, not a linen one. Sitting up brought the rest of the stadium into view. Beyond the football field, tiered seats surrounded him. A tattered placard announced "Go Bears!", so apparently Barry was in Chicago. There was no snow on the ground here. The sky above was blue, cheery and unclouded.

Back in my own time, he guessed.

But then Barry spied a figure lurching across the grassy field and he knew he'd guessed wrong. With another resigned sigh, this one deeper and more regretful, he watched the zombie teeter along until it noticed him. Then, with an angry hiss, the creature jerked to face the detective and shamble in his direction.

No—instead of returning home, Barry had awakened back in the post-apocalyptic nightmare. This broke the pattern set by the previous temporal displacements. What did this mean?

But his current circumstances didn't really afford Barry much time to ponder this mystery. Another zombie had spotted him and was reeling his way. The first one was only a few yards from him.

Clambering to his feet, he made a swift inspection of his resources. The parka and winter outfit were gone; now he wore khaki slacks and a short-sleeved polo shirt. There were no golf clubs or guns at his waist, even his pockets offered nothing that could serve as a weapon, not even a pack of cigs. Finding himself unarmed, his only choice was speedy flight.

His dash for freedom got too over-enthusiastic. After a few strides, his foot slid on the grass and he went tumbling on his belly. By the time he regained his feet, the first zombie was almost upon him. Momentarily postponing flight, Barry kicked the creature's legs out from under it. As it toppled, he ran off.

Racing along the 40th yard line, he reached the sidelines only to find the gate there was closed, locked. Beyond it shambled several undead shadows, so this wasn't the escape route he sought. He took off along the sidelines, heading upfield. Now that he was a moving target, he'd caught the attention of a few other zombies scattered throughout the football stadium. The ones on the field were were too far away to be immediate threats. The ones in the stands troubled him, though. Once he got off the field and into the stadium proper, he ran the risk of being trapped in a corridor or locker room as he fled these lurkers. He needed a weapon.

Secured by a tangle of chains, the next gate held at bay an undead gaggle. Barry continued on. Before the third gate, he came to a tunnel that led into the arena's depths; this was where the team members entered the field at the onset of games that would probably never again happen. The shadowed recess was empty of any figures, living or dead. He disappeared into it.

The deeper hallways were scrimpingly lit by sunlight bouncing along their winding lengths. He passed more than one fire station, but the braces mounted on the wall were lacking any fire axes; someone had grabbed them long ago as weapons against attackers. Twice he spotted jerkily animated figures down remote corridors, but he easily eluded them. His circuitous route had confused him, though; he no longer knew which direction led out.

Searching for a quick exit, Barry began trying doors as he moved along the corridors. A conference room, a business office, a room filled with tall gray file cabinets, a locker room that probably included showers—none of these offered him a way out. Nor did they provide anything he could use as a weapon. In the business office, he'd tried to smash a chair, hoping to use a broken leg or armrest as a bludgeon, but the damned thing was cast metal. As were the seats lining the conference table. There weren't even any ashtrays that could be thrown as missiles.

He never did find a proper exit. A second conference room featured a wall of bay windows. He used one of the metal chairs to shatter the glass. He'd believed he'd been wandering subterranean levels, but here he found himself on the second floor, looking out onto some rolling green hills.

Crawling out onto a short roof, he made his way down to the ground.

Those hills beckoned Barry with their idyllic promise of shelter, but as a city-boy he remained generally immune to their pastoral temptation. Besides, a sports stadium would have a big parking area, probably located around the other side of the arena—there would be cars. Maybe one of them could be coaxed to life. That'd be so nice; he was getting tired of walking.

For a moment, however, he couldn't be certain whether that exhaustion came from wandering the stadium's murky hallways, or from trudging through that blizzard. His life had become too disjointed. He was experiencing difficulty fixing memories in their correct order.

He began his circumnavigation of the arena. Along the way he found a fallen branch that was hefty enough to serve as a bludgeon. As he'd feared, zombies pervaded the exterior vicinity. Out here they could freely stagger back and forth.

The stragglers he simply outran. But this brought him into territory occupied by an undead herd. These, he tried to dodge, but whacking a couple of putrefied heads was necessary to make it past them unscathed. By the time Barry reached the parking lot, his spry activities had attracted the attention of the few hundred zombies who ambled about the asphalt expanse. *So many of them...all looking for live meat. Why can't they just eat each other?* Now progress was going to get more perilous. At least there was a decent selection of abandoned automobiles for him to chose between...if any of them still worked.

Swinging his branch like a proud barbarian, he smashed his way through a mounting crowd. Between clashes, he clumsily checked the doors of cars he passed. After six locked failures, Barry was finally able to yank open a door. He hastily retreated inside the SUV, closing and locking the door after himself.

Safe...for the moment.

Finding an unlocked vehicle had only been the first step in obtaining transportation. The SUV had to start, otherwise he was now trapped in a metal coffin that was going nowhere. Already zombies had clustered around the car, battering its roof with their moldered fists, gnawing at the window with their broken teeth.

No key protruded from the ignition.

Not a good beginning.

A search under the floor-mat produced a hidden set of keys.

Hurray!

Now, the last obstacle: would the SUV start up?

The zombies were starting to pile up outside. Climbing over each other, several had reached the roof where they formed a foundation for the next wave of climbers. Little light leaked past the tangled undead morass, consigning Barry to a grim darkness. Their hissing and gnashing and pounding created a primitive soundtrack for the tableau. His neck muscles clenched with dread at the prospects if the car didn't start. He could never fight his way through such a dense mob of the creatures. How long would the car's metal hull or its shatterproof windows survive against a relentless barrage of bloodless fists?

He twisted the key in its slot—and the SUV's engine started up as if it'd only been abandoned a few hours. A gust of grateful air rushed past his teeth.

Shifting the car into reverse, he tramped down on the accelerator. The vehicle lurched, but moved only a few inches. He switched the gear back to forward and again gunned the motor. This time the car crawled at least a foot before the heaped zombies halted its advance. Without hesitation, Barry repeated the process, rocking the SUV back and forth, gradually disrupting the integrity of the undead pile-on until ultimately one of the forward lurches succeeded in bursting free of the barrier of brittle corpses. Unleashed at last, the SUV tore across the parking lot.

While steering around the rest of the forsaken cars, Barry pointedly rammed every shambling figure he could. By the time he left the arena and reached a highway, the grill and hood of the SUV was splattered with decomposing fragments of a dozen undead individuals.

He found a pack of Marlboros in the glove compartment.

Lighting up, he headed east.

After some debate, Barry decided to return to the East Coast. As yet he was unsure if that journey would take him all the way to Manhattan. On one hand, it might be nice to be back among familiar surroundings. On the other hand, he wasn't sure he wanted to see those familiar surroundings in their post-apocalyptic state of decay. His few friends and acquaintances wouldn't be there—in fact, he was appalled by the notion that some if not all of them existed now as shambling zombies. In the end, he stuck with his eastward choice by default.

Not that any choices really mattered.

Lately, his mood had shriveled into a morose apathy. Barry's emotional decay was far from a new development. It had started once Emily had been diagnosed with ovarian cancer. Since then, his life had ridden a downward spiral, and nothing he had done had eased the crushing weight of his guilt and loneliness. He'd put on an optimistic face with Emily, but it'd had no effect on her suffering. For all his hope and confidence (he'd even resorted to prayer a few times during her last days), she had still died. And the solace he'd sought in the bottle had been no better. Instead of helping him escape, every drink seemed to fortify his despair. Between the booze and his waning soul, his work had gotten sloppy, a precursor for the state of abject misery he suspected lay ahead for him. He simply lost the capacity to give a shit about anything. He went through the motions, posing as a brave widower, pretending to be a cop, recklessly acting the hero, but nothing mattered to him anymore.

Losing Miss Collard had been the final straw. For all his police savvy, he'd been unable to save her from a grisly demise. If not for some unknown force that kept yanking him back and forth in time, he'd have shared her fate. And when the time had come for him to exact punishment against those responsible for her death, he'd been incapable of pulling the trigger. Justice or vengeance—whatever motive you wanted to pick, he'd failed on all counts.

A cunning psychiatrist might've tried to point out that none of these losses had been Barry Winsor's fault. He had not instigated his wife's cancer; nor was he the architect of the farmers' cannibal habits. He had fought these villains, not aided their terrible progress. But Barry had dealt with clever psychiatrists before; he knew how to sidestep their semantic games. He knew he hadn't induced Emily's cancer or caused Miss Collard's death—but as an officer of the law it was his job to protect people (loved ones or strangers) from the vagrancy of ill fortune.

He'd failed Emily. He'd failed Miss Collard. Even now, he was failing himself.

More than once while driving along, Barry entertained the notion of twisting the wheel and veering from the highway. A high-speed crash would put a quick end to his anguish. But he was unable to act on this recurrent impulse.

His survival instinct refused to let him secure oblivion. He was condemned to stay alive…so he could continue to suffer.

What was the old proverb? *Adversity makes you stronger.* Well, Barry didn't feel stronger. In fact, he felt quite the opposite. He was tired of dragging himself through each subsequent minute. Every hour only darkened his world.

Look at the world, he told himself. *Society gone, people dead or undead or fighting with each other instead of banding together against this terrible catastrophe. Everything I've seen tells me things will only get worse. There's no bright tomorrow out there. Why am I bothering to survive?*

Somehow, Barry feared that when he learned the answer to that question, it would ring as hollow as every other ambition he'd fought for.

At one point, while refueling the SUV, Barry had examined what was left on the shelves of the attached convenience store. The pickings were sparse. Apparently junk food had been high on every scavenger's list, followed by canned foods and dry goods. Even the countertop rotisserie had been stripped of all its over-cooked hot dogs. Cabinets that had once housed bags of ice now held no more than sacks of water. Nobody had bothered to pillage napkins or diapers. The cash register, though, had been pulverized and emptied.

Fat lot of good money was going to be for the survivors. It wasn't as if you could pay a zombie not to eat your brains. And the crazies—try to bribe them to let you pass unmolested and they'd just laugh and shoot you in the face. Then, depending on the depth of their lunacy, they might steal your money.

The local newspapers stacked by the cash register bore the date November 11, which told him nothing. Every paper he'd seen in this post-apocalyptic world had been from around this time. And he had only a hazy idea how long it had been since the zombie outbreak had hobbled civilization and put an end to any publishing industry. Maybe a current date might be found on a computer, but he'd encountered no working technology (not even in Glendale); understandable without a working power grid to supply electricity.

He told himself that dates were no longer relevant, but his inquisitive mind retained a latent curiosity about such things. The detective in him needed to know how many weeks or months the dead had been ambulatory.

But—what good would that knowledge actually be to him? Civilization had relied on numbers, but they had little value in this new world. They wouldn't help him survive.

If he was going to bother to survive…

He still hadn't decided about that.

His eastward journey made good time. Within two days Barry was back cruising through Pennsylvania's farmlands.

Along the way, he'd filled the back of the SUV with supplies. He'd also rearmed himself with a pair of hefty golf clubs—and a shotgun he'd found in an interstate toll booth.

So far, his encounters had been few and generally uneventful. He regularly saw zombies shambling through fields, but they were never close enough to cause him trepidation. The ones who stumbled along the side of the road reacted too slow to do more than pounce on the dust kicked up by his vehicle's passing.

On the first night, he'd taken shelter in a backwoods motel; he would never make that mistake again. Despite the noise traps he'd set, the undead had found their way indoors and only their abysmal stench had roused Barry in time to save himself.

He knew he stank from days on the road, but enough to be detected by undead nostrils? Did the zombies even have a sense of smell? If so, how could they scent anything past their own putrid stench? Maybe, just to play it safe, he would avail himself of a heavy bath on his next opportunity.

Ignoring exhaustion, he drove through the second night.

Soon, he planned to bear south. He had no desire to stray into Dusty's turf.

An hour or so after noon, he fell asleep at the wheel—

--and woke up cruising along another roadway.

He shook his head to clear it.

Almost dozed off there…

But then he noticed that the landscape had drastically changed. Instead of farmlands, now he traveled past chemical factories. The fires that had once stoked these industrial smokestacks were dormant, but an impressive array of unnatural colors tinting the surrounding marshes bore testament to their lasting residue. Moments ago (as far as Barry was concerned), the sun had been at its zenith in a clear sky; now, putrid clouds pervaded the heavens, masking the time of day.

I did more than doze off...

He had driven from mid-Pennsylvania to southern New Jersey and slept through a journey of nearly two hundred miles. Was that possible? Asleep, how had he navigated the car?—followed winding roads?—not died in a horrible crash?

Had he been asleep for this new lapse? Or had he time-slipped again?

As if I don't already have enough to cope with—now I get to beware random displacements?

This lack of continuity troubled Barry. How was he supposed to live with the prospect of suddenly ending up somewhere else?—or somewhen else? For all he knew, he was experiencing countless displacements during the course of a day, but simply didn't notice them. How could he trust that one moment followed the next? Without linear succession, his life was destabilized, uncertain, precarious.

He pulled the SUV over to the side of the road.

If this sort of thing was going on, driving could be hazardous.

But—he'd made it safely this far without accident.

He didn't know which premonition to heed.

He got out of the car and lighted a cig. Leaning his butt on the car's flank, Barry considered his options. In the distance, Manhattan's cityscape marked a misty horizon. A soft breeze stole away his exhaled smoke.

It was hard to concentrate. If he had indeed slept from Pennsylvania to New Jersey, it had not been a restful slumber. Exhaustion still gnawed at Barry's flagging mental focus. He was hungry too; all that food stashed in the car and he couldn't remember the last time he'd eaten.

As it was, Barry failed to notice the armored Buick as it appeared around a remote bend up the road. When the vehicle drew near, it promptly stopped; its inhabitant was obviously shocked to see a living person.

Or so Barry would have thought if he hadn't already been half-asleep on his feet.

The forgotten cigarette in his hand burned down and stung his fingers. This jolted him briefly alert.

In that fleeting instant of cognizance, he saw the fortified Buick. A figure had climbed out and was running toward him. Someone was shouting his name.

And then his fevered weariness dragged him down into welcome sleep.

He woke rested this time, but confused. By this point Barry was used to being confused. His life had become a disjointed series of unconnected moments. He tried not to be surprised by anything these days.

But this latest tableau in which Barry found himself confounded even his newfound indifference.

He no longer leaned against the SUV atop a hill overlooking the Hudson River. His position was horizontal. He tentatively parted his lids, but no sooty sunlight fell on his face. His surroundings were dark.

Another jump had occurred, a drastic one this time.

He tried to identify where (and when) he was. A soft surface pressed against his back. A mattress. Was he back home again?

The odors captured by his nostrils lacked the stale locker room smell generated by his bachelor lifestyle. In fact, a hint of jasmine lurked in the air

The smell closed a fist around his heart. Jasmine had been Emily's favorite perfume.

He moved slightly on the mattress. The squirm told him that blankets covered him; a soft pillow cushioned his head. It certainly felt like his own bed.

Then something moved beside him. Every muscle in his body tensed. During his time in the post-apocalyptic world, he had adopted an acute wariness in order to survive. That caution insisted he flee the bed immediately. Whatever lay next to him could only be an adversary. There were nothing but adversaries in Barry's life now. He was micro-seconds away from throwing aside the covers and tumbling from the mattress—when something draped across his chest. An arm. It was warm, so he doubted the limb was undead. And—somewhow—its weight was familiar. Its hand slowly spread its fingers to gently cup his side. The smell of jasmine grew stronger.

No—it can't be--

But then a voice whispered against his shoulder, a voice he knew, a voice he hadn't heard in years, a voice he still heard in some of his more pleasant dreams. It spoke only a sigh, but that demure exhalation brought tears to Barry's eyes. He closed them tight, to stifle any weeping and to shut out the false hope that threatened to fill his chest.

"Emily?"

Her reply was another nonverbal sigh, accompanied by an intimate hug.

It *was* her.

His control cracked and sobs exploded from his throat. Tears flowed to moisten his cheeks.

Roused from her light slumber by his outburst, Emily reached out and switched on a bedside lamp. She rolled against him and held him close. "It's okay, Barry. I'm here."

There could be no doubt, no denial—he lay with his wife in his own bed in their bedroom. He recognized the furniture, the ugly painting over the bed, those awful lime green curtains Emily had been so fond of... all the things that had driven him to relocate his sleeping arrangements to the den once she was gone. The date on the bedside digital clock confirmed his suspicion. His tears changed from shock to joy and he returned her hug.

This time, his temporal displacement had sent him back years, not just months. He had left that post-apocalyptic nightmare far behind him, and now he languished in the embrace of his beloved.

His dead wife.

But—she wasn't dead yet. Her cancer and all of her subsequent suffering lay in the future. She was alive and still healthy. And they were together again.

"You're here," he moaned. "You're okay."

He hugged her tight.

With a grunt, she disengaged herself from his frantic clutches. Sitting up, she stretched and fluffed her auburn tresses. With an aching heart he studied the muscles of her back, so familiar to him even after all these years. He couldn't believe she was here with him again.

"Are you okay, Barry?"

Get it together, boy, he admonished himself. *You probably look as if you've seen a ghost. Calm down and enjoy this.*

"I thought you were gone," he confessed, "but here you are."

"That was just a bad dream."

And this isn't. This is real.

"Come back to bed," cooed Barry. He patted the mattress between them.

With a warm smile, Emily leaned over and ran her hands over his chest.

His smile was even warmer.

It was a wonderful interlude. They drifted off in each other's arms, but when Barry woke he was alone.

It was dark again, but the mattress was far from comfortable beneath him. No one lay pressed again him. The air was dusty now, devoid of any perfume. He was back in the zombie infested future.

Dammit...

Fresh tears ran down his face.

I was so happy. Why couldn't I have stayed there?

This time he resisted investigating his new surroundings. He wanted to remember every detail of his brief time with Emily, but as he lay here in different darkness, the nuances slipped away, leaving him with only a vague memory of that wonderful reunion.

He wanted a cigarette—but not as part of some post-coital ritual. He wanted to drown his sorrows with a butt... *Or better yet,* he thought, *a stiff shot of whiskey. Hell, leave the bottle. It won't go to waste.*

"I think he's awake." The voice was masculine, gruff but muted slightly as if the person spoke from the other end of a tunnel.

Barry tried to sit up, but his head swam loosely around the room, forcing him to collapse back on the ratty bed.

Suddenly the darkness parted and a rectangle of light rushed in to blind him. He squinted and raised his hands to ward off this violent glare.

"Barry!" came an exclamation. This voice was female, younger, husky with worry. It came from nearby.

When he peered through his spread fingers, Barry gasped. Bending down to touch his arm was the very last person he expected. (Well, technically, the *very* last person would've been Emily, but he was never going to be that lucky again.)

"Miss Collard..." he moaned.

Other displacements had been traumatic, often dumping him into perilous circumstances, but *this*—this was torture. First Barry had been granted a taste of life with Emily before her ordeal, and now he'd been moved to a time prior to Miss Collard's ugly demise.

"I never thought I'd see you again," she was telling him.

She wore an orange tubetop accented her unremarkable bosom. Her mousy hair was bundled beneath a bandana wrapped around her head.

While it was nice to see her too, alive and exuberant, Barry sadly wondered if this encounter was going to be as short-lived as his reunion with Emily. He wanted to apologize for failing her, but Miss Collard wouldn't know what he was talking about. The poor girl had no inkling of the gruesome fate that loomed in her future. But Barry knew—and it tore his heart into pieces.

Suspicion was never far from his thoughts anymore. It only took a few moments before he started questioning his present situation. Searching for a memory that matched what was going on, he found nothing.

Back when those zombies had invaded that burning rowhouse, Barry had burst in to wake her from slumber, not the other way around. Besides, they'd spent most of their time together riding in that police black-and-white.

Here and now, with Miss Collard crouched at his bedside—this moment had no place in their mutual history.

Nor did the middle-aged man who lounged in the open doorway. He was a complete stranger.

Was it possible Barry had lost a chunk of memory?

"What happened to you back at the farm's picnic?" Miss Collard asked him.

"Huh?" Her query confused Barry. He had presumed this moment was before they'd reached the farm. How could she know about the cannibal picnic?

Unless this was a lost memory from their visit to Templar's farm. But…he couldn't imagine where it would plug into the sequence of events as he remembered them.

"How do you know about the farm?" whispered Barry.

"How could I forget?" she squeaked defensively. "I remember everything. How they lured us in and captured us. How they planned to cook us for their picnic."

How could she know about things that hadn't happened to her yet?

"They might've succeeded, too," she continued. "If not for Joey."

"Joey?" muttered the dazed detective.

"Joey Fulton…you remember him…that old guy's son… He's the reason I'm here today and not part of those villains' diet.'"

He remembered Joey Fulton. The kid had immediately developed a crush on Miss Collard once they'd arrived at the farm. But what did the love-struck teen have to with her being here now?

When the hell is now, *anyway?*

"I suspect your friend is still too weak for this," declared the old man. He strode from the doorway and stood behind Miss Collard, his hands resting with paternal reassurance on her bare shoulders.

And where'd she get that garish tubetop? She wore a camouflage outfit while we were on-the-road together.

It was slowly dawning on him that his temporal displacement hadn't dropped him into the timeline before Miss Collard's death…but somewhere else…

"Maybe you're right, Doc Toby," she mumbled.

"He needs more rest."

"No—wait—" Barry reached out and caught Miss Collard's arm. "I don't understand any of this."

She threw a worried look over her shoulder.

After some hesitation, the doctor mixed a nod with a shrug and remarked, "His fever could have caused some memory damage."

"Please," begged Barry. "I need to know."

Sitting on the edge of the bed, she took his hand and inquired, "If you don't remember Joey, what do you remember?"

"I remember the kid," grunted Barry. "And the picnic." He drew his left hand from underneath the coarse blanket and showed her his missing finger. "And the mayor doing this. The rest…is a blur…" Unsure how to explain his sudden disappearance from the picnic, he skirted that detail.

"No wonder," she chirped. "That's when all hell broke loose."

And Barry listened, entranced and stunned by her tale. Apparently, Joey Fulton had sabotaged the picnic. He'd set off a box of fireworks in one of the silos. Already hurt and barely conscious from the abuse she'd suffered at the hands of the farmhands who'd dragged her from the pit in the barn, Miss Collard's recollections of this period were hazy, but Joey had told her later about the riot. It'd been quite a melee, from his account. Believing the grain silo was aflame, half the farmers had rushed to extinguish a fire they couldn't find…while the more paranoid ones had immediately armed themselves and rushed to defend the farmland's perimeter against the attack they thought was happening. In the ensuing panic, Joey had managed to snatch Miss Collard and flee the farm with her.

"Joey was too afraid to sneak back and look for you," she informed Barry. "And he wouldn't let me go back to check either."

Barry had underestimated the kid's teenage crush. Whatever feelings Joey Fulton had formed for the girl had been powerful enough to overcome his loyalty for his own clan. It was amazing that he'd rallied the courage to disobey his family, much less oppose them concerning their plans to slaughter Miss Collard fo dinner. After going to such great lengths to rescue Miss Collard, it was entirely understandable that the kid would refuse to let her return to the farm and run the risk of being recaptured. Barry had to privately applaud Joey's obstinance in this matter; it had kept the girl alive.

It would have done no good for either of them to go back to look for Barry. There'd been no Barry to find; he'd been yanked from the picnic and dumped back home in bed, where'd he'd almost bled to death.

"I never knew whether you escaped or were still a captive," she confessed. Tears welled from her eyes.

He couldn't tell her what had really happened. She'd never believe the truth; Barry barely did himself. He disliked lying to her, but it was the only option he had.

"I don't remember the melee," he told her, "but I must have taken advantage of it to sneak away too." His head sank back on the bed, not from weariness but to avoid lying to her face.

Mistaking this for a sign of exhaustion, Doc Toby decreed, "That's enough, girl. He needs rest if he's going to recover." He gently urged her from the bedside and out of the room. Before closing the door, the man advised Barry to sleep."

And then he was back in darkness.

Apparently, exhaustion *had* been a factor for Barry Winsor...he'd just been too exhausted to realize it.

Sleep came quickly, a deep slumber uninterrupted by dreams, nightmares, or any more displacements. When he woke, he still lay in the coarse bed. Moments later, Doc Toby visited to check on his condition. He took his temperature and pulse, then gave Barry some pills.

"What are they?"

"Just aspirin," Doc Toby replied offhandedly. The doctor possessed an offhandedly relaxed manner that made one immediately trust him. Physically, he was a medium-sized black man starting to run to flab with a receding hairline—innocuous and not particularly strong-willed. Barry could detect a genuine benevolence in his myopic eyes. His puffy hair made his head appear overlarge, where it was actually long and bean-shaped. His prominent forehead pushed the rest of his features to the bottom of his face, a compression that gave him a permanent thick-lipped pout. Years of policework had taught Barry to trust his gut concerning new people, and he felt that his initial evaluation of Doc Toby was fairly accurate. In fact, Barry suspected the man harbored more care than he could cope with. "You're doing much better."

"I was sick?" Barry had presumed his collapse had been brought on by driving for so long without rest or food.

Doc Toby shrugged. "I lack the diagnostic equipment to be certain, but I suspect you were taken down by a mixture of fatigue and flu. You had a temperature, that much was obvious." The man ducked his head, exhibiting a trace of embarrassment. "I'm not exactly a medical doctor. I used to sell pharmaceuticals. I'm afraid I'm the best this settlement has."

"Settlement?"

Here was a question the man was less self-conscious about answering. The history of the Sanctuary settlement was short but impressive, all things considered. Escaping the Princeton riots, a group of professors had fled east and taken refuge in one of the chemical factories outside Newark. During the weeks immediately following the zombie outbreak, they had offered shelter to many of the shell-shocked survivors. These people had banded together with the intention of preserving civilization, and they had succeeded. A shantytown had sprung up around the factory to house this new society. Naturally, this success had attracted the jealous attention of several bands of outlaws, but so far Sanctuary had managed to fight off these marauders with bombs assembled from the factory's chemical stocks.

Barry was fascinated. He had hoped the country was littered with groups who were resisting a downfall into savagery, but how many of them were destined to succeed? For all his high ambitions, Dusty had only succeeded in assembling an army of miscreants; they were more interested in battle and pillage than any revival of order. While Templar's colony of cannibals had worn a facade of normalcy, that homespun civility had been no more than a mask for deep depravity. Barry was glad to hear of one settlement that had been able to flourish in the face of greedy and undead persecution.

"So…Miss Collard and Joey Fulton ended up joining you here after they fled the boy's family," ventured Barry.

"Yes," Doc Toby confirmed his guess. "Denise has only been here two months, and already she's made her mark. Her suggestions have improved Sanctuary's ability to defend itself. That gives the Board time to cook up new chemicals for more bombs."

That made sense. Miss Collard was a survivalist at heart. Countless times during their travels, the girl had offered sagacious advice regarding effective defensive measures. Now that she was part of this settlement, she would want to see Sanctuary properly safeguarded. Sanctuary was lucky to have such a valuable asset.

"She also likes to go cruising, looking for refugees to invite into our fold," continued Doc Toby. "The Board doesn't approve of her forrays, they worry about her safety, but she can be obstinate—and sneaky—when she wants. She sneaks off and always brings back new citizens. Like she did with you."

Although he done little more than listen, the discussion had exhausted Barry. Doc Toby could see this and recommended his patient indulge in some more rest. He left the detective in the dark again.

While he would've liked to mull over what he'd learned, Barry's fatigue won out and he sank into another peaceful slumber, undisturbed by dreams, nightmares, or displacements.

After another day of rest, Doc Toby proclaimed Barry was healthy enough to abandon his bedridden state and resume life.

Despite the Doc's tale of the settlement's success, surprise closed off Barry's throat when he was led outdoors and got his first real look at Sanctuary.

The shantytown that spread around him did not look hastily erected. The buildings were made of actual walls and roofs instead of sheets of propped-together corrugated metal. In fact, they looked like rural ranch houses, the type built by community services on television when tornadoes destroyed midwest towns. Behind panes of pristine glass, floral curtains hung. There were even small potted plants sitting on a few porches, although those plants didn't look all that healthy.

People strolled along the lanes between these quaint domiciles, their gait casual and untainted by fear. These refugees knew that no undead creatures would pounce on them and tear them to pieces. Here in Sanctuary, they were safe from such horrors.

A large structure formed a dreary backdrop for the pastoral neighborhood. It was like Sanctuary sat at the foot of a decrepit behemoth. Rows of windows, many shattered and dark, ran the length of this ominous monolith. Its walls had once been concrete, but years of exposure to grimy pollution had given them a tar-like countenance. Two squat smokestacks rose from the building's roof, belching forth toxic soot that fed an overcast of odious clouds. The factory. Doc Toby had mentioned that the professors were struggling to cook up more of the chemicals needed to increase their arsenal of bombs. The factory radiated the complete opposite of the shantytown's idyllic ambiance.

Confessing he had half-an-hour before his next appointment, the Doc offered to show Barry around.

They strolled past rows of those ranch houses. When Barry complimented their professional appearance, Doc Toby told him that one of Sanctuary's earliest refugees had been a smalltown construction engineer prior to the apocalypse. The man had welcomed the opportunity to fashion residential housing for everyone.

"This is our grocery. If you look out back, you can see the garden where we grow our own vegetables."

Following the man's guidance, Barry saw a medium-sized empty plot of land behind the store. "Your crops look rather sickly."

The Doc sadly concurred. "It's all the poisons in the soil from the factory. We've tried hauling in fresh dirt, but the contamination keeps resurfacing."

Glancing at the bilious cloudbank that filled the sky, Barry could understand why.

"We rely heavily on canned goods for our nutrition," the Doc told him.

Next was the town's clothing store (which specialized more in repairs than in selling new goods), followed by a day care center (where families could leave their children while they toiled to make Sanctuary a better place). Annexed to the latter was, according to the Doc, a recreation center (for folks to burn off stress after-hours). They came to a building under construction, which the Doc revealed was to be the town library. Nearby sat a freight truck filled with books (borrowed from a local town) awaiting the library's completion. "The professors know the importance of education," stressed Doc Toby.

"Not exactly a 'shantytown,' is it?"

"Oh, this is purely temporary. Our long-range plans involve a more metropolitan site for Sanctuary."

Before he could elaborate or Barry could inquire about these "long-range plans," a young couple rounded a corner and monopolized both the men's attentions.

"Barry!" squealed Miss Collard. Disengaging herself from her companion, she capered over to encircle Barry in a joyous hug. Instead of her usual fatigues, this time she wore an ankle-length peasant dress. "You're finally all better!"

"Yes," chuckled Doc Toby. "The make-believe physician has decreed Mr Winsor healthy once more."

Barry returned her hug. He was happy to see Miss Collard.

It took him a moment to realize that her companion was Joey Fulton. The boy had grown quite a bit during the few months since Barry had last seen him. A modicum of lanky muscles had filled out his wiry physique. His peach-fuzz has thickened into a furry facial covering that still couldn't be called a beard, but it was a start. His abrupt growth spurt made him seem a more appropriate escort for the twenty-something Miss Collard.

Suppressing any paternal suspicion, Barry shook hands with the young man.

"Hello, Mr Winsor," Joey remarked. "It's good to see you healthy."

"You mean alive."

The lad's face darkened. "I'm...sorry my family..."

"Tried to eat me?"

A wince momentarily bent Joey. "Uhh—"

He refrained from telling the boy that his family no longer existed. That information could wait until Barry was more certain of the lad's new alliegance.

"I think we can put all that behind us, eh, boy? I'm not going to judge you by the sins of your kin." He leaned over and drew Miss Collard close, his arm around her shoulders. "After all, you save my little honey here from that same fate."

Joey gave him a solemn smile, but Barry could detect a strong jealousy hiding behind that thin veneer of courtesy. Clearly, there was a romance going on here.

The detective tactfully stepped back so the lad could reclaim his beloved.

"Running into you is most fortuitous, Denise," announced Doc Toby. Openly consulting his wristwatch, he explained, "I'm already late for an appointment. Could you take custody of Mr Winsor and get him settled around town?"

She readily agreed.

With a cavalier wave, the Doc dashed off.

"So..." With one entwined with Joey's arm, Miss Collard hooked her other arm around Barry's and guided him along the street. "As you can see, Sanctuary is ever growing. This is going to be our library..."

Barry politely informed her that he knew about the library. And the recreation and day care centers and the clothing repair shop. "And yes, I've seen the grocery and the sad garden."

"Oh." A minor pout pursed her lips, but she recovered quickly, and her mouth relaxed into a warm smile. "Well, is there anything you'd like to see?"

Without hesitation, Barry declared, "I'd like to meet some of the professors who run this place." His gaze rose to study the dark factory. He presumed that was where the founding fathers dwelled.

His request startled the couple.

"They're nothing like my family," Joey earnestly assured him.

"They're usually busy in their labs," was Miss Collard's response.

Brushing aside their feeble excuses, Barry set off along a side street. "I'm sure I can find my way." The couple scurried after him.

"Of course," the girl asserted. "You're an ex-cop. They'd want to welcome you."

"Still a cop." Having reached where the short avenue dead-ended against the factory, Barry peered back and forth until he spotted the entrance to the big dark building. He trotted off in that direction.

A semicircle of asphalt surrounded the factory's entranceway. The settlement stopped just shy of this paved apron. Two metal stubs stood to one side; the sign they had once supported was long gone, with it any way of identifying the factory's prior name or owners. While the building's exterior doors were unguarded, Barry noticed video cameras that tracked his approach. As he passed indoors, he saw someone has crudely etched "Princeton II" over the threshold.

Being a factory, the facilities possessed few amenities devoted to social visitors. Past the entrance doorway, the foyer was dank and cramped; if any seats had originally lined the waiting area, they'd been removed, leaving the chamber starkly empty. A reception desk, also unattended, stood in front of a pro-industry painting that filled the opposite wall.

Surveying the valiant workers lifting their productive arms to the painting's glorious sunrise, he waited before the empty reception counter. The factory's unseen monitors had observed his entrance, so he expected that soon someone would appear to challenge his visit.

Miss Collard and her young beau had followed him inside, but they remained by the doors, clearly reluctant to venture further into the vacant foyer.

So, Barry reflected, *she isn't the renegade hellion Doc Toby thinks she is. She harbors some respect for—or fear of—these founding fathers.*

Moments passed before a figure stepped from a shadowed arch and came to face the detective. From the man's low brow and unshaven chin, Barry doubted he was one of the professors, more likely a member of the squad posted to guard the building.

"You must be new to Sanctuary," the security man addressed Barry. For all his punkish appearance, his voice carried a fair degree of puissance. "Otherwise you'd know visitors don't come here without an invitation."

Barry smiled, but before he could reply, Miss Collard's voice rang out behind him: "I invited him."

The guard turned to regard her as she moved to stand beside the visitor. Barry noticed that Joey remained by the entrance, an uncomfortable grimace distorting his features.

"This is Barry Winsor," she announced loudly, as if she was actually speaking to someone beyond the foyer's barren walls. "He's a police officer from New York City."

The security man studied Barry with more caution this time. Barry knew that look: an alpha dog evaluating a potential rival. Or maybe the man wondered if the law had come to punish him for aggressions he had indulged in before arriving here.

"I thought the Board would want to meet him," continued Miss Collard.

"Purely a social visit," Barry added. "I'm not here in any official capacity."

This remark softened the guard's wary expression, but only a little. He directed his reply to the girl, "You know how busy the profs are, girl. If you want to introduce this cop to the Board, you should follow protocol and make an appointment like anybody else."

"Detective, actually," Barry nonchalantly tossed out. "13th Precinct in Manhattan."

"But we're already here," Miss Collard pointed out. "Surely—"

"Bring them to Conference Room 3," a stern voice loudly reverberated in the chamber. No new person had entered, so Barry presumed it came from a hidden loudspeaker. As he'd suspected, some kind of supervisor had been monitoring the exchange.

Clearly unhappy with these orders, the guard hid his disapproval as he escorted Barry through the arch and down a murky hallway. Miss Collard accompanied Barry. After a moment, Joey Fulton scurried after them.

The corridor, undecorated by anything other than a coat of gray paint, revealed nothing about the nature of the building. Nor did the conference room to which they were brought. In Barry's experience all conference rooms were the same. This one reminded him of the meeting room he'd seen back at the Chicago football stadium. In fact, two of the landscapes hanging on the walls were identical to paintings back at the arena. The long table had been fashioned from different lumber, but its overall design was the same. The chairs were similarly familiar. Here, though, no expanse of windows looked out upon a pleasant view; here, four solid walls (three gray, one pink) enclosed the room.

The main difference lay in the fact that the stadium's conference room had been empty, while here two men waited.

One stood at the far end of the long table, his arms folded across his narrow chest. He was a trim man with thinning hair. He wore a white lab coat over a fluffy sweater and cotton slacks. All he needed was a pair of fisheye-lensed spectacles to make him a parody of what people pictured when they thought of college professors.

Seated when Barry and company entered, the other man rose to welcome them with an extended open hand. This one looked more like a real estate broker. A bright orange mane topped a florid face. A plethora of sales pitches had left his cheeks bulging in a permanent smile. He wore a light blue suit with matching tie.

"Welcome to Sanctuary, Detective Winsor. I am Professor Daniel Grauss." He nodded in the direction of the scowling man. "And this is Dr Heigl."

Heigl remained where he stood, making no overture at greeting the police official.

Barry took Grauss' hand and gave it a hearty clasp, not too tight, but enough to establish the clasper's vitality. Unable to naturally mirror the red-faced man's grimace of assurance, Barry settled for a brief, temperate smile.

"Is this how you apologize for your latest jaunt, Miss Collard?" snarled Heigl. His stance remained tall and firm. His deadpan expression didn't need to communicate any censure, his baritone voice rang with enough vivid disdain. "Your trips beyond our territory are unauthorized, but you persist in making them. You are compromising the security of this settlement."

Suddenly bristling with spunk, the girl declared, "Let's not forget who devised that security web for you, okay? None of my travels ever endanger Sanctuary. Besides, my 'jaunts,' as you so dismissively call them, always manage to bring back valuable new citizens for the settlement. Don't they, Dr Heigl?"

While Heigl gave no response, Grauss was quick to fuss over Miss Collard, praising her courageous efforts, congratulating her on the many talented newcomers she regularly brought into the fold.

The contrast of personalities was not lost on Barry. *Good cop, bad cop.* Grauss would be more forthcoming with information, but probably nothing of real value; while Heigl was the one who bore watching.

Gaining information was Barry's real goal with this meeting. Not just data on Sanctuary, but Barry hoped that a group of learned ndividuals might be able to tell him something viable about the causes of the zombie outbreak. Barry certainly put little faith in any of the theories he'd heard so far, like Sheldon's "farting asteroid" tale.

Alas, Barry could already sense that right now wasn't the best time to go fishing for answers, not with Mr Uncooperative Heigl around. The best he was going to get now were cursory introductions and a standardized "welcome to the fold" speech.

In fact, while Barry had been ruminating on these matters, Professor Grauss had already launched into the welcome speech. Barry listened as attentively as he could, nodding and smiling at appropriate points. These guys were just as proud of Sanctuary as Doc Toby had been, and admittedly they had reasons to be smug. Anyone could try to establish an island of civilization in the now-turgid sea of horrors, but few were able to hold out against the undead plague, much less the more dangerous threat posed by unscrupulous people seeking to usurp everything for themselves.

"Perhaps you'd like a tour of the factory," Gauss offered.

"Now is hardly the time for such unnecessary distractions," proclaimed Dr Heigl. "There are several ongoing matters that require our attention."

"My associate is right," Grauss apologized. "Other Board members are busy working on projects that are crucial to the settlement's survival, much less Sanctuary's ultimate ambition. We should really get back to the labs to assist them."

Another cryptic reference to some ulterior motive for Sanctuary's existence. Barry was very interested in learning more about this, but he recognized the wisdom of not pushing for more immediate information, at least not with Dr Heigl present.

"I understand," he responded. "Another time, perhaps."

"Yes, of course," Grauss smiled.

"Miss Collard can tell you how to make an appointment," added Dr Heigl, "even though she rarely does so herself."

Answering an unseen and unheard signal, the security guard opened the conference room's door and, still armed with his scowl, stood waiting.

I guess my "audience" is over, mused Barry.

"Well, it was good meeting you." He extended his hand and Grauss shook it goodbye. When Dr. Heigl made no move to acknowledge their departure, Barry was tempted to stride around the table and give the lofty professor a vigorous handshake goodbye, but he resisted the urge, knowing that such an audacious gesture would only earn him negative points. Instead he gave Heigl a slight nod, which (of course) was not returned.

He followed Miss Collard and Joey from the room. Stepping behind him, the guard crowded Barry and the others along the gray corridor, through the barren reception foyer and out the glass doors.

Once they stood on the asphalt apron, Joey Fulton released a plentiful "whew." Clearly, he had been uncomfortable during the entire visit. Only now, back outdoors under the sooty overcast, did the boy regain his proprietary attitude toward Miss Collard. Moving smoothly, he slid between Barry and the girl and took her arm.

To hide his amused smirk, Barry turned to regard the nearby shantytown. "Well, I suppose it's high time I got settled in."

"Yes," the girl chirped. "I'll show you to the barracks."

As they walked, she explained that newcomers were initially set up in the barracks. Food, lodging and other basic amenities were provided on credit. He could help around town to earn the bucks to pay off his debt. (Apparently, "bucks" were an intangible currency; everyone's accounts were tabulated and stored in the head of the town assessor.) Afterward, Barry could use his earnings to put a deposit on an empty household for himself, if he so chose.

If I decide to stay...

For a few days, Barry helped a work crew erect another house at the far end of town. Gradually, the settlement was expanding around the factory's circumference. The construction crew was hard pressed to keep pace with the influx of new citizens. The barracks were overcrowded.

Apparently Miss Collard wasn't Sanctuary's only source of new blood. While her "jaunts" were unauthorized, a certified team scoured the surrounding territory, putting down any zombies they saw and collecting survivors.

Barry kept a keen ear, but never heard any complaints among the citizenry. With good reason, he thought. The settlement provided more than the basic necessities of life, its people were bonded together by a sense of community in these hostile times. And safety—that was another benefit offered by Sanctuary. Here in town, the populace knew they were protected from any zombie or raider attack.

His one regret was the scarcity of alcohol in Sanctuary. Not that booze was forbidden, but the professors conscripted most of it for the chemicals they cooked. Upon consideration, Barry realized this was probably for the best. There was no place for a drunk in these survivalist times. Barry wanted to be a valuable asset to the settlement; indulging in alcohol binges would be counterproductie to achieving that renown. He put aside his vices and rechanneled any nervous energy into helping around town.

Cigarettes, though, were plentiful. Many of Sanctuary's citizenry smoked.

One morning, Miss Collard took him on a tour of the town's defense network. Most of the traps and devices were of her design; he even recognized a few she had utilized during their travels. She was a clever girl, with a strange acumen for life in wartime. He appreciated the tour. Now he knew what spots to avoid should he ever venture beyond the shantytown.

She asked him to meet her that afternoon at a copse north of Sanctuary.

When Barry arrived, she led him into the shrubbery where an armored Buick was hidden. This afternoon, she had abandoned effeminate attire and wore her gray-and-blue camouflage fatigues.

"I'm going out today," the girl told him, "and I thought you might like to ride along."

He did.

Once they were settled in the Buick, she pointed out an array of weapons strapped to the insides of the doors and under the dashboard.

"Expecting trouble?" he chuckled

"I always expect trouble. You know that."

That he did.

He chose a semiautomatic shotgun and stuffed a pistol into his right boot. So efficient was Sanctuary's defensive perimeter, the settlement's denizens had no need to carry weapons, and although Barry had honored that rule, he'd been uncomfortable doing so. As a cop, without a gun he felt naked.

Miss Collard followed a nearly nonexistent path through the trees. At the edge of the woods, she stopped and got out to disarm a pair of explosive traps that guarded this section of Sanctuary's perimeter. Once she had driven out into the meadow, she stopped again, to re-arm the traps. Beyond the meadow lay a road; she took it west.

"Are you happy here?" he asked.

"Yes, very much so."

"Even though you have to sneak away?"

"Oh, that's just Heigl. He's a stickler for rules. He can seem aloof, but he means well. The Board really do have the best interests at heart for the people they've accepted into Sanctuary."

"Not everyone is asked to join?"

"Oh, y'know," she chuffed dismissively. "There's always riffraff. And the gangs that try to raid the town. Nobody wants neighbors they can't trust."

He had to agree with her, but wondered who did the actual choosing of who could stay and who had to go.

"Grauss is a sweety, though," the girl confided as she took a ramp that brought her to a surprisingly clear highway. (Later, she revealed that members of the town had gone out and removed most obstacles from the nearby roads.) "Maybe that's because he taught philosophy courses at Princeton. The other profs are mostly hard science boys."

"What's Dr Heigl's field?"

"Comparitive Politics."

That figured. While the others applied their knowledge to improving Sanctuary's livelihood, Heigl was the one who decided policy.

"Don't let him bother you. The other profs are much nicer. Grauss has a secret passion for chocolate." For a while, she drove along the empty interstate. Finally, as she took an exit, she broke the silence with, "You should really stay, Barry. Sanctuary could use someone with your skills."

"Why? Are there many robberies of murders?"

"You know what I mean. Your survival skills."

"I think you've got more than enough survival skills to take care of the entire settlement."

"We can always use more," she mumbled. "Especially for what comes next."

Before Barry could ask her what she meant, Miss Collard turned into an almost indiscernible gap in the roadside bushes. After a few yards she stopped the Buick, but turned on its headlights. Unnecessary while driving in daylight, the twin beams revealed a vehicle hidden in the shrubbery: the SUV he had driven east.

"I was alone when I found you, Barry. I brought you back to Sanctuary, but had to leave your car out here. I hid it, though, so nobody would pillage your stuff. I couldn't help but notice that you've collected a significant amount of valuable supplies in your travels."

He thanked her, but remained seated in the Buick.

"This is where you make your choice, Barry. You can get in your car and drive away...or you can follow me back to Sanctuary."

The girl was offering him freedom or citizenry.

"The decision is yours," she told him.

What kind of future did he want? One of a loner wandering the countryside? Or one as part of a unified community?

An assortment of implications flowed through his mind as he considered what to do.

If he chose to join the settlement, did he want to relinquish the SUV and his stash of supplies to the town? The common good and all that.

But if he left the SUV where it was and returned with Miss Collard in the Buick, he'd be implying his choice to stay might not be completely earnest, that he was holding the car back as an emergency escape vehicle.

To be perfectly honest with himself, Barry didn't relish the prospect of heading off on his own. The world was a terribly hazardous place these days. One couldn't trust the living or the dead out there. Besides, he'd developed a camaraderie with Little Miss Survivalist. With her razor-sharp skills, he knew the girl hardly needed watching after, but she still sparked a protective sentiment in him.

And he still hoped to be able to question the professors about the cause of the zombie outbreak. If anyone might know what had started the dead walking, it would be men of learning. He could only hope that the theories they held in credence were less fanciful than Sheldon's leaky asteroid.

"I hope you stay. Like I mentioned, Sanctuary can really your expertise for the next stage."

"Yes, you mentioned that. And what does this 'next stage' involve?" He turned to face her. "If you don't mind my asking."

"The Board plan to take Manhattan."

The settlement welcomed the supplies Barry donated upon his return. A few of the professors actually came out to thank him, although two of them joked that Dr Heigl was going to publicly denounce Miss Collard's latest unauthorized jaunt, regardless of the booty she'd brought back.

They'd each returned, she and Barry, with their own loads of valuables. En route back to Sanctuary, Miss Collard had taken a detour to empty a fallout shelter which one of her previous refugees had told her about.

An exemption was declared and Barry Winsor was awarded the house he had just helped build over the last few days. To his surprise, he found himself living next-door to Miss Collard…and her live-in boy-friend.

Barry had to remind himself that as a single woman over the age of twenty-one she was entitled to make her own adult decisions. He still wasn't convinced that Joey Fulton was her wisest choice for a partner… but then, she knew him better than Barry did. He tried to get to know the lad, but Joey was ultimately too uncomfortable around Barry to relax. The boy couldn't get past the fact that his family had tried to eat the detective.

"They—they cut off your finger!"

"They did it, kid, not you."

"But—"

"But you were busy rescuing Miss Collard. That counts for a lot in my book."

"I'm so ashamed of their ugly habits. I assure you, I never ate any-thing at their special meals."

This time, Barry told the lad that his family had been punished for their crimes.

"Gasp! Was—was it you? Did you—"

"Most of the punishing was actually done by a gang of marauders."

"Dusty's Raiders?"

Barry nodded.

"Mayor Templar was always ranting about how the Raiders were go-ing to spoil everything."

"I didn't kill him…but I did put him down once he turned undead."

"Oh…"

In the long run, this admission turned out to have the opposite effect than what Barry had expected. Instead of easing the relationship between him and the lad, Joey grew distant and seemed to resent the man, now for entirely different reasons. This disappointed Barry, for not only did it foil his efforts to befriend the girl's chosen beloved, it indicated the lad har-bored some residue of fidelity for his family, regardless of their degenerate ways. He was loath to bring this to Miss Collard's attention, so he just kept a closer eye on the ex-cannibal. (The detective remained unconvinced by the lad's claim that he'd never partaken of human flesh. A family united by such a depraved habit would have made sure the next generation acquired the taste as young as possible.)

Remembering Miss Collard's remark about Professor Grauss' sweet-tooth, Barry watched the rec center for sign of the man. He put in an appearance after only one day of surveillance. When Barry abandoned his recon position and followed the prof indoors, he found Grauss already scooping candy bars from the desert counter. The prof eventually retreated to an isolated table to gorge himself.

Slipping into the booth across from the man, Barry greeted him as he ripped open one of the candy bars he'd grabbed en route to join the prof.

At first, Grauss' eyes widened with embarrassed guilt, but he relaxed somewhat once Barry started chowing down on his own slab of chocolate. The two men shared a vice, or so Grauss believed. Barry made a show of taking repeated bites and munching away, but in truth he consumed very little of the candy bar (not unlike how he'd stretched a single drink out for hours back in Glendale while carousing with the Raiders).

After a few minutes of munching, Grauss thanked Barry for the recent additions to Sanctuary's candy stash. The bars they were eating had come from the supplies carried in the detective's SUV.

Barry graciously accepted the man's gratitude.

For a while, Grauss ate and Barry pretended to.

Eventually, his lips and chin smeared with chocolate (Grauss had a sloppy sweet-tooth), the prof asked Barry how he was settling in.

"Pretty well," Barry responded. "I suspect this place is a lot nicer now than it was when you guys first got here."

"Oh yes. Certain problems plagued us from the onset When the outbreak happened, the workers abandoned the factory quickly, leaving many of the chemical vats still cooking. The place was filled with poison gas by the time we arrived. It took considerable decontamination before we could take up residence."

"You're all Princeton men, right?"

"Mostly." The sugar rush was making him chatty. "Let's see…Adams comes from Temple in Philadelphia. Kaufmann used to work for DOW. And Heigl is actually from Cambridge, but was a guest lecturer when the outbreak happened. Most of us—the members of the Board—were together at a party held at Dracy's place celebrating Heigl's lecture. An undead swarm hit the campus. We barely got out with our lives. Adams had a van, we all escaped in it. We fled east at Heigl's insistence, he believed that New York City would somehow fortify itself against the contagion."

Barry voiced a cynical grunt.

"Yes—we found only chaos in the city. So we retreated across the river and found this abandoned factory. It was Kaufmann's idea for us to commandeer the premises. He foresaw a need for chemicals if our survival was going to be long-term. Bombs and gun powder, defenses against the zombies." Grauss shook his head sadly. "Only Heigl predicted that we would have to beware living humans too. He believes that humanity is ruled by narcissism, that man will always choose violence over rational action."

"That's quite a negative outlook for a political professor."

Grauus shrugged. "It turned out there were a lot of crazies wandering the countryside. We were hit early on. Three of us died repelling the attack. We were lucky to have just finished cooking our first batch of explosives. Some of the bombs we used were faulty; two of our losses were caused by the premature detonation of our own bombs."

"Was it just you professors at that point? Or had you started taking in other people by then?"

"Oh, we began accepting refugees the day after we arrived here. But many of them were families—children and women. One woman— Maggie Simpson, wife of our housing contractor—was pregnant. Our fighting force was limited mostly to Board members during Sanctuary's early days."

"Why 'Board'? Aren't you guys more like a Ruling Council?"

"Heigl argued against conventional political systems. He stressed that we weren't going to make the same mistakes made by the lost civilization. We were going to craft a rational society using science as our basis. So, 'Board' fit better than any of the other suggestions."

"Listen…" Barry folded his arms on the edge of the small table and leaned forward. "What do you professors make of the whole undead situation? Do you have any credible explanations for the dead coming back to life?"

Grauss grimaced, took a big bite of chocolate and chewed a moment before he replied, "Oh, everybody has their pet theory. Heigl blames the zombie outbreak on a corporate lab experiment gone awry, and Kaufman denies any DOW culpability in the affair. Adams has a biology background, he thinks some natural virus mutated and is activating the corpses' neural system."

"What—like ebola?"

"Who knows? Biology isn't my field."

"I'd be interested to hear what *you* think happened."

"What—" He sat back and laughed. "Because I'm a philosphy professor, you think I'm going point the finger at some ethical cause? Maybe the species got so arrogant that their own karma raised their dead to exact punishment? Ha!"

"Kinda hard to imagine something as intangible as that happening."

"You want to know the truth—I have *no idea* what happened. None of the theories put forth by my learned associates click for me. I supose you could call me an agnostic on the subject."

"Or you're like me...you just haven't yet heard an explanation you can believe in."

Grauss laughed.

Barry joined him.

Barry experienced only one displacement during his early days at Sanctuary. Although a minor and brief one, it deeply disturbed him.

He went to sleep in his bed in the shantytown house he had helped build...

And woke up in his own bed back in the house he had shared with Emily.

But when he rose and went to peer outside, he found himself staring at post-apocalyptic ruin. Automobiles filled the street, abandoned and canted at awkward angles. The house across the way was burnt-out rubble. Stiff zombies shambled through the tableau.

Puzzled and more than a little frightened, he crawled back into bed.

And woke up back in Sanctuary.

He was pretty sure it hadn't been a dream.

One day, Doc Toby came to tell Barry he'd been summoned by the Board.

From his position winching a wall erect, Barry called to the Doc, "Just a minute...as soon as this—"

Another worker sidled over and attempted to relieve Barry of the rope he was hoisting. "The Board don't like being kept waiting."

A scowl did nothing to deflect the man, he managed to wrestle the rope free of Barry's grasp. For an instant the wall wobbled, threatening to topple back to the newly poured foundation, but Barry reached out to steady the panel before it came down. Together, they tugged and jostled the panel until it stood vertical. Two more workers quickly secured it in place.

"Come along," Doc Toby sighed.

Barry fell into step next to the mock doctor. "I should really stop for a quick shower and a change of clothes," grumbled Barry.

"They're in a pissy mood today. You shouldn't antagonize them with tardiness."

"Okay, okay." Barry wiped a sheen of perspiration from the back of his neck. Personally, he wasn't too worried about offending anybody. If the Board wanted to see him right away, they'd just have to settle for the way he stank when yanked off a strenuous construction detail. What could be so important, anyway, to warrant a midday summoning?

Possible reasons floated through his head.

Maybe Miss Collard had made another unauthorized jaunt and the Board intended to vent their displeasure on him instead of wasting time chastising the girl when she returned. A fat lot of good that'd do.

Maybe they were going to heap more hollow praise on him for donating the foodstuff stash he'd brought to town. Barry was getting rather bored with everybody's constant gratitude for that. It wasn't as if Sanctuary's supplies had been dangerously low.

Lately, Barry had been making the rounds, asking all the citizens their favorite explanation for the zombie outbreak. Was the Board going to censure him for doing this? A dose of curiosity was healthy, especially when it concerned so life-changing a matter as the undead.

Being too damned busy keeping themselves alive, most people hadn't deeply questioned what had happened. This didn't overly surprise Barry. So much of the pre-outbreak population had been couch potatoes who'd let authority figures push them around without complaint. A lack of curiosity went hand-in-hand with this vacuity.

Some, though, had pondered the mystery and come up with a variety of answers. Most of them were too fanciful or preposterous for Barry's serious consideration.

"Them damned UFOs caused it to wipe out mankind so they can fly in and repopulate the Earth with little green men."

""It was supposed to be the Rapture, but there were too many gays and the imbalance interfered with the heavenly process."

"Oh, this is all just an illusion forced on us by intelligent machines—like in that movie."

"You can blame those wacky California hippies with their magic crystals and vampire slayers."

"It's the Democrats' fault. They were so pissed off about losing the election, this was their payback."

So far, Barry hadn't gotten the opportunity to ask Doc Toby about his own theory. The man was intelligent and street-smart; Barry was interested to hear his thoughts on the matter. Now was as good a time as any...

"So, Doc, what's your pet theory about what started turning dead people into zombies?"

After a moment passed with no response from Doc Toby, Barry grunted, "Doc?"

"Can't help you there, Barry."

"What? No thoughts at all about it?"

"I certainly wouldn't trust anyone who claims they know the truth. Oh, everybody wonders, but there's no way to really know, is there? Not without going back in time and watching it happen."

"If time travel were possible, someone could go back and *stop* it from happening." Actually, this possibility had crossed Barry's mind more than once. But—two factors handicapped this course of action. One: he had no control over his temporal displacements, nor idea what was causing them. And more importantly, two: until he learned the real cause of the zombie outbreak, going back in time to stop it from happening was futile.

"I think that depends on what model of Time you believe in," remarked Doc Toby, "the steady stream or the multi-branching network."

"Huh?"

"In the steady stream model, events are predestined by the coexistence of the past and the future, so it would be impossible to change the past. No matter how drastic the changes you made were, events would realign to bring about the outcome you were trying to erase.

"While, according to the multi-branched model, every event has a variety of consequences, and each of them create a new timeline branching off from the original trunk, and that thread branches off into myriad new timelines with each subsequent eventuality. You drive up to an intersection in the road. You could turn left. You could turn right. Or go straight, or turn the car completely around and drive away, or even get out of the car—and then there are a hundred new branches for every direction you could take from that point. In this model, going back in time to change history would only create a new branch. Your actions in the past would have no direct effect on the future of the timeline you came from."

"I thought you sold pharmaceuticals before the outbreak."

"That was my job, Barry, not my entire existence. I—uh—I've read a lot of science fiction. I was just quoting what a consensus of authors have put into their time-travel stories."

"Does that mean you believe in time travel?" The introduction of this topic in their conversation seemed awkward to Barry, even suspicious. After all, Barry was the only one who knew about his temporal displacements. Or was he? Had Doc Toby somehow guessed that Barry was a hapless time traveler? Maybe Barry had babbled in his sleep, revealing his secret, while the Doc had been ministering to his recuperation. Doc Toby had been the who'd brought up time travel….to avoid talking about his opinions concerning the origins of the undead contagion—that alone was somewhat suspicious. Did the man know something about the zombies that he was reluctant to share? Or was he just trying to seed Barry's head with the idea of traveling back in time to stop the undead outbreak? But then, Doc Toby had just outlined why it was probably impossible for a time traveler to alter the past. Why would he suggest a plan that was inherently unfeasible?

"God, no," admitted the Doc. "Time travel is fiction."

"Like zombies."

"Okay. Zombies exist—but I suspect that's enough of a twist for our world. Adding time travel to the mix is pushing plausibility."

"And the dead walking around isn't implausible?"

They had reached the factory's entrance.

As Doc Toby pulled open the door and stood back to allow Barry to pass, the man muttered, "We're all walking talking dead men."

Inside, a security guard promptly whisked Barry across the foyer and down the gray corridor he'd seen before. In fact, he was escorted to the same conference room. Doc Toby tagged along.

This time, there were several Board members present. Dr Heigl occupied his spot at the head of the table. Barry saw Professor Grauss and a few others he'd met since he'd joined the Sanctuary settlement…Noel Adams (the biologist), Derek Kaufmann (the chemist), Oscar Devers (an engineer). There were three more he didn't know.

Grauss bid Barry to take the seat at the end of the table. From there, he looked down a gauntlet of founding fathers to the political maven at the table's far terminus. The guard left. Doc Toby stayed, but lingered by the wall.

With the exception of Heigl's permanent scowl, the other faces all trembled with anticipation.

Anticipation of what? mused Barry.

He sat back, making himself as comfortable as possible in the straight-backed metal chair. "What's up, boys?"

Dr Heigl's frown deepened at the flippancy. Barry had expected that.

The others leaned forward, as if bristling with a need for something.

It was Dr Heigl who finally spoke. "So, Detectve Winsor...what's your initial reaction to what we propose?"

"Huh?"

"You didn't brief him, did you, Toby?"

At the periphery of his vision, Barry saw the Doc twitch, then respond in a taciturn voice, "No. I didn't get the chance, Dr Heigl. Anyway—" He tossed his head and defiantly glared at the spindly man. "—I think your expansion scheme is mad. If you want to convince Barry to join your insanity, you'll have to do it yourself."

"It is not madness, Toby," barked Dr Heigl. "It's our sanest option if we expect to reestablish civilization."

"You're talking about your idea to reclaim Manhattan," Barry announced.

Heigl swiveled to bask Barry with his scowl. "So—you *have* been briefed."

It'd been a guess, but apparently an accurate one. Detective Barry had easily connected the fragments of the puzzle.

"Miss Collard mentioned it," he revealed.

"Good. Then—"

"In passing. No details. Why don't you fill them in for me, Dr Heigl?"

It was clear (from what he'd heard so far) that this was Heigl's scheme...and that not everyone thought much of it. *Let's hear what spin he puts on it...*

"First, you must understand that the Board are dedicated to reestablishing civilization. This—"

"A laudable ambition," grunted Barry.

"This settlement here is a temporary operation. Although the factory was integral in getting us started, the previous owners polluted the region with their chemical spill-off. This land is simply too contaminated for long-term habitation."

"No kidding."

"Um—yes. A more stable environment is required to rebuild civilization."

"If you think the Big Apple's a 'stable environment,' you're crazy."

This remark irritated Heigl—as Barry had known it would. He kept interjecting snide comments to rile the man. Not just out of fun—although it *was* quite amusing to keep poking Heigl with verbal sticks—but Barry hoped that by unsettling the man, he'd accidentally spill some piece of information he didn't want to.

"New York City was a cultural hub—"

"*Was*, Heigl—past tense. Trust me, now it's no different from anywhere else—filled with crazies and zombies. *Not* a stable environment for anyone except suicidal individuals."

"Naturally, such undesirable elements would have to be removed from the city," asserted Derek Kaufmann.

"By what army?" Barry scoffed.

"That is where you come in, Officer Winsor," declared Dr Heigl. "As a member of Manhattan's police force, you know the city in a way no one else could. Your expertise in law-keeping marks you as the obvious person to head the clean-up crew."

Barry's scoffing tone devolved into a guffaw.

"I would expect an honorable man like yourself to feel some civic responsiblity about restoring order in his hometown."

Aww—cheap-shot, Barry privately chafed. *But valid nonetheless...*

"Sanctuary cannot remain here, Officer Winsor," added one of the profs whose name Barry didn't know. "But Manhattan would offer the space and resources for a real colony to flourish."

"Look, guys," Barry admitted, "as I've already mentioned, restarting civilization is a laudable ambition. And it *would* be a lot easier to achieve in a city than out here in the boondocks—but Manhattan is just too savage a place to pick to do it. The city's full of aggressive threats—like the zombies and the crazies. It's awfully flattering that you believe I'm the man for the job—but you're asking the impossible. It'd take an army to purge the Big Apple of all its worms. And don't take this the wrong way, but Sanctuary is severely lacking when it comes to troops of trained fighters."

"I agree," remarked Doc Toby. The man had come up to stand behind Barry's chair. "I think their plan is dangerous, but..." He put his hands on Barry's shoulders. "...they're dead set on doing it, with or without you. If you don't take the job, they'll just find somebody who will."

"I suspect Miss Collard would jump at the chance," intoned Dr Heigl with a sinister smirk.

Another cheap-shot. Everyone knew that Barry was protective of the girl. And Heigl was right; considering her survivalist inclinations, she *would* jump at the chance to apply her skills to cleaning up Manhattan. Despite Barry's faith in the girl's abilities, there was no way she was equal to the task of coping with the violent madhouse that metropolis had become. If she tried, she would fail—and in the process lose her life and the lives of anyone reckless enough to follow her into battle. The only way Barry could prevent this from happening was to take the job himself. *Then I'll be the one who fails and leads everybody into a losing battle.*

He could always try to convince Miss Collard to leave Sanctuary with him. While seemingly a cowardly retreat, it would save everybody's lives. The Board could never take Manhattan with their only trained agents gone. But…Barry knew how much she liked it in Sanctuary, how attached she had gotten to the people here, especially that Fulton boy. If Barry asked her to go, Joey Fulton would demand she stay—or worse, demand to accompany her. Barry still didn't trust the lad; having him as a traveling companion would be an ordeal…one that would undoubtedly end with somebody getting their head twisted from their scrawny little neck. No, Miss Collard wouldn't leave, certainly not once they'd offered her the job of leading the charge to take Manhattan. It was the girl's hometown, she'd crow the value of cleaning out all the undead riffraff and returning civilization to the Big Apple. If he left, she would just step into the position he vacated.

He really didn't have much choice in this awful matter.

With his gaze narrowed to a dagger slit, Barry met Dr Heigl's defiant frown and held it for a protracted moment before he whispered, "Fine."

"A bit too ambiguous, Officer Winsor."

"Fine," Barry repeated. "I'll be your attack dog."

The ends of Heigl's lips curled up. "Fine, Commander Winsor."

"But mark my words, Heigl," grated Barry. "If she gets harmed in any way, your broken neck will be the price."

Behind him, Doc Toby coughed, then pointed out, "Be realistic, Barry. You know you'll never keep her out of it. A clean-up job like this, she'll demand to be involved."

Barry rose to his feet. He let the backs of his legs shove the chair into a loud topple to the floor. He glared first at the Doc, then included Heigl and the rest of the founding fathers in his angry regard. "If she gets harmed in any way, you all answer to me."

Without waiting for any response, he turned away. The guard tried to intercede when he reached for the door handle, but he shoved him back with a stiff palm to the chest. Yanking open the door, Barry left.

As he proceeded down the corridor, he heard someone remark from the conference room, "Well, that went better than we expected."

7

BARRY SEARCHED THE SHANTYTOWN, but saw no sign of Miss Collard. Eventually, he found her at home, although it took nearly five minutes of pounding on the door of her house to get her to respond.

"What?!" The door jerked open and Miss Collard stood there, rage darkening her sweet countenance. "What the hell do you want?" Then she saw who it was and her eyes softened. "Barry—what's wrong?"

"Get dressed," he growled. "We're going to take a ride."

Her only garment at the moment was a men's shirt, only partially buttoned, that barely came down to her hips. In the murky recesses of the domicile, a shadow moved: Joey Fulton peering from the bedroom.

"Not another unauthorized run, Denise," groaned the lad.

"Oh, don't worry, Joey dear. I'll be—"

"This run is authorized," snapped Barry.

"By who?" Joey challenged. "The Board would never approve of—"

"Authorized by *me*!" With that, Barry stormed off.

Fifteen minutes later, she came next door. He sat in his SUV, waiting for her. "What's all this about, Barry?"

"Get in."

He drove over to the shed that served as the settlement's armory. There, the same guard who had escorted him from the factory awaited Barry's arrival. Without comment, Barry began loading weapons into the car's rear bay. "Gettin' an early start, huh?" the guard sneered. He watched, but never offered to help.

Miss Collard remained silent throughout the loading up and as Barry navigated through the settlement's main gates. None of the sentries challenged the departure.

See? he told himself. *Word's already spread about my appointment. She'd have heard about it soon and immediately wanted in. If I hadn't taken her along on this run, she'd have come after me. At least, this way she gets to hear about it from me—my spin, my rules, my game-plan*

The SUV had put some distance between itself and the shantytown before the girl finally broke the silence.

"What's all this about, Barry?"

"In their eminent madness, the Board have decided to force civilization back on Manhattan. They've appointed me the man to clean up the Big Apple."

"Clean it up? You mean, drive out the zombies?"

"And the crazies too."

"Uhh…we're not headed off to do it right now, are we? Just the two of us?"

"Hell no, girl," he grunted. "This is just a recon run. I figured you'd want in."

"Well, of course!"

Your hometown…

"It's my hometown—of course I'd love to help clean it up!"

You wouldn't want to miss the fight…

"I wouldn't want to miss the action," she cackled. "This is great."

"Let's review the ground rules, okay? I'm in command, so you have to do exactly what I tell you to do. Always. I won't have you taking unnecessary risks."

"Okay, dad."

"No joking around, Miss Collard. This job is utter lunacy. Every second is going to ooze danger—real nasty danger. You remember how bad it was back when we were still there. We barely escaped alive. And now—to placate a bunch of over-ambitious highbrows, we're going to be returning to that pandemoniem."

"I can take are of myself," she bridled.

"I want your A-game, girl."

"You'll get it, sir."

"No lip."

"Sorry." For a moment her brow furrowed and she gazed out the window at the passing scenery. Then she turned back to him. "Cleaning up the city's going to require a bigger crew than the two of us."

"Can you think of anybody else back in Sanctuary who'd be up to helping us?"

"Uhh…not really…"

"So it's just you and me, kid."

The recon went smoother than Barry expected, despite the weird journey it turned out to be. The data they gathered was radically daunting.

First they had to run gauntlets in districts on the Jersey side of the Holland Tunnel. In all fairness, these selections of survivors were untrained and armed with sticks and hammers. Nevertheless, Barry and his traveling companion faced a few stressful moments as he wildly navigated through mazes of obstacles while she spread some covering fire. They made it through relatively unscathed, but Barry made a mental note about these xenophobic settlements—they might pose a problem when it came time to move Sanctuary's populace from the shantytown into New York.

But then, the likelihood of that exodus depended on him cleaning up Manhattan so they could move in. All those zombies and crazies and gangs, not to mention the half-eaten cadavers laying all over the place—cleaning up this mess was a lot for just two people to handle. Barry couldn't see any way to pull it off.

While the Tunnel itself was unnoccupied, maneuvering past the miasma of abandoned vehicles was treacherous. The lights had failed at some point, plunging the underground passage into torturous darkness.

Canal Street was worse. Here, the automotive obstacles were more numerous, and accompanied by a gaggle of shambling zombies. Adding to the fun: somebody fired a few shots at the SUV as Barry guided it along the cluttered avenue.

Further into midtown, the devastation increased exponentially. Multi-vehicle collisions had left damaged cars piled in heaps, blocking intersections better than any man-made barriers.

Eventually, Barry and Miss Collard had to abandon the SUV and continue their recon on foot. Even then, it was hard going. All kinds of rubble littered the streets: broken cars, shattered storefronts. goods that had been dragged from the latter and then left on the sidewalks, furniture and such that had been thrown from higher floors, and the ever-present bits of grisly anatomical detritus left behind by hungry zombies. Infected by the undead contagion, some of these partial carcasses twitched and crawled about in search of their own victims to assault.

While Barry just ignored these half-cadavers, Miss Collard summarily bashed in their heads, putting an end to their post-humous existence. Privately, he saluted her prudence. Dispatching them now meant less to deal with when clean-up time arrived. He let the girl vent her nervous aggression on these minor threats, and reserved his full attention for scanning their immediate territory for hidden perils.

Like up ahead...where a pair of freight trucks sat nose-to-nose, blocking the intersection like a metal wall. From his safe vantage, Barry spotted three men guarding the barricade: two behind the trucks and another on a nearby rooftop. More sentries probably lurked beyond his line of vision.

An enclave of survivors defending their turf, he reflected. Not surprising. New Yorkers were stubborn individuals, fighters. Those who made it through the initial rampage would band together to safeguard entire neighborhoods.

Groups like this posed additional problems for Sanctuary taking possession of the Big Apple. These people had stayed here and fought off dangers, defending their homes. If anything, the city belonged more to them than to any outsiders who might want to move in. In the eyes of these locals, Sanctuary's citizens would be invaders. And these locals would undoubtedly repel any incursion as wholeheartedly as they had fought off the native threats.

Again, these considerations were moot. There was no way Barry and his stalwart companion could successfully rid the city of its riffraff.

But...what if Barry found a way to recruit the locals to the task of cleaning up Manhattan? Having honed their battle skills defending their homes, these survivors could provide valuable assistance to a clean-up operation. That is, if they could be convinced to help.

Well, he mused, *no time like the present to find out.*

Leaning close to Miss Collard, Barry explained, "I'm going to make contact with these people, find out what I can about them. Maybe I can recruit them to help us."

She gave a grave nod.

"You stay out of sight," he continued. "You're my surprise back-up if I need it."

Again, Miss Collard nodded. She moved back, slipping into the shadows of a broken doorway to a lingerie shop.

Barry set forth, creeping from pile of rubble to crumpled car. When he was within twenty yards of the truck-barrier, he chose a suitable mound that would hide him from any rooftop lookouts. Then he called out, "Ahoy. I'm a traveler. I come in peace."

After a momenrt, someone shouted back, "Show yourself."

Plucking a piece of debris (possbly the top panel from a streetside newspaper vending box) from the ground, Barry slowly lifted it beyond the protection of his hiding place. Shots rang out immediately. The first bullet struck nearby, subsequent slugs pelted the raised metal sheet, knocking it from Barry's grasp.

Once the gunfire stopped, Barry yelled, "Uncool."

"Step out where we can see you."

"I don't think so."

"What do you want?"

"I'm passing through. Just wanted to say hello."

"Well then, hello back atcha. Turn around and pass through some-where else."

"Fair enough. I don't want any trouble. Hello…and goodbye."

He waited a minute, but no further communication was thrown from behind the wall of trucks. With a shrug, he retraced his path through the rubble.

When he reached the lingerie shop, Miss Collard hissed from the doorway, "That's it? You're not going to try to befriend them?"

"You saw what they did. They're not looking to make friends."

"But—"

"C'mon. The city's going to be filled with little fortresses like that."

"Maybe the next one will be friendlier."

Barry gave a curt guffaw. "Not likely. They'll all be xenophobic—that's how they've survived this long."

"Then how—"

"Don't worry about it. We're doing recon right now, not recruitment."

"Right."

They retreated along the avenue and headed off down another street.

While they crept through the wreckage, Barry rethought his overall strategy.

What he'd found so far basically fit his expectations. The city was rife with zombies and ruination. The survivors were filled with distrust—wisely so. Cleaning out the undead and the crazies was not just impos-sible, it would be a futile move. Hundreds of enclaves would defend their own territories against all incursions.

But this only gives me an overview of the way things are here. I need more specific information.

I need a snitch.

Reclaiming the SUV, Barry drove them uptown. It was not an easy jour-ney. Innumerable auto wrecks clogged Broadway, traveling more than a hundred feet along the avenue was impossible. He tried East 8th Sreet but the going was scarcely better. He took 8th Street over to head north on 4th Avenue, which proved to be less congested. Several times Barry had to detour around fortified enclaves.

When Miss Collard asked where they were going—and why—Barry gave vague responses. He knew she wouldn't understand. She'd call him foolish, reckless—and to a certain degree her accusation might be accurate. And the nearer he got, the more it looked as if he wasn't going to be able to reach his destination. His fourth detour brought him back to his original position. The 13th Precinct Police Station was completely encircled by barriers. It lay deep within the turf of some enclave.

The efficacy of the enclave's barrier was impressive. Barry even spotted a few gun towers built on rooftops along the perimeter. These people meant business. Back in his days as a detective, the neighborhood had consisted of a variety of shops, among them a deli, a bakery, a coffee cafe, a clothes cleaners, an appliance store, a jewelry outlet. The tradesmen who owned and operated these businesses were not the type to be this knowledgeable about fortification. What he saw now was far beyond anything they could've found in books. Maybe surviving law officers had helped them out. He remembered there was a gun emporium around the corner from the precinct; his fellow officers had preferred its gun range to the one at the station house. Whoever was responsible (perhaps even a conglomerate of militant and mercantile influences) had done a damned good job bottling up this urban fortress.

Finally, Barry was forced to confess his intention to the girl, now that he saw no way of achieving it. She disagreed—not with his goal, but with forsaking it so easily.

"It just so happens I have some familiarity with this neighborhood," she informed him. "Back before the undead outbreak, I used to attend a lot of parties and raves in this district."

"So? I used to work here, and this enclave has every access road barricaded. There's no way in—unless you're going to suggest we go Batman and cross the rooftops." He patted his belly. "And I'm not exactly in tiptop roof climbing condition."

"I was thinking more of a Jules Verne approach."

Images flashed through Barry's mind of sleek metal cylinders conquering outer space or the deepest oceans and crude dirigibles cruising through the clouds. Well, riding a balloon might be a way past the barricade, but where were they going to find such a thing?

"Like *Journey to the Center of the Big Apple*." She smiled, waggled her eyebrows, and continued, "As a cop, you should remember that most raves are staged in unauthorized locations. The crew breaks into a building or facility, sets up the dancefloor, stage and lights—while news of the rave's location gets distributed by texting or word of mouth. Everybody parties hard. And when it's over, the crew packs up and leaves…and the sites' owners are never the wiser."

"What do raves have to do with Jules Verne?"

"You're getting slow, old man," she teased him. "Raves get staged in warehouses, lofts, garages…*basements*."

"Oh."

He got it now. She was talking about the labyrinthine chambers that existed beneath Manhattan: subways, maintenance tunnels, underground parking garages, utility crawlways connecting subterranean generators, not to mention the miles of sewers that ran under the cty.

This enclave had set up barriers on every street and alleyway leading into their neighborhood…but they had probably forgotten about the network of burrows that lurked beneath their feet.

"Yes, a subterranean route could deliver me inside the walled-off territory," he muttered.

"Oh hey," protested Miss Collard. "My idea—I get to come along."

"Too dangerous. No, you stay out here."

"You want to waste hours hunting a safe way in? Or do you want a guide who already knows the way?"

Dammit—she has a point.

"I can do more than take care of myself," she announced. "I can take care of you."

Barry hated giving in, but she was right. Sneaking in there would be extremely dangerous, possibly more than he could handle alone. Backup might come in *very handy* if he ran afoul of the locals. He had no wish to put the girl in harm's way, but he was even less interested in wandering in the dark for hours only to stumble into a trap set to catch sneaky intruders. He was used to having a partner…and Miss Collard would actually make a pretty sharp one. She knew her stuff, had the necessary spunk, and was effective with a gun (or a knife, if silence was an issue).

"Okay," he relented.

They hid the SUV by parking it inside a delicatessen that had been gutted by a fire—her suggestion. (Already her spry mind was proving invaluable. The vehicle would be far safer here than left on the street, where a passing survivor might decide to steal it.)

"Where's the Police Station?" she asked.

He told her its address.

She nodded, retreating behind a pensive expression for a moment, then straightened to exclaim, "Okay—I know how we can get there from here."

Along the street to a tall business building she led him, then down into its basement via a ramp hidden in a tight alley. They moved from the basement to sub-levels, where a series of narrow crawlways took them to an underground reservoir. Not once during this underground journey did they encounter any trouble, alive or undead. The tunnels were vacant of any sentries.

The precinct building had an underground parking facility. This was perfect. She could take him direct to the station without once running into any of the locals. In and out without incident. Barry couldn't be happier.

Eventually, Miss Collard opened a metal door with a magician's flourish. The precinct's underground garage.

Before entering, Barry looked and listened for signs that anyone was out there. His acute hearing detected a murmur from deeper within the murky garage. After a moment, two figures came into view, crossing from an unseen section to the elevator that lay at the far end of the concrete expanse. The figures passed the elevator and disappeared into a dooray that he knew (from experience) let onto a stairwell that gave access to the upper floors of the station house.

He waited a few minutes to make sure no one else would appear. Confident the basement was unoccupied, Barry dashed into the man-made cavern. More than half of the parking spaces were occupied by orderly parked vehicles—black-and-whites, vans, even a bus ussually used to transport prisoners to more permanent incarceration. Some rubbish littered the expanse, but no bodies. A walled-off chamber on the right housed the shooting range which he and his fellow officers had disparaged in favor of the commercial target practice facilities just down the street. At the far end of the basement lay his target: a lone elevator—or more specifically, next to the elevator, the doorway leading to an ascending stairwell. Chances were the building lacked the power to run the elevator, and even if the thing still worked, using it was risky; someone might hear the machinery. Stairs were the ninja way upstairs.

Miss Collard followed closely and quietly on his heels. At this point, she deferred to his familiarity with the terrain.

They took the stairs cautiously, wary of anyone descending from above.

At the second floor landing, Barry cagily cracked the access door to study the region beyond. A few figures moved along the corridor, each intent on some duty. They were, he noted, dressed in casual garb, not police uniforms. After a few minutes, they vanished through doorways that lined the passage. Barry waited an additional few minutes before venturing forth down the hallway. Halfway along, a person stepped into the corridor, headed toward him.

He resisted the urge to halt or dive into one of the open doorways; instead he maintained his pace and adopted an attitude of someone who belonged here. As he and the man passed each other, neither gave any hint of noticing the other. Behind him, the man left the hallway through a door Barry knew led to a men's room. A backwards glance told him that Miss Collard was right behind him; she had waited in the stairwell until the man had gone. But even if he had spotted the girl, would he have raised a suspicios challenge? The locals had no reason to expect any intruders this deep within their territory.

Continuing on, Barry reached the doorway to the squad room and entered it. The room was empty of anyone else. He crossed to the desk that had been his once upon a time. Opening a drawer, he withdrew a palm-sized black notebook and shoved it into his pocket without checking it.

"Done," he announced in a whisper.

Lingering by the doorway, she guarded against any surprises.

Together, they retraced their way along the corridor.

Pausing at a window at the end of the hallway, Barry scrutinized the street outside. The enclave had a working generator. Some lights were hooked into this new power grid. The asphalt and pavement had been cleared of any gruesome refuse. There were no cars in sight, wrecked or still operational. He saw two people (a man and woman) stroll arm-in-arm along the unlittered avenue. At the end of the block, a cafe was lit-up, revealing several patrons inside. Within the boundaries of this enclave, society had been salvaged. This was exactly what the Board wanted to achieve.

Why was it necessary to oust these people and replace them with Sanctuary's populace? Why couldn't they simply coexist?

Because, he told himself, *everybody wants to rule the world.*

"Barry, c'mon!" insisted the girl. She was already halfway through the door to the stairs.

He was about to join her when two men appeared farther down the corridor. They wore police uniforms. They were headed his way. Miss Collard had already ducked inside the stairwell, closing the door behind her. Facing the window, Barry pretended to root through his pockets for something.

As the men drew near, Barry recognized one of the voices from their conversation. A furtive peek confirmed his auditory identification: Deputy Cheif Gann. His immediate superior had survived the zombie outbreak and was a member of this fortified enclave.

It was safe to presume from Gann's presence here that he was probably high up in the enclave's chain of command. That would mean the man was familiar with the ranks of other officers-from-the-old-days who still worked here. Gann would instantly recognize Barry Winsor and realize he did not belong.

What should I do if he spots me?

Before Barry could reach a decision, the men passed along the hallway and left without noticing him. They disappeared through a door that took them into a storage room.

Tension flowed from Barry like water from a punctured plastic bottle. He hadn't expected to run into anyone he knew. Having no familiarity with this enclave's history, how could he have explained his presence here? How many other officers that he knew from the old days—like Deputy Chief Gann—were here? For that matter, what about the Barry Winsor who belonged to this time? Was there another Barry somewhere else in the building?

He was unprepared to deal with these questions.

Abandoning such imponderables, he followed Miss Collard down to the basement and back through the maze of circuitous tunnels.

Early evening had arrived in the city by the time Barry and Miss Collard returned to the street.

Now that he had his notebook, Barry was armed with all his police contacts. Under present circumstances, this wealth of bureaucratic data might have seemed irrelevant—but a few pieces of info might still be valid.

The addresses of fellow officers weren't what he sought. Looking them up might be helpful at some point; if any remained alive and in-town, they could be recruited to his clean-up crew.

No, he wanted the seedier contacts. Details on the lawbreakers he'd been investigating—and the snitches who fed him crucial reports of their doings.

Barry was willing to bet that a good number of those criminals were still out there. A lot of crooks were screw-ups, but some hoodlums were survival types, willing to trample babies if they would profit from doing so. Zombies wouldn't faze them. And they'd thrive on the collapse of civilization.

He wasn't concerned with the hardcore felons right now, their time would come once the clean-up started. Snitches were Barry's immediate interest.

He consulted the list in his notebook.

And look at that—there's one only a few blocks away. Yowel Fredrickson, the snitch whose tip had sent Detective Winsor trailing bagman Titus Roth all over town. What a small post-apocalyptic world it was.

They decided to leave the SUV where it was and travel on foot to Fredrickson's address. Here, deeper into the city, only a few stray zombies wandered the deserted avenues. Miss Collard used her knife like a scythe. Barry wielded his trusty golf clubs. Any undead creatures that were brazen enough to threaten the recon team were easily put down. No active power grid reached beyond the enclave, leaving all the streetlamps dark. The going became problematic; more than once the pair had to retrace their steps to find a clear way along the inky avenues.

Barry recognized the spot without needing to consult the building's address. Years ago, on this very stoop, he had nabbed Fredrickson after chasing him from the grocery the boy had robbed. He remembered tackling the thief, then cuffing him to the iron railing that flanked the building's entrance, before dashing off to help a beat cop chase down Fredrickson's partner-in-crime. The latter had eluded the beat cop, but eventually Barry had coerced Fredrickson to give up his accomplice—in exchange for amnesty in the robbery. From that point on, the boy had been a C.I. for Detective Winsor. All this time and Barry had never realized he'd nailed the kid on the steps to the building in which he lived (which only went to illustrate how inept a crook Fredrickson was).

After all these years (and the collapse of civilization), Barry hoped the snitch was still holed up here; the tenement looked completely abandoned.

Together, Barry and his erstwhile traveling companion entered the building. The foyer was littered with trash, but no cadavers. The girl spotted the stairs and up they went. On the third floor, they skulked down a murky hallway to arrive at number 314, which matched the address in Barry's notebook. The door was locked, but Mis Collard swiftly picked it to admit them.

The apartment was tiny, ill-furnished, and bad-smelling. The snitch was not there.

"What now?" she asked.

"Not sure. I don't relish scouring the city to find other snitches from my list of Criminal Informants. That could take hours, and it's bound to be dangerous. Plus there's no guarantee we'll find any of them at the addresses I have. I don't even know for sure the punk I'm looking for is staying here now."

"Somebody is," she announced. She brought his attention to a styrofoam chest filled with dry goods: somebody's food stash.

So—maybe luck was with Barry on this. Someone occupied Fredrickson's old apartment. If it was him, he simply wasn't home right now. All Barry had to do was wait for his return.

He outlined his plan to Miss Collard. She concurred until he advised her: "You go downstairs and watch the front entrance."

"Oh no," she moaned. "I'm—"

"This time, you're going to follow orders." His tone was firm. "I need you downstairs to watch the street."

Grumbling under her breath, Miss Collard turned to leave with head lowered.

"Wait."

She peered back over her shoulder.

Pulling two walky-talkies from his satchel, he tossed one to her. "Take this. Warn me if anybody shows up."

"What about this Fredrickson guy?"

Barry gave her a quick description so she'd be able to identify the snitch. "If it's Fredrickson, let him pass, then stay downstairs in case someone else shows up."

"You don't expect him to be alone?"

"These days, I don't know what to expect, girl."

"Okay."

She left, and he settled down to wait.

An assortment of junk cluttered the apartment, booty (Barry assumed) from Fredrickson's scavenging. Two whole boxes were filled with pornographic DVDs and video games. In a corner, a pile of DVD players and game consoles sat atop a dusty television set. (A lot of good they were without electricity to power them.) Another box (a metal one, this time) was filled with loose jewelry and wads of bundled-together hundred dollar bills (more swag that was relatively useless post-apocalypse). The closet was packed with expensive Armani suits, all sealed in protective plastic bags. Shoeboxes on the floor of the closet contained more value-less currency. (No wonder Fredrickson lived in a hovel; all of his pillaging had been fixated on luxuries, not survival.) The bed itself was a cheap mattress thrown on a plank supported by cinderblocks—but the sheets were sumptuous satin. A bedside stack of dog-eared skin mags further revealed the snitch's frustrated libido. (Unable to play any of his porno DVDs, he'd apparently resorted to old school measures to satisfy his frustration.) A few pin-ups from the raunchy magazines were pinned to the wall. The styrofoam cooler Miss Collard had spotted contained only a meager selection of junk food, nothing of any nutritional value. A single lounger was the only place Barry felt comfortable sitting, and even then, first he got out a few of Fredrickson's Armani suits and draped them over the chair's questionably stained fabric.

Good God, Yowell, Barry reflected. *The city's an outlaw's paradise—you could crash in an expensive hotel suite, but you choose to live here. I always thought you were a loser—this just corroborates my suspicion.*

Boredom set in. With the passage of hours, that became lethargy, which led to drifting off.

Oh dammit, he fumed as he woke in a hospital bed. *Not now--*

But denial had no effect on the reality of his plight.

He'd been displaced…once again abandoning Miss Collard in a perilous situation.

So…where—or when—am I now?

Right away Barry knew something was wrong. Besides an overwhelming exhaustion, he was blind in one eye. When he raised his left hand to his face, he discovered he wore a conventional eye-patch. Even with his limited vision, he could tell this was a different hospital room than the one in which that crazy doctor had tranqed him. That had been a private room, where here several other beds, all unoccupied, lined the walls. Many more tubes ran from bedside machines to his reclining form. A large bay window looked out upon a grandiose cityscape with dawn spilling through majestic clouds. It took him a moment to realize the city he was looking at had suffered no apocalypse.

I'm back before the outbreak…but with an eye infection I don't remember having.

When the door opened, a matronly women entered. She was dressed in white like a nurse. He could not recall ever having met this woman, but there was something enigmatically familiar about her. In his lethargic condition, he couldn't concentrate. When she spoke, though, the years had not unduly changed her voice, and he recognized the woman as Miss Collard—a much older Miss Collard than he knew.

Damn…

This meant he hadn't been sent back. He'd been displaced forward into his own future.

"I see you're awake again, Mr Winsor," she remarked.

"And disoriented, I'm afraid," he confessed weakly. "How did I get here?" He almost asked what date it was, but judiciously stopped himself. To match the girl's advanced age, it was apparent that Barry must be in his seventies. No wonder he felt so tired.

A worried look crossed her weathered face. "Oh dear…"

"It's okay," he assured her. "I remember most everything else…who I am and who you are…our time together on-the-road…"

"Is this one of your I've-come-unstuck-in-time episodes?

She knew about his temporal displacements? Or…no—her tone was rich with commiserating disapproval. She was talking about an old man's delusions. At some point, he'd told her about his affliction, but she hadn't believed him. That made him feel sad.

Weariness crept up and doused Barry with an devastating wave of dizziness. What he could see with his single eye grew hazy and Miss Collard's matronly face retreated down a murky tunnel. Darkness ultimately embraced him.

This time, something woke Barry. A noise.

He came alert, but the unfamiliar surroundings confused him. He was seated, but his abrupt awakening sent him sliding from the lounge-chair. Something crinkled beneath him as he landed on the floor.

It was dark, but enough moonlight fell through a grimy window to reveal a tiny room cramped by boxes. He was on the floor by the lounge-chair with a pile of plastic-wrapped Armani suits under his ass. He was back in Fredrickson's hovel!

"What the hell—" came an exclamation.

He wasn't alone. Someone had just entered the room. A figure poised in the doorway for a fleeting second before whirling about and dashing away.

"Hey," Barry grunted. He tried to leap after the visitor, but his legs got tangled in the crumpled Armani suit. By the time he reached the door, the figure was gone. Barry ran down the hallway after it.

In the dark, he'd caught too brief a glimpse of the visitor. He couldn't tell if it had been Yowell Fredrickson or some other lowlife. Either way, chasing him seemed like the smart thing to do. When he got to the end of the corridor, Barry spotted no fleeing figure down either of the shadowy hallways that branched off at this point. But the stairwell door was just creaking shut. He wrenched it open and entered an even deeper darkness.

Why hadn't Miss Collard notified him that someone had entered the building?

He had pounded down half-a-dozen steps before he realized that the lowlife's fleeing footfalls came from above, not below. The guy was heading for the roof.

This was why no warning call had come from Miss Collard. The intruder had entered the building from above...and was using the same route for his hasty departure.

It's not Yowell, he told himself. Fredrickson wasn't this smart.

It didn't matter to Barry. Fredrickson or some other thug—either one would serve his purposes this evening.

Halting his descent, Barry scrambled around and headed up the stairs. After two flights at top speed, his heart was pounding in his chest louder than the echoing thunder of his feet striking the steps. Each breath was a gasp. He wasn't incapacitated, just winded.

All those damned cigarettes...

He caught up to the thug on the top floor. The fool had gotten his jacket caught in the jamb of the exit door as it had swung open. Completely unaware what had grabbed him, the intruder thrashed and cursed. He strained to escape, shoving the door open as far as it would go and consequently tigthening the grasp the jamb had on his jacket.

Barry got his attention by sticking the barrel of his semi-automatic rifle in the guy's face. This made the thug recoil. He lost his footing and ended up on his ass, staring up at Barry. Moonlight revealed the intruder's blunt gawk.

"Long time, Yowell."

Wonder replaced panic as Fredrickson gaped up at Barry. "Detective Winsor...?"

"Uh huh."

"Uh—imagine runnin' into you...after all tha's happened..."

Barry kicked him softly. "Up."

He led the snitch back downstairs.

"Thought I'd pop in and check up on you, boy."

"Umm...well, guess I'm doin' okay..."

"Really? Your life doesn't suck?" At gunpoint, he guided Fredrickson back into his disreputable apartment. "I mean, what with all the zombies and the collapse of civilization, everybody else's life sucks something awful these days. But—not you, huh, Yowell? You're doing okay? Coping? Flourishing?"

"Hey—don't try to pin any of that on me, man!" Fredrickson bridled, but indignity looked ridiculous on his doughy face. "I had nothin' to do with that shit. I'm jus' tryin' to stay alive, okay?"

"Living the high life, are you, in your tiny hovel with your porno mags?"

"What the hell do you want, copper? Y'know there's no more police force, right? Not since thin's fell apart—the 'collapse of civilization,' like you put it. So you ain't got no authority to push me around—"

"Shut up, Yowell."

"—or make any wild accusations or anythin'. Cuz I—"

Barry pumped a single shot into the wall next to Fredrickson's head. The snitch twitched, aghast and deafened, as he fell onto his bed. Sprawled there, Fredrickson gawked up at the detective.

"I told you to shut up, Yowel."

Dragging the loungechair from the wall, Barry positioned it facing the bed. Before seating himself, he pulled the crumpled Armani suit from the floor and draped it covering the chair. He settled into the chair with the rifle cradled in his lap, pointed at the figure cowering on the bed.

"I have some questions," he told the snitch, "and I'm really hoping you can help me out."

"Huh?"

"I have some questions," Barry repeated louder for the momentarily deaf punk.

"What kinda questions?"

"Current events. News around town sort of stuff."

"How would I know stuff like that?"

"Because you live here, Yowell. And if you didn't know the lay of the land, you wouldn't still be alive. I want to know everybody's dirty little secrets."

"What makes ya think I know anythin' like that?"

"You're a bottom-feeder, Yowell. You stay alive by knowing everybody's secrets—and selling them back and forth."

Fredrickson chewed his stubborn lip for a moment before responding, "Whadda I get in exchange?"

A belly laugh escaped from Barry. "That's pretty good, kid. I haven't had a decent laugh in a long time."

"Quid per quo, detective."

This time, Barry restricted his mirth to just a rueful smirk. "It's 'quid *pro* quo,' Yowell. And the rule doesn't apply when one of the participants has a gun pointed at the other's guts." The rifle barrel twitched in his lap to emphasize the point. "But out of respect for our history together, Yowell, I'm not going to shoot you. There must be another incentive I can find to get you to talk."

Stretching out his left leg, Barry hooked his foot around one of the shoeboxes and dragged it from the closet. He picked it up, tossing aside its cardboard lid and exposing stacks of bundled hundred dollar bills. All the while, he kept the rifle aimed squarely at Fredrickson. With his other foot, Barry moved a cheap tin trashcan over to the foot of the bed. He emptied half the currency from the shoebox into the trashcan. Balancing the lightened box on his thigh, he used his free hand to take out a cigarette and light it. Moving with exaggerated gestures, Barry held the still-lit match out before him and dropped it into the can.

Even before the match was halfway down, Fredrickson blurted "Hey!" and lurched on the bed, his butt sliding across the satin sheets. Barry's rifle barrel tracked his movement and halted the punk as he teetered on the edge of the mattress.

There was no satisfying *woosh*. The flame spread tediously from the curled carboard stump to the bills. Eventually, however, the trashcan contained a minor conflagration.

The snitch thrust out his jaw in an expression of angry refusal. After a moment of this, Barry tipped some more money from the shoebox into the trashcan. This time there was a *woosh* as the tongues of fire danced higher.

"Stop me when you're satisfied with the price," chuckled Barry. He tossed another bundle of bucks into the pyre.

"Okay okay—stop! I'll tell ya wha'ever ya wanna know! Jus' don't burn any more of my money!"

"Start with an overview of what's left of the city."

Relevant information gushed from the snitch's now-agile lips.

The town was mainly split between three factions. The Panthers held everything above 125th Street. The York Nostra's turf included everything east of Broadway. The Curly Boys ruled everything west. (No wonder Broadway had been such an obstacle course, the avenue served as a demarcation line between empires.) In truth, none of these self-proclaimed empires possessed the gumption to back up their claims. Consequently, local enclaves were popping up with the moxy to declare their own independence. Most of these groups were more into shouting matches than doing anything useful, though. Chaos and the undead threatened everyone. "Some days it's jus' impossible to go outside without havin' to fight yer way across the street, man."

Initially, Barry let the kid's outline flow freely and jotted a few particulars in his notebook. After a bit, though, Fredrickson's focus began to wander and Barry had to nudge him back on-course with specific questions.

"So, the three main factions are just blowhards who lack the firepower to enforce their dominion."

"Always issuin' proclamations an' stagin' stupid parades. But yeah, nobody pays much attention to 'em. People mostly banded together accordin' to neighborhoods."

That would mean hundreds of little kingdoms existed throughout Manhattan, each bound to zealously guard their sovereignty. "Cleaning-up" this mess could take years.

"There's this group of bankers on Wall Street," Fredrickson snickered. "They think money still runs everythin'. I'm a major broker for 'em. Nobody else bothered to stockpile hard cash."

So maybe Fredrickson wasn't as delusional as Barry had thought... hoarding all that currency in boxes in his closet. At least one of the snitch's clients dealt in obsolete cash.

Most of the city's utilities had still been functional when Barry left town months ago. Phones had been the first network to fail, along with that went the internet. Then the failure of the power grid had knocked out everything.

"What about the utilities?"

"Water still works, least in most parts of th' city. As far as electricity goes, a few small outfits have restored power, but th' best they've done is light up their own neighborhoods."

"Like the group a few blocks east of here."

"What, ya mean th' Local Blues? They're a nasty bunch, copper. You'd be smart to avoid them altogether."

Barry underlined the name he'd just written down.

"Why?"

"I jus' told ya—they're a nasty bunch. Bad-tempered an' armed to th' teeth, man."

"From their name—the Local Blues—can I presume this group was organized by local police officers?" Barry already suspected this, from Deputy Chief Gann's presence in the station house, but he hoped Fredrickson would confirm that suspicion. A strong ex-cop presence among the Local Blues also might explain why the snitch was so vehement about having no contact with them.

"Maybe at first, but a rougher crowd moved in an' took over a while back."

"Who?"

Fredrickson gave an insincere shrug. "Like I told ya, they're a nasty bunch. I stay away from them, an' so should you."

"Aw now, Yowell, the Q&A was going so good, and then you have to spoil things by withholding information." As Barry pouted, he reached over and plucked a pair of the snitch's bedside porn magazines to dangle them over the burning trashcan.

"Aw man, I'm not—"

"You expect me to believe you're living blocks away from this Local Blues group and you have no contact with them? I wasn't an idiot in the old days, Yowell, and fighting zombies hasn't made me any dumber."

"Okay okay—but I deal with scouts an' guys guardin' their perimeter, not the head honchos."

"But you know who they are."

Fredrickson released a long sigh, then confessed, "Yeah, okay, maybe I heard some rumors."

"Rumors can be satisfying…if they're good ones."

"Well, two of th' guys I trade with, they used to belong to Snappy's crew."

Barry knew who he meant. Snappy Rogers ran an enforcer crew out of a bowling alley south of Houston. But…Snappy was a thug; he lacked the brains to pull off an operation as big—and as *efficient*—as what Barry had witnessed. These days, the Detective suspected the enforcer answered to someone higher up the tainted foodchain.

Additional verbal probes failed to get Fredrickson to name anyone else, though, Either the snitch really didn't know, or he was *really* afraid of whoever ran the Blues.

"Why ya so interested in th' Local Blues, anyway?" whined Fredrickson. "Oh wait—yer old precinct house is over there, ain't it? Man, believe me, I'm bein' straight with ya when I tell ya to steer clear of the Blues, okay? They're a nasty bunch."

Barry smiled. "I appreciate your concern for my health, Yowell. I'll be sure to remember you in my prayers."

"Jus' tryin' to be helpful…"

"Oh, you've been a big help, Yowell." Barry tossed the nearly empty shoebox back into the closet. Sitting back, he flipped his notebook closed and hoisted the rifle to point at the ceiling. "We're done."

Squirming on the edge of the bed, Fredrickson grunted, "Uhh…"

"You can go."

"But—this is my place…"

With a theatrical sigh, Barry lowered the gun. "For heaven's sake, kid, get out of here before you ruin my good mood."

Rising, Fredrickson moved jerkily across the room. Just shy of the door, he paused to survey his possessions and moan, "Yer not gonna burn any more of my stuff, are ya?"

"Go, Yowell."

Yanking open the door, he came up short on the threshold. A figure stood outside in the hallway.

"Boo!"

With a terrified squeal, Fredrickson squeezed past and fled down the corridor.

A giggling Miss Collard stepped into the dingy room. "I'm sorry. I couldn't resist."

"I thought I told you stay downstairs."

"I checked in with you a while ago." She touched the walky-talkie clipped at her waist. "But you didn't answer. I figured you were busy. But then I heard a shot, I came running. When I got up here, I could hear you through the door. You had everything under control, so I hung back and waited to see what happened."

All plausible interpretations of events. Barry assumed her call had come through during his brief nap; his walky-talkie hadn't roused him because he'd been temporarily displaced to the far future. All things considered, abandoning her post wasn't all that grievous—she'd done so thinking she was coming to his aid. If their roles had been reversed, and Barry had been the one to hear a shot, he'd've gone to check on her. At least she'd been sharp enough not to barge in when she found the situation wasn't a hazardous one.

"Sounds like you got what you wanted."

He nodded. "More than enough."

"So—what's our next move?"

"Recon's done, girl. It's time for us to get the hell out of Dodge."

Sanctuary's Board of founding fathers did not like what Barry had to report about conditions in the Big Apple. Dr Heigl contributed no comments, but the other profs voiced more than enough complaints to compensate for his silence.

"All of this data is too abstract. Where are the specifics?"

"You conducted no interviews with any actual citizens of these enclaves you mentioned?"

"Did you spend time studying these enclaves? To verify any of the information your snitch gave you?"

"How are we supposed to believe anything this man told you? By your own description, he was a criminal back when you knew him before the outbreak."

"Perhaps we acted prematurely appointing you to handle this project. Maybe this is beyond the capabilities of a simple beat cop—excuse me, of a simple 'detective.'"

Suppressing exasperation, Barry reminded them they had asked him to condense and simplify his report. "Maybe the details you want will be in the long written report you expect me to write." But Barry had no intention of wasting his time scribing the details of his recon for posterity. Details were poignantly sparse in his account because they were rendered moot by the overall assessment. Any realistic appraisal of the basic facts showed how impractical the Board's clean-up project was. Details wouldn't change that reality.

Cleaning-up Manhattan was an impossible task. The city was rife with small enclaves who would resist any external interference. Many of these gangs were armed and dangerous.

"We have an ample supply of explosives," asserted Professor Kaufmann.

"And if you use enough bombs to crush these groups," countered Barry, "all you'll be doing to destroying the territory you intend to repopulate."

"We can be discreet in our targeting."

"Bombs aren't discreet. They destroy everything. You'll just end up with a lot of blown-up buildings."

"Perhaps if you had gathered more detailed information about these feudal states, their weaknesses would be more obvious."

"Besides," Barry insisted, "we lack the manpower to do anything."

"That deficiency is only temporary."

Finally, Dr Heigl spoke. "We thank you, Commander Winsor, for your inadequate report. You may go." He busied himself sorting a pile of papers before him.

As Barry left, Heigl tossed after him, "Please send in Miss Collard on your way out. We can only hope her account is more useful than yours."

The girl rolled her eyes for him as they passed each other in the open doorway. He sympathized with her attitude. Her report would satisfy them no more than his had.

"They're fools."

Doc Toby lifted his glass in support of Barry's declaration. "To the Board's stupidity," he toasted.

Upon leaving the factory, Barry had run into the mock doctor. Immediately sensing Barry's foul mood, the Doc had invited him back to the clinic to unwind. To facilitate this "unwinding," he produced a bottle of bourbon. "As a rule, the Board think they conscript all the alcohol—but I retain a certain supply for antiseptic...and other purposes."

Initially, Barry had accepted to be polite. He'd nursed his first glass for a while, but the Doc's relentless toasts had earned them both several refills. Soon, Barry had a warm buzz going.

"My assessment of the situation is accurate. It's my town, I know it better than they do."

"You would, yes."

"I was a cop there for fifteen years."

"Long time."

"I know the city better than they could ever hope to."

"To your superior understanding of the situation." The Doc hefted his glass in another toast.

"New Yorkers are stubborn bastards. They'll never let outsiders prance in and take over—not without a fight."

"And some of them are pretty well fortified, from your account."

"What makes the Board think they'll be better leaders than these enclaves already have?"

"Eminent arrogance," chuffed Doc Toby.

"Sanctuary doesn't have the trained manpower necessary to take even one of those enclaves, much less the entire city. Those fools're going to get everybody killed."

"Not that it matters…we're all dead already."

"Dammit—Miss Collard'll back me up with her report."

"Yeah, but the Board won't listen. They want to reclaim Manhattan—at any cost. They'll cut a deal with the devil if that's what's necessary to get it done."

"Well, I refuse to do it," announced an inebriated Barry. "I won't lead any squad of novices against those enclaves. I have enough blood on my hands already—I refuse to add to my sins."

"To our sins, Barry."

He awoke to find someone kicking him in the leg.

"What—"

"You idiot. Now is not the time for this bullshit! I thought you had your drinking under control."

My drinking?

Oh, right. Doc Toby had a bottle. He'd tried to keep his drinking to a minimum, but things had gotten out of hand.

Another kick, again to the same leg.

"Cut it out," he moaned.

Unable to return to the warm oblivion of sleep, Barry fished through his pockets until he found his cigarettes. He was fumbling one from the pack when someone slapped it from his clumsy fingers.

"Hey—"

"Wake up, dammit!"

So far, the voice had just been shrill and annoying, but enough cognition had crept back into Barry's brain for him to recognize the voice: Miss Collard. What was the matter? Why was she tormenting him like this?

"The Board have called a war council," she shouted at him. "This time, you really need to attend, Barry!"

He struggled past disorientation to catch the anger in the girl's tone. "You're pissed at me—why? What'd I do? I've been drinking with the Doc…"

Sitting up, he lurched to his feet, but didn't stay up for too long. With windmilling arms, he toppled back on the sofa. His fall jolted more awareness into him.

He sat in his own living room, not the clinic. And where was Doc Toby?

Have I suffered another displacement?

"You may've started with Doc Toby, but you've been on a binge for days, Barry."

"Days...?"

"You've already missed several war councils. Things are progressing out of control. They need a voice of stability. Lord knows, they won't listen to me."

Days? And the hazy details of the last few days rose from a murky pool in his mind. He'd started drinking with Doc Toby, but when the Doc had run out of booze, Barry'd come home to continue on his own. Where had he gotten the alcohol? It didn't matter; the bottles scattered around him were all empty. It had been a major binge. After all his efforts to cope with his drinking problem, his frustration with the Board's obstinate attitude had peaked, triggering a descent into besotted apathy. He felt embarrassed.

Especially so to have Miss Collard find him in this miserable state.

From her words, it seemed the girl had long been aware of his problem. She had never mentioned it to him (possibly out of respect?)—until now. She was really pissed off this time.

Something about him missing a bunch of war councils...

War councils?

Oh damn—the Board's going ahead with the clean-up!

"I need to be at this new war council," he grumbled. He tried to struggle to his feet, but couldn't manage it.

"Yes, you do," proclaimed Miss Collard. "But first you need to sober up—and take a bath—you stink."

A shower would shock some sobriety back into him. But...he couldn't get to the bathroom on his own. He had to suffer the additional humiliation of the girl helping him get there. Dumping him in the shower stall, she turned on the water. He slumped there, fully-dressed and drenched, but it worked. Within seconds, the cold water had freed him of the cloudy influence of his intoxication.

He divested himself of his sodden clothes and found a fresh shirt and slacks. He regarded himself in the bathroom mirror and was not too thrilled with what he saw. His mind might be clear now, but his face still retained all the earmarks of a drunk. His eyes were bloodshot behind wearily drooping lids. A nest of broken capillaries colored his nose. His hair (what little was left) refused to flatten against his scalp. His forehead was ridged by worry-lines that wouldn't go away. He repeatedly found his lips hanging slack and tightened them into a forceful grimace…but seconds later he would discover they'd relaxed again to hang ajar like some imbecile.

Back in the living room, an irate Miss Collard waited. "You still look awful," she shared her disappointment with his appearance.

"Yeah," he reluctantly agreed.

"Let's go—before they make any regretable decisions."

Halfway across the room, Barry spotted a bottle that still contained some liquid. Brown. Whiskey. He scooped it up and took a healthy swig.

A groan escaped the girl.

"Hair of the dog," he gasped before taking another gurgling gulp. "Trust me, this'll sort me out…" It sounded like a drunken excuse, but Barry knew that some truth lay in the ritual. A third hit was enough to sharpen his wits.

"Okay, let's go."

She tried to brief him on the things he'd missed while lost in his drunken stupor, but he couldn't concentrate on her words. The day was too bright, the air too crisp. A group of children played on a home's front lawn; their squealing penetrated his head like a nine inch spike. The colors tainting the soil underfoot started strobing in waves converging on the factory's entryway.

He was too distracted to notice the changes that had overtaken parts of the settlement. More vehicles were parked inside the main gate, which was now overlooked by armed guards. More sentries lurked around the entrance to the factory.

Oblivious to these things, Barry marched into the factory. Without breaking stride, he continued on into the depths of the building. Miss Collard followed on his heels, anxiously asking if he'd been listening to her.

The conference room was packed. Additional chairs surrounded the long table, all were filled. And rows of men with guns lined the walls. Although still somewhat bleary-eyed, Barry recognized a few of them.

Dr Heigl did not occupy the end of the table; instead he sat among the other profs, almost as if he was in hiding. Someone else stood at the head of the table: Dusty in his sex club black leather. As Barry froze just inside the doorway, several heads turned to acknowledge his presence.

"Damn," grunted Dusty. "I thought you were joking. But no—there he is, big as life and twice as ugly."

At his side, Runt scowled but added no derision to his master's greeting.

"You," Barry gasped.

Behind him, Miss Collard hissed, "I tried to warn you."

"Please come in, Commander Winsor." Professor Kaufmann forced another prof to vacate a seat on the near side of the table, then indicated Barry should take it. "We're glad you could finally make it to one of these meetings." His voice was rich with scorn.

"Where you been hiding yourself, Winsor?" laughed Dusty. "They told me you were around, but I was starting to believe you were just a figment of their imagination."

Barry's gaze scanned the room. Several of the men lining the walls were familiar to him from his time with the Raiders—Red Ryder, Petey Pete, and—big surprise—Sheldon Bowman. All of the founding fathers were present. As was Doc Toby.

Old facts fell into place inside Detective Winsor's head. Sheldon had mentioned being in contact with other learned individuals via shortwave radio. It wasn't all that surprising that Dr Heigl (or another of Sanctuary's profs) were among Sheldon's long-distance acquaintances. Heigl had reached out to enlist additional troops for his clean-up project, probably contacting several widespread pockets of intelligentsia besides Sheldon. Smelling a mother lode of loot and mayhem, Dusty had graciously volunteered the services of his Raiders. The founding fathers thought they had accumulated an army, but all they'd really done was open their gates to a swarm of vipers.

All this while Barry had been lost on a binge.

Struggling to maintain his cool, Barry wandered over and took the seat offered by Kaufmann. As he sat, he noticed a large map of Manhattan was spread on the table. The map bore numerous markings, some of these Xs were surrounded by red boxes. *The locations of enclaves? The boxes must indicate which ones had walled defenses.* Somebody had clearly conducted subsequent recons into the city, collecting data regarding the gangs' territories.

How long was my binge?

Looking up from the map, Barry's gaze met with Sheldon's. The egocentric Fix-It man curled his lip at Barry. *Yup, the gang's all here, and they brought along their trusty opinions.*

"So," Barry sighed, "you're really going through with this…"

"Of course," chirped Professor Adams.

"The city is aching for a restoration of law and order," Professor Kaufmann added.

"Aching," chuckled Dusty.

"They're all visionaries with their heads lost in the clouds," Barry announced with a sweeping gesture. He fixed his stare on the head Raider and continued, "But you, Dusty—I know you're realistic enough to see how impossible this is. You're looking at forcibly evicting thousands of New Yorkers from their homes. They're not going to go quietly into the night."

"Much less, all the zombies you'll have to deal with." Miss Collard had come to stand just behind Barry.

Dusty puffed up his chest. "I think my crew's up to it."

"You'd need an army ten times bigger to even begin to clean up the city," Doc Toby chided from the sidelines.

"Hardly," remarked Dusty. "Just careful planning…and a few handy bombs."

"We've been training his men to handle high explosives," Professor Kaufmann mentioned.

The Raiders were savage enough with their own guns and knives and distempers. Putting grenades in their hands was sheer madness. Nothing good could come of this. The marauders would slaughter everyone.

"It's one thing to propose cleaning all the zombies out of the city—that's a laudable ambition," Barry addressed the profs. "But you intend to treat everybody else as a hostile force. That's wrong—on so many levels. These people have managed to revive pockets of civilization on their own and you plan to destroy that—just to replace it with your own brand of civilized behavior. What makes your system any better than what they already have? How can you justify the use of force against them?"

"If they join us, there'll be no need for force," Professor Kaufmann defended their policy.

"But that's the problem—nobody's going to just 'join' you, not if you show up and start tossing bombs at them."

Professor Dracy smirked. "Now you're rearranging cause and effect, Commander Winsor. There'll be no need to deploy explosives if they accept our dominion."

"You mean if they surrender."

Several profs shrugged.

"This isn't semantics we're arguing here," protested Barry. "We're talking about people's lives. New Yorkers and ours. Because, trust me, you're going to find that these locals are tough mothers. They'll fight to defend their freedom."

"They can only truly be free by joining us," Dr Heigl finally contributed something. His conviction frightened Barry. Heigl earnestly believed that his doctrines were superior to all others. If you refused to live according to his rules, you were summarily relinquishing the right to live. Barry had thought Sheldon was the ego king, but Heigl had him beat by miles.

"Why would anyone prefer to live in squalor and oppression on their own?" Sheldon put forth.

They're all crazy. The Board thinks it has a divine right to "civilize" these primitive New Yorkers. While Dusty and his Raiders are only concerned with booty and bloodshed, preferably the latter before the former. They've all lost their common sense and common decency.

But—to openly condemn the Board's scheme won't help anybody. Dusty's men will throw me and all other dissenters into confinement right away—if they don't shoot us outright as traitors.

The wisest move is to play along...and see if there's some way to discredit the plan.

Reaching out, Barry fingered the map on the table. He muttered, "You can't do it all at once."

"Of course not," scoffed Dusty.

"It'll take a long time."

"Not necessarily. New troops can be recruited from each enclave we bring into the fold. Our ranks will continue to grow with each victory."

And you'll put these new recruits on the front line, sparing any more Raider losses.

A nod was called for here, so Barry dipped his head with thoughtful lassitude.

He tapped the map. "All these notations—they're accurate?"

"Of course," declared Dusty. "We've been sending scouts into the city for almost a week."

My binge lasted longer than a week?

"While you were off hiding, Commander Winsor, Dusty's men have been industrious little soldiers," Professor Kaufmann added snidely.

"That brings up a sensitive point," spoke Dr Heigl.

The other profs all turned to hear his announcement. Barry noticed Dusty notice this. For whatever reason, Heigl sought to blend into the ranks of the founding fathers, but the deference they all gave the man had betrayed him as the Board's real leader.

"I believe," Dr Heigl continued, "that Mr Winsor's recent disinvolvement in this project illustrates his lack of faith in it. I propose he be stripped of his Commander rank, and Mr Dusty be appointed to that position."

As one, the assembled profs banged the table with their palms and decried, "Aye!"

Demoting me—is that supposed to hurt my feelings?—make me less of a man?

For all of his political savvy, Dr Heigl was quite incompetent when it came to understanding human nature. As if taking away his title emasculated Barry.

"Why, thank you for your vote of confidence," beamed Commander Dusty. "I'd like to keep Winsor around, though."

A scowl darkened Heigl's brow. "But he openly denounces the project."

"As a consultant," Dusty qualified his judgment. "He knows the terrain better than any of my men."

"But—"

"As well as his little girlfriend," added Dusty. "She's exhibited enough spunk that I'll want her among my assault teams."

"They both are dissidents."

"I say they're invaluable to the project. Call it a *command* decision."

"What game you playing, Dusty?"

"Game? Hah—not me, Winsor. My entire agenda's right out there for everybody to see. Got no secrets, pal. Not like you—you're full of secrets, ain't you?"

After the meeting, the various parties went their separate ways. The founding fathers disappeared into the depths of the factory. Barry, Miss Collard and Doc Toby took refuge under the awning outside the clinic. They watched Dusty and his men retreat to a stretch of land away from the building and the settlement; they had parked their trucks and trailers by the gate just inside the fenced perimeter. After exchanging a few token insults regarding the Board's collective stupidity, the Doc went indoors to see a newly arrived patient. Joey Fulton strolled over and Miss Collard accompanied the lad back to their house. Barry lingered on the stoop of the grocery store, studying the Raiders. Eventually, Dusty (without his crony shadow Runt in tow) wandered over to offer Barry a drink from a bottle of whiskey he carried. Barry took a token sip, but refrained from any further consumption.

"You don't believe in the Board's recivilization dream," he accused the head Raider. "You're here to use their clean-up scheme as an excuse to plunder and slaughter innocents."

"You think those highbrows are so clueless they don't suspect that? Don't kid yourself. They know; they just can't do anything about it. All the suspicion in the world don't put any food on the table, y'know what I mean?"

"So why do you want me around?"

"Because you're our resident Manhattan authority. I wasn't bullshitting about that. Things'll go a lot easier with you around."

"Don't expect me to help you."

"Y'know your problem, Winsor? You let yourself get bogged down with outmoded ethics."

"Ethics are never outmoded."

"Hell they aren't. The world's changed. So have the definitions of right and wrong."

"In your dreams."

"No, really. Nowadays, if a zombie shambles on up to you, you can put a bullet in its head and everything's okay. Couldn't do that in the old days. That would've been—what?—desecrating a corpse. They'd've locked you up for that. But now, hell, you get a standing ovation."

"You can twist words all you want, but you aren't going to convince me that your way is acceptable. You and your crew get off on mayhem and killing."

"Look who's talking. The guy who conned the Raiders to wipe out a colony of cannibals."

"I didn't tell you to slaughter them."

"But you knew we would. Their blood's on your hands too, Winsor."

"The world's a better place without them."

"Mr Ethical gets judgmental. See? If you start thinking like that, today's world is an easier place to live in."

"I'll never be like you."

"Another one of your problems: you got no sense of self-preservation. Probably a hangover from your cop days, huh? All that pious attitude. To serve and protect. Well, times have changed, Winsor. The old ways are dead. You got to look out for number one now. Heh, but you're too busy keeping an eye out for zombies that want to chew on your face or crazies who want to cut off your ears and eat them. You got to beware of everybody these days. They all want a piece of you."

"Were you always this pessimistic?"

"Hell no. I'm a product of my environment. In the old days, everybody used to look down on me because I was a garbage collector. People thought I was scum—boy, sometimes I ached to haul off and kick them in their smug balls. How long would their precious society have lasted if nobody'd hauled away their trash? Well, today, I'll bet most of those assholes ended up as zombie dinners, while me—I'm a survivor." Dusty took a hard gulp from the whiskey bottle, then gave Barry a sideways glance. "So are you…I just ain't figured out how you pull it off, balancing your namby-pamby pacifism with your latent bloodthirsty nature."

"I am *not* bloodthirsty."

"Denial won't make it go away. But if you did succeed in purging yourself of every violent tendency, you wouldn't last an hour. Violence equals survival these days. And you're a survivor. So's your little girlfriend."

"Leave her out of this."

"Ooh, touchy, are we? Feeling a little guilty dipping the wick in such a young—"

Instead of being offended, Barry just laughed. "Sorry to disappoint you, Dusty, but we're not an item. She's just a friend. She has her own boyfriend."

"That punk kid I saw with her? Like *that's* going to last. Hell, I wouldn't mind a taste of that."

"Think of me as her father figure."

"Okay, sorry. I didn't mean to be vulgar. I was just kidding around. See? That's another problem you got: you have no sense of humor. You got a lot of problems, pal."

"We're a team. If you want her to help you clean-up Manhattan, you're going to need me along. We're a package deal."

"So, you've decided you'll help…"

"No—I'm telling you that if you want my help, you have to do things my way."

"Let me guess…your way involves no killing."

"And no unnecessary property damage."

"How do you expect us to convince these New Yorkers to join our cause if we can't use force? According to you, they're ready to fight all comers."

"There's a thing called diplomacy that's been known to work wonders."

Dusty gave a forced laugh. "Can you see me trying to get the Raiders to curtail their rambunctious nature?"

"They do what you tell them to…"

"No, Winsor. That's another of your problems. You think people faithfully follow directions—they don't. Most people don't like being told what to do. My Raiders do what I tell them—because I tell them to do what they already want to do. That's the earmark of a smart leader."

"Then you need to convince these New Yorkers they don't mind the Board moving in with a whole new set of rules."

"Ha! That's your job, Winsor. Why do you think I'm keeping you around?"

With that, Dusty took a final swig from the whiskey bottle and strolled away.

8

COMMANDER DUSTY KEPT THE TARGET of the project's initial strike a secret from everyone. The founding fathers voiced a token protest, but in truth they didn't care which enclave was going to be the first to fall to Sanctuary's new brand of civilization; they just resented being excluded from the loop. The Raiders didn't care, as long as, in the end, they were unleashed on a hapless crowd of New Yorkers.

Barry suspected that he was the one Dusty wanted to keep in ignorance. By doing so, the Commander avoided any argument Barry might produce to spare the enemy. Even Miss Collard had no idea which enclave was targeted on this premiere run.

Worry for the witless victims helped Barry lose sleep.

Lately, Barry had come to distrust sleep. It was always during slumber (or unconsciousness) that his displacements occurred. Now that the Board's clean-up project was about to start, Barry had resolved to remain at Dusty's side throughout the operation—to help or hinder, depending on which course would result in the least casualties. He couldn't afford to be whisked away at this crucial stage; not every displacement had returned him to his point of departure.

A voice of sanity was necessary at Dusty's side.

The convoy of Raider vehicles did not slow down as it neared the Hudson Tunnel. Barry rode with the Commander in his armored Ferrari.

"You should beware up ahead, Dusty," he confided. "Miss Collard and I encountered unfriendly groups guarding this end of the tunnel. This was all in our report of our initial recon."

Dusty was in the front passenger position. His sycophant crony, Runt, drove. Barry and Miss Collard rode in the cramped backseat.

Exhibiting a smug grin, Dusty twisted in his seat to address his consultants. "I read the girl's report, Winsor. Don't worry. My crew have spent the last two days eliminating any troublesome opposition we might encounter here."

Dammit, Barry grumbled to himself. The first strike hasn't even begun yet, and the bastard's already slaughtered a bunch of innocents. He sat back and folded his arms across his chest to brood.

The territory they rolled through showed no evidence of any battle. Either the mayhem had occurred farther back from the throughway, or the Raiders had cleaned up their gruesome handiwork. Somehow, Barry doubted the latter; he couldn't envision the marauders showing any tidiness after their bloodthirsty massacre.

Miss Collard leaned against him. When Barry shifted his gaze to her, she quietly informed him, "It's okay, Barry. I saw the footage of the assaults. These guys were holding women prisoner—"

"There's footage?!" Barry was horrified. "Dusty, you sick bastard—"

"Hey, reviewing our attack helped my crew refine their skills," remarked Dusty. "Don't act so outraged. We eliminated the slave traders and freed a bunch of girls." He threw a significant glance over his shoulder and added, "At least we assume they were slavers. For all we know, they were a group of cannibals planning to kill the girls and eat them."

Barry dimly recalled a pair of trucks arriving yesterday at Sanctuary and offloading a batch of haggard-looking women. He'd presumed they were refugees the settlement's routine scouts had stumbled on out in the wilderness.

"They deserved what they got, Barry," announced Miss Collard.

"And you showed her this training film you shot," Barry grated between grit teeth.

"I was able to offer some suggestions to tighten up their tactics," she explained.

"See? Your young ward has proven to be a valuable asset," Dusty chuckled. "Something you have yet to do yourself, Winsor."

Barry should have expected this. With Barry withholding counsel, Dusty had simply turned to his other "consultant." Objectively speaking, taping the attack had strategic value, just as showing it to Miss Collard had proven helpful with her suggestions. Barry resented that Dusty had outmaneuvered him by finding justifiable cause to involve the girl behind Barry's back. It was difficult to remember that cunning shared Dusty's head with his barbarous inclinations.

Swinging ahead of the Ferrari, one of the armored trucks took the lead position as the convoy entered the tunnel. At some point since Barry had ridden with the Raiders on their raid on the cannibal colony, the marauders had welded metal sheets to the flanks of cars, turning them into post-apocalyptic tanks; a few even sported machinegun or bazooka emplacements next to the drivers seat.

With the disappearance of the sun, Commander Dusty proceeded to explain his overall plan. "I was worried some of our trucks weren't going to fit through here, so I sent out a team to measure things. They also moved the bigger obstacles out of our way. This wasn't just for easy access. I wanted to insure we had a clear path in case we need to beat a hasty retreat. But—that's not going to happen, is it, Winsor?"

Barry offered no response, so the vainglorious commander continued his reverie, "Once we reach the city, we'll spend some time cleaning-up the area immediately adjacent to the tunnel entrance. I don't want any zombies interfering with this operation. In fact, there's a squad of men specifically appointed to watch our backs and put down any undead pests. So the main crew can concentrate on our target."

At least the man intended to spare some resources to deal with vermin removal.

The convoy churned along the tunnel at a fair clip. Headlights revealed the clear way mentioned in Dusty's crowing. Reverberating through the tunnel, a multitude of tires grinding on pavement became a bizarre din, like the humming of gigantic frogs.

"So," sighed Barry, "which enclave did you pick?"

Dusty grinned at him.

"The Local Blues, right?"

A double-take jerked Dusty around. "So—you guessed."

"Well, the three main factions are no real threat. The Blues would be your optimum choice, tactically speaking. They appear to be the best fortified group. Taking out the strongest adversary would intimidate the other, lesser enclaves, making them easier conquests for later on."

"My thoughts exactly," cackled Dusty. "See? You can be bloodthirsty when you want."

"Any connection you perceive between a strategy designed to minimize casualties and bloodlust is entirely delusional, Dusty."

"We'll see…"

The convoy exited the tunnel. Several vehicles disgorged troops who promptly set about dispatching any nearby zombies. The Ferrari led the other transports east on Canal until they reached 4th Street, where they headed north.

"Choosing the Blues makes it all the easier for us to avoid unnecessary bloodshed," Barry announced after a while. "As it happens, my old precinct lies inside their territory."

"I noticed that on the map," grunted Dusty.

"Well, I have friends there—friends I might be able to convince to surrender."

"Too bad the siege'll be over by the time you could get inside to sweet-talk your friends."

"Not necessarily..."

This time, Dusty turned in his seat to glare at the detective. "Meaning...?"

"There's a—" Miss Collard started to reply, but Barry silenced the girl with an elbow to her side.

"I know a way in," declared Barry.

"A safe way past their defenses?" Dusty inquired, but he directed his question to Miss Collard instead of Barry.

"A way in," elucidated Barry. "Not a—"

Keeping his piercing eyes on the girl, Dusty interrupted, "I'd rather hear about this from her."

"Tough. You're going to hear about it from me or not at all."

The two men matched stares, unwavering, resolved, defiant.

"Stop trying to protect me," complained Miss Collard.

"I'm not protecting you," Barry snarled at her. "I'm trying to avoid unnecessary bloodshed."

"I can take care of myself."

"Just stay out of this."

"Pull over," Dusty directed his driver.

"But—" protested Runt.

Smacking the crony in the head, Dusty repeated his order in a voice tense with impatience.

With no openings available along the avenue, Runt had to stop the Ferrari in the middle of the street. Behind, the rest of the convoy lurched to a halt. Several men clambered from the trucks, weapons ready, but Dusty waved them back as he climbed from the car. Stepping to the sidewalk, he signaled Barry to follow him.

"I warned you," Barry declared when he came to stand beside the irritated commander, "not to involve her in this."

Grabbing Barry's arm, Dusty pulled him behind a roadside van and cold-cocked him. As Barry sprawled on the pavement, Dusty growled, "This is the last time I'm going to remind you who's in charge, Winsor. If you're not willing to live up to your consultant position, I'll put a bullet in your head and Miss Collard can do your job, you hear me?"

Barry stifled any caustic reply as he slowly climbed to his feet.

"So—tell me about this secret way past their defenses."

Remaining mute, Barry shook his head. He met Dusty's angry glare with stubborn silence.

"I'm not screwing around, Winsor."

"Neither am I," whispered Barry. "I won't help you slaughter people."

"Look, I'd rather avoid any massacres today too. We could use the increase of personnel if we're going to clean this city up. So, if you've got a way to sneak past their defenses, all the better."

Again, Barry shook his head. "I go in alone or not at all."

"Dammit, Winsor…"

Barry shrugged. "My way…or you get to explain to Miss Collard why you shot me." Besides the camaraderie they had developed, he knew the girl thought of him as a figure of authority…but Barry belonged to the old guard, while Dusty was a commander of the new order. What would she do if Dusty killed him?

The two exchanged quiet defiance for several minutes before Dusty finally released an exasperated sigh and accepted Barry's terms.

"I'll give you an hour, Winsor. After that, we go in blazing."

"I'll need more time than that. Getting inside will take a while. Then I'll need to find my friends and convince them to join us…and they'll need time to convince their superiors."

The Commander made a noise that was half-cough, half-guffaw. "Don't push it, Winsor."

"Three hours."

"Two."

With that, Dusty turned and returned to his command vehicle.

The Ferrari took off as soon as he was back in the passenger seat. Barry had to run to catch up and clamber back aboard.

To guard his subterranean route into the Local Blues' enclave, Barry had the Raiders drop him off blocks from the spot he left the street level and went underground. Once inside the building he chose, he hid himself and waited to see if anyone followed him.

When two Raiders crept along behind him, Barry let them pass and enter a doorway he'd left ajar. Down those stairs, they'd find nothing more than a dead-end basement.

From the very beginning, Barry had known he couldn't trust Dusty.

Leaving the building via a side exit, Barry traveled down a series of exterior alleys until he reached the spot where Miss Collard had taken him underground. Even there he waited to make certain he wasn't being followed. Once he had determined that no spies were tagging his trail, Barry descended into the labyrinth of crawlspaces that ran beneath Manhattan. Here, his path became more haphazard.

Before departing from Sanctuary, Barry had gotten Miss Collard to review the route she had taken them on their initial recon. Despite his excellent memory, however, he got lost more than once while following the path he had memorized. Direction and distance were deceptive down here; the darkness conspired to undermine his attempts to retrace their route. If not for the chalk markings he'd made on his prior journey, he'd never have found his way.

It took him the better part of an hour to maneuver these tunnels and reach his old precinct's underground garage.

Dammit, he fretted, I'm running out of time before Dusty launches the assault.

Crossing the empty garage, Barry entered the stairwell and hurriedly ascended to the second floor. There, he hoped to find someone who could put him in contact with one of the Local Blues' chain of command. If he was lucky, it would be someone he knew from the old days; otherwise he'd have to waste valuable time convincing whoever he found that he wasn't a threat, that a greater threat lurked out beyond the enclave's fortified perimeter.

When Barry eased open the stairwell door, a ring of men awaited him. All were armed and every weapon was aimed at him.

"Hold on," he gasped. "I come in peace." His declaration sounded so cliche and futile. As he expected, it had little effect on the welcoming party. They knew I was coming. Some form of surveillance had spotted his furtive entry—but if that were the case, why hadn't the Locals detected his prior entry?

Slammed against a wall, Barry was swiftly searched and disarmed. He was brusquely escorted to a holding cell. There, handcuffs were applied to his wrists and secured to an interrogation table. A pair of men stood watch over him until an interrogator arrived.

It was Deputy Chief Gann. He'd put on a few pounds since the apocalypse, but was still the tall, stern figure of authority. Shocks of white ran through his ebony hair along the temples. Nests of crinkles surrounded his eyes.

Settling back in his chair, he regarded Barry, his brows beetled with pensive consideration. "You took your damned time reporting in for duty, Detective Winsor."

Barry shrugged. "World's gone to hell, Deputy Chief."

"That's no excuse."

Barry exhaled a deep sigh. "You always were a ball-buster, sir."

Gann's frown dwelled for a moment before his lips curled into a smile. "Still am, Winsor. So, is that why you're back? Seeking discipline?"

"Not really, sir. I'm here as an emissary."

"So—you're with the group who's trying to pull a sneak attack on us."

While tempted to disassociate himself from the Raiders, Barry realized it was best not to confuse things with personal differences. "They represent a group from Jersey who are looking to revive civilization by unifying small enclaves into a single social unit."

"Uh huh…" was Gann's neutral response.

"I'm here to try to avoid militant conflict with political negotiation," Barry continued.

"Ah." Deputy Chief Gann nodded.

Behind him, the two guards shared a sly smirk.

"The Local Blues are always receptive to assimilating other groups into our ranks," remarked Gann.

Barry countered, "My people seek a mutual unification."

"Ah well, now—"

The door to the interrogation room opened to admit someone. The guards promptly snapped to attention as the man entered. Deputy Chief Gann threw a glance over his shoulder; when he saw who it was, his posture stiffened.

"This is the invaders' advance agent?" the newcomer grunted.

"Yes sir," replied Gann in a respectful tone.

There was something vaguely familiar about this man. In his late thirties, he was of medium build, but his posture conveyed a sense of authority. His face was long, distinguished, with deep creases segregating his chin into a conspicuous extension of the head. A handsome silver mane adorned that head. His eyes were quick and never stopped darting back and forth. His arrogant attitude went hand-in-hand with the way the Deputy Chief and the two guards deferred to him—this marked him as someone of higher authority than Gann in the Local Blues.

Clearly, Barry reflected, if a truce is to be reached, I need to negotiate it with him, not Gann.

"I'd hardly call my people 'invaders,'" Barry commented.

The newcomer gave a caustic snort. "You come sneaking uninvited into our territory—that makes you an invader."

Deputy Chief Gann interjected, "Actually, Governor Banksy, he's one of the officers who were once under my jurisdiction here."

Banksy! Now Barry knew why the man had seemed familiar. Back before the zombie outbreak, Detective Winsor and his partner Detective Dumont had been investigating Theodore Banksy. Insulated by expensive lawyers, the man had repeatedly escaped any culpability for the criminal activities they'd believed he had masterminded. And here he was now—a leader in the Local Blues enclave. Barry couldn't imagine how such a gangster had managed to gain control of the 13th precinct.

This drastically undermined any approach Barry had intended to use to convince the Blues to peacefully surrender to Dusty's Raiders. Theodore Banksy was a control freak; his insolent nature would never acquiesce to anyone else's dominion.

"I don't care if he used to be the President of the United States," snarled Banksy. "He's an outsider now, Chief Gann. And if he's affiliated with these new invaders, he's an unwelcome intruder."

"You should consider me an emissary, sir, not an intruder," Barry explained. "I'm here to negotiate a truce between—"

"You can call yourself whatever you want," the man interrupted, "but it doesn't change your insignificant status."

Barry attempted to outline Sanctuary's scientific Board's fundamental intentions to Banksy, but he could tell the man remained unswayed by his summary. There was no point in trying to intimidate him with descriptions of the danger that Dusty's Raiders posed for the Local Blues enclave. The settlement was too well fortified to be threatened by anything the Raiders could throw against it.

Losing interest before Barry had finished his explanation, Banksy turned away. He curtly ordered Chief Gann to "get the details of his group, then dispose of him."

"But sir, Detective Winsor was a good officer. He could prove to be a valuable asset."

"If he's not with us, he's against us," snapped Banksy. "This colony has no use for anyone whose loyalty is questionable."

The guards edged back to allow the man to leave the interrogation room.

With sadness creasing his forehead, Gann faced Barry and embellished a shrug with a weary sigh. "I'm sorry, Winsor."

"The way things are going, Chief, we're all going to be sorry."

Turning in his seat, Gann advised the guards to go.

"You sure, sir?"

"I can handle this," he assured them.

Reluctantly, the men withdrew, closing the door behind them.

"You're not going to give up your group, are you, Winsor?"

"They're not my group, Chief. Frankly, I don't approve of their methods—but I can't stop them. Believe me, I've tried..."

"I know the feeling."

Barry could feel the man's regret. He sat straighter, leaned forward with his elbows on the interrogation table. "Dammit, Gann—Theodore Banksy? How the hell did he get control of this station?"

"The entire city was in chaos after the outbreak, Winsor. Officers I would have normally staked my life on abandoned their posts. Not that I can blame them. Everyone was more concerned about the safety of their families than protecting the public-at-large. We tried to summon back-up personnel from other precincts, but they were suffering the same depleted ranks. By the time Banksy's crew showed up, we were desperate for men. If we hadn't accepted his help, the neighborhood would've fallen."

Barry could well imagine how dire the situation had been. Between the zombies and the crazies, Manhattan must've been a rabid disaster zone. Without adequate personnel, Deputy Chief Gann had undoubtedly courted despair under these circumstances. When help had shown up, he couldn't question its price; public safety had taken precedence. And afterwards, Barry could imagine how Banksy had leveraged himself into a ruling position; he couldn't fault Gann for letting the criminal usurp control. Clearly but sadly, the resulting enclave had benefited from this arrangement.

"Banksy has established an impressive defensive grid, Winsor. Your group hasn't a chance of penetrating it."

"If I got in, so can they."

"All the more reason for you to reveal the weak spot you used to get in here."

"Plugging that weak spot won't stop their attack, Gann."

"You let us worry about that."

"No matter what happens, there's going to be a bloodbath. Your enclave may have superior fortifications, but the raiders have explosives."

Gann made a dismissive gesture. "Our defenses can handle a few grenades..."

"We're talking about explosives far more severe than just grenades, Gann."

This time, the Chief's expression faltered for a moment. He met Barry's gaze, probing and obviously reluctant to ask.

"Way more severe," Barry answered the question the man was unwilling to voice. "Big enough to bring down entire buildings."

"Jesus…"

"They have a factory over in Jersey that's been retooled to produce military grade explosives."

"They wouldn't use them, would they, Winsor? I mean—you claim they want to negotiate a truce…"

"I'm the one who wants a truce. The troops they've got outside your enclave are bloodthirsty bastards who'd be just as happy to wipe you guys out."

"Jesus…" Gann sat back, stunned and finally grasping the scope of the menace that faced his enclave. "Dammit, Winsor, you were a good officer. How'd you get mixed up with a group of psychopaths like that?"

"That's a long and complicated tale, Chief. Suffice it to say, the ones who run the factory aren't psychopaths, but they felt they needed warriors to enforce their goals. The ones they enlisted are more violent than they realize." Barry gave his ex-commander a knowing look. "I expect you know how that goes, eh?"

Gann gave a feeble grunt of acknowledgement.

An uncomfortable silence ensued.

Finally, Gann muttered, "So…we're faced with two groups who are too ruthless to back off. What can we do?"

With a shrug, Barry admitted, "I honestly don't know, Chief. Banksy didn't sound too interested in a truce. Do you think he'd change his mind if he learned how heavily armed the invaders are?"

Gann wearily shook his head. "He's too obstinate. He'd force us to fight to the death rather than relinquish his little empire."

Another awkward silence.

This time, it was Barry who spoke, "Sneak me out of here, Chief. Maybe I can talk my group into—"

Bedlam suddenly resounded, literally shaking the building.

My time's up, Barry realized. Maneuvering through the underground labyrinth had eaten up half of the two hours Dusty had given him, and Barry's capture and interrogation had wasted the rest. When he'd failed to return, an impatient Dusty had unleashed the Raiders on the Local Blues enclave.

"Too late," he advised Gann.

"Oh shit—" The Deputy Chief leapt to his feet. His chair loudly hit the floor as he dashed to flee the interrogation room.

"Hey!" yelled Barry as Gann yanked open the door. Poised in the threshold, the man gaped back at him, his eyes wide with earnest panic.

Beyond Gann, Barry could see that the two guards were gone. Frantic personnel raced back and forth along the trembling corridor, their excited cries blending with the remote detonations that rocked the precinct house.

Rattling the cuffs that secured him to the metal table, Barry shouted, "Don't leave me like this, man."

For a terrible moment, Deputy Chief Gann visibly struggled to overcome his fear. During his years of police service, the man had faced all sorts of stress, but never danger like this. Bombs ruptured the night. The building shuddered around him. These explosions were doing more than tearing apart masonry, they were annihilating the post-apocalyptic world as he knew it. Ultimately, Gann's common decency won out and he stumbled back into the room. The floor bucked and rocked under his feet as he fought his way across the interrogation table. He fumbled a set of keys from his pocket, but the ensuing pandemonium hampered his efforts to find the one that would unlock Barry's cuffs. Twice, Gann almost dropped the key ring; the third time, the ring did escape his clumsy fingers to clatter on the tipping table. Barry managed to snatch the ring before it disappeared into the powdery brume that was filling the chamber. It had been too long since he'd handled police keys, he couldn't recall which one went with the cuffs. Half-blinded by dust expelled from the quivering ceiling, he chose key after key, rejecting them when they refused to fit and moving on to try the next.

By the time Barry succeeded in uncuffing himself, Gann had returned to the open doorway. He cast a worried look back into the interrogation room as Barry lurched to his feet. Before Barry could reach the door, Gann had vanished, fleeing off down the corridor.

Dammit, Barry cursed to himself. I'd hoped Gann might give me a gun to defend myself— But panic had driven the Deputy Chief to bolt before Barry could voice his request.

He cautiously peered out into the hallway—just in time to see Gann push his way past a group of frantic others and disappear into the depths of the station house. The others spared no attention on the fleeing Deputy Chief, nor did they take any notice of Barry as he edged along the corridor. Everyone was swept up reacting to the overall tumult. By the time Barry had gotten halfway down the passage, gunfire echoed through the building. The attackers had breached the precinct.

Moving with heightened speed, Barry made for the stairs.

The bark of a multitude of weapons rang along the hallway, accompanied by screams of pain and angry shouts. As Barry wrenched open the door to the stairwell, a swarm of men stumbled into the hallway at its farthest point. All of them were firing at targets in their wake. Several of the men buckled and tumbled to the floor as bullets pelted them. Wild slugs gouged the walls, some reaching as far as Barry's position. One narrowly missed him, explosively creating a hole in the doorframe and sending shards to tear through his jacket. He lingered a second too long and witnessed a group of Raiders finish off survivors before rampaging down the corridor. Barry ducked into the stairwell and clattered down the steps, hoping no one had seen him.

His luck took him only a floor down before he encountered more Raiders as they stormed up the stairs. Pushing open the first floor doorway, he fell through the opening in time to avoid getting caught in a crossfire between them and defenders located on higher stories. Behind him, he heard shots shred the stairwell, punctuated by hoarse grunts as a few bullets punctured combatants, followed by meaty thuds as the wounded tumbled down the steps.

Stumbling along this new corridor, Barry sought shelter from the gunplay that dominated the passageway. The entire precinct house had become a war zone. No matter where he turned, defenders were falling before aggressive firepower wielded by the invaders.

So much for Banksy's impenetrable fortifications, mused Barry. Dusty's Raiders had clearly broken through the perimeter with bombastic ease. Their bombs must've taken everyone by surprise, atomizing the guards and blowing holes in the barricades. Stunned by this onslaught, the Local Blues were succumbing to the Raiders' swarming might. Drunk with their initial success, the marauders had gone on a killing spree.

Barry took refuge in a squad room off the main corridor. There, he found several bodies littering the area, evidence of an earlier stage of battle. Without hesitation, he relieved these cadavers of their weapons. Crouching behind the dispatch desk, he assessed his new armament and tried to ignore the ongoing commotion around him. He barely had time to confirm that the two pump shotguns were loaded before he needed to empty them as the corpses around him stirred with undead reanimation.

Typical of Dusty's moronic warriors to kill the locals and not take the time to shoot them in the head, grumbled Barry, so they won't come back to life as zombies. Now I've got to beware of everybody—living and dead.

Screw all of this, he fumed. I wanted no part of this invasion, and now I'm stuck in the middle of it. I need to get the hell out of here.

Leaving via the precinct's front entrance was clearly a hazardous prospect. The raucous noise outside revealed that a savage battle still endured on the street. But then, an equal level of mayhem existed within the station house. Indoors was no safer than the war-torn avenues. No matter which way he picked, he'd have to wade through crowds of trigger-happy combatants. His wisest choice was to head for the underground pathway he had used to penetrate the Local Blues' territory.

That meant backtracking through a shooting gallery of corridors littered with corpses. Despite his reluctance, this route offered less dangers than venturing onto the external battlefield.

He took a moment to gauge the activity inside the building. While the walls concealed troop movements from visual discernment, the cacophony of gunfire indicated conflict hotspots as they raged through the hallways. He waited until a lull occurred before he abandoned his hiding place and scurried across the open squad room, moving from desk to desk to prevent a lone warrior from catching sight of him. In the heat of battle, Barry wanted to avoid being shot by members of either the invaders or the defenders…while remaining watchful of the hostile attention of the plethora of fresh corpses that sprawled everywhere.

More than once the precinct house shook from explosions so tremendous they obviously came from inside the building. The air was thick with dust set in motion by these ongoing disturbances. A relentless pandemonium of screams and gunshots and explosions assaulted Barry's ears. If he hadn't known what was going on, he might have imagined another more forceful doomsday was crushing what was left of mankind.

All things considered, it was the end of the world for most of tonight's participants. Not all of the fresh cadavers belonged to the locals; the raiders were suffering their own share of casualties. Whichever side ended up claiming tonight's victory, their ranks were going to be drastically depleted. How much of a victory was it going to be if there were only a handful of survivors?

Barry's main concern was making sure that he was among those who lived to see the dawn.

Waiting for a safe moment was pointless, neither faction was going to let there be a lull in the brutalities—not until every opponent was dead. He launched himself across the squad room, entering the corridor in a crouch, hoping that vantage would spare him from the exchanged fussilades. Slugs zipped all around him, plucking at his clothing and gouging holes in the walls. For all the speed he sought, Barry needed to move with some care lest the mounds of dead foul his progress. At one point, a cadaverous hand reached forth from the abattoir mounds to clutch at his leg. His attempt to kick it aside proved futile, its crooked fingers tangling in the fabric of his pants. Twisting around (and hunching low to avoid the hail of bullets), he brought the butt of a shotgun down on the dead limb. A grisly crack signaled an ulna breaking under the impact, but the injury failed to dissuade the zombie from its murderous grasp. Brittle talons dug into the cloth in a manner that did more than slow him down. Against his wishes, Barry was dragged from his feet—just in time to avoid being caught by a salvo of automatic gunfire. A jagged maw opened in the hallway wall above his head. Ignoring this close call, Barry rolled across a surface of bodies that suddenly ceased to be dormant. Several undead hands clawed at him. He kicked and thrashed, striking out with barrels and butts of the weapons he carried. Everything in his immediate vicinity became an adversary to be pummeled down. He squirmed and twisted, frantic to evade anything that sought a grip on him. Newly dead lips hissed at his struggle. A tangle of limbs surrounded him, closing in, blocking his headway. He fought on, blindly, savagely, cursing, seeking a break in the reanimated obstacle course that clogged the hallway.

There—only feet away—lay the stairwell that led down to the parking garage, the ajar door taunting him with its potential succor.

The irony was not lost on him that he might escape unscathed by any living antagonists—only to be brought down by an undead morass.

When an arm crooked around his neck, he wrestled unsuccessfully to free himself. The chokehold was too resolute, refusing to release him. As he fought off other undead clutches, this one grip dragged him through the doorway's threshold. A voice rasped near his ear, but its message was lost in the overall bedlam.

A momentary darkness enveloped Barry as the door was pushed closed, liberating him from all other clutches. Although his stamina was spent, he called upon heaven to grant him a last burst of strength to fight his way free, but providence ignored his prayer.

"Cut it out," a voice hissed against the back of his neck.

His struggle lost its fervor, more out of exhaustion than because of any recognition. It took another rasped admonition to penetrate Barry's veil of enfeebled hysteria.

"Who—what—" he croaked.

"Stop fighting," came the voice. "Or I'll throw you back into the hall."

The voice was familiar, but Barry couldn't attach a face or identity to it.

"Damn, this place is a madhouse."

Then it came to Barry: "Red Ryder?"

"We need to find a way out of here." The arm encircling Barry's neck relaxed.

"Downstairs," Barry whispered. "There's a way out down there."

"Yeah? Okay, then let's go." The man's weight eased from against Barry's back as he retreated down the steps.

Barry started to follow him, then a panicky thought exploded in his head. He reached out and grabbed Red Ryder's arm in the dark. "Miss Collard—where is she?"

"Huh?" He tried to pull free, but Barry's fingers tightened on the man's arm.

"Where's Miss Collard?"

"How should I know?"

"Dusty threatened to send her in after me if I didn't return."

"He got fed up waiting for you, but he didn't bother with her. We used bombs to get past the barricades."

"Did she remain outside the perimeter?"

"Dammit, Barry—I dunno. I came in with the rest of the Raiders, through the breach in the barricade. We converged on the precinct house cuz that was where the locals ran to hide."

"I can't leave her in here…"

Shaking off his grip, Red Ryder tangled his fingers in Barry's jacket and pulled him in the direction of the basement garage. "You know a way out down here, you show me first," he growled. "Then you can run off after your girl—"

"Let go of me!"

Red Ryder's grip did not loosen, so Barry responded with a brusque shove. The Raider's hold tore free and he toppled away into the darkness. A series of thumps and curses marked his ignoble tumble down the steps. Before the man hit the bottom, Barry had wheeled about and burst from the stairwell back into the corridor filled with thrashing zombies.

The switch from the darkened stairs to the moderately lit hallway momentarily blinded Barry. He swung his rifle in a wide arc to ward off any immediate assailants, buying himself the seconds necessary for his vision to clear. When his eyes adjusted to the light, he saw that little had changed: the passage was still clogged with spasming corpses. Further down the corridor, murky figures were embroiled in combat with each other. Someone beyond this tableau was firing an automatic weapon into the crowd, indiscriminately wasting locals and marauders alike. The half-erect bodies of zombies shielded Barry from the onslaught. He reared back through the open doorway and lost his footing as the floor gave way to descending steps. Down he went.

He didn't land on Red Ryder, though. The Raider had already scrambled into the basement. Tumbling momentum carried Barry through after the man. He sprawled on his belly. Within seconds, his disorientation gave way to a somewhat jumbled view of the parking garage.

The basement was another active battlefield. Figures in police blues tangled with black-clad Raiders. Gunfire echoed in the underground enclosure, punctuated by angry shouts and wounded grunts. Overhead, a series of fluorescent lights flickered, bestowing an eerie strobescent illumination on the combatants. Barry couldn't pick out Red Ryder among the turmoil. Nor did he see any sign of Miss Collard—which relieved him; regardless of the girl's spunk, this battle was too severe for her.

He held on to that notion, praying Dusty hadn't insisted that she join the assault force. Hopefully, the girl was safe somewhere outside the under-siege enclave.

According to Red Ryder, Dusty hadn't bothered to force Miss Collard to show him the secret way past the guarded perimeter; he had resorted to more straightforward measures, literally "crashing" his way in. The man was true to his blustery nature.

But this meant the underground route would be empty—making it an expedient escape route.

If I can just make it past this brawl...

Girding himself for some hectic action, Barry launched himself. His course angled to the left, seeking to avoid the fray by sneaking along the wall.

He managed to dodge past the first brawlers he encountered, but the next struggle was too thick—a batch of Raiders had trapped a gaggle of Locals between two parked vans and were summarily slaughtering them—forcing him to detour off into the general mayhem. He squeezed his way past pairs of men locked in combat, escaping notice. He stepped over numerous bodies, some dead, some just wounded; he ignored anyone who tried to clutch him as he passed.

At one point, he reached a squad of Locals who were defending an armored police bus. Raiders ringed them in, but the Locals were holding them off, buying time for others to board the vehicle. He saw Theodore Banksy climb onto the bus. The gangster paused in the bus' doorway, and for an instant the man's savage gaze locked on Barry. He scowled and pointed a menacing finger at Barry—before vanishing into the bus' dark interior.

What? thought Barry. Don't blame this on me. If you hadn't been such an arrogant shit, this melee could've been avoided.

But that was the way assholes like Banksy thought. They took credit for every good thing regardless of whether or not it was achieved by them, but blamed all their mistakes on others.

Barry had paused too long. Suddenly one of the warriors turned their hostility on him. He didn't even get the chance to tell if the man was a Local or a Raider—another pounced on them, diverting their malicious attention from Barry. He staggered free for only an instant, though, before another took a swing at him. Dodging the man's bludgeon (this one was a Raider), Barry delivered a kick as he passed the assailant. Down he went— to be replaced by another. Somehow, Barry's dance between the combatants had taken him away from the wall and deeper into the fighting.

Disoriented, he was no longer sure which direction he wanted to go. He couldn't see enough of the garage to determine where the exit door lay. He wasn't given much opportunity to scan the background, assailants fixated on him only to become victims of others. Staying alive dominated his attention.

It was getting difficult to tell the difference between the living and the undead. He decided to save what little ammo was left in the guns he'd appropriated, so he struck out at his opponents with the butt of the rifle, bashing all comers.

Suddenly, a stocky dark mass roared through the mob. Its twin luminous eyes dazzled. Those who failed to get out of the way in time were crushed underneath the juggernaut's tires. Barry leaped back, but even so the bus careened past him barely inches from his elbow.

He got a clear view of Banksy through the slats of a window; the gangster glared at Barry with the fury of a rabid beast.

There's somebody who's going to hold grudge…

And then the bus roared past him and was gone. The combatants swarmed in to fill the gap its passage had made through the mob. Barry was thrown back into defensive mode. He swung about him, wildly, blindly, unconcerned whether he battered friend or foe.

He was outnumbered and lacked the killer instinct. All the others were bloodthirsty, while Barry's single goal was survival.

Somebody knocked him down. Before he could scramble to his feet, somebody else hit him over the head with something and—everything went black.

Surfacing from a dark warm place, Barry became aware of clammy weights upon him. He twitched reflexively, to cast off these burdens, but they proved too heavy. Clammy and cold and—what was that slimy part?—bloody.

He put his weight behind a gyration and succeeded in breaking through to the surface. He stared around him at the hundreds of bodies that littered the parking garage. The undead fed upon the dead. He saw no one who looked alive.

The battle was over. The spoils left for the scavengers—the revenants whose undead appetites set them chomping on each other. Only by being buried under a pile of already gnawed corpses had Barry escaped notice by the ravenous zombies.

And by fighting his way to the surface, he'd attracted their attention. Several abandoned their half-eaten meals to come lurching in his direction.

He was unarmed. He'd lost his guns during his time as part of the mound of bodies.

He groped about, searching the immediate casdavers for weapons. His fingers encountered something long thin and hard. He yanked it free of a body—a machete.

Getting to his feet was problematic. The "ground" was too lumpy and squishy to accommodate his uncertain sense of balance. He remained on his knees as he fought off the first onslaught of undead assailants. He swung the machete with as much force as he could muster. Limbs fell away. Wounds gaped across unbreathing torsos. He chopped fatal crevasses in indisriminate scalps. He even managed to lop off a head or two. He was holding his own…but he needed to do better than that.

Eventually they would overwhelm his defensive stance. They just kept coming, a seemingly endless surge of murderous meat. He needed to go on the offensive.

It was imperative that he reach the escape door—or even the stairs upstairs. Either one would suffice right now. He needed to ditch this undead crowd. Elsewhere, out in the open, he'd have a better chance for survival.

He spotted the elevator—and the stairwell doorway next to it. He headed in that direction.

These zombies were sluggish, perhaps weighed down by the raw flesh they'd just gorged upon. It proved easier to sidestep them than waste the energy dispatching them.

He won his way to the stairwell. Inside, a few bodies sprawled on the steps, but they were too badly mutilated to pose a threat.

Upstairs, the precinct house had become a necropolis. Corpses lay everywhere, a mixture of undead and half-eaten carcasses. Again, a torpidity slowed down these zombies, making them easy to dodge.

No living souls remained.

The raid had escalated into a mass slaughter, what looked to be mutual destruction.

He spotted Deputy Chief Gann, or least the undead thing had once been Barry's ex-commander. He took the time to dispatch this zombie, out of respect. Otherwise, he skirted the shambling creatures, crawled over inert corpses, and made his way out onto the street. Even there, bodies littered the asphalt.

He took the time to replenish his arsenal, robbing the dead of a rifle and two handguns. He held onto the machete.

He kept an eye out for Miss Collard, but saw no sign of her among the dead.

That's a good sign.

Many of the bodies *were* familiar, though. He recognized several men from his days with the Raiders. No Dusty, though. And there were others whom he vaguely remembered from the old neighborhood, shop owners and fellow officers he'd known back before the apocalypse. The landscape was not just gruesome, it was depressing. So many dead…

And who had won?

He saw no survivors. *You'd think there'd be some sign of the winners.* If the Local Blues had successfully defended their territory, why weren't they here? While if Dusty's Raiders had been victorious, why weren't they looting the station house or the neighboring stores? Were there so few survivors that he hadn't yet run into one of them?

I don't belong here, Barry told himself. Once upon a time, these streets had been his personal turf…but no longer. Now they were war-torn horrorshows.

All of this was the handiwork of the Raiders—and indirectly Sanctuary. Barry wanted no more part of this madness.

I need to find Miss Collard and get her away from those maniacs.

He desperately prayed that the girl had not taken part in the siege. That she had been smart enough not to put her life on the line to satisfy Dusty's bloodlust. He needed to believe that she had escaped the massacre.

If so, she would return to Sanctuary.

He came to an intersection that had been blocked by nose-to-nose trucks. Now, all that remained of the vehicles was debris cluttering two large craters that gouged the pavement. The Board's explosive concoctions had certainly done the job.

Beyond the enclave, only a few bodies littered the streets. He checked the spot where Dusty had marshaled his forces, but the Raiders were long gone.

It took him a while to locate a working car.

Then he embarked on his second exodus of his hometown.

The car ran out of gas a few miles into New Jersey.

He continued west on-foot.

So far, he'd seen no trace of the Raiders, nor any signs of life. Just shambling hungry corpses.

He came to a mall and found another car in the parking lot.

His journey was relatively uneventful.

But when he got to Sanctuary, he was startled to learn he was the first to return from the Manhattan assault.

"Where's everybody else?" demanded Dr Heigl. He and other members of the Board had come to the gate to witness his arrival. Additional citizens gathered with them.

Barry tried to explain what had happened, that by the time he'd recovered, everybody else was gone. No Raiders, no Locals. All he'd seen were dead bodies. "If there are any surviving Raiders, they should have showed up before I did."

The Board were horrified to learn of the slaughter. How could the enclave have refused induction into Sanctuary's populace?

Barry chose not to remind the professors of the Raiders' predilection for violence. In truth, he was too distracted to care about further placating the upset Board members. He was worried for Miss Collard's safety. Even if she hadn't left New York with the Raider remnants, she would've come here. The girl had faith in Sanctuary. She recognized the colony's flaws, but believed that time would temper the Board's ruthlessness. (Oh, if only she were here to witness the profs' witless shock that there'd been a massacre.) She felt a part of the community. She was cohabiting with that kid—Joey Fulton. Her life was back in the little township that had grown around the old chemical factory.

If she had survived, she'd have returned to Sanctuary.

If she had survived…

She wasn't here…so she hadn't survived.

Simple deduction.

But—Barry refused to believe the girl was dead. Perhaps she hadn't been able to find transportation. She might be traveling on foot. That would take her longer to get back here. She could be out there, stumbling along a roadside, fighting off random zombies and feral crazies.

When he announced he must go in search of the girl, Dr Heigl forbid him to leave the settlement. Barry punched him in the nose.

"With Dusty's men all missing-in-action," wailed another Board member, "you need to defend Sanctuary!"

"I'm not a one-man militia," Barry protested.

"You're the only one left with the necessary training…" Professor Grauss moaned.

"Which I intend to apply to finding Miss Collard. My loyalties lie more with her than with you lot."

"Coward," sneered Sheldon Bowman.

Barry scowled at the pompous Fix-It man. With the Raiders gone, Sheldon was no longer a person of importance. Now he was just another professor, a blowhard with an ego the size of the moon—and the Board already had its share of those.

"I think the coward's the one who didn't accompany his crew into battle," Barry declared.

Shrinking back, Sheldon took shelter among the throng of Board members—whose status had exempted them from physically participating in the raid. They were all too important. They were the generals sending the troops out to fight their battles.

Shoving his way through the group of profs, Joey Fulton cried, "Where's Denise?"

Barry filled him in on his suspicions.

"I'm going with you," proclaimed the lad.

Back on his feet, Dr Heigl snarled a reminder that no one was leaving the settlement. "That uppity bitch can find her own way home."

Stepping up, Joey Fulton punched him in the nose.

The Board members gasped with horror.

"You coming, kid?" Barry turned and marched over to claim his SUV from the few vehicles that remained of Sanctuary's transport pool. The boy trotted after him.

A vast expanse of countryside existed between Sanctuary and the Big Apple. Barry was at a loss where to start. A systematic sweep of the terrain was impractical—too much territory to cover.

He chain-smoked as he drove.

Joey was no help. He had no knowledge concerning any haunts the girl might have out in the field. She'd never taken him on any of her forays. "She claimed she didn't want to risk my beautiful ass." But Barry suspected the boy's basic non-reckless common sense had been a decisive part in the decision to remain warm and safe in Sanctuary.

At least he offered to come along in search of her, mused Barry as he cruised between chemical swamps. The kid had guts when in counted.

Barry couldn't remember any places they'd visited on their travels for which the girl had shown a fondness. Most of them had been nightmares. None of them would provide her with shelter.

A frustrated Barry pulled the SUV over to the side of the road. He got out and paced along the roadside. After a moment, Joey climbed from the car, but lingered beside it, watching the detective stomp back and forth.

"I can't just drive up and down every road between here and New York," Barry fretted aloud. "But what other choice do I have?"

"Maybe she never left the city," muttered Joey Fulton.

"Huh?"

"She lived in Manhattan, didn't she? Before the outbreak?"

He turned to face the boy.

"She never talked much about her pre-outbreak life. But she must've had an apartment, right? Maybe she went there."

It was a valid possibility. Barry cursed himself for not thinking of it.

"Probably," Barry admitted. He crushed a butt under his heel, then lit a fresh cig. "But I don't know the address."

"She could be in the book."

"The book…"

"The phonebook."

Again, Barry chastized himself for being muddle-headed and not understanding the common reference.

Yes, she might be "in the book."

They got back in the SUV and it drove off, headed east.

Denise Collard.

She was indeed listed in the phonebook.

Barry knew the neighborhood. Mostly students and actresses-cum-waitresses.

The building that housed her apartment was a grimy redbrick structure that looked old enough to have housed a horde of immigrants. Her room was on the third floor.

Her building was empty of any undead or zombie leftovers. Their footsteps on the worn wooden floors seemed thunderous to Barry in contrast with the harsh silence that dominated the gloomy hallways. Most of the wallpaper had peeled off long ago, but a few lingering scraps showed a drab floral pattern.

Her door was locked.

Calling upon old skills, Barry picked the lock.

They found her in the bedroom, nearly comatose on the floor.

"No visible wounds," remarked Barry.

"But she's unconscious. Could she have a concussion? Would that show?"

Barry shrugged. "No lumps on her head. A good amount of bruising, though."

"She's really hot."

"Fever."

"She needs a doctor!"

Barry agreed.

"Back in Sanctuary. Doc Toby will heal her!" The lad's voice almost cracked with desperation.

With the kid's help, Barry carried Miss Collard downstairs and settled her in the SUV's backseat. Joey sat with her, cradling her fevered head.

Barry hit the accelerator.

Back in Sanctuary, Doc Toby was overloaded with patients when Barry and Joey arrived with Miss Collard's fevered body.

The Raiders had finally returned, at least their few ragged survivors. The siege had decimated the ranks of Dusty's army. Dusty was among the survivors, but nowhere in sight; he was sequestered with the Board in the factory. The other Raiders were battered and lacerated.

Barry barged in to the clinic, bellowing for Doc Toby.

When the Doc appeared, he was haggard and somewhat blood-stained. Many of the Raiders' injuries had been severe. "Two men died soon after the group arrived."

"There's something wrong with her," Joey Fulton asserted, gesturing frantically at Miss Collard where they'd laid her on a gurney.

"She has a bad fever," added Barry.

Bulldogging through his weariness, Doc Toby examined the girl.

Barry and the boy stood by, anxious and attentive.

"Pneumonia," announced Doct Toby. "Complicated, no doubt, by her depleted condition. Was she in the siege battle?"

Barry confessed he didn't know.

"She's pretty bruised up."

Barry (and the boy) nodded.

"She must've had a hard time on the road, then she got sick." He stripped off his bloody gloves and drew a fresh pair onto his hands. "She'll be alright now."

Joey wouldn't leave the girl. The clinic was overcrowded, so they took Miss Collard back to her cottage to convalesce. Barry left her in the boy's care.

Guards tried to stop Barry from entering the factory, but he bullied his way past them.

The Board was in conference, reviewing Dusty's account of the siege—which differed somewhat from the account Barry had given.

According to Dusty, his men had faced superior foes, but the Raiders had triumphed in the end. The death toll was high, but Dusty insisted the victory justified the losses. "And our next victory will be just as glorious!"

Although surprised to see Barry, Dusty quickly regained his composure. "Thought you were dead when you didn't show up. Figured they iced you and your negotiations. Suppose it's good to see you, though, alive and all." He gave Barry a wicked grin. "At this point, we need all the able men we can get."

"You can't possibly be considering another assault so soon," argued Barry. "The few men you have left are in shit condition—I've just come from the clinic, I saw them, they couldn't take a batch of teenage girls right now."

"There are enough men around the settlement. They'll fill my army's ranks."

"With clumsy amateurs. The next enclave you hit will wipe them out."

"As long as we have enough explosives, we can't lose, Winsor."

Interrupting their terse exchange, Dr Heigl remonstrated Barry, "You have no official standing with this settlement, Winsor. Your opinions are of no interest to the Board."

"They're more than 'opinions', they're facts. And they should be of utmost interest, Heigl," Barry threw back at him. "You're making a big mistake by listening to this maniac. He and his crew were bloodthirsty savages. They didn't offer anybody the chance to join Sanctuary, they slaughtered everyone! And now all that's left of the Raiders are a batch of casualties—" He pointed to Dusty. "—and this trigger-happy lunatic!"

"Dusty's army won the battle, Winsor," remarked Professor Kaufmann. "Being the victor doesn't make them bloodthirsty."

"You weren't there; I was. What I saw was a massacre. They blew up buildings and slaughtered everybody."

"See?" Dusty addressed Dr Heigl. "I told you how invaluable the explosives were. That's why I need more."

"Hey!" yelled Barry. Once he had everyone's startled attention, he declared, "I thought you guys wanted to restore civilization—not blow it up."

A few of the profs nodded, muttering among themselves.

"Most of the groups out there are hostile," Dusty asserted. "You've got to force civilization on them."

"What he's describing is an Evil Empire," argued Barry. "Is that the society you want to build? You don't recreate civilization by force, you do it through cooperation and coexistence."

"If they resist joining us, then they must be treated as enemies.," Dr Heigl proclaimed.

"The man has a valid point, Dr Heigl," muttered Professor Grauss. "Violence isn't the only option. Surely we can negotiate alliances with some of these Manhattan enclaves."

"Trust me," Dusty grunted. "They can't be trusted. They'll stab us in the back. We need to strike first."

"There are so few people left," Barry pointed out. "Why would you advocate killing any of them?"

"Because most of them," Dusty snarled, "are cut-throat bastards. Society would be better without them."

Barry turned to address the Board members. "If your big goal is to revive civilization–then employ civilized methods to unify the survivors. Diplomacy is called for, not a slaughterfest."

A dire silence bloomed and lingered.

Finally someone muttered, "Historically speaking, violent societies never prosper."

"See?" urged Barry.

"This discussion has strayed too far from the topic," Dr Heigl insisted. "While we want to avoid killing anybody, if they resist, then we must be prepared to use force to assert our wisdom."

"Are you planning to establish a democracy? Or a dictatorship?"

The man bristled with indignation. "We are not power-mad individuals, Winsor. We are intelligent libertarians who seek the restoration of sanity to this post-apocalyptic world."

"Then act civilized."

Another silence endured. Barry hoped his words had finally swayed enough of the profs to regain their common decency.

This time, it was Dusty who spoke, "Fine. And when diplomacy fails, I'll take care of business."

Outside, Doc Toby was waiting for Barry.

"What's the matter?" he exclaimed. "Has Miss Collard's condition worsened?"

"No, she's alright. I was waiting to see you."

They strolled away, heads bowed with weariness.

"Get anywhere with them?"

Barry ruefully shook his head.

"Not surprising," muttered Doc Toby. "They're a pigheaded bunch."

"Dusty's convinced the Board to give him more explosives."

"So…further raids are in the offing." The Doc stumbled, and Barry suddenly realized the man was drunk.

"I'm afraid so." Barry sighed. "They won't stop until they've slaughtered eveybody…"

"Not that it matters. We're all dead anyway."

They had arrived at the clinic, but loitered outside. Doc Toby seemed disinclined to go in.

"How are your other patients doing?" Barry asked.

"All dead…everybody's dead."

That explained the man's unwillingness to return to his duties. It must've been a hard blow for Doc Toby, to lose all his patients. No wonder he'd hit the bottle; Barry could empathize with that escape route from life.

"That's not very doctorly of you."

"Ah, but remember—I'm not a real doctor, just a glorified pharmaceutical salesman. More to the point, I'm a realist."

But Barry wasn't paying attention. Noises from inside the clinic had distracted his attention from Doc Toby's laments. It sounded like there were people inside…people complaining.

"Did you—" Barry choked out, "—*deal* with their bodies?" Had the Doc not dealt with the last Raiders after their deaths? Had they reanimated during his absence? Was the clinic now infested with fresh zombies?

Doc Toby shrugged. "I patched them up as best I could."

Mystification confused Barry. Why would the Doc "patch up" a bunch of corpses?

"Those ruffians are trouble," muttered Doc Toby. "They're pissed off and itchy for a fight."

Barry's mystification pinnacled. What was the Doc talking about?

Finally, a visibly-dejected Doc Toby pushed open the door and shuffled into the clinic. A fearfully reluctant Barry followed him indoors, but his hand strayed to the pistol at his waist, preparing to draw and fire if any undead dispatches were called for.

But if these last Raiders were deceased, they were far more talkative than any zombies Barry had encountered. Most the men were confined to cots, but others whose wounds were less debilitating, paced about with edgy impatience, complaining about their injuries. A few of them called out insults to Doc Toby as he moved among them, checking their condition. Barry saw no sign of Red Ryder; the man must have failed to survive the siege. But—there was Runt, his leg splinted and wrapped in gauze, openly glaring in Barry's direction; even in pain, the crony had the energy to express his hatred for the detective.

"But," Barry sidled up to the Doc, "you told me they were all dead…"

Doc Toby snorted, not looking up from rewrapping a bandage on a Raider's arm. "They're dead, I'm dead, you're dead. Everybody's dead."

"What are you talking about?" blurted Barry.

"Yeah, Doc," grunted the Raider with the wounded arm. He gave a sardonic grin. "I sure don't feel dead."

"If you knew what I knew, you'd kill yourself," Doc Toby mumbled, half to himself. "Ha!—not that that would do anything."

Barry pulled the Doc away from the Raiders, leading him into an examination cubicle. He planted him in a chair and confronted him. "You need to sober up, Doc. You're babbling."

"Not babbling," Doc Toby protested weakly. "I don't babble…I abhor people who do…talking just to hear their own voices…senseless babble… you'll get none of that from me…"

"You're not making sense," insisted Barry. "Those men out there survived the siege. They're not dead, nor am I or you. We're—"

"All dead, all of us…you just don't know it…"

"You're drunk."

"Not drunk enough." Leaning over, he drew a bottle from behind the examination table. He lifted it to his lips and took a healthy swig of the whiskey. "I never manage to get drunk enough to forget the awful truth."

"What 'awful truth' is that?"

Instead of answering, Doc Toby took another gulp of whiskey. With his free hand, he took the stethoscope from the pocket of his coat and tossed it to Barry.

"What am I supposed to do with this?" he muttered.

"Go ahead—use it. See if you can find your heartbeat."

He hesitated, more out of puzzlement than dread, but then clipped the nozzles into his ears and lifted the end and pressed it to his chest.

Nothing. Silence.

"Can't find it, huh?"

Barry gawked at the Doc. Confusion swarmed in his mind, pitting disbelief against denial, empirical evidence against reality. "Of course I have a heartbeat— This thing must be broken."

"Nothing wrong with the 'scope," an inebriated Doc Toby replied. "You're the broken one. We're all broken. Nobody's got a heartbeat anymore. Because everybody's dead."

"I'm not dead," Barry insisted. "I'm alive. What are you—"

Doc Toby waved a dismissive hand at Barry. "Don't get it, do you? The zombie outbreak didn't just affect the dead—whatever happened, it *killed everybody*. But nobody noticed—because we were all animated dead men."

"That's absurd. How could we *not* notice we were dead?"

Doc Toby leaned forward and fixed a knowing eye on the befuddled detective. "Before the apocalypse, that might've been a valid point. But ever since the fall of civilization, everybody's been busy struggling to survive. Think about it—when was the last time you checked your pulse or blood pressure? Forever, right? Because you've been busy surviving. Everybody's been too distracted to think of getting a formal physical examination. And I doubt there are many reputable doctors left out there. Those who've discovered the truth are probably keeping it to themselves—" He sat back to hug the whiskey bottle. "—like me. It's safer that way."

"But you're not keeping it to yourself. You're telling me."

"You take all this way too seriously, Barry. Now maybe you can relax. There's no point in fighting to survive—none of us did."

"But…I'm still living a kind a life. This body may be dead, but my mind is still going. I'm not completely dead."

"In the old days, medical science strived to keep the body alive even if the brain was dead. Now we have the reverse: living brains in dead bodies."

"But—the zombies—their brains are dead…"

"Some people suffer enough bodily damage that their systems shut down, approximating a state of death. But they stay reanimated as undead."

"All the work you did on those Raiders' injuries…"

"Mostly cosmetic. Simple wounds and bruises appear to heal, just at a decelerated rate."

"What about illnesses?" Barry demanded. "Is Miss Collard going to fully recuperate?"

"Most of the sick people I've 'treated' got better. Not that it matters much in the long run."

Although the idea was fantastic—everybody being dead—was it any stranger than people coming back as zombies? Besides, it was impossible to explain away Barry's lack of a heartbeat. No heartbeat meant no pulse, no point in breathing to oxygenate the unmoving bloodstream. Did he still need to sleep? Why was he bothering to eat? Was he defecating the entirety of what he comsumed? So—what fuel was his dead body using to maintain itself? The zombies were compelled to eat human flesh, but Barry felt no such deviant urge.

As a detective, Barry consciously relied on evidence when reaching any conclusion. He attached a certain degree of value to gut feelings, but empirical data won out every time. He could not ignore the verifiable facts, no matter how horrifying was the result.

We're all dead...

Somehow, this realization didn't hit Barry as hard as it had apparently affected Doc Toby. The truth had filled the Doc with a rigid fatalism, where Barry's perceptions were more pragmatic. Knowing he was dead brought no change to Barry's self-referential status. As far as he was concerned, he was alive—just subjected to some strange state of organic inactivity—but still sentient and self-aware. Alive, dead, both conditions had become identical.

Death has become a standard for everyone.

But even the dead can die—and afterwards they become undead.

And then there's a third stage of death, when someone damages the brain and kills the zombie.

"Do you have any idea what caused all this?"

Doc Toby laughed, drained the bottle, and then gave a whiskey burp before responding. "Not the foggiest, sorry, Barry. I know you're obsessed with finding out what caused the outbreak...but I can't help you. We're all dead and we'll never know why."

Burdened with this awful knowledge, Barry took his leave of the clinic. For a while, he wandered, lost in unresolvable thoughts.

He couldn't imagine the consequences of everybody being dead. The medical implications seemed ridiculous. How could the body function without functioning organs? Okay—most of the organs weren't working—but the brain was. He was still thinking, so electrical synapses were still firing off inside his cerebellum. Was that the primary difference? Biochemical biology had ceased, but electromagnetic impulses remained unaffected.

If biological functions were dead, then women couldn't get pregnant. No more children. Would the surviving kids grow older?—or stay stunted corpses?

All of this was bound to change the revival of civilization. What kind of a society would a dead populace make? Could everybody's dead status somehow be influencing them to act bloodthirsty? *No wonder nobody can coexist. But it doesn't matter—there'll be no more children. This is the last generation. Once we die off, mankind is gone.*

Rebuilding society was pointless.

He visited Miss Collard. The girl was still sleeping, but Joey Fulton reported that her fever was down.

How can she have a fever with no active blood flow?

How much of an atrocity had Templar's colony of cannibals been guilty of...? They'd eaten human flesh, but they (like their victims) were already dead. No—in this instance, categorical details were immaterial. Those bastards had believed they were killing people and eating them—their evil intentions condemned them regardless of the deceased nature of their prey.

Barry did not share his new knowledge with the boy. What was the point? The lad had enough worries. He was better off not knowing. Doc Toby was right--everybody was better off not knowing.

Leavng the girl in Joey Fulton's capable hands, Barry retreated to a remote part of the settlement, deep in a nearby stand of trees barely surviving the toxic soil, to conduct his penultimate rumnations.

There, he reached the conclusion that he wanted no part in the Board's desire to spread Sanctuary's dominion by assimilating the various enclaves of Manhattan. With or without his Raiders, Dusty would spread mayhem and murder to further the Board's impractical scheme. And that scheme of restoring civilization was a waste of time, at best a short-lived solution that would eventually fail as the new society's population slowly died out.

Human civilization had reached its summit, and the contagion behind the zombie outbreak had destroyed that cultural plateau. Everything that followed were simply racial death throes.

Barry failed to aspire to be a part of that painful downward spiral.

If he stayed, he would be compelled to fight the Board at every point of their operation. That was, he knew, unreasonable—and futile. He was one man against many. The profs could easily rally the entire settlement against Barry, branding him a troublesome danger to everyone's safety. He'd end up cast out or assassinated.

It was easier to just leave of his own volition.

He was loath to abandon Miss Collard...but the girl was better off here. The settlement's warped ambitions would keep her busy, and hopefully she would remain unaware of her true dead condition. She would *die* happy in that ignorance.

The time had come for Barry to leave Sanctuary and never look back.

Dusty caught up to him as Barry was loading supplies into his SUV.

"Splitting, huh?"

Barry offered no comment; he had no interest in engaging in a discussion with the bloodthirsty maniac. Barry continued piling boxes into the car's rear.

"No hard feelings, okay?"

That jarred Barry. "Huh?" *What the hell is that supposed to mean?*

"I know you only want the best for the settlement—and I respect you for that, really—but your approach is just too passive to work. The job of rebuilding civilization needs a forceful hand, not a peacekeeping one. It's stupid to waste time trying to negotiate with your enemies. We need to crush them and move on to the rebuilding part."

The poor fool, he actually believes civilization can be force-fed to a captive populace.

"It's nice that you've found a job that gives you an outlet for your antisocial hostilities," Barry snarled.

"We both want the same thing, Winsor; we just disagree on how to achieve it."

What would Dusty think if he learned that everybody was already dead? Would that rob his hostility of any satisfaction? Or launch him on a killing spree? Those questions were moot. Barry had no intention of sharing the secret with the maniac. While everyone else was better off in ignorance, this man didn't deserve to know the truth.

"You wait, though," Dusty advised. "Come back in a year and you'll be surprised by all I'll have achieved."

Mayhem and destruction and wanton slaughter and bombed-out buildings…the fool would ruin the city along with its population. If Barry ever revisited his hometown, there'd be nothing to see but a tortured wasteland.

He was tempted to shoot Dusty and spare everyone the hell the man intended to unleash. But no…if it wasn't Dusty, the Board would find somebody else to take the reins and lead Sanctuary's army against all comers. Besides, killing was Dusty's go-to solution, not Barry's.

Granted, Dusty deserved to die. His crimes were excessive. But…he was already dead. He just didn't know it.

9

A **FEW DAYS OUT,** Barry's dead wife began appearing in his dreams.

In these nightmares, he encountered Emily during his travels…but she was undead and chased him across a cornfield and then through a shopping mall. The real horror wasn't in the chase, it came when she initially shambled into view and his heart stopped at the realization that here was his beloved, now contaminated by the unholy undead taint. That instant of recognition stretched out until it seemed to last for hours, the two of them locked in a tragic scenario: him standing there, and her shuffling toward him with barred teeth.

These nightmares plagued him to the point that he stopped sleeping for days on end. Then, when he finally collapsed, exhaustion consigned him to somnambulant depths beyond the reach of any dreamlands.

He chanced upon a backwoods tavern whose stock was relatively intact. He welcomed the opportunity to go on a binge. Alcoholic escape was a familiar psychic salve. It solved nothing, but for a while it sedated the drinker, numbing him into hassle-free oblivion.

He spent more than a month in a savage stupor, but lacking a calander, he remained oblivious to that. He remained oblivious to pretty much everything. He lost weight. He grew a bushy beard. He wasted no time on bathing. He devoted every conscious moment to drinking. He drained bottle after bottle, heedless whether they were high-end liqueurs or inexpensive swill. It was amazing that he survived the bender.

His retreat from reality came to an abrupt end one afternoon.

Squeals of terror roused Barry from his stupefaction. Reacting with a mixture of cop instinct and post-apocalyptic survivalism, he instantly came awake and grabbed up his weapons, ready to defend his domain. Murky shadows infested the tavern, but Barry could detect no threats lurking in those inky corners.

Must've been part of a dream, he counciled himself.

227

But another round of screams contradicted this assumption; they came from outside. Resenting the disturbance, Barry crawled across the tavern's sticky, debris stewn floor. A pair of ornate trestles flanked the doorway; he used them for support, laboriously dragging himself to his unsteady feet. For a moment (it seemed long, but might only have been a handful of seconds), he stood there, weaving physically and mentally, perched precariously between alertness and apathy.

A third chorus of distress sounded, throwing him into full vigilance. He shouldered the door open and staggered outdoors. The fierce daylight hurt his eyes, he squinted in a feeble effort to ward off the brilliance. He knew the landscape wasn't really spinning, but he couldn't focus on anything amid the teetering spectacle. He shook his head, but that only left him with a blurred double image of things. It looked as if a hundred zombies were closing in on him.

Hefting his pair of golf clubs into position, Barry swung into action. He lay into the undead throng, dispatching the creatures with remarkable acumen considering his exceptional intoxication. But then, wielding his knobbed bludgeons was an unruly defense, devastating anything that came within reach. He fought without uttering a sound. The zombies advanced with hissing hunger, and went down with squelchy thuds. Somewhere, on the fringe of everything, human voices still squealed with fear. Barry ignored them, letting nothing interfere with his battle. His concentration was locked on a fuzzy set of movements: waving his arms back and forth, putting as much vicious force as he could behind each swing.

He was drenched with sweat and gore by the time he realized no further adversaries were left. A mound of brutalized corpses surrounded him. His clubs were bent and caked with viscera. His breath came in ragged gasps. The light still hurt his eyes.

Turning away from his destructive handiwork, Barry stumbled back inside the tavern. The shadows embraced him, cooling his damp skin and anesthetizing his weary mind.

Barry woke to discover he was no longer alone.

In his delerious condition, he was dimly aware of women who ministered to his needs. They spoke to him in soothing tones. Neither of them resembled or sounded like his late wife, which possibly helped him relax, since lately Emily only showed up in his terrifying nightmares. A swarm of children bustled about, weaving in and out of his view during his brief moments of consciousness.

Eventually, Barry recuperated enough to learn what had happened.

The women were Anne and Heather. "We don't think last names matter much these days." Anne was a short matronly woman, dark haired with a pug nose and full lips. Heather was a willowy blonde, long-limbed and pale-skinned; the younger of the two, she might've been a showgirl if not for her hawk-nosed profile. These ladies had traveled together ever since they'd lost their respective husbands to zombie attacks, supporting each other and guarding their collective brood against all threats.

"We ran afoul of some zombies just outside of town," Anne explained. "They chased us here. We were looking to hide inside the tavern, but then you appeared. You single-handedly fought them off."

"But then you collapsed," added Heather.

"You were suffering from fatigue and malnutrition," Anne resumed. "You were a mess. Heather and I bathed and fed you. We nursed you back to health."

"Uhh, thanks," Barry responded. His voice was hoarse.

"You saved us from those dead things," chimed in one of the children, a six-year-old girl with red pigtails.

He gave the kid a warm smile.

With hesitant inquiries, the widows coaxed Barry to tell his tale, although he pruned it down considerably. Barry (he judiciously left his surname unspoken), used to be a police officer back in Manhattan before the outbreak. Since then, he'd wandered the countryside, "just surviving."

"You were drunk," accused the pigtailed kid. Her name was Daphne. "Daddy used to drink a lot…back before the dead things came out."

Heather hushed the kid.

"No, it's okay," muttered Barry. Addressing the child, "Yeah, well, when times get tough, sometimes adults get drunk. But little kids shouldn't do that. They need to stay clearheaded and strong to take care of their mommies."

"You was real tough, Mr Winsor, when you whupped all those dead things. Was that cuz you was drunk?" inquired a tow-headed boy whose name was Butch. "Our dad used to get real tough when he would drink. I betcha he'd've taken care of those mean dead things that took him away if he'd been drunk."

"There are better ways to be a tough fighter than getting drunk," Barry told them, although he wasn't entirely sure of the veracity of that declaration. Apparently, he'd fought like a bloodthirsty madman when he'd dispatched the zombie horde that had chased the refugees to the tavern. He'd definitely been plastered. So, the booze *had* enhanced his hostility. He didn't like the sound of that. Previously, he'd used alcohol to withdraw from reality. But now, it seemed to be bringing out the worst in him…fighting with a ferocity more easily attributable to a maniac like Dusty.

The kids were full of questions. Some he had no problem answering; others left him helplessly confounded. Fortunately, he was able to avoid their relentless inquisitions by feigning restorative naps.

During his recuperative period, the mothers had found a wealth of foodstuffs in a hidden room down in the basement. (Too focused on the booze, Barry had never bothered to look for edibles other than nuts and stale chips.) Now, everybody ate well. A stash of comic books served to occupy the kids most of the daylight hours.

When Barry was well enough to walk, he discovered that someone had removed the piled corpses from the tavern's parking lot. "Anne and I took them out back and burned the bodies," Heather told him. "We did it while the kids slept. We didn't want them to see any of that."

"They'll have to learn at some point," remarked Barry, "if they're going to survive in this new world."

"Surely these zombies will decrease in numbers with time. I mean, the more people put down, the less of them there are."

Barry shrugged. Alas, everytime somebody died, the ranks of the undead got replenished. But Heather was right, in a way unknown to her; sooner or later, Earth's people would die off and the last zombies would wander the countryside in search of extinct prey.

The kids would never constitute a fighting force, at least not until they grew up (if they ever would; that remained to be seen). They were too small. There weren't enough guns to go around, which would leave them fighting with knives, but their short arms drastically limited the effective reach of those blades. Anne and Heather were scrappers, but he was loath to risk either of them; a dead mother would traumatize the kids.

Objectively, the tavern was a relatively safe haven. Well off the main roads, it was hidden by decorative stands of trees. They had an ample supply of food. A well out back gave them fresh water. Whenever the group might want other sundries, Barry could always visit a nearby town and loot whatever the families needed. All it needed was a sturdy fence to keep away the undead.

But when he proposed fortifying a perimeter, the women surprised him with their desire to move on. "We're looking for civilization, not a hole to hide in," Heather explained. "The kids need other people if they're going to learn socialization skills." Anne added, "It's too hard living out in the wilds." Although the mothers appreciated the temporary security the tavern offered, they were adamant about continuing their pilgrimage. There had to be places out there where people had united to recreate their lost society. Sooner or later, they would find paradise.

While he admired their ambitions, Barry knew from personal experience how disappointed the moms were going to be. In his travels, he had seen a variety of places that had claimed to have reestablished civilization, but each one had been flawed in some fashion, flawed enough to taint their brand of civilized behavior, rendering their society unacceptable. At least, unacceptable to Barry's standards.

As an ex-cop, he felt his ethics were the only trace left of the old law and order. So far, human nature had thoroughly disappointed Detective Winsor.

Inevitably, Barry couldn't let the families venture forth unescorted. If they planned to wander the wilderness, they would need protection from the many dangers that populated the post-apocalyptic world. For a while, he would act as their protector.

To serve and protect: still his motto after all this time.

And who knows, he mused, *maybe these feisty ladies will actually find the paradise they're looking for.*

They traveled west through North Carolina seeking a peaceful settlement they could make their home. Most of the little pocket societies they encountered were aggressively xenophobic or deviant. Avoiding them wasn't always that easy. But Barry managed to stay a step ahead of the locals.

He developed a fondness for the kids, and a degree of respect for their mothers, who proved to be able fighters in a pinch. While he was careful to spread his attention evenly among these adopted children, Little Daphne was his favorite. He imagined his Emily had been like this when she'd been young: so full of inquisitive life.

The child possessed a unique perspective on the zombie outbreak. Being a youngster, she had not yet gained a true understanding of what was and wasn't possible. In this whimsical state, she still believed in fairies and wizards. So, zombies were easily accepted into her worldview, just bogeymen who'd escaped from the closet to wander the countryside. They still frightened her, but little Daphne wasn't as shocked as the adults were about the existence of zombies in the first place. The undead were just a part of the world in which she lived, like trees and clouds and frogs and chocolate. "Although," she admitted, "chocolate's become really rare anymore." Gradually, the girl's memory of her last candy bar would fade until chocolate was no different than fairies: never seen, but eternally hoped for.

Exchanges like this threatened to move Barry Winsor to tears.

To facilitate coping with his new responsibilities, Barry swore off alcohol. Much to the unspoken approval of the kids.

Without fail, he protected the family.

By this point, they'd all started thinking of themselves as the "family" instead of two "families."

They never did find paradise.

The family made it as far as Tennessee.

For several hours, they'd trekked through hilly country. Most of those hills had been covered by trees, often the lush woods completely obscured the sky. So when the family reached a relatively open slope that revealed a rare glimpse of distant regions, they paused to rest—and appreciate the view. Fair weather had left most of the sky empty; to the west a mass of dark clouds stretched along the horizon.

"You can see for miles from up here," noted Anne.

"Pretty," one of the kids remarked.

"Look—over there." Heather pointed to the north. Visible from this high vantage, several thin trails of smoke rose from beyond the hills. "A settlement?"

"Could be," Barry intoned. If there'd been only one trail, it might've been the beginning of a wild fire, but from their number and the delicate way they ascended into the air, their origin was unquestionably civilized.

This development infected the children with an optimistic agitation. The mothers gathered their offspring and advised them to be patient. The family would investigate.

Only Barry harbored caution. Time and again, their discovery of settlements had generated enthusiasm—only to be replaced by disappointment when observations revealed the enclaves' unsavory nature. He wondered how long the kids would put up with these delays. Already, Daphne's impatience was repeatedly surfacing.

"Why's it taking so long, Mr Winsor?"

"Some thing's just take time, honey," he tried to assuage her curiosity.

"But we keep finding people. Why couldn't we join them?"

How could children comprehend the social nuances practiced by mankind, much less fathom that some were unhealthy, even dangerous?

"Well, Daphne, those people weren't right."

"Not right how?"

He chewed his lip. "They were...bad people."

"How could you tell? You just spied on them. You never spoke with them."

"I could tell."

She squinted up at him, her mouth arched to express her dubious attitude.

"It's a cop thing, honey."

"Oh." Her face resumed its juvenile innocence, full of trust and acceptance. Within seconds, she was off on another topic, asking him about how birds could fly.

He scanned the sky while trying to explain the aerodynamic properties of wings. What had made her think of birds? He saw none flittering about overhead. In fact, the woods had been noticeably devoid of wildlife. But maybe the girl had spotted something that had escaped his detection; her young eyes and ears were more acute than his.

This new colony was still some distance away. The family would have to get closer before the detective could assess the settlement's temperament.

Surveying the terrain, Barry saw no easy route. While the incline that spread out below the family featured few trees, the slope was steep and densely clogged with vegetation. Progress would be slow and difficult.

He regretted making the children traverse such harsh topography, but travel along manmade roads was risky. Undead and living threats could catch the family out in the open. Consequently, Barry had taken the group through thick woodlands to avoid any hazardous contact. Fortunately, most of the kids still thought country hiking was fun.

After a brief meal of nuts and jerky, the family gathered their belongings and wits. They set off to move down the slope. Dense shrubbery covered the terrain, impairing any easy descent. Even the machetes they'd picked up during their travels proved fruitless against the robust thickets. On more than one occasion, the group had to backtrack and seek other routes through clusters of scrub that proved equally impenetrable. Most of the time the shrubbery completely surrounded them. Their stalwart persistence took them more than halfway down the escarpment.

Although intent on hacking away at the brush, Barry had noticed that distant stormcloud was sweeping across the landscape. He didn't like the look of it. By the time it darkened the sky overhead, it was too late. The foliage masked the brunt of the storm until the downpour reached a torrential state. Eventually, the tempest became forceful enough to penetrate the leafy canopy and drench everyone.

"Back!" Barry called out to them.

The moms struggled to round up their brood. The kids were all laughing. Barry's footing was reduced to sloshing in mud.

"Back," he urged everyone. "Back up the hill."

"Aww," groaned several childlike voices.

"We're so close to the bottom," Heather protested.

"Now! Everybody move it!" Barry had a very bad feeling about this.

The torrential downpour increased in strength. The rain pelted the vegetation like solid pellets, literally tearing holes in the leaves. The mud was getting runnier. Visibility was drastically diminished.

So far, these clouds had offered no thunder—but suddenly a mammoth rumble shook the hill.

What the hell—

He felt the flash flood before its rising tide became visible. A wash of water coursed through the shrubbery, ripping foliage from the twigs, uprooting bigger shrubs. The ground joined the fluid in its mad rush. Abruptly, there was no longer anything solid on which to stand.

Snagging the bough of a stout bush and holding on for dear life, Barry tried to grab a nearby smudge that looked like a flailing child—but failed. His hands were too slippery, the kid's velocity too great. The youngster disappeared in the deluge.

Barely audible over the roaring flood, a chorus of screams brought his heart up into his throat. He bellowed instructions, warning them to grab the sturdiest bush and not let go, but he could hardly hear himself over the bedlam.

What had been a surging current suddenly became an angry wall of water, tearing almost everything from the slope: mud, scrub, bushes and humans. The violent flood wrenched his stout shrub free of the soil, taking Barry with it. He tumbled on a horizontal trajectory along the escarpment. He lost hold of his uprooted anchor. Branches raked him. Large debris pummeled him. He fought to stay conscious; he couldn't afford to pass out and be yanked away to another year.

Carried by the same flood, something large collided with Barry. A big bush, he surmised, as its twigs scraped away more of his skin. He clutched at it and managed to wrap the fingers of one hand around a robust branch. A moment later, he succeeded in snatching another branch with his other hand. He held on as if his life depended on it—which it likely did.

His ride was arduous as he bopped in the flood as it tore through the valley between hills. This furious wave hauled away everything it stripped from the slope. The tumultuous flow tossed Barry about like a piece of flotsam in a maelstrom of arboreal debris. Submerged, he strained to resist the urge to gasp for air. A host of new bruises joined his daily retinue of aches.

Suddenly his violent journey ended. His shoulder slammed into a broad hard surface. The surging water pressed his back against this barrier, while the brunt of the flow held him in place. He spread his limbs to extend his contact with whatever it was. Resisting the deluge's urgency, Barry carefully twisted around until he lay spread-eagled on his belly. He could tell now it was a boulder, a large rock embedded in the slope firmly enough to withstand the fervor of the torrent.

The water splashed over him in ragged waves. When his head erratically broke the surface, he gulped air to last him until his next gasp. Torturously, he crawled up the boulder until he liberated his torso from the rushing water. Finally able to breath, he rested—but never too much, lest he lose his grip on the salvation crag.

Immediate stress overwhelmed Barry's mind for a time. He had no idea how long he clung there. The flash flood seemed to last forever. Ultimately, though, the pellmell torrent dwindled, and he found himself alone on a generally denuded escarpment.

Long moments passed before the first sob erupted from his throat. Shuddering with grief and the wet cold, he wept.

The flood swept everyone away. Only Barry survived. He searched, but never found any of their bodies.

Once again he had failed to save those under his protection.

This tragedy plunged Barry into another depressive spiral. Ignoring the settlement to the north, he struck off at random. The next deserted town he hit, he sought out an abandoned bar and drank himself unconscious.

When the booze ran out, sobriety returned, bringing with it Barry's deep-seated guilt—just as he'd expected. He'd hoped, though, that his binge might extend to a point whereat dehydration and hunger might take him out. Alas, his constitution was stronger than he'd thought it would be, lasting longer than the bar's supply of alcohol.

For some time, he wallowed in despair, damning fate for failing to end his misery—and, more important to him, condemning the miseries his company seemed to bring others. His wife, his partner, his fellow officers, Anne and Heather and their collective family, especially young Daphne—Barry's affection had brought them nothing but suffering and death. He had failed so many people. It had become his scourge.

Meanwhile, he'd reached a point where he'd accepted abandoning Miss Collard—she would be better off without his curse hanging over her. There were a select few among Sanctuary's poulation for whom Barry had developed a kind of fondness. They should all be safe now because he'd left before his poisonous influence could doom them.

But he knew that was spurious logic. The world had become a maliciously dangerous place; bad shit didn't just happen these days, disasters had a way of actively seeking out human targets. Life expectancies were way down from the old days...*ha, especially,* he reminded himself, *since everybody's already dead.*

Barry was tired of losing people, but at the same time a part of him yearned to protect everybody, from the undead, from the crazies, even from themselves. This new world suffered from a severe lack of law and order. It needed individuals like him who were willing to fight for human values and common decency.

"I'm just so tired of losing people," he muttered.

"Then you need to get better at protecting them."

Sprawled on the bar's dirty floor, Barry turned his head to find someone standing over him. "Go away. Leave me alone."

The figure chuckled, but the laugh lacked any real mirth. The man crouched down, moving laboriously, as if the simple action of stooping involved painful exertion, and Barry could see his face now.

It was Barry...well, sort of Barry. He wore an eye-patch and his face sagged with wrinkled flesh. Despite the war scars and years of stress, though, his features were familiar enough for even drunk Barry to recognize this much older version of himself. Drunk Barry didn't take it seriously, though, so grumbled, "A bad booze hallucination."

"More like a handy displacement," older Barry replied. He offered drunk Barry a plastic bottle filled with a clear liquid.

Thinking it might be vodka, the man on the floor sat up, opened the bottle and took a hard chug—before spitting it out. "Water!"

"Don't waste it," admonished older Barry. "You're badly dehydrated." He rose to his feet and hobbled over to examine the looted empty shelves behind the bar.

"Who cares…"

"I do," he threw over his shoulder. "Which means—later on—you will too."

"What are you supposed to be?" snarled drunk Barry. "Future me, come back to get me to change my ways?"

"It's that obvious, huh?"

"What happened to our eye?"

The older Barry turned away for a moment, an unsuccessful attempt to hide a scowl. "A stroke."

"You're *old*…"

"With age comes experience and wisdom."

"So—you can control the temporal displacements?"

"Not likely. They're still random. This one just happens to be personally advantageous."

"Not to me," drunk Barry complained as he dragged himself from the dirty floor. He perched his butt on a nearby cocktail chair.

"Like I told you—not yet. But trust me, by the time you get to be me, you'll agree that a lot of what we did was worthwhile. You'll thank yourself for this intervention."

"You're too late for an intervention," laughed drunk Barry. "There's no booze left for me to drink, so I have no choice but to sober up."

Plucking a bottle from the shadowy recesses of one of the shelves he'd been examining, older Barry held it up and declared, "All gone—except for this one bottle."

"Huh?" Drunk Barry staggered from the chair. "I don't believe you. Let me see. Give it here."

While toying with it, older Barry deftly kept the bottle beyond drunk Barry's reach.

"Give it to me!"

"Fat chance," grunted older Barry. "This is my reward for getting you to stop."

Drunk Barry's legs got tangled up with each other, returning him to a spread-eagled position on the floor.

Caressing the bottle like a lost lover, older Barry teased its cork from the bottle's mouth. "I've stayed clean all these years because I had to—to see things got done right. But now, my responsibilities are near an end. And I deserve a stiff shot for all my efforts." He threw drunk Barry a sympathetic look. "The stuff you're going to do is really going to matter. You mustn't screw up."

Drunk Barry propped himself up on his elbows and cursed, "Stupid alkie dream."

"You need to believe—" Older Barry came over and kicked drunk Barry in the ribs. "—that I'm real."

"Ow!"

"Hallucinations don't leave bruises, pal," proclaimed older Barry. He settled on a bar stool and tipped the bottle to his lips. His first sip was tenuous, crinkling the lines around his rheumy eyes. His next gulp was hungry. He sat back with the wistful smirk of an addict reunited after all these years with his poison of choice.

Drunk Barry squimed around until he managed to get into a crosslegged sitting position on the floor. Holding the water bottle in his lap, he glared at his elder self and grumbled, "Hallucinations don't steal a guy's last bottle, either."

Pausing between sips, older Barry responded, "Another fact in my favor. Anyway, I need this far more than you do." He set the now slightly depleted bottle (it looked like rum) on the bar and tilted his head to peer in his younger self's direction. "Right now, your job is to sober up and get your ass back to Sanctuary. I'm not sure how long I have left here—your memory of this encounter is, at best, clouded by a hangover. So you need to pay extra attention to what I'm telling you."

"All you're telling me to do is to listen to you."

""And to sober up!"

"Yeah, well, since you're drinking my last bottle, I don't have much choice about that, do I?"

"Sober up and stay sober, then."

Younger Barry laughed at that.

"Was I really this cynical?" older Barry lamented to himselves.

"You can call it what you want. I prefer to think of myself as realistic."

"Don't bullshit yourself. You wouldn't be so maudlin all the time if you didn't miss the good times. They happened, and they can happen again. But not as long as you refuse to see opportunity."

"Opportunity for what?"

Older Barry waved an expressive hand at him. "For the potential of every moment. Each passing moment holds the potential for a thousand emotions, from sad to serious to silly. You need to take advantage of that potential, instead of avoiding them because you're worried about the consequences. Consequences are as plentiful as emotions. They dont always land on the sorry side."

Drunk Barry put a hand to head and winced. "Jeez, when do I turn into a dreary philosophy scholar?"

"Even though we're both participating in this discussion, it uniquely belongs to you. You're not the only one who's going to benefit from your sobriety. And this time I don't mean me—I mean Miss Collard and Doc Toby and hundreds more."

"Only hundreds?" drunk Barry sardonically threw back. "I'm not destined to save the world?"

With a dark frown, older Barry confessed, "If you don't hurry up, the world population just might be down that low by the time you get to Sanctuary."

"Umm…"

Drunk Barry watched as his doppleganger faded away, leaving the half-full bottle of rum on the bar. Long after future Barry was gone (if he'd even been there in the first place), drunk Barry stared hard at the bottle. The last bottle of booze remaining here at the bar. The last chance to resume oblivion. The last temptation.

Is that why he left it behind? reflected Barry. *A last temptation to overcome before I do his bidding?*

Clambering to his feet, Barry snatched the bottle from the bar and took a healthy swig.

Too bad, future me. Right now, I'm not up to any challenges or responsibilities.

As it was, even a taste of the rum was enough to tip Barry back into pervasive inebriation. Sedated, he sank back to the floor and peacefully closed his eyes.

I'll sober up when I do…

And found himself standing in a white room.

An hospital room with rows of beds. Life-sustaining machinery surrounded one bed. A bay window looked out upon an intact New York City skyline.

Wobbling with unsteadiness, Barry edged closer to the occupied bed.

It was him—Barry Winsor—specifically, older Barry.

As Barry drew near, older Barry opened his one visible eye and scowled at him. Barry could smell the rum on his breath.

"You weak-willed idiot," older Barry spoke softly. "I knew you'd let me down. So I spit in the rum, hoping it might draw you ahead to me once you drank it."

Drunk Barry frowned. His alcohol-addled brain was having difficulty grasping what was happening. Somehow he'd been displaced to older Barry's point in the time stream, but instead of occupying the Barry body, he was here as a duplicated extension of himself. *This displacement is different from all of the others.* It came to him as a slap-in-the-face shock: this was a *controlled* displacement. Not a random one. *Somehow, older Barry has intentionally pulled me here...to do what? Chastise me for drinking the rum? But—why is he pissed at me for drinking the rum? He expected me to...*

What weaseled its way to the surface of this miasma of realizations was: "You can control the displacements!"

"They're all in your head. You need to get your shit together. I mean it." Reaching out, he took the bottle of rum from drunk Barry and cradled it to his own breast. "You want me to say it? If I have to, I will..."

"Say what...?"

"You save the world! But only if you get your shit together and get back to Sanctuary!"

His older self looked so fragile. Drunk Barry reached out to touch him...and his hand passed through the chest as if it weren't there.

More specifically, *he* was the one who was ceasing to exist here in the old man's hospital room. Gradually, the features of the murky bar rose into focus around drunk Barry. He was back. If he harbored any doubt that the displacement had happened, the confirmation was the rum bottle he no longer held.

Sneaky bastard...

Back in the hospital room, old Barry hugged the bottle of rum with a sly grin. Nurse Collard would not approve of him imbibing, but he had no intention of giving up the bottle. He'd snatched it from the past, not an easy trick. It was his now. After such a long sobriety, he deserved some booze in his final moments. A reward for all his efforts—his successes and his failures.

He regretted having to lie to his younger self.

His prior visit to the past had failed to have the desired impact on his younger (stubborn) self. Further contact had been required. A more grandiose carrot had been necessary this time, but old Barry believed he'd finally gotten through to the crotchety drunk.

Hopefully, he won't make the same mistakes I made...

Settling back on his mound of pillows, he closed his one good eye and waited to see what changes might occur within his memory.

Barry never intended to return to Sanctuary leading a throng of refugees in tow—but life was full of surprises.

Not all of them pleasant.

During his travels, Barry had encountered several people. Some were wretched examples of humanity, but there were others who needed protection from the former crazies. And the multitude of walking un-dead posed a perpetual threat; their numbers never seemed to decrease. Without intending to do so, Barry ended up playing the role of the hero for each of these needy individuals. Whether they needed rescuing from hungry zombies or homicidal crazies or just lonely despair, Barry was there to do the saving.

To serve and protect, both consciously and involuntarily.

As they drew near Sanctuary's turf, Barry was surprised to see no recon scouts guarding the territory. That should've been his first clue, but he was too eager to see Miss Collard again after all this time; his caution had been shouldered aside by jocund expectations.

He halted the group's progress atop a hill. The view looked down on Sanctuary, but instead of a thriving settlement, all that was left were ragtag ruins. Scorched, torn-to-pieces husks surrounded the masonry skeleton of the chemical factory. The colony had not just been "hit," it'd been obliterated.

Barry's gut threw a name to his lips with no more rationale than raw instinct: "Banksy."

Vindictive bastard that he was, Theodore Banksy blamed Barry Winsor for the destruction of his Manhattan enclave. So he had destroyed Barry's Sanctuary as payback for the massacre of the Local Blues settlement. Genocide for genocide. That was the way Banksy thought.

At this point, there was no evidence to support Barry's suspicion, but he knew to trust his gut. The devastation made him sick. He staggered into Sanctuary's remains with tears streaming down his drawn cheeks. Clearly, explosives had been used to decimate the factory; the town's houses had suffered secondary damage before they'd been torched. Sickeningly colorful chemical spills ran from the factory's corpse, creating a kaleidoscopic moat around the settlement. Unmindful of stench or sizzle, Barry waded the moat to examine the wreckage. He found humanoid cinders scattered among the residential debris. The cadavers were too badly burned to be identifiable.

His followers were as stunned as he by what remained of Sanctuary. They'd been promised shelter from the savage new world, but all they'd found at the end of their long hard road were ruins.

Barry refused to believe the slaughter had been complete. There had to be survivors.

He sent out parties to search the neighboring area for any refugees from this disaster. They all came back empty-handed.

Stunned and suddenly lacking purpose, Barry set up camp on a hill overlooking the Sanctuary ruins. He sat for hours, gazing down upon the scorched earth. The others began to worry for his sanity.

Not only had he failed Miss Collard and the others, he'd failed himself. After all the effort his older self had gone to in order to come back and counsel him at a time of need…and he'd screwed up. He'd returned too late. Sanctuary was gone. Miss Collard lost, along with Doc Toby, that asshole Dusty, the pompous Board and the innocent citizens—everybody dead. Banksy may have ordered the massacre, but Barry blamed himself for letting it happen. He should have known better, should never have left Sanctuary. If he'd stayed, maybe he could've helped defend the settlement.

No…he knew that was implausible. His presence wouldn't have mattered against the vengeful brutality of Banksy's frustrated Blues. If he had been here, he'd be dead too.

But that wasn't much of a consolation.

His future self had insisted that Sanctuary's salvation was his responsibility. How could Barry have failed so dramatically?

He told no one he was leaving. He snuck off one night, this time vowing never to revisit this site of misery.

Consequently, he missed the return of a batch of Sanctuary survivors. To escape Banksy's vengeance, the refugees had fled far north into the thicker woodlands of the Pine Barrens. Only now, more than a month after the attack, the refugees were back…because they had nowhere else to go. Among these refugees were Miss Collard, Joey Fulton, Doc Toby, and a pair of disillusioned Board members, Professors Grauss and Dracy. Together with those who had followed Barry Winsor here, they decided to build a new Sanctuary, uphill from the ruins of its predecessor, where the site's poisons wouldn't impair the new settlement, but would remain as a dire reminder of foolhardy violence.

Already gone, Barry never learned of the girl's survival or the fate of his other acquaintances.

10

NO LONGER DID BARRY TRAVEL WITHOUT PURPOSE. There was vengeance on his mind. He didn't care whether or not it was honorable. He lusted for Theodore Banksy's blood, and *nothing* was going to deprive him of this gruesome accomplishment. He would slaughter anyone who got in his way. And if Barry should fall in the course of his revenge, he vowed that his zombie would finish the job for him. Only then could he sleep easy.

Everyone had lied to Barry. The Bible, his pastor, his parents, his immediate superiors in the police force, even his dead wife—all had assured him that good always triumphed over evil. Even his future self had lied to him, forcing him to sober up and run back north, where he'd been led to believe he would save Sanctuary. But…he hadn't.

Maybe the blame was his. Maybe he'd taken too long to sober up. Perhaps he hadn't traveled fast enough. More likely, he'd screwed up by trusting his older self.

But he wasn't going to fail this time. Banksy's punishment would happen, and Barry Winsor's hand would be the instrument that delivered the deathblow.

While he traveled alone, Barry made a point of questioning anyone he encountered. He sought traces of an armed force, the last of Banksy's Blues. Initially, his enquiries were rather intense, scaring the pathetic people he unearthed hiding throughout the countryside. Even when he subdued his attitude, his interrogations frightened most individuals into unwilling silence.

In truth, the few that had seen the army Winsor sought remembered them as a savage, bloodthirsty lot. They killed without dispatching the resulting zombies. This was an unforgivable sin in the new world.

When someone finally mentioned this habitual omission, Barry's fury doubled.

He followed a sparse selection of clues west, through farm country and around the shoreline of Lake Michigan. It seemed that Banksy was headed for Chicago. Styling himself as some post-apocalyptic Al Capone, perhaps the gangster planned to start a new empire in history's most infamous criminal city.

En route, Barry collected an impressive arsenal to use against Banksy's murderous army. Completely by accident, he found a National Reserve office whose cellar turned out to be not as well-hidden as its designer had intended. The weapons cache contained there supplied him with brutal automatic rifles and even a bazooka. His arsenal got too cumbersome to carry alone, so he conscripted the use of a ratty pickup truck whose rear he loaded with these implements of destruction.

As he drove, he concocted colorful, elaborately grisly ways to exact his revenge on Theodore Banksy. Lost in these unhealthy thoughts, he took an elevated curve too fast and sent the vehicle plummeting down a steep slope. The rocky slope punished the truck, and Barry barely leapt free before it hit bottom—where the explosives stashed in it exploded, atomizing the wreck.

The loss pissed him off, but it also brought him his best lead in tracking Banksy's army. He waited on the wooded slope. Once the blaze died out, he hoped to root through the wreckage for weapons that had survived the blast. Someone else got there first.

As he watched, a pair of crudely armored cars arrived on the elevated road. The vehicles disgorged a squad of men who carefully descended the hill to examine the still-burning wreckage. Although Barry could not overhear the squad, he knew what was afoot when they split up to scout the surrounding hills. He hid under a large slab jutting from the slope like a basalt tongue.

He hadn't counted on the man who searched this immediate region being an accomplished tracker. The man easily spied traces of Barry's clamber to crouch beneath the ledge. Moving slightly downhill, casually never casting a glance in the rock's direction, the tracker reached a position that exposed the underside of the ledge to his gun. He fired a warning shot, then advised whoever was hiding to come out. The warning shot had been awful close; Barry was unwilling to risk getting hit by another volley. Voicing his surrender, he crawled from his earthen shelter.

As Barry stood erect, two other squad members arrived, summoned by the tracker's shot. They searched Barry, relieved him of his weaponry, then bound him with plastic ties. His binding told Barry these men had, at some time in the past, been involved with law enforcement; only cops carried plastic ties for this purpose. Besides, he recognized their outfits; these men belonged to Banksy.

His foremost urge was to remain mute when questioned, but then it occurred to him that opening up to these men (with a tale of complete falsehood) might help his ultimate goal. If he could convince them that he was like them, they might welcome him into their ranks. Instead of sneaking into Banksy's camp, the gangster's own troops would get him in. He liked the irony of that.

So, Barry introduced himself as Bud Wycotte and spun a tale designed to appeal to an ex-cop. He told how Bud had been a cop before the outbreak, but Internal Affairs had busted him on trumped up charges. Bud had been incarcerated in Hartford, Connecticut, when all hell had broken loose; he'd barely escaped alive. Bud hoped some of those zombies got to gnaw on the faces of the IA reps who'd had him falsely locked up.

The men nodded in agreement with Barry's muttered wish. They were entirely sympathetic to Bud's unjust plight.

"Who cares that you were innocent, though," one remarked.

Another added, "The real trick is not getting caught."

Barry laughed along with the troops.

"I was headed west," he continued. "There's talk of some group who are trying to restore order in Chicago."

"We'd be part of that group," declared the tracker.

"Hey." A fellow elbowed him in the side.

"Aw, c'mon," ventured another man, "this guy belongs with us."

"Yeah. He ain't no wasteland wussy."

They cut the plastic ties off Barry and escorted him up the hill to their armored cars.

The accident may have taken away his impressive arsenal, but it had eventually led to a free pass into the heart of his target.

He could not believe how easily he infiltrated their ranks.

The army had settled into Chicago's prestigious Drake Hotel. The neighborhood still bore traces of the battle Banksy's troops had fought to oust whatever feudal lord had previously ruled the territory. Apparently, Banksy was unwilling to spare the men to finish the clean-up.

The army numbered just under two hundred men; one fifty of whom had come from New York, the remaining men had been picked up along the way—like Bud. The troops were bivouacked in plush hotel located across the street. An impressive array of military vehicles, appropriated from army bases north of the city, were parked in front of the Drake's steps. He found the police bus from the 13th NYCP garage out back, with other transport vehicles. Banksy's troops had amassed a lot of nasty hardware during their cross-country trek.

Once Bud had been given a billet, he was assigned to a squad guarding the transport vehicles. In a neighboring lot was parked a selection of luxury cars, Audis, Ferraris, even a vintage red Corvette. These, he was informed, belonged to the commanders. Barry wondered which one was Banksy's personal ride.

It would take some time to acclimate himself to life among the ChiTown Blues. He needed to pass as one of them: a good cop gone bad. As long as he didn't have to kill or abuse anyone, he was confident he could pull off the ruse.

For now, it appeared as if Banksy's army was still settling in, learning the ropes of ruling the Windy City. Other local enclaves existed and needed to be put down, but apparently Banksy was biding his time, allowing his reputation to hold any enemies and rivals at bay.

Barry could help undermine that informal cease-fire.

During his offhours, Bud Wycotte showed a fondness for bar-hopping. He appeared to consume volumes of alcohol (but never got drunk) and to wear out a string of gymnastic prostitutes (whom he never touched, but used roofies to maintain his status as an insatiable stud). He was a party hound. Other troopers enjoyed his company, but they rarely remembered much about their outrageous evenings out (Again, a liberal distribution of roofies kept Barry operating in a shadowy zone beyond anyone's radar.) He was able to secretly spread dissent, even convincing a few groups of rowdy locals to stage open protests of Banksy's dominion. Not that these rallies ever posed a viable threat to the ChiTown Blues, but monitoring their subversive existence wasted the time and energies of personnel. Barry was able to leak the locations of several food hoards to starving immigrant families who squatted among the lakeside warehouses—more small but annoying potatoes.

All the while, Barry gathered information. Troop deployments, the location of secret ammunition depots, the daily routines practiced by Theodore Banksy and his other co-commanders. Somewhere along the way, Banksy had accepted two strangers to share in his ruling class. He learned their names and histories, but they were recent additions and thereby exempt from the vengeance Barry planned for the Blues' decimation of Sanctuary. One of them, a Neil Hample, had previously been a politician of some local popularity; Barry actually respected the man for his stands and the departments he had recreated to handle restoring the city's utilities. The other, a Carl Lundquest, had been a measly loan shark, and might've been overlooked in the power struggle if not for his fiercely loyal older, bigger brother, Ken, a disgraced ultimate fighting champion. The Lunquests' lust for power was top-heavy and would eventually topple their over-ambitious interests. While Hample might just be the man to take over and run the city once Barry had wiped out the rest of the guilty Blues.

Barry's seditious endeavors kept him busy, but he was always on the lookout for data concerning Banksy's personal itinerary. The gangster maintained a 24/7 trio of burly thugs to guard his safety. Even when he took his Corvette out for an adventurous spin, one of the guards rode shotgun. The tramps he favored were roomed separately from the other ladies. His food was prepared by chefs assigned to exclusively cater to his every dietary whim. Finding a hole in his defenses was going to be problematic.

He no longer cared about asserting a sense of law and order in this terrible world. His future self had lied to him about saving Sanctuary, so it made sense that his claim about Barry "saving the world" was no more than an exaggeration to goad him back to sobriety. Only vengeance mattered to Barry Winsor now, punishing Banksy and his murderous Blues for what they'd done to Sanctuary.

But Barry would bide his time, plan carefully, and avoid risky stunts that might endanger his position: the secret wolverine in the hen-house.

But fate was impatient and forced a disastrous confrontation on the lurking dissident.

Bud was serving a shift guarding the transport vehicles, one of two men on duty. His companion, Nick, had just snuck off to take a leak, leaving Barry to contemplate a bit of random sabotage. He wandered across the parking area to peer at the rows of luxury cars reserved for the higher Blues echelons. Tampering with one of the sports cars might spoil some commander's personal outing; although minor, Barry felt that even trivial inconveniences helped his cause. Anything that annoyed the ruling class or impaired its ability to mete out oppression was a worthy endeavor.

Strolling amid the luxury vehicles, he chose one at random and popped its hood. Leaning down, he loosened a spark plug—not enough to cause a malfunction, but just enough so that the vibrations of the car once it got moving would eventually disconnect the plug in its socket. He stood back, closed the car's sleek yellow hood, and realized two figures stood there. While Barry had been busy with his vandalism, they must've come from the master building and crossed the lot.

"What're you doing there?" demanded one of the men.

It was Theodore Banksy with one of his personal guards.

"Uh…checking out the motor, sir," Barry produced a handy excuse. "This is some slick car, boss. I—" His on-the-spot concoction was cut short by Banksy's sudden outcry.

"You!"

Dammit—

Despite the dim lighting, the gangster had recognized Barry as the man he blamed for the downfall of his Manhattan enclave.

There was no way of fast-talking his way out of this. Barry had to cast off his role as a spy and go on the offensive—quick, before Banksy's guard drew his weapon.

Stepping in close, Barry drew his revolver and drove it into the guard's lantern-jaw. As the guard collapsed, Barry swung his gun to fire a succession of shots at the lead gangster—but the bastard wasn't there. Banksy had taken advantage of the brief assault and fled, diving behind one of the other luxury cars.

Dammit—

Dashing along the row of dormant headlights, Barry replaced his clip as he moved. But there was no sign of the escaping gangster between the cars.

He could hear muttering and the crackle of a radio signal. Banksy was calling for help.

Dammit—I'll never get a better chance to ice the bastard. But if I can't find him before others arrive, I'll have to fight them all off. I haven't got enough ammo to handle a bunch of adversaries.

Where are you, you tricky bastard?

He slipped between two cars, checking the gaps deeper in the arranged rows. By racing back and then across, he should optimize his chances of spotting the hiding gangster.

And there he was.

But before Barry could fire a shot, Banksy shot at him, forcing the detective to duck back. The two exchanged some shots from their vantages, inflicting wounds only on the cars' sleek fuselages.

"You worm!" cursed Banksy from the darkness.

"You slaughtered everyone at Sanctuary," Barry called back.

"Did you lose some friends there? Maybe a wife or a mistress? Serves you right, you scumbag. You ruined everything back in Manhattan."

It was futile for Barry to try to set the gangster straight about the siege on his enclave. Banksy wouldn't care that Barry had opposed the assault. He blamed Barry for its downfall. In payback, Banksy had destroyed Sanctuary. "Now," announced Barry, "each of us has a reason to want the other dead."

"If I don't get you here," Banksy vowed, "I'll track you down to the ends of the earth."

"Good to know. But—let's finish this here. Just you and me."

Banksy barked a bestial laugh. "Any minute now, my men will be here to capture you. Then I can take my time torturing you. That sounds much better to me."

And the bastard was right. Barry had to force a face-to-face confrontation—and soon, before any unwelcome cavalry showed up. The only viable way of achieving that was to throw all caution to the wind and—

Flinging himself from cover, Barry rushed the gangster. He fired some covering shots, but received no salvo in return...because Banksy had moved on. Now he was lost again among the parked cars.

A slug struck a fender by his hip. He dodged back, returning fire, but for only a brief instant—before the revolver clacked uselessly in his hand. He'd emptied this clip. And a quick search revealed no more tucked at his belt. He was out of ammo.

A savage volley of shots zoomed out of the darkness, chipping paint from the Audi against which Barry leaned. He recoiled, falling to his knees and hastily retreating.

Dammit—

Buried in the shots Barry could hear cries of newcomers. He'd run out of time. Banksy's cavalry had arrived.

The time had come to get out of here. Unarmed, Barry couldn't fight them off. If he fled, he might live to get another shot at the guilty gangster.

Reaching under the nearest car, Barry cut the fuel line with a knife he pulled from his boot. He flicked a lighter to life with his free hand and dropped it under the vehicle. Running in a crouch, he moved swiftly along a line of cars until he reached the northern end of the lot. He yanked open the driver's door and scrambled aboard a convertible parked in the front row.

Flames rose at the far side of the collection of luxury vehicles, first tiny licks low to the ground, then boisterous tongues striving for greatness, soon followed by a tumultuous blast as the gas tank combusted in an eruption that sent the car leaping high into the air. It came down with a crash and all hell broke loose. Attracted by the explosion, the cavalry clustered around the automotive prye. Their voices raised in excited protests.

All of the luxury cars waited with their keys in their ignitions, so the commanders could take off without undue formalities. Barry knew this from his stint as parking lot guard. He started the convertible's engine and launched it across the lot. Swerving to avoid hitting a few men who still trailed from the building into the parking area, he slammed the side of the car into one of the solemn police transports. The sporty car bounced back with spry resilience. He deftly steered it from the lot and around into the alley that led to the front of the Drake building.

Behind him, a pair of headlights winked on, testimony that someone had moved nimbly enough to give chase in another of the luxury cars.

Barry sent his vehicle careening into the night.

Being unfamiliar with Chicago's streets, Barry drove like a madman. He noisily took corners at speeds much too high. He miraculously avoided crashing into the autos whose wrecks still lingered on the throughways. He hoped there was enough fuel in the car to get him beyond the metropolitan district. Outside the city, he would find anoither, more innocuous vehicle to finish his getaway.

That is—if he got the chance.

Behind him, someone was in full pursuit. Their high-beams glittered through the dust kicked up in his wake. Barry veered down anonymous streets, hoping to lose his tail, but whoever was after him, they were a better driver than he. Their vehicle might even be faster than the one he'd chosen. Being an urban child, Barry had lived most of his life never needing a car to get around the Big Apple. In the course of being a police officer, though, he had become a competent driver. And since finding himself stranded in this post-apocalyptic world, his driving exploits had grown audacious, even foolhardy, predicated by perilous circumstances.

This evening was putting his driving skills to a grueling test.

He had better luck once he got past the concrete jungle. As structures began to dwindle in size, his serpentine route managed to shake his pursuer. He did not slow down, but chose his turns with more judicious care.

Dammit—

He could not get over how close he'd come to killing Banksy—only to fumble the ball and blow it. No, that was unfair. Although it rankled Barry to admit it, Banksy had proven to be an agile adversary—quick and quick-witted. The gangster had doled out with the same resolve as Barry put into slaying him. They were equally matched opponents. A worthy nemesis? No—Barry refused to credit the bastard with any trace of honor. Banksy was a criminal, a murderer, a power-crazed feudal lord who could not be allowed to reign in these post-apocalyptic times.

I had my chance and I blew it.

Would Barry find another opportunity? Or had he once again defended his unofficial title as all-time biggest loser? He'd failed everyone… and now he couldn't even live up to his own promises.

A car barreled from a sidestreet and narrowly missed broadsiding Barry's stolen convertible. He reflexively crushed the accelerator pad underfoot, resulting in a reckless spurt of velocity. Momentarily out of control, he careened down the roadway. He smashed a fruit stand to pieces, sending rotten produce tumbling everywhere, but missed colliding with the truck parked next to it. His erratic trajectory plunged him off the asphalt and for a stretch he raced along behind a roadside line of sturdy fir trees.

On the other side of the arboreal barrier, the pursuit car paced his helter-skelter progress.

Dammit—I thought I shook him…

A sharp metallic *twang* told Barry that his pursuer was shooting at him. The trees blocked most of the shots, but a few were making it through to hit the convertible. Barry veered away from the line of firs, disappearing into a hilly gap between two country houses. Crossing the grassy expanse was treacherous, more than once he nearly ran into isolated statuary decorating the lawn. As soon as he spotted a roadway, he returned his tires to the pavement.

At one point, he threw the car across several dividers to reach a ramp leading to an elevated highway. Here, he tried to coax his escape craft to greater velocities.

He drove this way for nearly half-an-hour, and was almost ready to congratulate himself for losing his tail—when two pinpricks of light grew in his rearview mirror to dazzle like a dragon's angry gaze.

Dammit—this guy just won't give up.

His gut warned him who it probably was—because terrible luck never seemed to abandon Detective Winsor. Moments later, the pursuit car, a vintage red Corvette, pulled up beside Barry's stolen convertible as they raced down the interstate—and Barry saw that the driver was Theodore Banksy. There was no one else with him in the car, he had come alone after Barry.

In the old days, nobody could link Banksy to any crime; he had been way too careful. These days, though, the gangster had become a do-it-yourself kind of guy. He wanted Barry dead and he was going to do it himself. The main difference, of course—in the old days the man had feared legal retribution; but now he considered himself the new ruling class. If any laws existed today, Banksy believed he was above them, his will a celestial force.

This bastard might really chase me to the ends of the earth…

He caught a glimpse of Banksy raising a pistol from his lap. Before the man could aim his weapon, Barry heeled the brakes, sending the pursuit vehicle zooming ahead of him. The gangster's rear blinkers vanished in the nocturnal distance. Barry extinguished his own lights, then cut across the highway's partially clogged lanes. He worked on rebuilding his velocity while weaving between abandoned vehicles. A near collision with a bank security van tore the sideview mirror from the passenger side of the convertible. He sought an off-ramp that would allow him to escape from the interstate before his pursuer found him again, but his traveling speed and the murky evening conspired to hide any such exit from him. Dodging automotive obstacles kept his eyes locked on the road ahead of him.

By the time Barry spotted a large green sign announcing an impending exit, his stalker had reappeared. The red Corvette approached from behind at breakneck speed. Barry waited until the last possible instant before he veered to the left. A jumble of cars almost blocked the ramp. He angled his convertible past this ancient accident and left the highway behind.

As he drove away along residential roads, Barry couldn't tell if Banksy had succeeded in following him. He saw no headlights in his wake, but that meant nothing. He couldn't trust in the gangster's tracking ability to wane at this point, and he knew better than to rely on his own luck. He concentrated on taking as circuitous a route as possible. He cut through the parking lot of an unlit shopping mall. The roads he traveled grew smaller and cruder until Barry was piloting his stolen convertible along a graveled backroad. This brought him to a train-yard where discarded freight cars loomed in disarray. Resisting the urge to abandon the convertible and seek a hiding place in the night, Barry searched for a way out of this railroad maze.

He found himself driving along a country road through woodlands. Finally, he eased up on the accelerator.

And suddenly, glaring lights snapped on behind him.

Dammit—

How was Banksy able to pick up his trail so relentlessly? No matter what Barry did, he could lose the Corvette but only briefly. Was the man half Indian? Had he gained some supernatural tracking sense? Or—as Barry suddenly guessed—did Banksy have a GPS unit linking all the Blues' vehicles? That seemed the most logical way to explain the man's uncanny ability to find Barry 's convertible every time he thought he'd shaken his tail.

Seconds later, something rammed into his rear, urging the convertible to add a lurch to its forward momentum. Barry floored the pedal, but the red Corvette remained tight on his tail. The country road was getting progressively serpentine, twisting its way through a dense forest. More than once, both vehicles ripped shrubbery asunder as they barely navigated around curves at reckless speed.

Fortunately, the lane was too narrow to allow the Corvette to pass Barry's convertible. Banksy tried repeatedly to squeeze by, but ended up just stripping roadside trees of their bark. At least the gangster couldn't force him off the road or stop him by getting ahead of him and blocking his vehicle. It was still a harrowing ride, one Barry really could have done without.

A few times, Banksy released gunfire at him, but Barry had the feeling they were just warning shots. Had his shots damaged the convertible or its tires, an accident would have promptly resulted—an accident guaranteed to swallow the Corvette along with its prey.

He doesn't want me to die in a car crash. He has more grisly plans for me...

If only I had a gun...

But Barry had none; he'd discarded his weapon back in the luxury parking lot once it had run out of ammo.

It suddenly occurred to him to check the convertible's glove compartment. It was awkward leaning over to unlatch the hatch and root through the compartment on the far end of the dashboard. He found a box of undersized condoms and a lot of official paperwork, but no guns.

How about under the seats?

Still nothing.

He wondered how long this chase could go on? Sooner or later, one of the vehicles had to run out of fuel. Which one would sputter dry first?

A worried glance at the fuel gauge showed the needle dancing at the half-way mark.

Okay—so running out of gas wasn't an immediate concern. At least not for Barry. And somehow he just knew Banksy had more fuel than he did—that was the way the detective's luck always went.

So I need to find another way of giving Banksy the slip.

Maybe he could force the gangster to lose control of his car…

Edging back ever-so-slightly on the accelerator, Barry began to drive in a smooth curve, swinging back and forth across the narrow roadway. The Corvette dropped back. When Barry resumed speed, his pursuer promptly rode his tailgate. He tried the maneuver a few more times. On the third such move, Barry succeeded in cagily decreasing his velocity at the precise instant and crowding the Corvette against the edge of the forest. A thunder of crunching wood punctuated the roar of the twin engines. It sounded terrible, but for all the noise, the impact didn't seem to have incapacitated his stalker.

Dammit—

The woods were petering out on the left side of the road. The trees receded into the darkness. A guard rail swept into play, beyond which the edge of the dirt path dropped off into an abrupt slope. A queer light flickered in the distance.

Oh shit—it's—

Barry was quick to react once he realized what had happened—but Banksy was quicker.

Edging to the right, the Corvette pounced forward and squeezed its way between the convertible and the remaining wall of stout trees. Once there, it was easy for the gangster to sharply cut left and bully Barry's vehicle from the road.

The guard rail proved to be a flimsy barrier, parting like cardboard before the convertible's bumper. The car careened out into empty space and plummeted into the lake. The impact threw Barry's head against the windshield. Illusionary lights crowded his vision. He struggled to remain conscious.

The convertible hit the lake nose-first, just as it had the first time. The car sank fast, as if eager to reach its sunken grave. The water-level rose, swallowing and filling the vehicle.

Everything was blue, but a darker blue than he remembered.

He couldn't breathe, but this time he knew why. Panic did not consume him or impair his ability to cope.

Wasting no time trying to open the car doors, he reached up and tore himself an escape hatch in the convertible's fabric top. Squirming through the rip, he was free. He rose from the sinking automobile.

He didn't swim directly to the surface; this time he knew for sure that an enemy waited lakeside with a gun ready to shoot him if he survived drowning. He angled off to the side and kicked strongly to put distance between himself and the crash site. When he finally broke the surface, he gulped a lungful of air and immediately resubmerged himself. He swam horizontal beneath the water for as long as he could before his aching lungs forced him up again. This time he took quick stock of things.

The lake was dark. He could see the broken section of guard rail, but not well enough to tell if anybody lurked there. No glaring headlights blared from the lakeside road. And as far as he could tell in that brief instant, no gunshots were peppering the water.

Okay.

Taking a hefty breath, he reimmersed himself for another underwater swim.

When Barry decided he'd gone far enough, he drifted up to gently break the surface. This new, extended survey of the region brought him no additional information. The area was still steeped in an inky darkness. Right before his car had been forced from the road, he'd seen a wobbly light; it was still there—a reflection of the moon on the softly rippling water. After a moment, his eyes adjusted to the gloom, but not sharply enough to detect any menacing shapes moving along the lakeshore. The night was still, but for him the silence had an ominous undercurrent, for he knew that somewhere out there, Theodore Banksy waited with revolver in hand, itchy to spot his prey and put a bullet in his head.

It certainly did look like Barry had finally given the gangster the slip.

Turning in place, Barry scanned the far reaches of the lake. Nothing was different from the last time he'd lived through this incident.

He'd come full circle, returning to where his first temporal displacement had deposited him, only this time he'd reached the spot by living out the days leading up to the crash.

As before, he swam for the remote side of the lake, avoiding any chance of contact with his stalker—if Banksy still lurked out there. And Barry was sure the gangster was still out there; after coming this far, the bastard wasn't about to give up...or accept Winsor's death without seeing the body firsthand.

The hellbent car chase had left Barry enervated and exhausted, but the cold water jumpstarted his resolve so that this final leg of his swim did not unduly exhaust him.

By the time he reached the far shoreline, however, and dredged himself from the chilly waters, Barry was weary...but this time his fatigue was unplagued by uncertainty or bewilderment. This time he found himself on familiar turf, with a clear-cut itinerary: survival.

Barry's survival was paramount, otherwise Sanctuary wouldn't be avenged.

Despite the inclement temperature, he stripped off his clothes and squeezed as much water from them as he could manage. When he redressed, the garments were clammy, but no longer squishy

Without hesitation, he headed off into the woods.

The last time Barry had done this, he'd marched into the unknown with no specific destination other than "away" from the lake. This time, he knew what to expect of his forest trek; he wasn't sure how much of it he wanted to duplicate, though. He could do without encountering zombies in the dark woods, but at least this time he was more adept at dispatcing them.

As he crawled through the overgrown brush, Barry kept an eye peeled for anything that might serve as a weapon. Despite the improvements he'd gained in his fighting skills, especially when it came to dealing with undead adversaries, he would feel a lot better once he had something to use as a bludgeon. Initially, he tore a bough from a tree, but eventually he found a fallen branch of superior configuration for his purposes.

And with little time to spare, for even now Barry heard the noise of something stumbling through the remote foliage. He was tempted to circle around the advancing zombie and avoid any confrontation, but his sense of law and order impelled him to dispatch the creature here and now, sparing anyone else from running into the thing.

There was a problem with that decision. Too close together and thicketed by dense shrubbery, the trees afforded Barry no room to swing his bludgeon. First he had to knock the zombie down to the ground; from that vantage Barry could crush the thing's head with a vicious stab of his stout branch. It worked, but the zombie made a lot of noise, hissing and thrashing about, before a deathblow could be delivered. This ruckus attracted the attention of other undead creatures in the area.

During his first run-through, only one zombie had assaulted Barry. In all the mayhem of that previous attack, had Barry failed to notice these others? Or—had things changed?

Was reality *that* mutable? Could subtle differences in his own conduct result in drastic alterations to the scenarios ahead of him?

Already, he could think of several discrepancies. Originally, he'd experienced panic and confusion when the car had sunk into the lake, while this time he'd escaped the submersible with speed and agility. Also, he'd taken the time to find and fashion a sturdy weapon for himself, where before he'd stumbled along, defenseless and intimidated by the region's eerie environment. Not to mention, he'd had all five fingers when he'd first visited this woodland nightmare, and now he only had nine.

I can no longer rely on things being the same as they were the first time I got lost in these woods.

Rather than chance a complicated encounter with numerous zombies in these woods, Barry chose to slip away and avoid these supplementary adversaries.

For all the different choices he'd made, Barry's aimless wandering brought him to the same puzzling structure lost in the woods.

There it was: the strangely radiant concrete bunker.

This time, curiosity changed his actions. Ignoring the RAM Charger parked nearby, Barry approached the building. As before, the building's windows were darkened. The disturbing luster came from the bunker itself.

If not for its abnormal glow, Barry might've believed that it housed a radio station's transmitter generator. He'd seen one like it on an old TV comedy, *WKRP in Cincinnati*; in the episode, the disc jockey was doing a remote broadcast from out in the woods. But no transmitter tower stood nearby this radiant structure.

There was no heat involved in that glow; in fact, it seemed to leech what little warmth there was and make the night even colder. What kind of radiation could produce a bizarre glow like this?

The answer lay inside the building. Was he daring enough to venture inside to find out?

The door sported a remarkably expensive-looking lock, somewhat incongruous on a shabby building like this. The panel had been painted drab gray to match the rest of the bunker. Lightly tapping a fingertip on the door, Barry determined it was metal: heavy and inches thick. The thing belonged on a battleship, not a radio station's remote transmitter.

It could be a bomb shelter, situated this far from civilization. Or maybe it's a survivalist compound…

If it was a survivalist outpost, the RAM Charger indicated it was probably occupied. Some refugees had found the old bomb shelter and were using it as a home base.

None of which explained the thing's unearthly luminescence.

He was reaching out to knock harder on the door when a voice crowed from behind him.

"Holy shit—"

Wheeling about, Barry discovered a figure standing by the RAM Charger. He recognized the man right away, but it took a moment for him to accept who it was. During that befuddled pause, the man dropped the lunchbox he'd retrieved from the car and pulled his pistol from its holster. As he aimed the weapon at Barry, a toothy grin split his face.

"Detective Winsor," laughed Dusty. "I told him he was crazy, but here you are. Son of a bitch…"

Running into the head Raider here was a surprise, but one that paled next to the fiery resentment that immediately boiled in Barry: *Miss Collard is dead, but* this *bastard survived the Sanctuary massacre. That's not fair.*

Dusty took a few steps toward him, but then halted. With a scowl, he jiggled the barrel of his pistol. "The stick—drop it."

Reluctantly, Barry discarded his bludgeon.

A few more waggles of the gun instructed Barry to move to the left of the door. Once the detective stood aside, Dusty casually strolled up and kicked the door open. Not only unlocked, it had been ajar, but Barry hadn't realized that.

"In you go." With another twitch of his wrist, Dusty warded Barry to precede him inside. He followed, keeping a safe distance.

Before entering the building, Barry had been calculating the odds of jumping the Raider and taking his gun, but once he crossed the threshold his mind was swept away by a wave of awe and further unexpected familiarities.

Now it was his turn to utter, "Holy shit…"

The bunker's interior was crowded with machinery: a row of squat turbines hummed as they generated massive amounts of electrical energy; lights and gauges flickered on various consoles stacked everywhere; a wall of CPU servers were interconnected by a nest of cables. To one side sat a network of rods topped by metal spheres roughly six inches in diameter, their surfaces reached out to each other with lush electrical discharges.

Turning from a bank of controls, a second figure saw Barry and greeted him with a knowing nod. "I told you," the man told Dusty.

"Okay, okay," whined Dusty. "You were right, Sheldon. You're always right."

While Sheldon bustled about like an unruly bird, changing hundreds of settings on the control consoles, Dusty used extraneous cabling to tie Barry to a chair.

"Nothing personal, Winsor. I just know better than to trust you."

With head hung low, a dejected Barry muttered, "I'm still going to find a way to kill you…"

"That's what happens when two alpha dogs clash. Sooner or later, one of them wins out."

"You're not an alpha dog, you're a rabid animal."

"Tight enough for you?" Dusty drew the cable painfully taut around Barry's chest before knotting it around his wrists.

If Barry had gone indoors the first time he'd visited this bunker, these men would have been strangers to him. At that point in his subjective timeline, Barry had not met them. Only later would he come in contact with Dusty the Raider and his Fix-It Man, Sheldon Bowman, those interactions resulting in some unpleasant consequences. Now Barry was reliving his visit to the bunker, only to find these men here. Barry wasn't sure what you could call that: irony?—misfortune?—destiny?—just weird?

Initially, Barry's second pass of these circumstances had offered some beneficial differences…but now things were going rotten. *I should've ignored the damned bunker like last time,* Barry remonstrated himself, *and just stole the car and gotten out of here again.* But no, this time curiosity had guided him into disaster.

After a while, Sheldon stood back to survey his handiwork. He gave a satisfied nod, then wandered over to where Dusty continued to tease Barry with insults.

"Leave him alone," Sheldon warned his accomplice.

Grumbling under his breath, Dusty stood back with arms folded across his chest and his lips drawn into a frown.

"Where's that cheese sandwich?"

Dusty grunted, then weakly gestured. "Still outside. I got it from the car, but then I ran into him."

"Well, go get it. I'm hungry."

A cowed Dusty scuffed across the chamber and out the door.

This new Sheldon worried Barry. The shift in the relationship between Glendale's Fix-It Man and Dusty was wholly unexpected—disturbingly so. Previously, Dusty had been the Lord and Master, able to intimidate Sheldon with an unhappy glance…but now the Raider leader deferred to the intellectual like a pet left out in the rain.

Dusty's no longer the alpha dog, mused Barry. *Now he's more like an abused puppy.*

Now that they were alone, Sheldon turned to examine Barry. "I was worried you weren't going to make it this time." His expression was bland, almost bored.

"You were expecting me."

"Of course." Clearly insulted, Sheldon gave him a condescending look before he loosened the cables that bound Barry. Halfway done, he turned away to root through a cardboard box of stuff.

"I…don't understand…" Barry finished unwrapping the cables from himself. He massaged his newly bruised throat.

Sheldon's shoulders slumped. Abandoning his search, he sighed deeply. "You have a job to do. All that's required is your compliance. Whether or not you understand anything will have no bearing on the success of your assignment."

"I don't know what happened to make Dusty your lapdog, Sheldon, but don't expect me to jump when you snap your fingers. I still think you're a pompous ass."

"Oh, he still is a pompous ass," spoke Dusty from the doorway. He entered, closed the battleship hatch, then threw a small white-paper-bundled package at Sheldon. "But if we aren't nice to him, he isn't going to save the world."

A burst of laughter escaped from Barry's lips. "*Sheldon's* going to save the world? From what—freedom of choice?"

Sheldon clumsily grabbed the white paper package as it bounced off his shoulder. Coming unraveled, a cheese sandwich was revealed. In a paroxysm of pique, he threw it at Barry.

Still overwhelmed with humor, Barry let it hit him and fall to the floor.

"Did you explain things to him?" Dusty barked at Sheldon.

"I don't have to explain anything!"

"Don't expect him to play along unless he knows what's at stake, you ass."

The tension between the two men drew Barry from his giggling fit. He stared at them, then muttered, "You're serious…" Of course Dusty was serious. The man had an abundance of faults, but lying was not among them. He had no use for falsehoods; usually relying on his bluster to get things done.

"What the hell is going on here?" demanded Barry.

"And usually, Sheldon's so keen on bragging about his accomplishments. He did that all the time back in Glendale, blathering on and on about how he knows everything about everything. I used to tune him out. I'll bet you did the same back then. A mistake we both made." Dusty paused to shake his head, as if taking a private moment to chastise himself for being so foolish.

Then he continued, "All along, little Shelly's been playing everybody, getting us to do his bidding. He convinced me to let him be Glendale's Fix-It Man, giving him full access to the hamlet's limited technology. Remember his tales about all the smart people he knew? He wasn't bullshitting, he was in contact via short-wave radio with a lot of displaced scientists and professors scattered across the country—like Sanctuary's Board. It was Sheldon who relayed their request for mercenary assistance…because relocating there served his purposes. It got him together with Professor Dracy and Professor Grauss and the rest of those eggheads…so they could work out the details of their master plan."

"Reuniting Manhattan by force," muttered Barry.

"Hardly," Sheldon scoffed. "That was Dr Heigl's pet project. We were concerned with greater goals."

"I'm sorry—I may have disagreed with Heigl about how to go about restoring civilization, but what's a greater goal than that?"

Bridling as if he'd suddenly sat on a catcus, Sheldon proclaimed, "Stopping the fall of civilization from ever happening in the first place!"

A wide-eyed Barry held back any retorts. Instead, he turned his inquisitive look on Dusty.

The Raider tilted his head and gave it a few bobs. "I know, it sounds crazy…but hear him out."

Barry turned to give Sheldon his full attention, but when the intellectual remained silent, the detective chided, "I'm listening."

Sheldon rolled his eyes and heaved a humongous sigh. "You're all so thick. I have to spell it out for you, don't I?"

"For those of us who aren't as incredibly intelligent as the High and Mighty Big Brain Sheldon…yeah."

"The logic is so simple I cannot believe you don't see it. Clearly, the only way to stop the zombie outbreak from happening is to go back and prevent it from happening."

"Back in time, you mean."

With another eye-roll, Sheldon conceded, "Yes."

"So—you and the bomb chemists got together and cooked up a time machine at the factory."

"The theories were refined at the factory, but the apparaus was mostly assembled here, away from Sanctuary."

"Good thing they didn't, either," added Dusty. "It'd've been destroyed along with everything else."

"I knew that was going to happen," muttered Sheldon.

Barry blurted: "You knew about the attack—"

"Of course. It was obvious the Local Blues survivors would seek vengeance for the destruction of their little kingdom."

Launching from the chair, Barry paced to and fro, his arms flailing in the air. "And you did nothing?"

"I couldn't risk the machine's destruction, so I secretly moved it here."

"Don't get your police panties in an uproar, Winsor," interjected Dusty. "We warned the Board, but they refused to listen. They even forbid Sheldon from moving the device…so we had to steal it and sneak off."

"And leave Sanctuary to be destroyed…"

Sheldon raised a strident finger. "Need I remind you, if we can successfully prevent the zombie outbreak from ever happening, Sanctuary will consequently never exist to be destroyed."

"This is the part that loses me," grumbled Dusty. "The whole bit about retightening the timeline."

"The correct term," Sheldon pointed out, "is 'rewriting history.' Without a zombie outbreak, events will play out differently, creating a new timeline."

"Yeah, I get that part," complained Dusty. "I'm not stupid, Sheldon. But if no zombie outbreak creates a different timeline, then none of us will ever meet…and you'll never build your time machine to go back and stop the outbreak from happening. That's the part I don't grasp. Going back negates the time machine's construction, thereby preventing anybody from going back in the first place."

Barry nodded. "It's a self-generating paradox." Thanks to his discussion with Doc Toby about the vagrancies of time travel, Barry could see that.

A haughty Sheldon waved a dismissive palm at them. "You're getting lost in a semantic construction. Time travel is entirely mathematical in nature, and according to the math, the process and its outcome are valid by quantum definition."

Jeez, fretted Barry. *He acts as if he's completely figured out how Time works. And of course, whatever he's deduced is right—because* he *figured it out.*

With a sigh, Dusty advised, "Take his word on it, Winsor—or he'll start spouting numbers that'll make your head spin. I really don't want to sit through that again."

And Dusty believes him.

"This is all a practical joke," Barry exclaimed with a sour tone. "Right?"

Throwing up his hands, Dusty turned away.

A blank-faced Sheldon gaped at him.

Okay, maybe that *was a stupid question,* Barry admitted to himself. *Neither of these guys have ever shown any signs of a sense of humor.*

But—if they weren't joking around...

"You're telling me you actually built a real time machine?"

Putting fingertip to his own nose, Dusty turned back to face Barry.

A blank-faced Sheldon gaped at him.

"And it works?" demanded Barry. He glared at Dusty. "You've seen it in action?"

Dusty's finger sank from his nose as his face drooped with contrition. "Well...not exactly..."

"You're taking *his* word that it works," Barry accused the man.

"Of course the process works," insisted Sheldon.

Barry reseated and folded his arms across his chest. He sneered, "And your opinion is unquestionable."

"Of course." A flash of relief flew across Sheldon's face as he presumed that the detective had finally accepted his superior intelligence, but then vanished as he realized the man was only being sarcastic. Sheldon added with a scowl, "When the time comes, you'll see it in action."

"Good to know," grunted Barry.

"Pointlessly secretive right up to the end, huh, Shelly?" snarled Dusty. "You keep expecting everybody to do what you tell them to do, but you won't tell them that you need them to do it."

Up flew Barry's hand to point a stern finger at Sheldon. "Aha! You were waiting for me to show up. You need me to do someth...ing..." His demonstrative accusation lost its force as realization broke through Barry's mind. "You...you want me to..."

"Finally—the big reveal!" Dusty crowed. "And now our hapless victim understands his role in this affair. You thought you were an alpha dog, Winsor—as far as Shelly's concerned, you're just a lab animal."

Barry rose abruptly from the chair, his fists clenched and face twisted with anger. But then he spied Dusty's revolver (deftly drawn in the last few seconds) pointed casually at him. He returned his butt to the chair.

"No thank you," Barry promptly protested.

"Y'see?" Dusty admonished Sheldon. "This is why I tied him up in the first place. I knew he wasn't going to agree to your crazy scheme. Now I've got to—"

"Hold on—" interrupted Barry. (A surprise idea had arrived in his mind and he quickly reviewed it. Already, Barry was plagued with temporal displacements. Was it possible those anomalies stemmed from what Sheldon planned to do to him? Had Barry finally reached the point of origin regarding his time-skipping problems? The possibility filled him trepidation.) "Exactly what are you planning to do to me?"

"No stalling," Dusty grumbled. "Now, pick up that cable and start rewrapping yourself."

"Oh, put that away, Dusty," Barry reprimanded the man. "If you shoot me, Sheldon loses his test subject. You know he'd never let you do that."

A suddenly devious Dusty took a step back and swiveled his revolver to point at Sheldon. "Uh-uh-uh!" Halting his sneaky approach, Sheldon fingered the iron bar he held.

"Feel free to kill each other, if that's what you want," Barry counseled them. "Just remember, you need me alive."

Dusty lowered his gun.

Sheldon handed his metal rod to the Raider. "If he acts up, just knock him out."

Without comment, Dusty took the bar and settled in a position just behind Barry in the chair.

Sheldon declared, "As far as what I expect to do to you, Detective Winsor, you will be the subject I send back in time to before the zombie outbreak."

"Why not go yourself?" asked Barry.

Sheldon frowned. "I'm the only one who knows how to operate the apparatus."

"How convenient."

"I trust the math, Detective Winsor."

"But not enough to risk your ass, huh? Mine'll do nicely."

"That is uncalled for," Sheldon protested. "If I had a choice, I'd be the one going. I know *I* am capable of successfully completing the job.

You—you are an unknown quantity; admittedly a better one than Dusty, but still potentially unreliable."

"Thanks," grunted Dusty. "I wouldn't go if you paid me."

"And what do you expect me to do when I reach the past?" Barry inquired. "I mean, how do I convince the world there's a zombie outbreak in the offing? Are you going to give me hard evidence they'll believe? Some gruesome films? Maybe a living zombie—that'd wow them. More likely, they'll think I'm a nutcase and toss me into an asylum. My warnings won't stop anything."

"Of course not," Sheldon asserted. "You're not being sent back to publicize the impending disaster. You'll be sharing the data with an exclusive crew, men intelligent and influential enough to do what's necessary to avert the catastrophe."

The notion of how to convince anybody of the imminent apocalypse had long been a topic for Barry's internal reflection. With him slipping back and forth along the timeline, the opportunity existed for him to alert the world. But countless ruminations had all hit the same obstacle: they'd laugh at him and call him crazy.

But…had Sheldon found a way around that disbelief factor? For all his arrogance, the man had a shrewd brain. *Intelligent men…influential enough to do what's necessary to avert the catastrophe…*

"I detect a minor snag in your scheme," Barry announced. "Nobody knows what caused the contagion. How can anybody prevent it from happening if its origins remain a mystery?"

"Don't be stupid, Winsor. Of course I know what caused the outbreak. I told you about that back in Glendale."

"Your farting asteroid theory?" Barry gasped.

"Yes, now I recall--you scoffed at my explanation. Cast off your narrow-mindedness and pay attention then. I'll review the circumstances— this is the data you need to convey to the scientists you will visit in the past.

"Back then, an asteroid is approaching our planet. While some authorities inaccurately believe it will strike the Earth, the rock will actually only graze the stratosphere. But this near-miss will have dire consequences. Friction from the asteroid's passage through the fringes of the atmosphere will burn away a portion of the rock's surface, exposing a gas pocket. The chemical contents of this pocket will leak out and mingle with our air, ultimately spreading all across the globe to contaminate all forms of life. The contagion results in the mindless reanimation of dead flesh.

"This explanation is not a theoretical hypothesis; it's a factual account. Scientists documented the process as it occurred. You will offer affidavits confirming all this information, signed by the scientists' future selves. Each of them have provided private messages designed to convince their younger selves that they are actually hearing from future versions of themselves.

"These scientists are all in positions that will enable them to devise a method of preventing the asteroid from reaching the Earth. With no alien chemicals released into our atmosphere, the zombie plague will never happen. Civilization will go on as it was."

"Damn," muttered Barry. He had to admit, Sheldon had concocted a remarkably rational scheme. Realizing a public announcement would be laughed at, he'd decided to target certain individuals whom he knew, scientists and professors from his radio contacts. They could convince their younger selves to believe the fantastic tale.

That was where Sheldon's meticulous scheme fell apart. His belief that a crazy asteroid fart had caused the zombie contagion—this delusion was going to ruin the warning. Whether or not this near-miss even happened, Barry couldn't believe that it had any causal links to the undead plague. Siccing the scientists on chasing off the asteroid would have no bearing on the imminent apocalypse.

But there was no point arguing this with Sheldon. The farting asteroid was his pet theory, a wild concoction of his normally-quite-intelligent brain. As such, it was an unquestionable fact as far as the man was concerned.

It seemed clear to Barry that this proposed trip to the past was the cause of his temporal displacements. For all his brilliance, Sheldon's math was just a little off—enough to generate a side effect in the test subject, somehow robbing him of his innate ability to sequentially ride the timeline, inducing him to pop back and forth without rhyme or reason.

Well, no…while often a nuisance, these temporal displacements had been beneficial on more than one occasion—like snatching him away from the cannibal picnic as they were getting ready to cut him up and fry him—and his escape from the shootout at the gangsters' stag party back in Waldo's Gym. Did he want to give up those rescues by refusing to go along with Sheldon's plan?

For that matter, what would actually happen if he overpowered everybody and nobody sent him back in time? Spared any exposure to strange temporal energies, perhaps he would never end up sliding back and forth along the timeline? But--would the displacements never happen?...or endure because his memories of them locked them into existence?

Questioning the entire affair was a farce. The outcome of sending Barry back in time was already a part of his life. It was futile to debate whether or not to start the process in motion just because the cause came sequentially after its consequences.

"Okay, sounds straightforward enough," conceded Barry. "You need somebody to save the world—I'm your guy."

"You are just a courier," Sheldon replied. "Carrying vital information to the proper individuals. You will be instrumental, though, in saving the world."

"A little messenger boy," cackled Dusty. "All you'll be doing is passing notes in class to smart guys who'll do all the actual work. They'll be the heroes, not you."

"This plan depends on Detective Winsor following a precise set of instructions," Sheldon admonished the Raider. "I'd appreciate it if you'd stop disparaging him. You're just undermining his confidence. You want this plan to succeed, don't you, Dusty?"

The Raider made a nondescript sound. Since he stood behind Barry, the detective had no glimpse at his face to help attach meaning to his grunt.

Barry could envision a side of Dusty that was quite comfortable with the post-apocalyptic world. The zombie outbreak had given him reason to unleash his violent inclinations. A peaceful world would afford him no reason to be that way, would in fact brand him as a criminal. From the Raider's point-of-view, he was far happier guarding the world from an undead menace. If Sheldon's scheme succeeded, Dusty would revert to being a garbage collector. This made him a dubious ally of Sheldon whose ambition was to eradicate the undead threat from ever having existed at all.

Returning to the cardboard box, Sheldon withdrew a sheaf of papers which he handed to Barry. "Protect these with your life," he instructed him.

"How do I find these scientists?" asked Barry. "The ones you want me to give this data to..."

"Contact information is included in the papers you now hold. I am one of the individuals you will be visiting. Perhaps you should start with me."

Yes, it made perfect sense that Sheldon would include his younger self in the crew to carry out his scheme. It was his way of guaranteeing his inclusion in saving the world.

With an indifferent nod, Barry stuffed the papers into a pocket of his still-soggy jacket.

Suddenly noticing the damp condition of the detective's clothing, Sheldon remarked, "You can't enter the time field in wet clothes. Doing so might upset my careful calculations."

And there it was: the unknown variable that would transform Barry's conventional trip through time into recurrent temporal displacements.

Not that learning the why daunted his decision to go through with this. Avoiding the trip would only cancel the displacement he'd already lived through, resulting in him not surviving those instances.

Sheldon turned his disapproving glance on Dusty. "Switch clothes with him."

"No way!" declared Dusty. "Besides, my stuff won't fit him. He's too big." He gave a fleeting smirk. "And by that I mean too fat."

"Well, he definitely won't fit into my clothes," protested the intellectual scarecrow. "And we have nothing else here. I am reluctant to postpone his departure."

"There might be some stuff in the Charger," Dusty muttered.

"Then go fetch them, you fool," chided Sheldon.

"You're so concerned, go get them yourself."

Sheldon's spindly height increased an inch as he lifted his head aloft to glare at his recalcitrant lackey. "My presence is required *here*. I have further instructions for Detective Winsor."

Releasing a gust of exasperated air from his lungs, Dusty threw down the metal rod and stormed from the bunker.

With Dusty out of earshot, Barry confronted Sheldon. "You know this isn't going to work, don't you?"

The man met his gaze, unflinching.

"I thought so. You hate my guts, Sheldon, and this is just your way of getting rid of me."

Still, Sheldon offered no response. But his fiery glare revealed the veracity of Barry's impromptu accusation.

"You aren't sure how it's not going to work, but I am." Leaning forward, Barry pantomimed sharing a deep confidence. "And I'll be taking that secret with me—to my grave, into the past, or wherever I end up."

"If you feel this way," grated Sheldon, "then why are you going through with it?"

"Ah, Sheldon—that's another part of the secret you never get to find out."

"If this is what you want, then what's to prevent me from not sending you back?"

Barry had to laugh. "There's only one thing powerful enough to stop you from abandoning your grand scheme on the cusp of its fruition, Sheldon...your unconquerable ego."

A twitch down-curled the end of one of Sheldon's lips. His eyes narrowed, fury reddened his usually pale complexion...but initially he declined to dignify Barry's reckoning with any verbal denial. A moment passed, though, and Sheldon had to have the last word. His acerbic comment was lost in a sudden roar of gunfire outside the bunker.

The outburst brought Barry and Sheldon both whirling about to gawk through the bunker's open door. Out there, moonlight illuminated a ghastly scenario. Halfway back from the RAM Charger, Dusty contorted and twitched as a volley of shots tore his torso to shreds. He looked like a puppet dancing in the control of an incompetent handler. Within seconds, he fell to bleed all over the graveled courtyard. The ground-mist swallowed his body.

A voice rang outside: "Found you, you scumbag! Thought you could escape me by linking up with your buddies, huh? Not going to happen!"

Barry immediately recognized the voice: Theodore Banksy. *How the hell did he track me all the way from the lake through the woods to this radiant bunker?*

Moving with startling speed, Sheldon leaped to slam the battleship hatch. As he dashed over to man the wall of flickering consoles, he yelled, "Winsor—quick—step onto the launch pad!"

Dumbfounded by Dusty's abrupt murder, Barry was aghast. After doling out pain and suffering to so many, the Raider boss had finally been punished—but in such an excessive manner. *Live by the sword, die by the sword.* Frozen by shock, it took Sheldon's shout to jar Barry back to reality.

"Launch pad?" *Oh—the machine!*

As he dove toward the network of rods topped with spheres, Barry suddenly realized that Sheldon had no idea who was out there, vowing doom and disaster. And since the world revolved around Sheldon Bowman, this new enemy was obviously here to stop Sheldon from implementing his anti-apocalypse scheme. So naturally, his immediate reaction was to hurry the scheme to fulfillment.

Suddenly, this trip into the past would serve a multitude of purposes. Not only engaging Sheldon's complex scheme, it would deliver Barry beyond the wrathful reach of Theodore Banksy. But—in doing so, it would rob Barry of any chance of punishing the gangster for the Sanctuary massacre. Was he really willing to let that go? Wouldn't it amount to another failure on his part?

Halting inches from the launch pad, Barry gulped and shook his head. "No…" He couldn't fail Miss Collard another time. He needed to stay here and kill Banksy before he could take on the greater task of saving the world.

Dusty had disarmed him outside, leaving his bludgeon branch out there. The only weapon inside the bunker was the metal bar the Raider had discarded before going outside.

As Barry turned away from the machinery with the intention of snatching up the steel rod and trying to brain Banksy when he barged into the bunker—something hit Barry from the side. Gaunt fingers dug into his soggy sleeves and yanked him to a halt.

Abandoning the controls, Sheldon had rushed to halt Barry's eleventh-hour change-of-mind.

"You don't—" Barry tried to exclaim.

A sharp shove sent Barry stumbling back into the grip of the machine. It consisted of a chromium disc on the floor. A network of rods protruded from the base, rising to cage in anyone standing on the disc. The grapefruit-sized balls that tipped these shafts all blazed right now with nests of miniature electrical storms. Into this three-dimensional puzzle went Barry. Desperate to break his fall, his hands grasped at the crackling spheres as he tumbled into their embrace.

A strange tingle suddenly tickled Barry's skin. His head felt hot.

The battleship hatch flung open to admit Theodore Banksy. (Apparently Sheldon had neglected to lock the thing when he'd slammed it shut.) Still dressed in a tuxedo, the gangster wielded an automatic rifle. His hair was perfect.

"You die tonight, Winsor!" he yelled.

He sprayed the bunker's crowded interior with a savage salvo.

Past the rising tide of the machine's interlacing discharges, Barry watched the machinery crumple and burst into flame under the fusillade of slugs. He saw Sheldon fall before a hail of hot lead; as the man went down, a bullet drove a fist-sized hole into his face, sending most of his ever-so-brilliant-brains spilling out the back of his head.

Had Sheldon realized before he died that the attacker had come for Barry and not him?

As everything faded away, Barry hoped so. One last dig to remind the creep he wasn't the center of the universe.

11

WAKING UP, BARRY WAS ALMOST DISAPPOINTED to find himself in his own bed in the house he had shared with Emily for so many good years.

If not for his missing little finger, he might have convinced himself the entire affair had been born out of a drunken binge. But it was hard to explain away the finger, especially when its cruel detachment had been such a traumatic moment from his nightmarish world of zombies.

The sheaf of papers he discovered shoved inside his pajamas cemented the deal. They were certainly not a product of his own hand, nor could anyone have slipped the wad under his PJs while he slept.

Sheldon's machine had worked. Despite Barry's soggy clothes (which curiously had not joined him on his trip into the past) and heedless of the damage Banksy's gunfire had inflicted on machinery as the process had initiated—regardless of all these disturbances, the device had safely delivered him to the pre-apocalyptic past.

This last bit he confirmed by consulting the date on a newspaper in the kitchen. September 15; months before the outbreak. Sheldon's machine had returned Barry to the launch point of his first temporal displacement, bringing him full circle.

According to his memory, when he reported to the precinct later that morning, Yowel Fredrickson would show up and give him that lead on Titus Roth which would eventually lead Barry to the shootout at the gangster stag party. But first, Barry would learn that Frankie Dumont, his partner, would not be able to join Barry on that adventure—Frakie's mother was sick in Houston—something about a possible ebola infection.

Sitting at his kitchen table, Barry spent the predawn hours digesting all this and organizing the events into a chronological sequence untampered with by time travel.

While he felt a certain responsibility to carry out Sheldon's plan, Barry could not overlook the chance to arrest all of those criminals attending the stag party. Before, he'd stumbled into things and a crisis had ensued. But now, with his knowledge of what actually waited inside the decrepit gym, Barry could handle things differently. *Forewarned is forearmed.* Instead of going in alone, Barry would take an entire SWAT team in with him. The gangsters would be taken by surprise. And if they decided to shoot it out, this time they'd be outgunned.

And as an added bonus, Barry could take down Theodore Banksy long before they ever clashed in the apocalyptic future, for he recalled briefly glimpsing the man among the assembled thugs at the party. Fate had given Barry a surprise bonus chance to get the gangster.

Of all the duties spinning around in his head, the most important to Barry Winsor was proving that, in the end, he hadn't failed Miss Collard.

Visiting Sheldon's scientist buddies could wait a few days.

Since Barry already knew what Yowel the Criminal Informant was going to tell him, the detective saw no need to show up at the police station to hear it again. Skipping the encounter would also save him from paying the CI out of his own pocket. Instead, once the morning reached a decent hour, he drove out to Frankie's house in the Bronx.

There, he helped his partner cope with the bad news, which came via telephone fifteen minutes after Barry's arrival. By the time he gave Frankie a lift to the airport, his partner had calmed down somewhat.

Barry told him about Yowell's tip concerning Titus Roth's money drop. Here, he embellished the snitch's tale with details about how prominent gang lords would be attending this private stag party in a downtown boxing gym. "A chance to nab a whole houseful of mobsters," cackled Barry. To which Frankie replied, "You can't pass that up, Bar. Take backup, though." "Of course," grunted Barry; this time, he meant it.

Once Frankie was in the air, Detective Winsor hit the 13th Precinct's squad room and reported news of the stag party to Deputy Chief Gann. (It was nice to see the man again, alive and looking healthier than he had in the Local Blues enclave—the future had not been kind to Gann.) Excitement ran high as a SWAT team was summoned to help organize the raid.

Gloves kept anyone from noticing his missing pinky. Although he'd lost the finger in the future, the injury had landed him in the hospital back in this time period. He'd been able to credit the wound to the stag party shootout; a white lie that would not work hours before the stag party raid.

Gann agreed to let Barry tail the Roth kid as he collected monies throughout the city. That way, if the kid's route changed, the police would immediately know about it. With Frankie Dumont out-of-town on "personal business," another officer, was assigned to accompany Barry as he kept track of Roth. Officer Evan Pyle was not directly known to Barry, but word on the guy satisfied Barry that he'd suffice as a partner-for-an-afternoon. He was a gruff individual with big hands and a perpetual smile.

The rest of the team would be waiting to storm the gym as soon as Roth showed up.

His memory of the route the kid had originally taken was hazy in Barry's mind; too much had happened since that afternoon. Now (as then), the route seemed relatively random as Roth pedaled from barber shop to pool joint to stripper club to corner deli, adding parcels to the bag strapped to his bicycle. Neither Barry nor Evan Pyle observed any behavior that would indicate the kid had made them.

"Wasting a lot of gas doing it this way," remarked Pyle.

"Except he's on a bike," Barry pointed out. "He's not wasting any gas."

"Why's he keep doubling back to visit places? Why didn't he do those pickups when he first passed them?"

"Maybe there's some kind of pecking order to the pickups. Like the early pickups contain smaller amounts of money. That way if somebody tries to rob him, his losses won't be so great."

"So the pickups toward the end of his route would be the bigger pay-offs," mused Pyle. "We should remember them for later. They'd be the gang's more profitable dives."

"Good point."

"Give me the radio," Pyle chirped. "I'm going to suggest to Deputy Chief Gann that he send officers to shut down these places once the kid's made his pickups."

Barry nodded as he maneuvered his Impala through Manhattan traffic. He liked the idea. It would make it seem as if this afternoon's raid was part of a big operation. Put a nice scare into anybody that escaped the net.

After conferring with the precinct house, Pyle reported that Gann had loved the idea. "He wants us to tape the kid visiting each place, to establish a connection between them."

While Barry saw the wisdom in that suggestion, he had to ask, "Tape him how?"

"With our cell phones, idiot," chided Pyle, who was half Detective Winsor's age and belonged to a generation who owned cells that did everything except flush the toilet.

"I'm driving…"

"Okay, okay." Rooting through his rumpled sports jacket, Pyle produced his own cell. While he watched Roth cruise along the curb, his fingers tapped away, activating the device and setting it up to shoot digital video footage.

"Ready," Pyle finally announced.

"Fine," grunted Barry. "You handle that while I deal with traffic."

Following the Roth kid from pickup to pickup was boring, especially so for Barry since it was his second time. He chain-smoked through half-a-pack that afternoon. It was anticipation that made him nervous, the knowledge that he was going to turn the day around for himself and the police. On his first run, Barry had stupidly blundered alone into a room full of armed thugs, resulting in a monstrous shootout. But now, knowing what waited in the gym, Barry was showing up with full SWAT backup. The gangsters were in for quite a surprise.

A sudden displacement had saved Barry from being shot to pieces that first time, but no rescue was going to be necessary today. This time, he was bringing his own cavalry.

He did wonder, though…would the same displacement occur again, removing him from the raid on the stag party? What had triggered it in the first place? Stress? Most of his displacements had happened while Barry was asleep or unconscious. Were they even initiated by him?—or did they occur according to some cosmic schedule?

It was too late to fret over such things. Barry had to stay frosty, focused and alert. It would be the ultimate failure (to himself and everyone) if he got sloppy and was killed during the raid. He'd never see the gangsters locked up. He'd never see Banksy punished. And he'd never get around to contacting Sheldon's scientist pals and arrange the undoing of the impending zombie outbreak.

I'll just have to watch my ass, he told himself as the Roth kid's bike turned onto the block where the gymnasium was located downtown. *I always try to.*

Cruising past the rundown building, Barry turned at the next intersection and eventually pulled up beside an innocuous van that housed the raid's command center. Two more dark vans were parked further along the avenue; they were empty now, the SWAT team having taken up covert positions surrounding the gym. Barry and Pyle left their car and climbed aboard the surveillance van.

"All set?" asked Barry.

"Roth just reached the gym," answered one of the technicians manning the equipment. An array of screens showed camera views carried by several SWAT members. A few others showed neighboring scenes to afford an overview of the area.

His prior familiarity with the location gave Barry a certain advantage over these newcomers, but he could see the SWAT team had selected optimum spots around the gym's exterior. They were all well hidden with easy access nearby.

"Okay, he'll go right into the party," Barry predicted. "I'll signal the go-ahead once Pyle and I get in position." With that, Barry vacated the van, followed by his afternoon partner.

They quickly reached the front of the gym. Two officers flanked the entry door, their weapons drawn and ready. Hesitating only a second, Barry lifted his arm and brought down a closed fist. The two officers flew into action, storming through the doorway. Pyle tumbled after them. Barry paused a moment, checking the street for any sign of a lookout who might have spotted the breach. Each pedestrian continued on their way, most of them utterly oblivious to the police raid; the few who did notice ignored things with the ironclad indifference of native New Yorkers.

By the time Barry got inside, somebody had tasered the grizzled doorman; his twitching body slumped across the counter. Pyle and the other cop were already at the inner door. From deeper in the building came the sound of authoritative commands followed by angry protests, then gunshots. Before Pyle could push open the door, it swung wide and smashed him in the face. As he teetered back, Pyle took the nearest officer down with him. The first thug through the door stumbled over them, but never lost his footing. Expecting trouble, the second escapee came out with guns blazing. Barry shot the first thug in the leg. Somehow, the cop under Pyle managed to poke his revolver past the tangle of limbs and take out the wild gunslinger. Abandoning the unconscious doorman, the other policeman was laying down cover fire so the two fallen officers could safely get off the floor. Swept up in the thrill of the moment, Barry rushed into the stag party.

Frantic gangsters rushed to and fro while strippers scrambled for refuge under the party tables. Upon entering the room, the SWAT team had split up to take postitions evenly spaced around the chamber. Secure behind exercising equipment, the cops had the bad guys surrounded. Heedless of that (or maybe unconvinced of the futility of their situation), the thugs were firing about indiscriminately, often hitting their own compatriots. Barry edged behind a pile of wrestling mats (just like before), but this time he wasn't everybody's choice target. He was able to carefully return fire, wounding the hoodlums instead of blowing them away.

The bulk of the gangsters were fighting to reach what must have been the back door, but SWAT officers defended it against their rush. To one side, Barry saw a panicking Titus Roth dragging his bicycle after him under a table; a wet stain marked his baggy shorts. Barry's gaze kept moving, searching the chaos for Theodore Banksy. The gangster had been here before, there was no reason to expect him to be absent this time. He was the one Barry wanted to find and take down.

During the drive back and forth through the city, Barry had considered the morality of his intentions. As a sworn officer of the law, it was his job to apprehend lawbreakers, leaving determination of guilt and sentencing to the justice system. During his time in the apocalyptic future, survival instincts had been called for, relegating protocol to a luxury status. There, evil-doers were not just thieves and embezzlers—most were openly crazy, hostile and armed. A quick response was necessary, a lethal one if you intended to survive the encounter. Barry had tried his best to restrict inflicting mortal injuries to those who actually deserved them; there were more than enough of those opponents to deal with.

But now, Barry was back in the civilized world, where law and order still meant something. *To serve and protect* was a valid doctrine once again. On most matters, he was entirely willing to conform to current rules and ethics.

There was an exception—there are always exceptions—and it involved Theodore Banksy.

In Barry's eyes, Banksy was to blame for the Sanctuary massacre. Miss Collard's and everyone else's blood stained the gangster's hands. He deserved to be punished for those murders. Barry had sworm to avenge their deaths.

The core of the quandary involved the fact that the massacre lay months in the future. How ethical was it for Barry to punish the gangster for crimes he hadn't yet committed? Barry had witnessed enough to know this man was evil and dangerous—now or months older. If anything, the apocalypse would unleash a bloodthirstier version of the gangster. He *deserved* to die for his sins.

But…was it right for Barry to be the executioner?

The deciding point in this debate turned out to be: Barry's adamant need to punish Miss Collard's murderer. He refused to fail her again.

If his choice violated morality, tough nuts. A cosmic balance must be struck.

So, when he finally spotted Theodore Banksy, Barry acted without hesitation. He took aim and was ready to empty his clip at the villain—but then their eyes locked on each other. A rictus of intense hatred marked the gangster's expression. Why? While Barry certainly had adequate reason to hate the man, vice versa seemed odd, especially since the two had not yet met. Was Banksy *that* upset over the disruption of his stag party?

Barry's microsecond pause was enough for Banksy to jerk out of the detective's sights. By the time Barry caught sight of the man, he'd dodged back among the thugs trying to shoot their way out the backdoor. As Barry watched, Banksy assaulted one of his men and wrestled a gun from the dazed hoodlum. With manic haste, Banksy pointed his gun in Barry's direction and released a volley of shots.

Slugs pelted the wall around Barry, forcing him to duck back behind the stack of wrestling mats.

This was ridiculous. Granted, Barry was behind this afternoon's raid, but how could Banksy know that? Yet, with one glimpse, the gangster had developed a deep and fierce hatred for Detective Winsor.

Barry didn't care. His own enmity was quite mature in his own mind and, in his opinion, trumped this Banksy's newborn malice.

Peering from his crouch, Barry discovered the man was making a run for it. *A run where?* The SWAT team had every exit covered. *The bastard must know of a secret escape route.*

Ignoring all caution, Barry darted into the thick of the melee. Bullets zipped around him as he dashed through one crossfire and into another exchange of gunplay. He was adding to the pandemonium, too, firing his own shots at Banksy's fleeing figure.

The gangster had reached a seemingly innocuous row of steel lockers set against the wall. But then he yanked open one of the narrow cabinets and disappeared into the locker.

As Barry drew near, he could see the locker was bigger inside than it should've been—it was, in fact, the threshold of a passage that led deeper into the building. Without breaking stride, Barry plunged inside. The width was narrow, he had to twist sideways to move along the tunnel. It was little more than an oversized gap between two sheet-rock panels, separating other rooms in the gymnasium. He moved along this crawlspace as quickly as he could. Somewhere ahead of him, Banksy was escaping the raid.

You're not getting away this time, Barry swore.

The crawlspace led to a dead end—which proved to be just a closed panel when Barry hit it with his shoulder. The door popped open, revealing a storage room. Rows of shabby metal shelves were filled with dry-goods boxes and jars of condiments. Cartons of fruit were piled everywhere. The crawlspace didn't just lead deeper into the gym, it connected with the next shop on the block, what looked like a deli or restaurant. There was no sign of the gangster—or anybody—in the storage room. A doorway in the far wall hung open.

Barry gave chase. Out of the storage room, down a hallway filled with more haphazardly piled cartons, through a tiny kitchen that stank of grease and cheese, past a startled cook, behind a counter where he had to step over a cashier who'd been knocked to the floor. He caught Banksy in the middle of the dining area, grabbing him from behind and spinning him around to connect with a fist waiting to smash into the gangster's face. Patrons scattered from the sudden violence. Tables toppled, sending half-eaten meals down to create a slippery surface for the struggle that ensued.

Banksy fought back from the onset, but the instant he saw who he was brawling with, his wrath increased and he started cursing Barry by name. He tried to shoot Barry, but at such close range, the detective was able to slap the gun away from his opponent. The gangster responded with a harsh kick to Barry's gut. As Barry folded over, he reached out and wrapped Banksy in a clumsy bear-hug, trapping him beneath his fall. For a moment, they thrashed on the floor, battering each other with fists and feet and knees.

"Damn you, Winsor," hissed the gangster. "How I despise you!"

Barry felt certain Banksy couldn't know him, not at this point. It would be months before Barry infiltrated the Local Blues' enclave and met the gangster for the first time. Technically, in this pre-apocalypse moment, Barry only knew of Banksy from his criminal reputation; every officer on the force had worked hard to find a way to legally connect the villain with his crimes, but the bastard's lawyers were always too skillful.

And yet, here was Banksy ranting about how much he specifically hated Barry.

"And here you are again, Winsor—ruining everything!"

Again?

Their combat had brought them almost nose-to-nose, Banksy snarling like a deranged beast, Barry grimacing with righteous hostility. This close, Barry suddenly realized what was going on. This wasn't a younger Theodore Banksy—this was Barry's post-apocalyptic nemesis.

"Do you know how hard it was to convince all those cops that I should run the Local Blues?" snarled the gangster. "I was finally their Boss, but then you came along and destroyed my little empire!"

"You don't belong here," Barry grated at him.

"I had to go somewhere. All that machinery was exploding. And you were gone—" His assault intensified into crazed ferocity. "—I couldn't let you get away!"

The gangster had escaped the bunker and followed Barry into the past!

And—just as Barry had resumed his life in conformity with this point on the timeline—Theodore Banksy had done the same, slipping back into his role as a Manhattan crime kingpin. Had Banksy occupied his younger self's body (as Barry had), or had the gangster simply eliminated this era's Banksy and taken his place? (Did it really matter?) Fate seemed determined to keep Barry and Banksy together...until their differences could be resolved. And as far as both of them were concerned, the only acceptable outcome could be the other's annihilation.

At some point in the struggle, Banksy had regained possession of his gun. He shoved it into Barry's belly, and with a mad cackle, squeezed the trigger hard.

But no shots occurred. The gangster had emptied his gun during the shootout in the gym.

While Barry—well, Barry wasn't sure how much ammo he had left. He too had been shooting it up in the gym. He knew he had extra clips on him, but reloading wouldn't exactly be an easy option right now, as the two men rolled back and forth, kicking and punching at each other.

Barry tried to maneuver one of his arms into a chokehold around the gangster's neck, but Banksy was more agile. All told, a higher percentage of Banksy's bulk was made up of muscle, and he was at least a decade younger than the detective. Not to mention, the gangster's raving fervor better fueled his rampage. Barry fought hard, but his dedication to justice was no equal for Banksy's arrogant entitlement.

Shifting the gun in his grasp until he held it by the barrel, Banksy hammered at Barry with the metal butt. While the detective managed to block most of the blows, a few made their way past his defensively raised arm and struck his shoulder, his neck, and finally his head.

A blow to his temple dazed Barry. Darkness crept in, reducing his vision to a pinprick. For a moment, his muscles went lax. He didn't drop his revolver, but the weapon dangled at the end of a slack limb. He barely heard the villain's final declaration.

"I could finish you, Winsor, here and now—but that'd be too easy—too *painless* for you. When the time comes, you asswipe, I'm going to make sure you *suffer!*"

Thrashing at the encroaching gloom, Barry bullied his way back to consciousness. He found himself sprawled on the floor, scraps of food clung to his pants and the sleeves of his jacket. At the periphery of his vision, a blur kicked open the cafe's entrance and slipped outside. *He's getting away...* All around him, aghast patrons ogled the detective from where they had withdrawn from the violent fray. As Barry's wits oriented themselves, he saw a pair of thugs from the stag party dash out of the cafe's kitchen. These hoodlums stumbled into the wreckage of the dining area and grabbed bystanders as hostages. Unarmed, they used physical force to hold their captives.

Immediately, Barry brought his gun up to bear on the thugs. He fired a shot that hit one thug in the leg, then swung his aim to the other. As his barrel came into alignment with thug number two, the man danced back, throwing his arms wide and high and sending his hostage staggering off to safety. "Don't shoot, man, I surrender!" Similarly losing hold of his hostage, thug number one grabbed his leg and wailed with pain as he crumpled to the floor.

Within seconds, SWAT members rushed onto the scene to take custody of the two thugs.

Flocking around Barry, the diner's patrons slapped his shoulders with congratulations and babbled gratitude. Oblivious to their good intentions, Barry pushed his way free of the throng. He headed for the door.

Outside, he hastily scanned the street for sign of a fleeing figure...but saw nothing that fit that criteria.

Dammit—he got away...

His chest hurt with the pang of this fresh failure. Once again, despite his best efforts, Barry had failed to get Banksy. The bastard was like an eel with a guardian angel, he managed to squirm or bludgeon his way out of every trap set to catch him.

And this time, the Banksy on the loose was even more dangerous. Armed with knowledge of the impending future, who knew what deviltry the villain could stir up?

"What a pity," mumbled someone nearby.

"Damn straight," cursed Barry.

"He ran right out into the street without looking."

"The bus driver didn't see him."

"Somebody call an ambulance."

"I saw the whole thing."

"So tragic."

What are they talking about?

A crowd had gathered in the street. Barry had to elbow his way through the mob. At its center he found a timeless urban scenario.

Someone had rushed out into traffic and gotten hit by a bus. The vehicle stood there with its crumpled front grill, the driver and passengers spilling forth to join the collective gawkers. The victim lay on the asphalt: his body spread-eagled on his belly, while his head stared heavenward at a wholly unnatural angle.

Normally, accidents like this were appalling and sad. But this one brought a smirk to Barry's tight lips.

You didn't get very far, did you, you bastard?

When it arrived, the only thing an ambulance could do now was deliver Theodore Banksy to the morgue.

Deputy Cheif Gann was ecstatic over the success of the raid.

Forty-seven criminals had been apprehended. A wealth of funds had been found in the Roth kid's satchel. Tons of damning evidence had been unearthed in the gym's backrooms, paperwork that tied the gang to everything from narcotics to murder, even a counterfeiting press in the basement. The minute the captured thugs heard about Banksy's unfortunate accident, more than half of them had begged to trade info for suspended sentences. With the loss of the Boss, no shyster was going to waste time on small fry. By nightfall, offered data had led to fifty-two more arrests across the city. Not counting the hoodlums that had been caught red-handed when officers had hit each establishment the Roth kid had visited. Gambling, prostitution, protection rackets—an entire criminal empire fell that day.

And Detective Barry Winsor was the hero of the hour.

He could endure only so much fame, though. Well before sunset, he went to hit the can and simply never returned to the celebration.

Borrowing an unmarked car from the precinct's underground garage, a very satisfied Barry headed home.

The rest of the precinct had been thrilled by the damage the raid had delivered to Manhattan's criminal landscape. Although he shared their elation over this, Barry relished a more private accomplishment. Seeing Miss Collard's murder avenged was a major achievement for the time-battered detective. He had finally atoned for his sins of failure.

Granted, Barry had intended to have more of a hands-on involvement in Banksy's demise. But Fate had intervened, leaving his hands unbloodied. At least he derived some satisfaction for whipping the gangster into such a frenzied state that the man had run recklessly out into the street, heedless of ongoing traffic. *It was the least I could do for the bastard.* Now, Barry could deal with other responsibilities…

No point in putting this off, he told himself. He'd taken care of the one thing he'd deemed more important than Sheldon's scheme. Now his evening was wide open. *It might be nice to catch a nap—I'm feeling* really *wiped out—but if I don't get this done, I may never get around to it.* While Sheldon had been an asshole for most of the time Barry had known him (first at Glendale, then later at Sanctuary), Barry had to admit he owed the pompous ass a debt of gratitude. If not for his wacky time machine, Barry might still be trapped in an apocalyptic world with nothing to look forward to but a head full of regrets.

The documents Sheldon had entrusted to him were stashed in the safe box at Barry's house. Before he could start visiting Sheldon's scientist pals, he needed to retrieve those papers. Without them, his story was no more than a lunatic's jabber.

Once he reached his house, Barry dashed inside with the single-minded intention of just grabbing Sheldon's documentation, but before he got the chance to hit the road, his cell rang. It was his partner.

"Frankie!" exclaimed Barry. "I forgot to call you. The raid was a big success!"

"No shit? That's awesome!" came Frankie's prompt glee.

"How's your mom, Frankie?"

"Looks like we both got good news for each other. Mom's okay."

"No ebola?"

"All she has is a bad rash. They're ebola-crazy down here in Dallas, what with those other cases."

Barry recalled: after several outbreaks in Africa, a few infected people had made it to American soil. The CDC was in a panic, taking almost draconian measures to contain the disease.

He was glad to hear his partner's mother was not one of those poor individuals.

"That's wonderful news, Frankie."

"Thanks. And hey—kudos to you for the big bust."

"Yeah."

After a few more pleasantries (Frankie would be back by Moday, he wanted to spend a few days with his mom), they rang off.

Relief over news about his partner's mom's health joined forced with his advanced state of fatigue. A wave of exhaustion sent him reeling. He barely reached the bed in his den before falling asleep on his feet.

Checking his watch upon awakening, Barry wasn't surprised to discover he'd slept more than eighteen hours without interruption. His bladder, though, was not happy about this and immediately signaled its displeasure with a pang to his gut. He staggered into the bathroom and relieved himself.

Afterward, he sat on the edge of his bed and thought about things.

How committed was he really to carrying out Sheldon's wild scheme?

On one hand, despite his personal feelings concerning Sheldon Bowman, Barry couldn't deny the man's intelligence. When he wasn't posturing like an asshole, he could be quite brilliant.

On the other hand, a lot of Sheldon's beliefs sounded ridiculous to a layman like Barry. His farting asteroid theory was one of his more ridiculous assumptions.

But—what if?

During his future travels, Barry had hunted far and wide for an explanation for the zombie outbreak, but none of the tales he'd heard had shown any evidence to prove their liability. They were all little more than wild guesses. If every tale seemed equally dubious, then logic dictated that none of these implausible explanations could be ruled out. Despite their lack of supporting evidence, any one of them might be the real answer.

At this point in Barry's life, he'd already been forced to accept some outrageous things—like the walking dead, like time travel. He'd learned that anything was possible, no matter how absurd it sounded like.

So—what if a farting asteroid had caused the undead contagion? If there was a chance of preventing the outbreak, wasn't it worth some effort?

If there was any chance that Sheldon's farting asteroid theory had any validity, then the sooner the better his "pals" got started on whatever they were going to do to stop the disaster.

So I should get off my ass and get moving...

Despite his new resolve, Barry took the time to cook and eat a hearty meal before leaving. It'd been a long time since he'd enjoyed Canadian bacon and his favorite marmalade—and after his recent adventures (the raid on the stag party) and ordeals (crashing into the lake and then trekking through the woods) Barry felt he deserved some rewards.

It was late-afternoon before Barry headed out.

Consequently, by the time he reached Princeton, the university was mostly empty. The offices were closed, and none of the night classes could provide him with useful information. He retreated to an on-campus coffee shop to consider his options.

I should've called ahead, he remonstrated himself over a humongous cup of expresso. *Set up some kind of appointment...or at least gotten Dracy's home number from the school's offices.*

He felt stupid. It annoyed him that he couldn't get on with this matter. The others on Sheldon's list were scattered across the country, from MIT to Livermore. Barry had intended to convince Emmanuel Dracy, then enlist his help contacting the rest of the scientists. They might be more receptive hearing from him than getting a cold call from a Manhattan police officer with a strange tale to tell.

He checked a phonebook in a booth just inside the cafe, but there was no Dracy, E. listed.

He could drop by a local police station, flash his badge and run a trace on the professor...but he wanted to keep all this off-the-radar. If any of it backfired, Barry wanted plausible deniability. What if Dracy turned out to be vigorous skeptic and reported Barry's insane tale to the authorities? If Barry expected to return to his normal job after all this, he needed to be able to disappear into the shadows when the affair was rolling.

His only other option was to hang around until tomorrow. Come morning, the university offices would open and Barry could track down Professor Dracy. Barry didn't like it, but what choice did he have? Driving back to Manhattan and revisiting Princeton tomorrow seemed awfully pointless—a waste of time, gas and energy.

Frustrated at sitting here brooding over his expresso, Barry sat back and let his eyes wander over his surroundings. The other patrons reminded him of Miss Collard. They were about her age, although he doubted many of them could match the girl in combat. If nothing else, she'd been a premium fighter. He wondered what her younger self was doing this evening…out dancing with her vacuous friends?—hunting for a nice guy? He hoped she found someone better than Joey Fulton; Barry had never completely trusted that boy.

His gaze froze as he laid eyes on a familiar face—familiar, yes, but not one he'd ever expected to see again.

Sitting in a booth on the far side of the coffee house was Sheldon Bowman. Dressed in a muddy brown sweater and dark slacks, the man was waggling his superior finger in someone's face. A second shock: Sheldon was arguing with Professor Grauss.

Okay—Grauss was a professor based here at Princeton, Barry called that up from his memory. But not Sheldon—*he* had taught at another school, Barry couldn't recall which one. So, finding Grauss here was not all that startling, but Sheldon? His presence challenged any odds Barry could apply to the situation.

Had Sheldon too followed Barry into the past? Not likely; Barry'd seen Sheldon's head explode back in the bunker. There was no surviving that, not even as a zombie.

So—what was Sheldon doing here?

A third man shared the booth with them. At first he was no more than a stranger, but gradually Barry came to imagine he'd seen him before. Could this be Emmanuel Dracy? Barry had probably seen him on more than one occasion, but as just another unsympathetic face among the Board members the times he'd denounced them.

The patrons' diverse conversations blended together to form a gestalt numble, behind that the coffee house's jukebox music comprised a foundational hum to that murmur. It was impossible to pluck any identifiable words out of that babble.

Until a lull occurred—a gap between songs on the jukebox. Once that background rumble was eliminated, however briefly, cogerent fragments emerged from the tangled sentences being batted about the cafe.

Barry's alert hearing caught: "—Dracy has enough room at his house—'

He innocuously moved to a seat closer to the three professors. Now he could better hear their conversation.

"It's not my house," protested the man whose identify until now had been uncertain. "It belongs to my parents. I've told you that time and again, Sheldon."

"And you just mentioned they were out of town this weekend," came Sheldon's whiny reply. As usual, he wanted someone to do something and the only way he knew how to ask was to grumble.

Now, as in Sanctuary, Professor Grauss was adept at defusing awkward confrontations.

"Now now, Professor Bowman," Grauss remarked in his smooth voice, "I'm sure a room can be found for you at Faculty Hall."

Sheldon's face contorted into a mask that Barry knew well. His features scrunched up, as if falling into the center of his head. This convergence seemed to accentuate each feature's intensity. Combined, his stern mouth and protruding nose and scowling eyes became a cartoon parody of disapproval.

Acting purely on impulse, Barry approached their booth and interrupted their dispute. "Excuse me, are you Professor Dracy? Emmanuel Dracy?"

All three men turned to stare at this intruder. Grauss looked mildly interested. Sheldon fumed at the interference. Dracy clearly welcomed the distraction.

"I'm Dracy," he announced. He gestured for Barry to join them, but the detective remained standing.

Flashing his badge, Barry introduced himself: "Detective Barry Winsor, Manhattan PD."

"Oh dear," grunted Professor Grauss.

"Um—" Dracy's welcome expression disintegrated into confused turmoil. "What is this about, detective?"

"I was wondering if I could have a few minutes of your time," muttered Barry in a congenial voice.

"Why, certainly. Sit down and join us."

"Well," Barry muttered, "I'd rather speak with you alone, Professor Dracy."

Immediately, thirsty curiosity replaced Sheldon's rancor.

Professor Grauss just arched a noble eyebrow.

"Am I under some sort of suspicion, officer?"

"Not at all," Barry promptly assured him.

"Then have a seat. I've nothing to hide—from you or from my friends."

With a shrug, Barry settled into the vacant spot next to Sheldon, across from Dracy.

He's hoped that the presence of an officer of the law would have the standard reaction on the men; innocent or guilty, people tended to walk away from a cop if given the chance. But Sheldon and Grauss weren't retreating. More so, Dracy had invited them to stay. How was Barry supposed to tell his outlandish tale to such a wide audience? But then—Grauss was generally a stoic personality, he would hear Barry out and even then might not voice an open opnion of what he'd been told. And Sheldon—this was his scheme; there was a certain ironic symmetry to him witnessing it happening. Besides, Sheldon had made sure his name was among the individuals Barry was supposed to summon together to fight the asteroid menace. There were handwritten affidavits from each of these men among the papers Barry carried. This new development offered him the opportunity to contact three of the people on his list.

In fact, why should Barry bother trying to explain anything to these men? Why not let their own words do it instead?

Throwing caution to the wind, Barry drew the sheaf of papers from inside his jacket. He handed them to Professor Darcy.

Taking the papers, Dracy perused them. He slowly flipped from page to page, periodically punctuating his reading with mild grunts. When he had finished, he reviewed the first page again for a long moment before raising his gaze to meet Barry's.

"I presume this is a joke."

Barry slowly shook his head.

A broad grin broke out on Dracy's face. "Come now, you've had your fun. Who put you up to this? Dr Finkelstein? Some of my students?"

Barry decided against sharing a smile with the man.

"What is it?" demanded Sheldon. Throughout Dracy's reading, the man had fidgeted and repeatedly tried to sneak peeks at the papers. Now, he openly grabbed to take them from Dracy's hands.

At first, Dracy held fast. His gaze shifted from Sheldon to Barry, where his eyes asked the obvious question.

Barry shrugged. *In for a penny, in for a pound.*

The documents were transferred to Sheldon's greedy clutches. He declined to pass any pages along to Professor Grauss until he had digested each sheet. Once he was finished, he voiced a derisive noise.

Professor Grauss examined the papers with no apparent judgment.

"I'm afraid I don't understand," Professor Dracy finally offered.

"It's obvious," interjected Sheldon, his tone patently derogatory. "This man is attempting to implicate you in some scam that will damage your professional standing. He's probably not even a police officer."

"But he showed us his badge…"

"Anyone with access to Photoshop can create a believable badge, that doesn't make it real."

"But—" Dracy's forehead arched with stress. "The testimonies—they claim to be from future versions of ourselves…"

"Listen to yourself, Emmanuel. Are you actually putting any credence in such absurdities as zombies and time travel?"

"But the testimony that's supposed to come from an older me--it includes information only I could know…"

"Just like the one attributed to a future me," scoffed Sheldon. "All that proves is that this con man has invested some effort investigating us before attempting to perpetrate this scam."

Well, *this* was unexpected. Or maybe not. Barry had assumed that Sheldon would instinctively support a plan that was (unknown to him) completely of his own design. Instead, though, young Sheldon had dismissed the entire affair as a fraud. Wasn't a response like that precisely in line with the pompous Sheldon he knew? Anything that violated the man's preconceived notions of reality was indisputably bogus.

Holding his tongue, Barry ignored Sheldon and kept his eyes matched with Dracy's bewildered gaze.

With a polite cough, Professor Grauss handed the sheaf of papers back to Professor Dracy. Then, he commented, "I cannot help but note that Detective Winsor offers no verbal defense of these questionable facts."

Barry sighed, then confessed, "To tell you the truth, I think the whole thing is pretty flaky. I can verify the existence of a zombie outbreak in the near future; I've seen it firsthand."

"Through time travel…" Dracy hesitantly mumbled.

Barry nodded, then continued, "As far as this farting asteroid theory goes, however, that part I can neither confirm nor deny. It's *his* theory, not mine." Barry tilted his head in Sheldon's direction. "So was this entire idea of sending me back to prevent the outbreak before it happens."

"Then why didn't I come instead of you?"

Barry shrugged. A touch of a smirk colored his reply, "Because, Sheldon, for all your genius, you're a coward. You believed your scheme would work, but you couldn't risk your own brilliant ass to the process' test run. So you sent me—because you hate my guts and if it killed me, you wouldn't lose any sleep over it."

Shocked, a reddening Sheldon bridled with indignation. "How dare you insult me like that—"

"Whoever you are, Detective Winsor," chuckled Professor Grauss, "you've certainly done your homework."

"What?!" Sheldon blurted.

"If this were a scam," Grauss remarked, "wouldn't it have been prudent to include testimony from myself in this documentation you've shown us?"

"Sheldon assembled the information. I'm just the courier," admitted Barry. "You *are* one of the Board members that run Sanctuary, Professor Grauss. I've only spoken with you a few times, but you struck me as a pretty levelheaded guy. You'd have to ask Sheldon why he neglected to include you."

"You mean, I'd have to ask this future Sheldon. Surely, this Sheldon—" He nodded toward the man seated across the booth from him. "—would have no knowledge of the motives of his future self."

"You know him better than I do," confessed Barry. "Harsh post-apocalyptic living conditions changed future Sheldon, as they will inevitably change everyone."

"I'm curious..." ventured Professor Dracy. He leaned forward to shuffle the papers before him. "This message from the future warns of the disastrous consequences of the asteroid's brush with Earth's atmosphere, but it offers no suggestions to prevent that near-miss."

"Again, I'm just the courier. But really—do you expect your future selves to solve everything? Haven't they already done enough? Future Sheldon inferred the time machine was his, but I suspect it was actually a collaborative accomplishment. So—those guys already did their part. Now it's *your* turn."

"This is absurd!" exclaimed Sheldon. "You're actually discussing this man's ludicrous claims? He's repeatedly slandered me, and now he's succeeded in scamming you. We should call the police and have him arrested!"

Ignoring him, Dracy and Grauss conferred together.

"Several physicists claim that time travel is theoretically possible."

"Even if you concede that point, the matter of a zombie outbreak is somewhat unprecedented."

"But then, according to the documents' explanation, chemicals released by this asteroid mix with our atmosphere, creating an alien contagion. Who can predict the effects such a poison would have on human biology?"

Actually, it affected animals too, not just people, Barry mused, but decided to not confuse things with this minor correction. The same went for Doc Toby's belief that everybody had died and only a few became zombies.

"By the time zombies existed to study, it would already be too late. The contamination would have reached global saturation. There's no way the medical community could cope with an outbreak of such unique symptoms."

"Civilization would collapse. Anarchy would reign. And—if these zombies are real—then the survivors have to fight them off on a daily basis."

Amused, Barry watched them analyze the circumstances. Instead of relying on physical evidence, their examination concentrated on a hypothetical reconstruction of post-apocalyptic conditions.

"A majority of the survivors would band together against these threats. But others, scientists and thinkers, would seek a way to undo the catastrophe."

"Suddenly, time travel becomes a potentially useful course of research. Driven by imperative necessity, these future scientists succeed in finding a way to transmit a person back in time."

"Now this traveler must face the problem of convincing the people in the past that his warning is true."

"Affidavits from the scientists' future selves would help."

"The ethical burden is suddenly shifted from the future scientists to their past selves. These younger individuals must decide whether to accept the warning as truth…or reject it as a wild hoax. The fate of the world may rest on their judgment."

"If they choose the wrong interpretation, the catastrophe that follows will be their fault."

"Our fault…"

"This is madness!" announced Sheldon. He banged his palm on the table, sending everyone's plates and glasses dancing. "How can you justify placing any credence in this deception?"

Turning a solemn face on Sheldon, Dracy explained, "To ignore a global threat like this would be madness, Professor Bowman."

"But—it isn't real!"

"According to these documents, *you* are the main architect of this attempt to prevent catastrophe. Don't you feel some responsibility to your own handiwork?"

A livid Sheldon raged, "It isn't me! This is all a fraud!

Actually, Barry enjoyed seeing Sheldon so vehemently condemn his own scheme. The entire affair had been the crowning achievement of Sheldon's intellectual career—and here, his younger self scoffed at the whole thing. (And he wasn't really all that *younger* than future Sheldon. Only a handful of months separated them. As Barry had pointed out, the decisive difference was the apocalypse. Witnessing the fall of civilization had changed Sheldon Bowman, making him more arrogant about his own opinions.) This turnaround would've horrified future Sheldon. To have his own genius denounced by himself—the irony was so perfect.

"These other names on the list," Dracy consulted with Grauss. "We should contact them and show them these documents."

Nodding, Grauss agreed. "They should be given the chance to contribute to solving this problem."

Barry decided the time had come for his polite withdrawal. His job was done. Dracy and Grauss would carry Sheldon's warning to the proper hands, who would then find some means of preventing the asteroid from dumping its noxious chemicals into the Earth's atmosphere. The matter was out of Barry's hands now.

Slipping from the booth, Barry took his leave of the coffee house. He lingered for a moment to study the sky. Although clouds masked most of the heavens, a few stars glittered through the overcast.

"Hey—you—"

Turning, Barry found an angry Sheldon stomping from the coffee house.

"What's the catch?" he demanded.

"No catch, Sheldon. I just delivered the message—*your* message. You can heed it or ignore it, I couldn't care which."

"If you dare to try to publicize this fraud, I will denounce you."

Barry had to chuckle.

"I'm serious! I won't have something like this taint my career!"

"I can see where you'd want no part in saving the world."

The man continued to rant, to indict, to threaten, to vow the direst penalties. With a weary shake of his head, Barry left him to shout at the night.

12

BACK IN THE HOSPITAL ROOM, old Barry hugged the bottle of rum with a sly grin. Nurse Collard would not approve of him imbibing, but he had no intention of giving up the bottle. He'd snatched it from the past, not an easy trick. It was his now. After such a long sobriety, he deserved some booze in his final moments. A reward for all his efforts—his successes and his failures.

He regretted having to lie to his younger self.

Control his temporal displacements? What a ludicrous idea. In fact, since Sheldon's machine had deposited Barry back in his normal time period, he had experienced no further time jumps...at least, until this last one, in which his older, wiser self went back to read the riot act to his younger stubborn self. And, as with all the others, even this trip had been involuntary.

But young Barry had needed to believe that someday he might gain control over the displacements. Where was the harm making him think he had that to look forward to? A more grandiose carrot had been necessary. Old Barry prayed he'd finally gotten through to the crotchety drunk.

Hopefully, he won't make the same mistakes I made...

Settling back on his mound of pillows, he closed his one good eye and waited to see what changes might occur within his memory.

In older Barry's opinion, younger Barry had handled himself pretty well.

A lot of hostile surprises had been thrown in his way, but he'd managed to survive each one. On some of those occasions, he'd eventually cast off procrastination and made the right choice. For the most part, it was a life Barry could be proud of.

He'd resumed his life as a Manhattan police officer.

By the time Frankie Dumont returned from Dallas, the last details of the stag party raid had been wrapped up. Frankie and Barry devoted their attention to a car-jacking ring they suspected were working out of a garage up on 116th Street.

One morning he showed up in the squad room with a bandaged hand. "Stupid accident cutting some wood for a set of shelves," he confessed with a self-deprecating grimace.

Months later, Barry saw an Army official announce on the news that an asteroid was headed for Earth. Surprised that the US military was taking the threat seriously, he followed the story with more than a little curiosity. A few days later, it was reported that missiles had been launched and their detonations had knocked the asteroid into a different trajectory, one that would safely bypass the Earth and ultimately deliver it to the heart of the sun.

Son of a bitch— Sheldon's scheme had worked! Working behind the scenes, his scientist pals had convinced the military that the asteroid was a threat. *They probably focused on the dangers of a direct collision,* he mused. Revealing what they knew about any hidden gas pocket filled with toxic chemicals would only have confused the generals.

Of course, the zombie outbreak was still a few weeks away, so it remained to be seen if Sheldon's farting asteroid theory had any real bearing on the undead plague.

When that deadline came and went, however, without any zombie outbreak happening, Barry had to admit he was surprised. Sheldon had been right all along. If only he hadn't been an asshole, maybe somebody would've trusted him more.

Initially, Barry had given Professor Bowman the benefit of the doubt. He'd been an ass when Barry had known him in the future, but the detective had always assumed coping with the apocalyptic world had turned him into one. But no, having encountered a younger, pre-apocalyptic version of Sheldon, Barry had learned that the man had always been an ass.

It was probably better that the world would never know it had been saved by an asshole.

But then, the world would never know it had been saved—because the zombie apocalypse had never happened. No tangible catastrophe existed anymore. So there was no worldwide gratitude for Sheldon's unsung efforts.

Barry almost felt sorry for Sheldon…being deprived of such a lofty accomplishment—but then he remembered what an ass Sheldon was and the brief sputter of pity fizzled away.

At the time, Barry wondered what that group of scientists thought about the role they'd played in sparing mankind from a zombie holocaust.

Being intellectuals, they surely understood better than Barry the nebulous nature of their secret claim to fame. They could take pride in averting the asteroid's near-collision, but even that accomplishment had been orchestrated in camera.

Sometimes, Barry wished he could think of that future which no longer existed as a fanciful half-remembered nightmare…but his memories were too vivid, too saturated with regret for his failures, too ecstatic over his few redemptions. These memories refused to be suppressed or to fade with the passage of the years.

A decade later, he could still picture himself and Miss Collard, side-by-side, opposing the Board's absurd ambition of uniting all of Manhattan under Sanctuary's banner. Upon occasion, he would wax nostalgic about the people with whom he'd shared that post-apocalyptic landscape. Doc Toby, that untrained healer. Dusty, that bloodthirsty bastard. Dr Heigl, that egocentric bully. Even Joey Fulton brought a certain warmth to Barry's heart.

Often, he wondered what had become of them. When civilization had failed to collapse, what had they made of their lives?

Hopefully, without a food shortage brought about by the zombie hordes, the Templars had not resorted to cannibalism. Did Joey still work his father's farm? Had the lad found a pretty girl to marry and start a family?

Was Doc Toby still plugging away as a pharmaceutical salesman? Barry liked to imagine that the man had walked away from that soulless trade to become something that better fit his temperament, like a veterinarian.

How was Dusty coping with his bloodlust in a world less tolerant of open violence? Maybe he was an ultimate fighter on one of those shows on cable.

Sometimes Barry envisioned this football scholarship jock taking Dr Heigl's political science class to impress a curvy coed, and when the pompous teacher makes some derogatory comment about sports, the jock punches him in the face.

Did Mrs Simpson have her kid? Was it a boy or a girl?

The only one Barry ever looked up was Miss Collard.

He had developed too much affection for the girl during their time together. She was like the daughter he and Emily had never had. He'd never really gotten over all the times he had failed the girl; he'd carry that guilt to his grave, regardless of having changed the future and eradicating all those delinquencies. Hers was the only saved ife he really cared about.

So he checked up on her. Apparently she led a nondescript life. There was nothing on her in police records. Deeper investigation revealed she was studying to be a nurse. Over the years he covertly kept track of her, monitoring the life of the girl he had once fought beside against zombie mobs. Like any paternal figure, Barry disapproved of the men she dated; he especially disliked the one she married, but in the long run the guy turned out to be okay, a loving companion for Miss Collard…who was now Mrs Nelson. In the end, Barry had called in a few favors to insure that his failing years were consigned to the hospital where she worked, so he could have her around for his last days.

She was hardly the only person he watched grow old. There was Frankie Dumont, who unwillingly retired at fifty-five because of heart problems, then passed away in his sleep.

And Deputy Chief Gann. After thirty years on the force, the poor guy fell down the stairs at home and broke his neck.

And me… after my stroke, I ended up here in a hospice.

As the years rolled on, Barry often wondered if he had ever actually traveled through time. Or was it all just the product of an old man's scrambled memories? Age had weathered some of the details from his mind. Reviewing his life, much of its unsequential nature could be blamed on him remembering stuff out of chronological order.

But then, once Sheldon had sent him back to stop a zombie outbreak from happening, all of these apocalyptic memories were reduced to a fantasy world that had never existed. Holding onto these memories became progressively more difficult as his new life had unfolded.

He had believed that his experience with Sheldon's machine was what had made him come unstuck from the normal time-flow, but in actuality it had put an end to his temporal displacements.

If not for Miss Collard (now Mrs Nelson), Barry could have rejected the whole thing as a delusion. She was the one linchpin that undermined the illusion.

Even so, it seemed silly to believe in a world that had never happened.

Until today, when he'd found himself metaphysically pulled from bed and thrown back so many years to confront his younger self. At first, it had felt like another dream, but the younger Barry's drunken skepticism had vexed older Barry, goading him into a more solid belief in that nightmarish world of zombies and feudal enclaves. That annoyance had fueled his arguments. And when the stubborn fool had scoffed at elder Barry's advice, he'd tossed in a few lies to motivate the fool.

Upon returning to his hospital bed, Barry fretted that he hadn't convinced the fool to clean up his act. And so—fully in keeping with a dream-like sequence—young Barry had showed up here, giving him a second chance to browbeat some sense into his younger self.

Only now that younger Barry was gone did he fully accept all of his post-apocalyptic memories. They were not figments of an elderly brain.

The bottle of rum he clutched was all the proof he needed.

Of course, acceptance brought with it no epiphany concerning how any of it had happened. That really didn't bother him, though; there were lots of unexplained things in life…and he'd lived through more than anybody's share of them.

After all these years, Barry Winsor had finally reached the hospital room of his dreams. For a while he'd imagined the white room existed primarily in his dreams. He'd seen it a few times via his displacements, but had never really given it much thought until he'd actually met the room's elderly occupant.

That visit had tested his self-confidence—or lack of self-confidence. Getting criticized by an older and wiser Barry Winsor had set him back on-course, convincing him to swear off the booze and focus on what was really important: survival. Not just his survival, but more importantly: everybody's survival.

Once you shaped up, you made me proud, old Barry told himself. He took a hefty swig from the rum bottle. It burned his throat, but it was a nostalgic burn, one he hadn't tasted in long decades. Now that it was all over, he could fall off the wagon and celebrate.

The big difference was: this time he wasn't getting drunk to escape anything. This bottle (at least, what remained of it) was his reward…

For being a good person.

For being a good cop.

For protecting Miss Collard as best he could.

For saving the world.

For reaching the end of the line.

ABOUT THE AUTHOR

Perhaps best known as the writer/artist of the Those Annoying Post Bros. *comic book series, Matt Howarth has many outlets for his twisted creativity. And all of them are notoriously "strange".*

During his career of four decades, Matt has authored and drawn a variety of unconventional comic books and graphic novels, and contributed graphic fiction to numerous publications in the field of comics and science fiction... and music. For, among all of Matt's creative outlets, there runs the insidious influence of alternative and electronic music. He has found several ways to achieve this crossover of diverse genres.

Matt Howarth's Attic
www.matthowarth.com

Sonic Curiosity
www.soniccuriosity.com

Bugtown Mall
www.bugtownmall.com